TRANSREAL CYBERPUNK

NINE STORIES BY

RUDY RUCKER
&
BRUCE STERLING

INTRODUCTION BY
ROB LATHAM

Transreal Cyberpunk
Nine stories by Rudy Rucker & Bruce Sterling
Copyright © Rudy Rucker & Bruce Sterling 2016.
Introduction copyright © Rob Latham, 2016.

Paperback: ISBN 978-1-940948-14-0
Hardback: ISBN 978-1-940948-15-7
Ebook: ISBN 978-1-940948-16-4

Cover photos by Sylvia Rucker and by Rudy Rucker.

First edition published February, 2016
Transreal Books, Los Gatos, California
www.transrealbooks.com

Acknowledgements

Thanks, first of all, to the editors who abetted, bought and published these stories: Shawna McCarthy, Gardner Dozois, and Sheila Williams of *Asimov's Science Fiction*—and Patrick Nielsen Hayden at *Tor.com*.

Thanks to Rob Latham of the University of California at Riverside for writing his great introduction.

And thanks to the generous readers who supported the Transreal Books campaign to raise money for the book. Here are their chosen names, alphabetized by first letters.

@genebecker, @msilver, @screenhugger, @soupdiver, @stevegio, @tamberg, @TGTstudios, 50-50, ∞, Adam Weiss, Adrian Howard, AgentKaz, Ahmet A. Sabancı, Aidan Williamson, Al Billings, Alex Baxter, Algot Runeman, Allan Schnoor, Allen Varney, André cardozo, Andrew Beirne, Andrew G White, Andrew Hatchell, Andrew Lindsay, Andrew Peake, Andrew Tischaefer, Andrew Ward, Andrija Popovic, Andy Ward, Anon, Aris Alissandrakis, artlung, ATOMIC_REQUIEM, Baba Z Buehler, baohx2000, Benjamin Stough, benwf, BiL Castine, Bill Woodcock, Blazej Bucko, Bob Huss, Brandon Aycock, Brendan Fisher, Brendan Sheehan, Brian Anderson, Brian Dysart, Brian Repinski, Bruno Boutot, Caleb Monroe, Cameron Cooper, Carl Rigney, Carlos Pascual, Chad Bowden, Chaos82, Charlie Meetze, Chriftor Marovsk, chris bodhi, Chris McLaren, Chris Mendis, Chuck Ivy, Chuck Shotton, Clay Hinson, Cliff Winnig, CMFW, Cody Mingus, Collin Bennett, Connor Sites-Bowen, Conor McQuaid, COSMO, Cosmo Kairos, Dale Innis, Daniel Eisenman, Darwin Engwer, Daryl Davis, Dave Bonner, Dave Holets, Dave

Neurovagrant, NICHOLAS BESHER, Nicolas Toper, None, just happy to help make the book real, Noriyo Asano, Ominous Ohnemus, Ook, Osmium, Owen Rowley, Patrick Di Justo, Paul Leonard, Peer Stritzinger, Peter T., Peter Yeates, Philippe van Nedervelde, Pojo, Pookie, Profesor Cyfra, r0b1ns0n, Rafael Fajardo, Ramón Cahenzli, Raucous Raven, Ray Cornwall, Raymond Nordin III, Raymond Rigo Jr, Razormaid, real name, Renata Lemos Morais, Rez N. / @zproc, RGL/DHL, Riccardo Sartori, Richard Kadrey, Richie O'Hara-Beamand, Rick Ayre, Rick Crain, Rnx, rob alley, Rob Szarka, Rod Mearing, Roger Strunk, Roger Thomas, Rohan Pearce, Ron Corral, Ronald Pottol, Roy C., rudetuesday, Russell Davies, Samuel Backlund, Samuel Hansen, Sandy McAuley, Sarah J Brown, Scott G Lewis, Scott Meisburger + HK Meissen, Scott Pemberton, Scott Wiener, Sean Elias, Sean O'Donnell, Sean Richmond, Sean W Scully, Sebastian Klapp, sekari, Shay Brog, Sq, Srđan Đukić, Sruli Recht, Stan Yamane, Stary Mundek, Stephanie Rieger, Steve Garriott, Steve H., Steve Siwy, Steve Craig, Steven Shaviro, Stuart Murnain, Surse, Suzanne McBride, t1deman, Taylor Cox, Terry Bennett, The Ducharme Family, The Hackers Conference, Thomas Bøvith, Thomas Gideon, Thomas Werner, Tieg Zaharia, Tim Borsilli, Tim Conkling, Timothy Wyitt Carlile, Tom Velebny, Tony Gatner, Torben Steeg, Transknition, Trey Blalock, Tyler Battle, U.N.Spacey, Ulrik Hogrebe, Victor Simon, void-fraction, Wade Goyens, Walter F. Croft, William H D Sked, William Maddler, Yoshio Kobayashi, and Zach Peters.

What a crew!

Enjoy the book, everyone.

Rudy Rucker & Bruce Sterling
February 1, 2016.

Contents

Introduction by Rob Latham

Science fiction, like science, is a collaborative enterprise, in two ways. First, there's the encompassing "megatext" of the genre that all writers dip into, borrow from, contribute to, and collectively revise over the course of their careers. William Gibson invents cyberspace, and countless other writers jump on, adding and tinkering and retrofitting; somebody attaches hydraulic tubes and chrome handlebars and, *voila!*, we have steampunk. This is how the field grows, and always has.

But SF, uniquely among popular genres, is also literally collaborative, rife with famous writing partnerships: Pohl and Kornbluth, Kuttner and Moore, Niven and Pournelle. Harlan Ellison published an entire volume of collaborations with other authors, *Partners in Wonder*. For some reason, cyberpunk in particular has inspired much close teamwork: three of the stories in Gibson's seminal collection *Burning Chrome* are collaborations; Sterling and Gibson coauthored the steampunk novel *The Difference Engine*; and Rucker has coauthored stories with seven writers, including fellow *Mirrorshades* authors Paul Di Filippo, Marc Laidlaw, and John Shirley.

So on the one hand, there's nothing unusual about *Transreal Cyberpunk*, Rudy Rucker and Bruce Sterling's collection of the nine stories they wrote together between 1985 and 2015. On the other hand, this book is unlike any other collaboration I know of in the field, an example where the whole is not only greater than the sum of its parts, but wilder, and weirder, and more wondrous.

Both authors are essentially satirists, but their temperaments couldn't be more opposed. Sterling's satire is cold, precise, analytical, almost machine-like in its distanced bemusement at human foibles, while Rucker's is warm, good-natured, slapstick, with a forgiving fondness for human idiosyncrasy. Sterling's methods combine punk irony and hardheaded extrapolation, while Rucker's mix Beat goofiness and gonzo improvisation. How can such disparate aesthetics possibly fuse?

Well, it wasn't easy, as the authors detail in their individual notes on the stories. Each tale was apparently a struggle of wills, involving multiple drafts, in-person spitballing, endless bickering via phone and email, and (one gets the sense) sometimes tense standoffs and uneasy negotiations. But despite their many differences, the authors are clearly the best of friends: they love each other, as well as science fiction, avant garde literature, and visionary forms of technology. They are both gadflies in their peculiar ways, and both are drawn to that odd technocultural junction where the marginal meets the cutting-edge. Both have done their time in the lecture halls of interdisciplinary conferences and the boxy cubicles of entrepreneurial start-ups, where all manner of possible and abortive futures get incubated. And both, I think it is fair to say, have done their share of mind-altering drugs.

Certainly the fiction they produce together is psychedelic in its effects, a strobing mindfuck of ideas that comes at the reader helter-skelter. Sometimes you feel the need to drop the book and grab ahold of your chair. The volume is like a fictional zoo thronging with crazy critters of all kinds: reincarnated space dogs, flying jellyfish, string-theory ants, biotech leeches. Metamorphosis runs rampant: characters turn into writhing blobs, spacetime twists and explodes, and the prose itself shifts and mutates. Rucker and Sterling are big fans of William Burroughs, and one can sense his mordant presence in the occasional eruptions of collage and biomorphic horror.

But the writer I was reminded of most while reading these tales was Thomas Pynchon, who has the same wacko energy, the same fondness for oddball characters, and the same sharp-eyed, loveable ferocity. There's even a wink to Pynchon in one story, a reference to his made-up drug oneirine, from *Gravity's Rainbow*. According to that novel, oneirine's phenomenological effects are "like stuffing wedges of silver sponge, *right, into*, your *brain!*" And that pretty much summarizes the singular impact of reading *Transreal Cyberpunk*.

Even readers familiar with Rucker and Sterling writing on their own will be amazed by what their combined impudence and erudition yields. Despite all the zany invention, there are recurring themes and locales, of course. Apocalypse scenarios run rampant, from the historical (the Tunguska explosion) to the highly unlikely (twelfth-dimensional cosmic collapse). In one of his story notes, Sterling even refers to their compositional methods as "a ridiculous catastrophe." And the sites the authors are drawn to are spaces where innovation in all its forms can range free: scientific outposts, high-tech labs, digital media workshops, blogger confabs.

Most of the stories are set in some real or imaginary version of California, with its ethos of libertarian license and subcultural self-fashioning. It's a world Rucker knows quite well—indeed, it's his home base: he's one of the finest chroniclers of West Coast outlawry since the early Steinbeck (who gets a shout-out in one of the stories). In this laidback technotopia, Sterling is like a visitor from another planet, skeptical where Rucker is accepting, dubious where Rucker is sanguine, a hipster rather than a hippie. Sterling's instinct is always to hide behind the pose of a no-nonsense, dispassionate, if not slightly blasé raconteur, while Rucker's main urge is towards the heartfelt, the confessional, the whimsically revelatory. Yet both are audacious, captivating storytellers, and their contrasting styles bring out the best in one another: Sterling lets his hair down, gets a little funky, while Rucker takes on a harder, more cynical edge. The result is nothing less than astonishing.

For those unfamiliar with the concept, "transrealism" is a term of Rucker's coinage designed to refer to a combination of science-fictional inspiration and quotidian, if not memoiristic authenticity—or, as Sterling puts it at one point, a "mix of the visionary and the mundane." Influences range from Burroughs to Hunter S. Thompson to Philip K. Dick, the effect being of an everyday world shot through with veins of hallucinatory wonder, fissured with portals into strange dimensions. Rucker's early novels, *Software* and *Spacetime Donuts*, are classics of the form, and it was a newspaper review of those works by Sterling that first drew the two authors together. They met in 1983, and by 1985 had become, if not kindred spirits, then partners in crime, authoring a hilariously surreal take on the origins of the space age, "Storming the Cosmos," for *Asimov's Science Fiction*. As their story notes here make plain, they met infrequently over the years, but when they did, the sparks of inspiration flew, giving birth to some of the oddest works of contemporary SF I know of.

The transrealism of these stories lies in the fact that each contains a mismatched pair of friends, refractions of Sterling and Rucker, with the authors sometimes speaking for themselves, sometimes ventriloquizing one another. The history of SF is full of "buddy story" cycles, from Asimov's *I, Robot* to Lem's *Cyberiad*, but *Transreal Cyberpunk* differs from these precursors since the identities of the protagonists don't stay fixed. In one story, we're given a pair of Russian cosmo-nuts who discover an alien stardrive while zonked on psychedelic mushrooms, in another a pair of digital tinkerers dealing with an extra-dimensional ant invasion. The genders and sexualities of the duo morph from story to story—at one point forming a romantic couple facing down the end of the universe together. The pairs fight, they flirt, they fend off mutant "petware." What stays consistent is a bantering tone drawn from classic screwball comedy, as the brainiac buddies debate Big Ideas while dashing from one mad escapade to another.

While this might sound somewhat formulaic, that is not the effect at all. Indeed, these aren't just SF buddy stories, they're metafictional reflections on buddy stories—and, more than that, potent fictive meditations on the virtues and vicissitudes of friendship itself. They don't just reflect, they *embody* collaboration, dialogue, disputation. The stories are organized chronologically, and the characters seem to grow older together, the tones darkening, the humor taking on a sharper edge. The final story, written expressly for the volume, features a serene sage who faces down an ecological catastrophe with stoic bemusement. But he has not lost his youthful exuberance: after all, he has a kraken for a sidekick!

Transreal Cyberpunk is a labor of love from two of the most protean SF authors of the past three decades. It is also a goofball chronicle of a unique and admirable friendship. As with most friendships, the book loses its temper at times, or makes a brazen fool of itself, but it also rises to rapturous heights of zonked-out fellow feeling you're unlikely to find anywhere outside the pages of Kerouac or Rabelais. Science fiction is the richer for it.

Storming the Cosmos

I first met Vlad Zipkin at a Moscow beatnik party in the glorious winter of 1957. I went there as a KGB informer. Because of my report on that first meeting, poor Vlad had to spend six months in a mental hospital—not that he wasn't crazy.

As a boy I often tattled on wrongdoers, but I certainly didn't plan to grow up to be a professional informer. It just worked out that way. The turning point was in the spring of 1953, when I failed my completion exams at the All-Union Metallurgical Institute. I'd been working towards those exams for years; I wanted to help build the rockets that would launch us into the Infinite.

And then, suddenly, one day in April, it was all over. Our examination grades were posted, and I was one of the three in seventeen who'd failed. To take the exam again, I'd have to wait a whole year. First I was depressed, then angry. I knew for a fact that four of the students with good grades had cheated. I, who was honest, had failed; and they, who had cheated, had passed. It wasn't fair, it wasn't communist—I went and told the head of the Institute.

The upshot was that I passed after all, and became an assistant metallurgical engineer at the Kaliningrad space center. But, in reality, my main duty was to make weekly reports to the KGB on what my coworkers thought and said and did. I was, frankly, grateful to have my KGB work to do, as most of the metallurgical work was a bit beyond me.

There is an ugly Russian word for informer: *stukach*, snitch. The criminals, the psychotics, the parasites, and the beatniks—to them I was a *stukach*. But without *stukachi*, our communist society would explode into anarchy or grind to a decadent halt. Vlad Zipkin might be a genius, and I might be a *stukach*—but society needed us both.

I first met Vlad at a party thrown by a girl called Lyuda. Lyuda had her own Moscow apartment; her father was a Red Army colonel-general in Kaliningrad. She was a nice, sexy girl who looked a little like Doris Day.

Lyuda and her friends were all beatniks. They drank a lot; they used English slang; they listened to jazz; and the men hung around with prostitutes. One of the guys got Lyuda pregnant and she went for an abortion. She had VD as well. We heard of this, of course. Word spreads about these matters. Someone in Higher Circles decided to eliminate the anti-social sex gangster responsible for this. It was my job to find out who he was.

It was a matter for space-center KGB because several rocket-scientists were known to be in Lyuda's orbit. My approach was cagey. I made contact with a prostitute named Trina who hung around the Metropol, the Moskva, and other foreign hotels. Trina had chic Western clothes from her customers, and she was friends with many of the Moscow beatniks. I'm certainly not dashing enough to charm a girl like Trina—instead, I simply told her that I was KGB, and that if she didn't get me into one of Lyuda's bashes I'd have her arrested.

Lyuda's pad was jammed when we got there. I was proud to show up with a cool chick like Trina on my arm. I looked very sharp too, with the leather jacket, and the black stove-pipe pants with no cuffs that all the beatniks were wearing that season. Trina stuck right with me—as we'd planned—and lots of men came up to talk to us. Trina would get them to talking dirty, and then I'd make some remark about Lyuda, ending with "but I guess she has a boyfriend?" The problem was that she had lots of them. I kept having to go into the bathroom to write down more names. Somehow I had to decide on one particular guy.

Time went on, and I got tenser. Cigarette smoke filled the room. The bathroom was jammed and I had to wait. When I came back I saw Trina with a hardcore beatnik named Starsky—he got her attention with some garbled Americanisms: "Hey baby, let's jive down to Hollywood and drink cool Scotch. I love making it with gone broads like you and Lyuda." He showed her a wad of hard currency— dollars he had illegally bought from tourists. I decided on the spot that Starsky was my man, and told Trina to leave with him and find out where he lived.

Now that I'd finished my investigation, I could relax and enjoy myself. I got a bottle of vodka and sat down by Lyuda's Steinway piano. Some guy in sunglasses was playing a slow boogie-woogie. It was lovely, lovely enough to move me to tears—tears for Lyuda's corrupted beauty, tears for my lost childhood, tears for my mother's grave.

A sharp poke in the thigh interrupted my reverie.

"Quit bawling, fatso, this isn't the Ukraine."

The voice came from beneath the piano. Leaning down, I saw a man sitting cross-legged there, a thin, blond man with pale eyes. He smiled and showed his bad teeth. "Cheer up, pal, I mean it. And pass me that vodka bottle you're sucking. My name's Vlad Zipkin."

I passed him my bottle. "I'm Nikita Iosifovich Globov."

"Nice shoes," Vlad said admiringly. "Cool jacket, too. You're a snappy dresser, for a rocket-type."

"What makes you think I'm from the space center?" I said.

Vlad lowered his voice. "The shoes. You got those from Nokidze the Kazakh, the black market guy. He's been selling 'em all over Kaliningrad."

I climbed under the piano with Zipkin. The air was a little clearer there. "You're one of us, Comrade Zipkin?"

"I do information theory," Zipkin whispered, drunkenly touching one finger to his lips. "We're designing error-proof codes for communicating with the ... you know." He made a little orbiting movement with his forefinger and looked upward at the shiny dark bottom of the piano. The Sputnik had only been up since October. We space workers were still not used to talking about it in public.

"Come on, don't be shy," I said, smiling. "We can say 'Sputnik,' can't we? Everyone in the world has talked of nothing else for months!"

It was easy to draw Vlad out. "My group's hush-hush," he bragged criminally. "The top brass think 'information theory' has to be classified and censored. But the theory's not information itself, it's an abstract meta-information ..." He burbled on a while in the weird jargon of his profession. I grew bored and opened a pack of Kent cigarettes.

Vlad bummed one instantly. He was impressed that I had American cigarettes. Only cool black-market operators had classy cigs like that. Vlad felt the need to impress me in return. "Khrushchev wants the next sputnik to broadcast propaganda," he confided, blowing smoke. "The Internationale in outer space—what foolishness!" Vlad shook his head. "As if countries matter anymore outside our atmosphere. To any real Russian, it is already clear that we have surpassed the Americans. Why should we copy their fascist nationalism? We have soared into the void and left them in the dirt!" He grinned. "Damn, these are good smokes. Can you get me a connection?"

"What are you offering?" I said.

He nodded at Lyuda. "See our hostess? You see those earrings she has? They're gold-plated transistors I stole from the Center! All property is theft, hey Nikita?"

I liked Vlad well enough, but I felt duty-bound to report his questionable attitudes along with my information about Starsky. Political deviance such as Vlad's is a type of mental illness. I liked Vlad enough to truly want to see him get better.

Having made my report, I returned to Kaliningrad, and forgot about Vlad. I didn't hear about him for a month.

Since the early '50s, Kaliningrad had been the home of the Soviet space effort. Kaliningrad was thirty kilometers north of Moscow and had once been a summer resort. There we worked heroically at rocket research and construction—though the actual launches took place at the famous Baikonur Cosmodrome, far to the south. I enjoyed life in Kaliningrad. The stores were crammed with Polish hams and fresh lamb chops, and the landscape of forests and lakes was romantic and pleasant. Security was excellent.

Outside the research complex and block apartments were *dachas*, resort homes for space scientists, engineers, and party officials, including our top boss, the Chief Designer himself. The entire compound was surrounded by a high wood-and-concrete fence manned around the clock by armed guards. It was very peaceful. The compound held almost fifty *dachas*. I owned a small one—a kitchen and two rooms—with large garden filled with fruit trees and berry bushes, now covered by winter snow.

A month after Lyuda's party, I was enjoying myself in my *dacha*, quietly pressing a new suit I had bought from Nokidze the Kazakh, when I heard a black ZIL sedan splash up through the mud outside. I peeked through the curtains. A woman stamped up the path and knocked. I opened the door slightly.

"Nikita Iosifovich Globov?"

"Yes?"

"Let me in, you fat sneak!" she said.

I gaped at her. She addressed me with filthy words. Shocked, I let her in. She was a dusky, strong-featured Tartar woman dressed in a cheap black two-piece suit from the Moscow G. U. M. store. No woman in Kaliningrad wore clothes or shoes that ugly, unless she was a real hardliner. So I got worried. She kicked the door shut and glared at me.

"You turned in Vladimir Zipkin!"

"What?"

"Listen, you meddling idiot, I'm Captain Bogulyubova from Information Mechanics. You've put my best worker into the mental hospital! What were you thinking? Do you realize what this will do to my production schedules?"

I was caught off guard. I babbled something about proper ideology coming first.

"You louse!" she snarled. "It's my department and I handle Security there! How dare you report one of my people without coming to me first? Do you see me turning in metallurgists?"

"Well, you can't have him babbling state secrets to every beatnik in Moscow!" I said defensively.

"You forget yourself," said Captain Bogulyubova with a taut smile. "I have a rank in KGB and you are a common *stukach*. I can make a great deal of trouble for you. A very great deal."

I began to sweat. "I was doing my duty. No one can deny that. Besides, I didn't know he was in the hospital! All he needed was a few counseling sessions!"

"You fouled up everything," she said, staring at me through slitted eyes like a Cossack sizing up a captured hog. She crossed her arms over her hefty chest and looked around my *dacha*. "This little place of yours will be nice for Vlad. He'll need some rest. *Poor* Vlad. No one else from my section will want to work with him after he gets out. They'll be afraid to be seen with him! But we need him, and you're going to help me. Vlad will work here, and you'll keep an eye on him. It can be a kind of house arrest."

"But what about my work in metallurgy?"

She glared at me. "Your new work will be Comrade Zipkin's rehabilitation. You'll volunteer to do it, and you'll tell the Higher Circles that he's become a splendid example of communist dedication! He'd better get the order of Lenin, understand?"

"This isn't fair, Comrade Captain. Be reasonable!"

"Listen, you hypocrite swine, I know all about you and your black market dealings. Those shoes cost more than you make in a month!" She snatched the iron off the end of my board and slammed it flat against my brand new suit. Steam curled up.

"All right!" I cried, wringing my hands. "I'll help him." I yanked the suit away and splashed water on the scorched fabric.

Nina laughed and stormed out of the house. I felt terrible. A man can't help it if he needs to dress well. It's unfair to hold a thing like that over someone.

§

Months passed. The spring of 1958 arrived. The dog Laika had been shot into the cosmic void. A good dog, a

20

Russian, an Earthling. The Americans' first launches had failed, and then in February they shot up a laughable sputnik no bigger than a grapefruit. Meanwhile we metallurgists forged ahead on the mighty RD-108 Supercluster paraffin-fueled engine, which would lift our first cosmonaut into the Infinite. There were technical snags and gross lapses in space-worker ideology, but much progress was made.

Captain Nina dropped by several times to bluster and grumble about Vlad. She blamed me for everything, but it was Vlad's problem. All one has to do, really, is tell the mental health workers what they want to hear. But Zipkin couldn't seem to master this.

A third sputnik was launched in May 1958, with much instrumentation on board. Yet it still failed to broadcast a coherent propaganda statement, much less sing the *Internationale*. Vlad was missed, and missed badly. I awaited Vlad's return with some trepidation. Would he resent me? Fear me? Despise me?

For my part, I simply wanted Vlad to like me. In going over his dossier I had come to see that, despite his eccentricities, the man was indeed a genius. I resolved to take care of Vlad Zipkin, to protect him from his irrational sociopathic impulses.

A KGB ambulance brought Vlad and his belongings to my *dacha* early one Sunday morning in July. He looked pale and disoriented. I greeted him with false heartiness.

"Greetings Vladimir Eduardovich! It's an honor and a joy to have you share my *dacha*. Come in, come in. I have yogurt and fresh gooseberries. Let me help you carry all that stuff inside!"

"So it was you." Vlad was silent while we carried his suitcase and three boxes of belongings into the *dacha*. When I urged him to eat with me, his face took on a desperate cast. "Please, Globov, leave me alone now. Those months in the hospital—you can't imagine what it's been like."

"Vladimir, don't worry, this *dacha* is your home, and I'm your friend."

Vlad grimaced. "Just let me spend the day alone in your garden, and don't tell the KGB I'm antisocial. I want to conform, I do want to fit in, but for God's sake, not today."

"Vlad, believe me, I want only the best for you. Go out and lie in the hammock; eat the berries, enjoy the sun."

Vlad's pale eyes bulged as they fell on my framed official photograph of Laika, the cosmonaut dog. The dog had a weird, frog-like, rubber oxygen mask on her face. Just before launch, she had been laced up within a heavy, stiff space-suit—a kind of canine straitjacket, actually. Vlad frowned and shuddered. I guess it reminded him of his recent unpleasantness.

Vlad yanked my vodka bottle off the kitchen counter, and headed outside without another word. I watched him through the window—he looked well enough, sipping vodka, picking blackberries, and finally falling asleep in the hammock. His suitcase contained very little of interest, and his boxes were mostly filled with books. Most were technical, but many were scientific romances: the socialist H. G. Wells, Capek, Yefremov, Kazantsev, and the like.

When Vlad awoke he was in much better spirits. I showed him around the property. The garden stretched back thirty meters, where there was a snug outhouse. We strolled together out into the muddy streets. At Vlad's urging, I got the guards to open the gate for us, and we walked out into the peaceful birch and pine woods around the Klyazma Reservoir. It had rained heavily during the preceding week, and mushrooms were everywhere. We amused ourselves by gathering the edible ones—every Russian knows mushrooms.

Vlad knew an "instant pickling" technique based on lightly boiling the mushrooms in brine, then packing them in ice and vinegar. It worked well back in our kitchen, and I congratulated him. He was as pleased as a child.

In the days that followed, I realized that Vlad was not anti-Party. He was simply very unworldly. He was one of those gifted unfortunates who can't manage life without a protector.

Still, his opinion carried a lot of weight around the Center, and he worked on important problems. I escorted him everywhere—except the labs I wasn't cleared for—reminding him not to blurt out anything stupid.

Of course my own work suffered. I told my co-workers that Vlad was a sick relative of mine, which explained my common absence from the job. Rather than being disappointed by my absence, though, the other engineers praised my dedication to Vlad and encouraged me to spend plenty of time with him. I liked Vlad, but soon grew tired of the constant shepherding. He did most of his work in our *dacha*, which kept me cooped up there when I could have been out cutting deals with Nokidze or reporting on the beatnik scene.

It was too bad that Captain Nina Bogulyubova had fallen down on her job. She should have been watching over Vlad from the first. Now I had to tidy up after her bungling, so I felt she owed me some free time. I hinted tactfully at this when she arrived with a sealed briefcase containing some of Vlad's work. My reward was another furious tongue lashing.

"You parasite, how dare you suggest that I failed Vladimir Eduardovich? I have always been aware of his value as a theorist, and as a man! He's worth any ten of you *stukach* vermin! The Chief Designer himself has asked after Vladimir's health. The Chief Designer spent years in a labor camp under Stalin. He knows it's no disgrace to be shut away by some lickspittle sneak ..." There was more, and worse. I began to feel that Captain Bogulyubova, in her violent Tartar way, had personal feelings for Vlad.

Also I had not known that our Chief Designer had been in camp. This was not good news, because people who have spent time in detention sometimes become embittered and lose proper perspective. Many people were being released from labor camps now that Nikita Khrushchev had become the Leader of Progressive Mankind. Also, amazing and almost insolent things were being published in the *Literary Gazette*.

Like most Ukrainians, I liked Khrushchev, but he had a funny peasant accent and everyone made fun of the way he

23

talked on the radio. We never had such problems in Stalin's day.

We Soviets had achieved a magnificent triumph in space, but I feared we were becoming lax. It saddened me to see how many space engineers, technicians, and designers avoided Party discipline. They claimed that their eighty-hour work weeks excused them from indoctrination meetings. Many read foreign technical documents without proper clearance. Proper censorship was evaded. Technicians from different departments sometimes gathered to discuss their work, privately, simply between themselves, without an actual need-to-know.

Vlad's behavior was especially scandalous. He left top-secret documents scattered about the *dacha*, where one's eye could not help but fall on them. He often drank to excess. He invited engineers from other departments to come visit us, and some of them, not knowing his dangerous past, accepted. It embarrassed me, because when they saw Vlad and me together they soon guessed the truth.

Still, I did my best to cover Vlad's tracks and minimize his indiscretions. In this I failed miserably.

One evening, to my astonishment, I found him mulling over working papers for the RD-108 Supercluster engine. He had built a cardboard model of the rocket out of roller tubes from my private stock of toilet paper. "Where did you get those?" I demanded.

"Found 'em in a box in the outhouse."

"No, the documents!" I shouted. "That's not your department! Those are state secrets!"

Vlad shrugged. "It's all wrong," he said thickly. He had been drinking again.

"What?"

"Our original rocket, the 107, had four nozzles. But this 108 Supercluster has twenty! Look, the extra engines are just bundled up like bananas and attached to the main rocket. They're held on with hoops! The Americans will laugh when they see this."

"But they won't." I snatched the blueprints out of his hands. "Who gave you these?"

"Korolyov did," Vlad muttered. "Sergei Pavlovich."

"The Chief Designer?" I said, stunned.

"Yeah, we were talking it over in the sauna this morning," Vlad said. "Your old pal Nokidze came by while you were at work this morning, and he and I had a few. So I walked down to the bathhouse to sweat it off. Turned out the Chief was in the sauna, too—he'd been up all night working. He and I did some time together once, years ago. We used to look up at the stars, talk rockets together ... So anyway, he turns to me and says, 'You know how much thrust Von Braun is getting from a single engine?' And I said, 'Oh, must be eighty, ninety tons, right?' 'Right,' he said, 'and we're getting twenty-five. We'll have to strap twenty together to launch one man. We need a miracle, Vladimir. I'm ready to try anything.' So then I told him about this book I've been reading."

I said, "You were drunk on working-hours? And the chief Designer saw you in the sauna?"

"He sweats like anybody else," Vlad said. "I told him about this new fiction writer. Aleksander Kazantsev. He's a thinker, that boy." Vlad tapped the side of his head meaningfully, then scratched his ribs inside his filthy house robe and lit a cigarette. I felt like killing him. "Kazantsev says we're not the first explorers in space. There've been others, beings from the void. It's no surprise. The great space-prophet Tsiolkovsky said there are an infinite number of inhabited worlds. You know how much the Chief Designer admired Tsiolkovsky. And when you look at the evidence—I mean this Tunguska thing—it begins to add up nicely."

"Tunguska," I said, fighting back a growing sense of horror. "That's in Siberia, isn't it?"

"Sure. So anyway, I said, 'Chief, why are you wasting our time on these firecrackers when we have a shot at true star flight? Send out a crew of trained investigators to the impact site of this so-called Tunguska meteor! Run an information-theoretic analysis! If it was really an atomic-powered spacecraft like Kazantsev says, maybe there's something left that could help us!'"

I winced, imagining Vlad in the sauna, drunk, first bringing up disgusting prison memories, then babbling on about space fiction to the premier genius of Soviet rocketry. It was horrible. "What did the chief say to you?"

"He said it sounded promising," said Vlad airily. "Said he'd get things rolling right away. You got any more of those Kents?"

I slumped into my chair, dazed. "Look inside my boots," I said numbly. "My Italian ones."

"Oh," Vlad said in a small voice. "I sort of found those last week."

I roused myself. "The chief let you see the Supercluster plans? And said you ought to go to Siberia?"

"Oh, not just you and me," Vlad said, amused. "He needs a really thorough investigation! We'd commandeer a whole train, get all the personnel and equipment we need!" Vlad grinned. "Excited, Nikita?"

My head spun. The man was a demon. I knew in my soul that he was goading me. Deliberately. Sadistically. Suddenly I realized how sick I was of Vlad, of constantly watchdogging this visionary moron. Words tumbled out of me.

"I hate you, Zipkin! So this is your revenge at last, eh? Sending me to Siberia! You beatnik scum! You think you're smart, blondie? You're weak, you're sick, that's what! I wish the KGB had shot you, you stupid, selfish, crazy ..." My eyes flooded with sudden tears.

Vlad patted my shoulder, surprised. "Now don't get all worked up."

"You're nuts!" I sobbed. "You rocketship types are all crazy, every one of you! Storming the cosmos ... well, you can storm my sacred ass! I'm not boarding any secret train to nowhere—"

"Now, now," Vlad soothed. "My imagination, your thoroughness—we make a great team! Just think of them pinning awards on us."

"If it's such a great idea, then you do it! I'm not slogging through some stinking wilderness ..."

"Be logical!" Vlad said, rolling his eyes in derision. "You know I'm not well trusted. Your Higher Circles don't understand me the way you do. I need you along to smooth things, that's all. Relax, Nikita! I promise, I'll split the fame and glory with you, fair and square."

§

Of course, I did my best to defuse, or at least avoid, this lunatic scheme. I protested to Higher Circles. My usual contact, a balding jazz fanatic named Colonel Popov, watched me blankly, with the empty stare of a professional interrogator. I hinted broadly that Vlad had been misbehaving with classified documents. Popov ignored this, absently tapping a pencil on his "special" phone in catchy 5/4 rhythm.

Hesitantly I mentioned Vlad's insane mission. Popov still gave no response. One of the phones, not the "special" one, rang loudly. Popov answered, said, "Yes," three times, and left the room.

I waited a long hour, careful not to look at or touch anything on his desk. Finally Popov returned.

I began at once to babble. I knew his silent treatment was an old trick, but I couldn't help it. Popov cut me off.

"Marx's laws of historical development apply universally to all societies," he said, sitting in his squeaking chair. "That, of course, includes possible star-dwelling societies." He steepled his fingers. "It follows logically that progressive Interstellar Void-Ites would look kindly on us progressive peoples."

"But the Tunguska meteor fell in 1908!" I said.

"Interesting," Popov mused. "Historical-determinist cosmic-oids could have calculated through Marxist science that Russia would be first to achieve communism. They might well have left us some message or legacy."

"But Comrade Colonel ..."

Popov rustled open a desk drawer. "Have you read this book?" It was Kazantsev's space romance. "It's all the rage at the space center these days. I got my copy from your friend Nina Bogulyubova."

"Well ..." I said.

"Then why do you presume to debate me without even reading the facts?" Popov folded his arms. "We find it significant that the Tunguska event took place on June 30, 1908. Today is June 15, 1958. If heroic measures are taken, you may reach the Tunguska valley on the very day of the 50th anniversary!"

That Tartar cow Bogulyubova had gotten to the Higher Circles first. Actually, it didn't surprise me that our KGB would support Vlad's scheme. They controlled our security, but our complex engineering and technical developments much exceeded their mental grasp. Space aliens, however, were a concept anyone could understand.

Any skepticism on their part was crushed by the Chief Designer's personal support for the scheme. The chief had been getting a lot of play in Khrushchev's speeches lately, and was known as a miracle worker. If he said it was possible, that was good enough for Security.

I was helpless. An expedition was organized in frantic haste.

Naturally it was vital to have KGB along. Me, of course, since I was guarding Vlad. And Nina Bogulyubova, as she was Vlad's superior. But then the KGB of the other departments grew jealous of Metallurgy and Information Mechanics. They suspected that we were pulling a fast one. Suppose an artifact really were discovered? It would make all our other work obsolete overnight. Would it not be best that each department have a KGB observer present? Soon we found no end of applicants for the expedition.

We were lavishly equipped. We had ten railway cars. Four held our Red Army escort and their tracked all-terrain vehicles. We also had three sleepers, a galley car, and two flatcars piled high with rations, tents, excavators, Geiger counters, radios, and surveying instruments. Vlad brought a bulky calculating device, Captain Nina supplied her own mysterious crates, and I had a box of metallurgical analysis equipment, in case we found a piece of the UFO.

We were towed through Moscow under tight security, then our cars were shackled to the green-and-yellow Trans-Siberian Express.

28

Soon the expedition was chugging across the endless, featureless steppes of central Asia. I grew so bored that I was forced to read Kazantsev's book.

On June 30, 1908, a huge, mysterious fireball had smashed into the Tunguska River valley of the central Siberian uplands. This place was impossibly remote. Kazantsev suggested that the crash point had been chosen deliberately to avoid injuring Earthlings.

It was not until 1927 that the first expedition reached the crash site, revealing terrific devastation, but—*no sign whatsoever of a meteorite*! They found no impact crater, either; only the swampy Tunguska valley, surrounded by an elliptical blast pattern: sixty kilometers of dead, smashed trees.

Kazantsev pointed out that the facts suggested a nuclear airburst. Perhaps it was a deliberate detonation by aliens, to demonstrate atomic power to Earthlings. Or it might have been the accidental explosion of a nuclear starship drive. In an accidental crash, a socially advanced alien pilot would naturally guide his stricken craft to one of the planet's "poles of uninhabitedness." And eyewitness reports made it clear that the Tunguska body had definitely changed course in flight!

Once I had read this excellent work, my natural optimism surfaced again. Perhaps we would find something grand in Tunguska after all, something miraculous that the 1927 expedition had overlooked. Kulik's expedition had missed it, but now we were in the atomic age. Or so we told ourselves. It seemed much more plausible on a train with two dozen other explorers, all eager for the great adventure.

It was an unsought vacation for us hardworking *stukachi*. Work had been savage throughout our departments, and we KGB had had a tough time keeping track of our comrades' correctness. Meanwhile, back in Kaliningrad, they were still laboring away, while we relaxed in the dining saloon with pegged chessboards and tall brass samovars of steaming tea.

Vlad and I shared our own sleeping car. I forgave him for having involved me in this mess. We became friends again. This would be real man's work, we told each other.

Tramping through the savage taiga with bears, wolves, and Siberian tigers! Hunting strange, possibly dangerous relics—relics that might change the very course of cosmic history! No more of this poring over blueprints and formulae like clerks! Neither of us had fought in the Great Patriotic War—I'd been too young, and Vlad had been in some camp or something. Other guys were always bragging about how they'd stormed this or shelled that or eaten shoe leather in Stalingrad—well, we'd soon be making them feel pretty small!

Day after day, the countryside rolled past. First the endless, grassy steppes, then a dark wall of pine forest, broken by white-barked birches. Khrushchev's Virgin Lands campaign was in full swing, and the radio was full of patriotic stuff about settling the wilderness. Every few hundred kilometers, especially by rivers, raw and ugly new towns had sprung up along the Trans-Sib line. Prefab apartment blocks, mud streets, cement trucks, and giant sooty power plants. Trains unloaded huge spools of black wire. "Electrification" was another big propaganda theme of 1958.

Our Trans-Sib train stopped often to take on passengers, but our long section was sealed under orders from Higher Circles. We had no chance to stretch our legs and slowly all our carriages filled up with the reek of dirty clothes and endless cigarettes.

I was doing my best to keep Vlad's spirits up when Nina Bogulyubova entered our carriage, ducking under a line of wet laundry. "Ah, Nina Igorovna," I said, trying to keep things friendly. "Vlad and I were just discussing something. Exactly what *does* it take to merit burial in the Kremlin?"

"Oh, put a cork in it," Bogulyubova said testily. "My money says your so-called spacecraft was just a chunk of ice and gas. Probably a piece of a comet which vaporized on impact. Maybe it's worth a look, but that doesn't mean I have to swallow crackpot pseudo-science!"

She sat on the bunk facing Vlad's, where he sprawled out, stunned with boredom and strong cigarettes. Nina opened her briefcase. "Vladimir, I've developed those pictures I took of you."

"Yeah?"

She produced a Kirlian photograph of his hand. "Look at these spiky flares of suppressed energy from your fingertips. Your aura has changed since we've boarded the train."

Vlad frowned. "I could do with a few deciliters of vodka, that's all."

She shook her head quickly, then smiled and blinked at him flirtatiously. "Vladimir Eduardovich, you're a man of genius. You have strong, passionate drives ..."

Vlad studied her for a moment, obviously weighing her dubious attractions against his extreme boredom. An affair with a woman who was his superior, and also KGB, would be grossly improper and risky. Vlad, naturally, caught my eye and winked. "Look, Nikita, take a hike for a while, okay?"

He was putty in her hands. I was disgusted by the way she exploited Vlad's weaknesses. I left him in her carnal clutches, though I felt really sorry for Vlad. Maybe I could scare him up something to drink.

§

The closest train-stop to Tunguska is near a place call Ust-Ilimsk, two hundred kilometers north of Bratsk, and three thousand long kilometers from Moscow. Even London, England, is twice as close to Moscow as Tunguska.

A secondary-line engine hauled our string of cars to a tiny railway junction in the absolute middle of nowhere. Then it chugged away. It was four in the morning of June 26, but since it was summer it was already light. There were five families running the place, living in log cabins chinked with mud.

Our ranking KGB officer, an officious jerk named Chalomei, unsealed our doors. Vlad and I jumped out onto the rough boards of the siding. After days of ceaseless train vibration we staggered around like sailors who'd lost their land-legs. All around us was raw wilderness, huge birches and tough Siberian pines, with knobby, shallow roots. Permafrost was only two feet underground. There was nothing but trees and marsh for days in all directions. I found it very depressing.

31

We tried to strike up a conversation with the local supervisor. He spoke bad Russian, and looked like a relocated Latvian. The rest of our company piled out, yawning and complaining.

When he saw them, our host turned pale. He wasn't much like the brave pioneers on the posters. He looked scrawny and glum.

"Quite a place you have here," I observed.

"Is better than labor camp, I always thinking," he said. He murmured something to Vlad.

"Yeah," Vlad said thoughtfully, looking at our crew. "Now that you mention it, they *are* all police sneaks."

With much confusion, we began unloading our train cars. Slowly the siding filled up with boxes of rations, bundled tents, and wooden crates labeled SECRET and THIS SIDE UP.

A fight broke out between our civilians and our Red Army detachment. Our Kaliningrad folk were soon sucking their blisters and rubbing strained backs, but the soldiers refused to do the work alone.

Things were getting out of hand. I urged Vlad to give them all a good talking-to, a good, ringing speech to establish who was who and what was what. Something simple and forceful, with lots of "marching steadfastly together" and "storming the stars" and so on.

"I'll give them something better," said Vlad, running his hands back through his hair. "I'll give them the truth." He climbed atop a crate and launched into a strange, ideologically incorrect harangue.

"Comrades. You should think of Einstein's teachings. Matter is illusion. Why do you struggle so? Spacetime is the ultimate reality. Spacetime is one, and we are all patterns on it. We are ripples, Comrades, wrinkles in the fabric of the ..."

"Einstein is a tool of International Zionism," shouted someone.

"And you are a dog," said Vlad evenly. "Nevertheless you and I are the same. We are different parts of the cosmic One. Matter is just a ..."

"Drop dead," yelled another heckler.

"Death is an illusion," said Vlad, his smile tightening. "A person's spacetime pattern codes an information pattern which the cosmos is free to ..."

It was total gibberish. Everyone began shouting and complaining at once, and Vlad's speech stuttered to a halt.

Our KGB colonel Chalomei jumped up on a crate and declared that he was taking charge. He was attached directly to the Chief Designer's staff, he shouted, and was fed up with our expedition's laxity. This was nothing but pure mutiny, but nobody else outranked him in KGB. It looked like Chalomei would get away with it. He then tried to order our Red Army boys to finish the unloading.

But they got mulish. There were six of them, all Central Asian Uzbeks from Uckduck, a hick burg in Uzbekskaja. They'd all joined the Red Army together, probably at gunpoint. Their leader was Master Sergeant Mukhamed, a rough character with a broken nose and puffy, scarred eyebrows. He looked and acted like a tank.

Mukhamed bellowed that his orders didn't include acting as house-serfs for egghead aristocrats. Chalomei insinuated how much trouble he could make for Mukhamed, but Mukhamed only laughed.

"I may be just a dumb Uzbek," Mukhamed roared, "but I didn't just fall off the turnip truck! Why do you think this train is full of you worthless *stukachi*? It's so those big-brain rocket boys you left behind can get some real work done for once! Without you stoolies hanging around, stirring up trouble to make yourselves look good! They'd love to see you scum break your necks in the swamps of Siberia ..."

He said a great deal more, but the damage was already done. Our expedition's morale collapsed like a burst balloon. The rest of the group refused to move another millimeter without direct orders from Higher Circles.

We spent three days then, on the station's telegraph, waiting for orders. The glorious 50th Anniversary of the event came and went and everything was screwed up and in a total shambles. The gloomiest rumors spread among us. Some said that the Chief Designer had tricked us KGB to get us out of the way, and others said that Khrushchev himself was behind it. (There were always rumors of struggle between Party and KGB at the Very Highest Circles.) Whatever it meant, we were all sure to be humiliated when we got back, and heads would roll.

I was worried sick. If this really was a plot to hoodwink KGB, then I was in it up to my neck. Then the galley car caught fire during the night and sabotage was suspected. The locals, fearing interrogation, fled into the forest, though it was probably just one of Chalomei's *stukachi* being careless with a samovar.

Orders finally arrived from Higher Circles. KGB personnel were to return to their posts for a "reassessment of their performance." This did not sound promising at all. No such orders were given to Vlad or the "expedition regulars," whatever that meant. Apparently the Higher Circles had not yet grasped that there *were* no "expedition regulars."

Nina and I were both severely implicated, so we both decided that we were certainly "regulars" and should put off going back as long as possible. Together with Vlad, we had a long talk with Sergeant Mukhamed, who seemed a sensible sort.

"We're better off without those desk jockeys," Mukhamed said bluntly. "This is rough country. We can't waste time tying up the shoelaces of those Moscow fairies. Besides, my orders say 'Zipkin' and I don't see 'KGB' written anywhere on them."

"Maybe he's right," Vlad said. "We're in so deep now that our best chance is to actually *find* an artifact and prove them all wrong! Results are what count, after all! We've come this far—why turn tail now?"

Our own orders said nothing about the equipment. It turned out there was far too much of it for us to load it aboard the Red Army tractor vehicles. We left most of it on the sidings.

We left early next morning, while the others were still snoring. We had three all-terrain vehicles with us, brand new Red Army amphibious personnel carriers, called "BTR-50s," or "*byutors*" in Army slang. They had camouflaged steel armor and rode very low to the ground on broad tracks.

They had loud, rugged diesel engines and good navigation equipment, with room for ten troops each in a bay in the back. The front had slits and searchlights and little pop-up armored hatches for the driver and commander. The *byutors* floated in water, too, and could churn through the thickest mud like a salamander. We scientists rode in the first vehicle, while the second carried equipment and the third, fuel.

Once underway, our spirits rose immediately. You could always depend on the good old Red Army to get the job done! We roared through woods and swamps with a loud, comforting racket, scaring up large flocks of herons and geese. Our photoreconnaissance maps, which had been issued to us under the strictest security, helped us avoid the worst obstacles. The days were long and we made good speed, stopping only a few hours a night.

It took three days of steady travel to reach the Tunguska basin. Cone-shaped hills surrounded the valley like watchtowers.

The terrain changed here. Mummified trees strewed the ground like jackstraws, many of them oddly burnt. Trees decayed very slowly in the Siberian taiga. They were deep-frozen all winter and stayed whole for decades.

Dusk fell. We bulled our way around the slope of one of the hills, while leafless, withered branches crunched and shrieked beneath our treads. The marshy Tunguska valley, clogged and gray with debris, came in to view. Sergeant Mukhamed called a halt. The maze of fallen lumber was too much for our machines.

We tottered out of the *byutors* and savored the silence. My kidneys felt like jelly from days of lurching and jarring. I stood by our *byutor*, resting my hand on it, taking comfort in the fact that it was man-made. The rough travel and savage dreariness had taken the edge off my enthusiasm. I needed a drink.

But our last liter of vodka had gone out the train window somewhere between Omsk and Tomsk. Nina had thrown it away "for Vlad's sake." She was acting more like a lovesick schoolgirl every day. She was constantly fussing over Vlad, tidying him up, watching his diet, leaping heavily to his defense in every conversation. Vlad, of course, merely sopped up this devotion as his due, too absent-minded to notice it. Vlad had a real talent for that. I wasn't sure which of the two of them was more disgusting.

"At last," Vlad exulted. "Look, Ninotchka, the site of the mystery! Isn't it sublime!" Nina smiled and linked her solid arm with his.

The dusk thickened. Huge taiga mosquitoes whirred past our ears and settled to sting and pump blood. We slapped furiously, then set up our camp amid a ring of dense, smoky fires.

To our alarm, answering fires flared up on the five other hilltops ringing the valley.

"Evenks," grumbled Sergeant Mukhamed. "Savage nomads. They live off their reindeer, and camp in round tents called yurts. No one can civilize them; it's hopeless. Best just to ignore them."

"Why are they here?" Nina said. "Such a bleak place."

Vlad rubbed his chin. "The record of the '27 Kulik Expedition said the Evenk tribes remembered the explosion. They spoke of a Thunder-God smiting the valley. They must know this place pretty well."

"I'm telling you," rasped Mukhamed, "stay away. The men are all mushroom-eaters and the women are all whores."

One of the shaven-headed Uzbek privates looked up from his tin of rations. "Really, Sarge?"

"Their girls have lice as big as your thumbnails," the sergeant said. "And the men don't like strangers. When they eat those poison toadstools they get like wild beasts."

We had tea and hardtack, sniffling and wiping our eyes from the bug-repelling smoke. Vlad was full of plans. "Tomorrow we'll gather data on the direction of the treefalls. That'll show us the central impact point. Nina, you can help me with that. Nikita, you can stay here and help the soldiers set up base camp. And maybe later tomorrow we'll have an idea of where to look for our artifact."

Later that night, Vlad and Nina crept out of our long tent. I heard restrained groaning and sighing for half an hour. The soldiers snored on peacefully while I lay under the canvas with my eyes wide open. Finally Nina shuffled in, followed by Vlad brushing mud from his knees.

I slept poorly that night. Maybe Nina was no sexy hard-currency girl, but she was a woman, and even a *stukach* can't overhear that sort of thing without getting hot and bothered. After all, I had my needs, too.

Around one in the morning I gave up trying to sleep and stepped out of the tent for some air. An incredible aurora display greeted me. We were late for the 50th anniversary of the Tunguska crash, but I had the feeling the valley was welcoming me.

There was an arc of rainbow light directly overhead, with crimson and yellow streamers shooting out from the zenith towards the horizons. Wide luminous bands, paralleling the arch, kept rising out of the horizon to roll across the heavens with swift steady majesty. The bands crashed into the arch like long breakers from a sea of light.

The great auroral rainbow, with all its wavering streamers, began to swing slowly upwards, and a second, brighter arch formed below it. The new arch shot a long serried row of slender, colored lances towards the Tunguska valley. The lances stretched down, touched, and a lightning flash of vivid orange glared out, filling the whole world around me. I held my breath, waiting for the thunder, but the only sound was Nina's light snoring.

I watched for a while longer, until finally the great cosmic tide of light shivered into pieces. At the very end, disks appeared, silvery, shimmering saucers that filled the sky. Truly we had come to a very strange place. Filled with profound emotions, I was able to forget myself and sleep.

Next morning everyone woke up refreshed and cheerful. Vlad and Nina traipsed off with the surveying equipment. With the soldiers' help, I set up the diesel generator for Vlad's portable calculator. We did some camp scut-work, cutting heaps of firewood, digging a proper latrine. By then it was noon, but the lovebirds were still not back, so I did some exploring of my own. I tramped downhill into the disaster zone.

I realized almost at once that our task was hopeless. The ground was squelchy and dead, beneath a thick tangling shroud of leafless pines. We couldn't look for wreckage systematically without hauling away the musty, long-dead crust of trees. Even if we managed that, the ground itself was impossibly soggy and treacherous.

I despaired. The valley itself oppressed my soul. The rest of the taiga had chipmunks, wood grouse, the occasional heron or squirrel, but this swamp seemed lifeless, poisonous. In many places the earth had sagged into shallow bowls and depressions, as if the rock below it had rotted away.

New young pines had sprung up to take the place of the old, but I didn't like the look of them. The green saplings, growing up through the gray skeletons of their ancestors, were oddly stunted and twisted. A few older pines had been half-sheltered from the blast by freaks of topography. The living bark on their battered limbs and trunks showed repulsive puckered blast-scars.

Something malign had entered the soil. Perhaps poisoned comet ice, I thought. I took samples of the mud, mostly to impress the soldiers back at camp. I wasn't much of a scientist, but I knew how to go through the motions.

While digging I disturbed an ant nest. The strange, big-headed ants emerged from their tunnels and surveyed the damage with eerie calm.

By the time I returned to camp, Vlad and Nina were back. Vlad was working on his calculator while Nina read out direction-angles of the felled trees. "We're almost done," Nina told me, her broad-cheeked face full of bovine satisfaction. "We're running an information-theoretic analysis to determine the ground location of the explosion."

The soldiers looked impressed. But the upshot of Vlad's and Nina's fancy analysis was what any fool could see by glancing at the elliptical valley. The brunt of the explosion had burst from the nearer focus of the ellipse, directly over a little hill I'd had my eye on all along.

"I've been taking soil samples," I told Nina. "I suspect odd trace elements in the soil. I suppose you noticed the strange growth of the pines. They're particularly tall at the blast's epicenter."

"Hmph," Nina said. "While you were sleeping last night, there was a minor aurora. I took photos. I think the geomagnetic field may have had an influence on the object's trajectory."

"That's elementary," I sniffed. "What we need to study is a possible remagnetization of the rocks. Especially at impact point."

"You're neglecting the biological element," Nina said. By now the soldiers' heads were swiveling to follow our discussion like a tennis match. "I suppose you didn't notice the faint luminescence of the sod?" She pulled some crumpled blades of grass from her pocket. "A Kirlian analysis will prove interesting."

"But, of course, the ants—" I began.

"Will you two fakers shut up a minute?" Vlad broke in. "I'm trying to think."

I swallowed hard. "Oh yes, Comrade Genius? What about?"

"About finding what we came for, Nikita. The alien craft." Vlad frowned, waving his arm at the valley below us. "I'm convinced it's buried out there somewhere. We don't have a chance in this tangle and ooze ... but we've got to figure some way to sniff it out."

At that moment we heard the distant barking of a dog. "Great," Vlad said without pausing. "Maybe that's a bloodhound."

He'd made a joke. I realized this after a moment, but by then it was too late to laugh. "It's just some Evenk mutt," Sergeant Mukhamed said. "They keep sled-dogs ... eat 'em, too." The dog barked louder, coming closer. "Maybe it got loose."

Ten minutes later the dog bounded into our camp, barking joyously and frisking. It was a small, bright-eyed female husky, with muddy legs and damp fur caked with bits of bark. "That's no sled-dog," Vlad said, wondering. "That's a city mutt. What's it doing here?"

She was certainly friendly enough. She barked in excitement and sniffed at our hands trustingly. I patted the dog and called her a good girl. "Where on earth did you come from?" I asked. I'd always liked dogs.

One of the soldiers addressed the dog in Uzbek and offered it some of his rations. It sniffed the food, took a tentative lick, but refused to eat it.

"Sit!" Vlad said suddenly. The dog sat obediently.

"She understands Russian," Vlad said.

"Nonsense," I said. "She just reacted to your voice."

"There must be other Russians nearby," Nina said. "A secret research station, maybe? Something we were never told about?"

"Well, I guess we have a mascot," I said, scratching the dog's scalp.

"Come here, Laika," Vlad said. The dog pricked her ears and wandered toward him.

I felt an icy sensation of horror. I snatched my hand back as if I had touched a corpse. With an effort, I controlled myself. "Come on, Vlad," I said. "You're joking again."

"Good dog," Vlad said, patting her.

"Vlad," I said, "Laika's rocket burned up on re-entry."

"Yes," Vlad said, "the first creature we Earthlings put into space was sentenced to be burned alive. I often think about that." Vlad stared dramatically into the depths of the valley. "Comrades, I think something is waiting here to help us storm the cosmos. I think it preserved Laika's soul and reanimated her here, at this place, and at this time ... It's no coincidence. This is no ordinary animal. This is Laika, the cosmonaut dog!"

Laika barked loudly. I had never seen the dog without the rubber oxygen mask on her face, but I knew with a thrill of supernatural fear that Vlad was right. I felt an instant irrational urge to kill the dog, or at least give her a good kick. If I killed and buried her, I wouldn't have to think about what she meant.

The others looked equally stricken. "Probably fell off a train," Mukhamed muttered at last.

Vlad regally ignored this frail reed of logic. "We ought to follow Laika. The ... Thunder-God put her here to lead us. It won't get dark till ten o'clock. Let's move out, comrades." Vlad stood up and shrugged on his backpack. "Mukhamed?"

"Uh ..." the sergeant said. "My orders are to stay with the vehicles." He cleared his throat and spat. "There are Evenks about. Natural thieves. We wouldn't want our camp to be raided."

Vlad looked at him in surprise, and then with pity. He walked towards me, threw one arm over my shoulder, and took me aside. "Nikita, these Uzbeks are brave soldiers but they're a bit superstitious. Terrified of the unknown. What a laugh. But you and I ... Scientists, space pioneers ... the Unknown is our natural habitat, right?"

"Well ..."

"Come on, Nikita." He glowered. "We can't go back and face the top brass empty-handed."

Nina joined us. "I knew you'd turn yellow, Globov. Never mind him, Vlad, darling. Why should you share your fame and glory with this sneaking coward? I'll go with you—"

"You're a woman," Vlad assured her loftily. "You're staying here where it's safe."

"But Vlad—"

Vlad folded his arms. "Don't make me have to beat you." Nina blushed girlishly and looked at the toes of her hiking boots. She could have broken his back like a twig.

The dog barked loudly and capered at our feet. "Come on," Vlad said. He set off without looking back.

I grabbed my pack and followed him. I had to. I was guarding him: no more Vlad, no more Globov ...

Our journey was a nightmare. The dog kept trying to follow us, or would run yipping through ratholes in the brush that we had to circle painfully. Half on intuition, we headed for the epicenter of the blast, the little hillock at the valley's focus.

It was almost dusk again when we finally reached it, battered, scratched and bone-tired. We found a yurt there, half-hidden in a slough off to one side of the hill. It was an Evenk reindeer-skin tent, oozing grayish smoke from a vent-hole. A couple of scabby reindeer were pegged down outside it, gnawing at a lush, purplish patch of swamp moss. The dead trees around had been heavily seared by the blast, leaving half-charcoaled bubbly lumps of ancient resin. Some ferns and rushes had sprung up, corkscrewed, malformed, and growing with cancerous vigor.

The dog barked loudly at the wretched reindeer, who looked up with bleary-eyed indifference.

We heard leather thongs hiss loose in the door flap. A pale face framed in a greasy fur hood poked through. It was a young Evenk girl. She called to the dog, then noticed us and giggled quietly.

The dog rushed toward the yurt, wagging her tail. "Hello," Vlad called. He spread his open hands. "Come on out, we're friends."

The girl stepped out and inched toward us, watching the ground carefully. She paused at a small twig, her dilated eyes goggling as if it were a boulder. She high-jumped far over it, and landed giggling. She wore an elaborate reindeer-skin jacket that hung past her knees, thickly embroidered with little beads of bone and wood. She also had tight fur trousers with lumpy beaded booties, sewn all in one piece like a child's pajamas.

She sidled up, grinning coyly, and touched my face and clothes in curiosity. "Nikita," I said, touching my chest.

"Balan Thok," she whispered, running one fingertip down her sweating throat. She laughed drunkenly.

"Is that your dog?" Vlad said. "She came from the sky!" He gestured extravagantly. "Something under the earth here ... brought her down from the sky ... yes?"

I shrieked suddenly. A gargoyle had appeared in the tent's opening. But the blank, ghastly face was only a wooden ceremonial mask, shaped like a frying pan, with a handle to grip below the "chin." The mask had eye-slits and a carved mouth-hole fringed with a glued-on beard of reindeer hair.

Behind it was Balan Thok's father, or maybe grandfather. Cunningly, the old villain peered at us around the edge of his mask. His face was as wrinkled as an old boot. The sides of his head were shaven and filth-choked white hair puffed from the top like a thistle. His long reindeer coat was fringed with black fur and covered with bits of polished bone and metal.

We established that the old savage was called Jif Gurd. Vlad went through his sky-pointing routine again. Jif Gurd returned briefly to his leather yurt and re-emerged with a long wooden spear. Grinning vacuously, he jammed the butt of it into a socket in the ground and pointed to the heavens.

"I don't like the look of this," I told Vlad at once. "That spear has dried blood on it."

"Yeah. I've heard of this," Vlad said. "Sacrifice poles for the thunder-god. Kulik wrote about them." He turned to the old man. "That's right," he encouraged. "Thunder-God." He pointed to the dog. "Thunder-God brought this dog down."

"Thunder-God," said Jif Gurd seriously. "Dog." He looked up at the sky reverently. "Thunder-God." He made a descending motion with his right arm, threw his hands apart to describe the explosion. "Boom!"

"That's right! That's right!" Vlad said excitedly.

Jif Gurd nodded. He bent down almost absentmindedly and picked little Laika up by the scruff of the neck. "Dog."

"Yes, yes," Vlad nodded eagerly. Before we could do anything, before we could realize what was happening, Jif Gurd reached inside his greasy coat, produced a long, curved knife, and slashed poor Laika's throat. He lifted her up without effort—he was terribly strong, the strength of drug-madness—and jammed her limp neck over the end of the spear as if gaffing a fish.

Blood squirted everywhere. Vlad and I jumped back, horrified. "Hell!" Vlad cried in anguish. "I forgot that they sacrifice dogs!"

The hideous old man grinned and chattered excitedly. He was convinced that he understood us—that Vlad had wanted him to sacrifice the dog to the sky-god. He approved of the idea. He approved of us. I said, "He thinks we have something in common now, Vlad."

"Yeah," Vlad said. He looked sadly at Laika. "Well, we rocket men sacrificed her first, poor beast."

"There goes our last lead to the UFO," I said. "Poor Laika! All the way just for this!"

"This guy's got to know where the thing is," Vlad said stubbornly. "Look at the sly old codger—it's written all over his face." Vlad stepped forward. "Where is it? Where did it land?" He gestured wildly. "You take us there!"

Balan Thok gnawed her slender knuckles and giggled at our antics, but it didn't take the old guy long to catch on. By gestures, and a few key words, we established that the Thunder-God was in a hole nearby. A hidden hole, deep in the earth. He knew where it was. He could show it to us.

But he wouldn't.

"It's a religious thing," Vlad said, mulling it over. "I think we're ritually unclean."

"Muk-a-moor," said the old man. He opened the tent flap and gestured us inside.

The leather walls inside were black with years of soot. The yurt was round, maybe five steps across, and braced with a lattice of smooth flat sticks and buckskin thongs. A fire blazed away in the yurt's center, chunks of charred pine on a hearth of flat yellow stones. Dense smoke curdled the air. Two huge furry mounds loomed beside the hearth. They were Evenk sleeping bags, like miniature tents in themselves.

Our eyes were caught by the drying-racks over the fire. Mushrooms littered the racks, the red-capped fly agaric mushrooms that one always sees in children's books. The intoxicating toadstools of the Siberian nomad. Their steaming fungal reek filled the tent, below the acrid stench of smoke and rancid sweat.

"Muk-a-moor," said Jif Gurd, pointing at them, and then at his head.

"Oh, Christ," Vlad said. "He won't show us anything unless we eat his sacred mushrooms." He caught the geezer's eye and pantomimed eating.

The old addict shook his head and held up a leather cup. He pretended to drink, then smacked his rubbery, bearded lips. He pointed to Balan Thok.

"I don't get it," Vlad said.

"Right," I said, getting to my feet. "Well, you hold him here, and I'll go back to camp. I'll have the soldiers in by midnight. We'll beat the truth out of the old dog-butcher."

"Sit down, idiot," Vlad hissed. "Don't you remember how quick he was with that knife?"

It was true. At my movement a sinister gleam had entered the old man's eyes. I sat down quickly. "We can outrun him."

"It's getting dark," Vlad said. Just three words, but they brought a whole scene into mind: running blind through a maze of broken branches, with a drug-crazed, panting slasher at my heels ... I smiled winningly at the old shaman. He grinned back and again made his drinking gesture. He tossed the leather cup to Balan Thok, who grabbed at it wildly and missed it by two meters. She picked it up and turned her back on us. We heard her fumble with the lacing of her trousers. She squatted down. There was a hiss of liquid.

"Oh Jesus," I said. "Vlad, no."

"I've heard about this," Vlad said wonderingly. "The active ingredient passes on into the urine. Ten savages can get drunk on one mushroom. Pass it from man to man." He paused. "The kidneys absorb the impurities. It's supposed to be better for you that way. Not as poisonous."

"Can't we just eat the muk-a-moors?" I said, pointing at the rack. The old shaman glowered at me, and shook his head violently. Balan Thok sashayed toward me, hiding her face behind one sleeve. She put the warm cup into my hands and backed away, giggling.

I held the cup. A terrible fatalism washed over me. "Vladimir," I said. "I'm tired. My head hurts. I've been stung all over by mosquitoes and my pants are drenched with dog blood. I don't want to drink the poison piss of some savage—"

"It's for Science," Vlad said soberly.

45

"All my life," I began, "I wanted to work for the good of Society. My dear mother, God bless her memory ..." I choked up. "If she could see what her dear son has come to ... All those years of training, just for this! For this, Vlad?" I began trembling violently.

"Don't spill it!" Vlad said. Balan Thok stared at me, licking her lips. "I think she likes you," Vlad said.

For some weird reason these last words pushed me over the edge. I shoved the cup to my lips and drained the potion in one go. It sizzled down my gullet in a wave of hot nausea. Somehow I managed to keep from vomiting.

"How do you feel?" Vlad asked eagerly.

"My face is going numb." I stared at Balan Thok. Her eyes were full of hot fascination. I looked at her, willing her to come toward me. Nothing could be worse now. I had gone through the ultimate. I was ready, no, eager, to heap any degradation on myself. Maybe fornication with this degraded creature would raise me to some strange height.

"You're braver than I thought, Nikita," Vlad said. His voice rang with unnatural volume in my drugged ears. He pulled the cup from my numbed hands. "Considered objectively, this is really not so bad. A healthy young woman ... sterile fluid ... It's mere custom that makes it seem so repellent." He smiled in superior fashion, gripping the cup.

Suddenly the old Siberian shaman stood before him guffawing crazily as he donated Vlad's share. A cheesy reek came from his dropped trousers. Vlad stared at me in horror. I fell on my side, laughing wildly. My bones turned to rubber.

The girl laughed like a xylophone, gesturing to me lewdly. Vlad was puking noisily. I got up to lurch toward the girl, but forgot to move my feet and fell down. My head was inflamed with intense desire for her. She was turning round and round, singing in a high voice, holding a curved knife over her head. Somehow I tackled her and we fell headlong onto one of the Evenk sleeping bags, crushing it with a snapping of wood and lashings. I couldn't get out of my clothes. They were crawling over me like live things.

I paused to retch, not feeling much pain, just a torrent of sensations as the drug came up. Vlad and the old man were singing together loudly and at great length. I was thumping around vaguely on top of the girl, watching a louse crawl through one of her braids.

The old man came crawling up on all fours and stared into my face. "Thunder-God," he cackled, and tugged at my arm. He had pulled aside a large reindeer skin that covered the floor of the yurt. There was a deep hole, right there, right in the tent with us. Fighting the cramps in my stomach, I dragged myself toward it and peered in.

The space in the hole was strangely distorted; it was impossible to tell how deep it was. At its far end was a reticulated blue aurora that seemed to shift and flow in synchronization with my thoughts. For some reason I thought of Laika, and wished again that Jif Gurd hadn't killed her. The aurora pulsed at my thought, and there was a thump outside the tent—a thump followed by loud barking.

"Laika?" I said. My voice came out slow and drugged. Balan Thok had her arms around my neck and was licking my face. Dragging her after me, I crawled to the tent flap and peered out. There was a dog-shaped glob of light out there, barking as if its throat would burst.

I was scared, and I let Balan Thok pull me back into the tent. The full intoxication took over. Balan Thok undid my trousers and aroused me to madness. Vlad and the old man were lying at the edge of the Thunder-God hole, staring down into the growing blue light and screaming to it. I threw Balan Thok down between them, and we began coupling savagely. Each spastic twitch of our bodies was a coded message, a message that Vlad and Jif Gurd's howls were reinforcing. Our filth and drug-madness became a sacred ritual, an Eleusinian mystery. Before too long, I could hear the voice of ...

God? No ... not god, and not the Devil. The voice was from the blue light in the pit. And it wasn't a voice. It was the same, somehow, as the aurora I'd seen last night. It liked dogs, and it liked me. Behind all the frenzy, I was very happy there, shuddering on Balan Thok. Time passed.

RUDY RUCKER & BRUCE STERLING

At some point there was more barking outside, and the old man screamed. I saw his face, underlit by the pulsing blue glow from the Thunder-God hole. He bounded over me, waving his bloody knife overhead.

I heard a gunshot from the tent-door, and someone came crashing in. A person led by a bright blue dog. Captain Nina. The dog had helped her find us. The dog ran over and snapped at me, forcing me away from Balan Thok and the hole. I got hold of Vlad's leg, and dragged him along with me. There was another shot, and then Nina was struggling hand to hand with the old man. Vlad staggered to his feet and tried to join the fight. But I got my arms around his thin chest and kept backing away.

Jif Gurd and Nina were near the hole's jumpy light now, and I could see that they both were wounded. She had shot the old man twice with a pistol, but he had his knife, and the strength of a maniac. The two of them wrestled hand-to-hand, clawing and screaming. Now Balan Thok rose to her knees and began slashing at Nina's legs with a short dagger. Nina's pistol pointed this way and that, constantly about to fire.

I dragged Vlad backwards, and we tore through the rotting leather of the yurt's wall. An aurora like last night's filled the sky. Now that I wasn't staring into the hole I could think a little bit. So many things swirled in my mind, but one fact above all stuck out. *We had found an alien artifact.* If only it was a rocket-drive, then all of the terrible mess in the yurt could be forgotten ...

An incandescent blast lifted Vlad and me off the ground and threw us five meters. The entire yurt leapt into the sky. It was gone instantly, leaving a backward meteor trail of flaming orange in the sudden blackness of the sky. The sodden earth convulsed. From overhead, a leaping sonic boom pressed Vlad and me down into the muck where we had landed. I passed out.

Vlad shook me awake after many hours. The sun was still burning above the horizon. It was another of those dizzying, endless, timeless summer days. I tried to remember what had happened. When my first memories came I retched in pain.

Vlad had started a roaring campfire from dead, mummified branches. "Have some tea, Nikita," he said, handing me a tin army mug filled with hot, yellow liquid.

"No," I choked weakly. "No more."

"It's tea," Vlad said. I could tell his mind was running a mile a minute. "Take it easy. It's all over. We're alive, and we've found the star-drive. That blast last night!" His face hardened a bit. "Why didn't you let me try to save poor Nina?"

I coughed and wiped my bloodshot, aching eyes. I tried to fit my last twelve hallucinated hours into some coherent pattern. "The yurt," I croaked. "The star-drive shot it into the sky? That really happened?"

"Nina shot the old man. She burst in with a kind of ghost-dog? She burst in and the old man rushed her with his knife. When the drive went off, it threw all of them into the sky. Nina, the two Evenks, even the two reindeer and the dog. We were lucky—we were right at the edge of the ellipse."

"I saved you, Vlad. There was no way to save Nina, too. Please don't blame me." I needed his forgiveness because I felt guilty. I had a strange feeling that it had been my *wish of finding a rocket drive* that had made the artifact send out the fatal blast.

Vlad sighed and scratched his ribs. "Poor Ninotchka. Imagine how it must have looked. Us rolling around screaming in delirium and you having filthy sex with that Evenk girl ..." He frowned sadly. "Not what you expect from Soviet scientists."

I sat up to look at the elliptical blast area where the yurt had been. Nothing was left of it but a few sticks and thongs and bits of hide. The rest was a muddy crater. "My God, Vlad."

"It's extremely powerful," Vlad said moodily. "It wants to help us Earthlings, I know it does. It saved Laika, remember?"

"It saved her twice. Did you see the blue dog last night?"

Vlad frowned impatiently. "I saw lots of things last night, Nikita, but now those things are gone."

"The drive is gone?"

"Oh no," Vlad said. "I dug it out of the crater this morning."

He gestured at our booty. It was sitting in the mud behind him. It was caked with dirt and weird, powdery rust. It looked like an old tractor crankcase.

"Is that it?" I said doubtfully.

"It looked better this morning," Vlad said. "It was made of something like jade and was shaped like a vacuum cleaner. With fins. But if you take your eyes off it, it changes."

"No. Really?"

Vlad said, "It's looked shabby ever since you woke up. It's picking up on your shame. That was really pretty horrible last night, Nikita; I'd never thought that you ..."

I poked him sharply to shut him up. We looked at each other for a minute, and then I took a deep breath. "The main thing is that we've got it, Vlad. This is a great day in history."

"Yeah," agreed Vlad, finally smiling. The drive looked shinier now. "Help me rig up a sling for it."

With great care, as much for our pounding heads as for the Artifact itself, we bundled it up in Vlad's coat and slung it from a long, crooked shoulder-pole.

My head was still swimming. The mosquitoes were a nightmare. Vlad and I climbed up and over the splintery, denuded trunks of dead pines, stopping often to wheeze on the damp, metallic air. The sky was very clear and blue, the color of Lake Baikal. Sometimes, when Vlad's head and shoulders were outlined against the sky, I seemed to see a faint Kirlian shimmer traveling up the shoulder-pole to dance on his skin.

Panting with exhaustion, we stopped and gulped down more rations. Both of us had the trots. Small wonder. We built a good sooty fire to keep the bugs off for a while. We threw in some smoky green boughs from those nasty-looking young pines. Vlad could not resist the urge to look at it again.

We unwrapped it. Vlad stared at it fondly. "After this, it will belong to all mankind," he said. "But for now it's ours!"

It had changed again. Now it had handles. They looked good and solid, less rusty than the rest. We lugged it by the handles until we got within earshot of the base-camp.

The soldiers heard our yells and three of them came to help us.

They told us about Nina on our way back. All day she had paced and fidgeted, worrying about Vlad and trying to talk the soldiers into a rescue mission. Finally, despite their good advice, she had set off after us alone.

The aurora fireworks during the night had terrified the Uzbeks. They were astonished to see that we had not only survived, but triumphed.

But we had to tell them that Nina was gone.

Sergeant Mukhamed produced some 200-proof ethanol from the de-icing tank of his *byutor*. Weeping unashamedly, we toasted the memory of our lost comrade, State Security Captain Nina Igorovna Bogulyubova. After that we had another round, and I made a short but dignified speech about those who fall while storming the cosmos. Yes, dear Captain Nina was gone; but thanks to her sacrifice, we, her comrades, had achieved an unprecedented victory. She would never be forgotten. Vlad and I would see to that.

We had another toast for our cosmic triumph. Then another for the final victory. Then we were out of drinks.

The Uzbeks hadn't been idle while Vlad and I had been gone. They didn't have live ammo, but a small bear had come snuffling round the camp the day before and they'd managed to run over him with one of the *byutors*. The air reeked of roast bear meat and dripping fat. Vlad and I had a good big rack of ribs, each. The ribs in my chunk were pretty broken up, but it was still tasty. For the first time, I felt like a real hero. Eating bear meat in Siberia. It was a heck of a thing.

Now that we were back to the *byutors*, our problems were behind us and we could look forward to a real "rain of gold." Medals, and plenty of them. Big *dachas* on the Black Sea, and maybe even lecture tours in the West, where we could buy jazz records. All the Red Army boys figured they had big promotions coming.

We broke camp and loaded the carriers. Vlad wouldn't join in the soldiers' joking and kidding. He was still mooning about Nina. I felt sorry for Vlad. I'd never liked Nina much, and I'd been against her coming from the first. The wilderness was no place for females, and it was no wonder she'd come to grief. But I didn't point this out to Vlad. It would only have made him feel worse. Besides, Nina's heroic sacrifice had given a new level of deep moral meaning to our effort.

We packed the drive away in the first *byutor* where Vlad and I could keep an eye on it. Every time we stopped to refuel or study the maps, Vlad would open its wrappings and have a peek. I teased him about it. "What's the matter, comrade? Want to chain it to your leg?"

Vlad was running his hand over and over the drive's rusty surface. Beneath his polishing strokes, a faint gleam of silver had appeared. He frowned mightily. "Nikita, we must never forget that this is no soulless machine. I'm convinced it takes its form from what we make of it. It's a frozen idea— that's it true essence. And if you and I forget it, or look aside, it might just vanish."

I tried to laugh him out of it, but Vlad was serious. He slept next to it both nights, until we reached the rail spur.

We followed the line to the station. Vlad telegraphed full particulars to Moscow and I sent along a proud report to Higher Circles.

We waited impatiently for four days. Finally a train arrived. It contained some rocket-drive technicians from the Baikonur Cosmodrome, and two dozen uniformed KGB. Vlad and I were arrested. The Red Army boys were taken in custody by some Red Army brass. Even the Latvian who ran the station was arrested.

We were kept incommunicado in a bunk car. Vlad remained cheerful, though. "This is nothing," he said, drawing on his old jailbird's lore. "When they really mean business, they take your shoelaces. These KGB are just protective custody. After all, you and I have the greatest secret in cosmic history!" And we were treated well—we had red caviar, Crimean champagne, Kamchatkan king crab, blinis with sour cream.

The drive had been loaded aboard a flatcar and swathed down under many layers of canvas. The train pulled to a halt several times. The window shades on our car were kept lowered, but whenever we stopped, Vlad peeked out. He claimed the rocket specialists were adjusting the load.

After the second day of travel I had grave doubts about our whole situation. No one had interrogated us; for cosmic heroes, we were being badly neglected. I even had to beg ignominiously for DDT to kill the crab-lice I had caught from Balan Thok. Compared to the mundane boredom of our train confinement, our glorious adventure began to seem absurd. How would we explain our strange decisions—how would we explain what had happened to Nina? Our confusion would surely make it look like we were hiding something.

§

Instead of returning in triumph to Kaliningrad, our train headed south. We were bound for Baikonur Cosmodrome, where the rockets are launched. Actually, Baikonur is just the "security name" for the installation. The real town of Baikonur is five hundred kilometers away. The true launch site is near the village of Tyuratam. And Tyuratam, worse luck, is even more of a hick town than Baikonur.

This cheerless place lies on a high plain north of Afghanistan and east of the Aral Sea. It was dry and hot when we got there, with a cease-less irritating wind. As they marched us out of the train, we saw engineers unloading the drive. With derricks.

Over the course of the trip, as the government rocket experts fiddled with it, the drive had expanded to fit their preconceptions. It had grown to the size of a whole flatcar. It had become a maze of crooked hydraulics, with great ridged black blast-nozzles. It was even bound together with those ridiculous hoops.

Vlad and I were hustled into our new quarters: a decontamination suite, built in anticipation of the launch of our first cosmonauts. It was not bad for a jail. We probably would have gotten something worse, except that Vlad's head sometimes oozed a faint but definite blue glow, and that made them cautious.

Our food came through sterilized slots in the wall. The door was like a bank vault. We were interrogated through windows of bulletproof glass via speakers and microphones.

We soon discovered that our space drive had been classified at the Very Highest Circles. It was not to be publicly referred to as an alien artifact. Officially, our space-drive was a secret new design from Kaliningrad. Even the scientist already working on it at Tyuratam had been told this, and apparently believed it.

The Higher Circles expected our drive to work miracles, but they were to be miracles of national Soviet science. No one was to know of our contact with cosmic powers.

Vlad and I became part of a precedence struggle in Higher Circles. Red Army defense radars had spotted the launching of the yurt, and they wanted to grill us. Khrushchev's new Rocket Defense Forces also wanted us. So did the Kaliningrad KGB. And of course the Tyuratam technicians had a claim on us; they were planning to use our drive for a spectacular propaganda feat.

We ended up in the hands of KGB's Paranormal Research Corps.

Weeks grew into months as the state psychics grilled us. They held up Zener cards from behind the glass and demanded that we guess circle, star, or cross. They gave us racks of radish seedlings through the food slots, and wanted us to speak nicely to half of them, and scold the other half.

They wanted us to influence the roll of dice, and to make it interesting they forced us to gamble for our vodka and cigarette rations. Naturally we blew the lot and were left with nothing to smoke.

We had no result from these investigations, except that Vlad once extruded a tiny bit of pale blue ectoplasm, and I turned out to be pretty good at reading colors, while blindfolded, with my fingertips. (I peeked down the side of my nose.)

One of our interrogators was a scrawny hardline Stalinist named Yezhov. He'd been a student of the biologist Lysenko and was convinced that Vlad and I could turn wheat into barley by forced evolution. Vlad finally blew up at this. "You charlatans!" he screamed into the microphone. "Not one of you has even read Tsiolkovsky! How can I speak to you? Where is the Chief Designer? I demand to be taken to Comrade Sergei Korolyov! He'd understand this!"

"You won't get out of it that way," Yezhov yapped, angrily shaking his vial of wheat seeds. "Your Chief Designer has had a heart attack. He's recovering in his *dacha*, and Khrushchev himself has ordered that he not be disturbed. Besides, do you think we're stupid enough to let people with alien powers into the heart of Moscow?"

"So that's it!" I shouted, wounded to the core at the thought of my beloved Moscow. "You pimp! We've been holding out on you, that's all!" I jabbed my hand dramatically at him from behind the glass. "Tonight, when you're sleeping, my psychic aura will creep into your bed and squeeze your brain, like this!" I made a fist. Yezhov fled in terror.

Silence fell. "You shouldn't have done that," Vlad observed.

I slumped into one of our futuristic aluminum chairs. "I couldn't help it," I muttered. "Vlad, the truth's out. It's permanent exile for us. We'll never see Moscow again." Tears filled my eyes.

Vlad patted my shoulder sympathetically. "It was a brave gesture, Nikita. I'm proud to call you my friend."

"You're the brave one, Vlad."

"But without you at my side, Nikita ... You know, I'd have never dared to go into the valley alone. And if you hadn't drunk that piss first, well, I certainly would never have—"

"That's all in the past now, Vlad." My cheeks burned and I began sobbing. "I should have ignored you when you were sitting under that piano at Lyuda's. I should have left you in peace with your beatnik friends. Vlad, can you ever forgive me?"

"It's nothing," Vlad said nobly, thumping my back. "We've all been used, even poor Chief Korolyov. They've worked him to a frazzle. Even in camp he used to complain about his heart." Vlad shook his fist. "Those fools. We bring them a magnificent drive from Tunguska, and they convince themselves it's a reaction engine from Kaliningrad."

I burned with indignation. "That's right. It was our discovery! We're heroes, but they treat us like enemies of the State! It's so unfair, so uncommunist!" My voice rose. "If we're enemies of the State, then what are we doing in here? Real enemies of the State live in Paris, with silk suits and a girl on each arm! And plenty of capitalist dollars in a secret Swiss bank!"

Vlad was philosophical. "You can have all that. You know what I wanted? To see men on the moon. I just wanted to see men reach the moon, and know I'd seen a great leap for all humanity!"

I wiped away tears. "You're a dreamer, Vlad. The Infinite is just a propaganda game. We'll never see daylight again."

"Don't give up hope," Vlad said stubbornly. "At least we're not clearing trees in some labor camp where it's forty below. Sooner or later they'll launch some cosmonauts, and then they'll need this place for real. They'll have to spring us then!"

§

We didn't hear from the psychic corps again. We still got regular meals, and the occasional science magazine, reduced to tatters by some idiot censor who had decided Vlad and I were security risks. Once we even got a charity package from, of all people, Lyuda, who sent Vlad two cartons of Kents. We made a little ceremony of smoking one each, every day.

Our glass decontamination booth fronted on an empty auditorium for journalists and debriefing teams. Too bad none of them ever showed up. Every third day three cleaning women with mops and buckets scoured the auditorium floor. They always ignored us. Vlad and I used to speculate feverishly about their underwear.

56

The psychics had given up, and no one else seemed interested. Somehow we'd been lost in the files. We had been covered up so thoroughly that we no longer existed. We were the ghosts' ghosts, and the secrets' secrets, the best-hidden people in the world. We seemed to have popped loose from time and space, sleeping later and later each day, until finally we lost a day completely and could never keep track again.

We were down to our last pack of Kents when we had an unexpected visit.

It was a Red Army general with two brass-hat flunkies. We spotted him coming down the aisle from the auditorium's big double doors, and we hustled on our best shirts. The general was a harried-looking, bald guy in his fifties. He turned on our speakers and looked down at his clipboard. "Comrades Zipkin and Globov!"

"Let me handle this, Vlad," I hissed quickly. I leaned into my mike. "Yes, Comrade General?"

"My name's Nedelin. I'm in charge of the launch."

"What launch?" Vlad blurted.

"The Mars probe, of course." Nedelin frowned. "According to this, you were involved in the engine's design and construction?"

"Oh yes," I said. "Thoroughly."

Nedelin turned a page. "A special project with the Chief Designer." He spoke with respect. "I'm no scientist, and I know you have important work in there. But could you spare time from your labors to lend us a hand? We could use your expertise."

Vlad began to babble. "Oh, let us watch the launch! You can shoot us later, if you want! But let us see it, for God's sake—"

Luckily I had clamped my hand over Vlad's mike. I spoke quickly. "We're at your service, General. Never mind Professor Zipkin, he's a bit distraught."

One of the flunkies wheeled open our bank vault door. His nose wrinkled at the sudden reek of months of our airtight stench, but he said nothing. Vlad and I accompanied Nedelin through the building. I could barely hold back from skipping and leaping, and Vlad's knees trembled so badly I was afraid he would faint.

"I wouldn't have disturbed your secret project," the general informed us, "but Comrade Khrushchev delivers a speech at the United Nations tomorrow. He plans to announce that the Soviet Union has launched a probe to Mars. This launch must succeed today at all costs." We walked through steel double-doors into the Tyuratam sunshine. Dust and grass had never smelled so good.

We climbed into Nedelin's open-top field car. "You understand the stakes involved," Nedelin said, sweating despite the crisp October breeze. "There is a new American president, this Cuban situation ... our success is crucial!"

We drove off rapidly across the bleak concrete expanse of the rocket-field. Nedelin shouted at us from the front seat. "Intelligence says the Americans are redoubling their space efforts. We must do something unprecedented, something to crush their morale! Something years ahead of its time! The first spacecraft sent to another planet!"

Wind poured through our long hair, our patchy beards. "A new American president," Vlad muttered. "Big deal." As I soaked my lungs with fresh air I realized how much Vlad and I stank. We looked and smelled like derelicts. Nedelin was obviously desperate.

We pulled up outside the sloped, fire-scorched wall of a concrete launch bunker. The Mars rocket towered on its pad, surrounded by four twenty-story hinged gantries. Wisps of cloud poured down from the rocket's liquid oxygen ports. Dozens of technicians in white coats and hard-hats clambered on the skeletal gentry-ladders, or shouted through bullhorns around the rocket's huge base.

"Well, comrades?" Nedelin said. "As you can see, we have our best people at it. The countdown went smoothly. We called for ignition. And nothing. Nothing at all!" He pulled off his brimmed cap and wiped his balding scalp. "We have a very narrow launch window! Within a matter of hours we will have lost our best parameters. Not to mention Comrade Khrushchev's speech!"

Vlad sniffed the air. "Comrade General. Have you fueled this craft with liquid paraffin?"

"Naturally!"

Vlad's voice sank. "These people are working on a rocket which misfired. And you haven't drained the fuel?"

Nedelin drew himself up stiffly. "That would take hours! I understand the risk! I'm not asking these people to face any danger I wouldn't face myself!"

"You pompous ass!" Vlad screeched. "That's no Earthling rocket! It only looks like one because you expect it to! It's not supposed to have fuel!"

Nedelin stared in amazement. "What?"

"That's why it didn't take off!" Vlad raved. "It didn't want to kill us all! That drive is from outer space! You've turned it into a gigantic firebomb!"

"You've gone mad! Comrade, get hold of yourself!" Nedelin shouted. We were all on the edge of panic.

"This blockhead's useless," Vlad snarled, grabbing my arm. "We've got to get those people out of there, Nikita! It could take off any second—everyone expected it to!"

We ran for the rocket, shouting wildly, yelling anything that came into our heads. We had to get the technicians away. The Tunguska device had never known its own strength—it didn't know how frail we were. I stumbled and looked over my shoulder. Nedelin's flunkies were just a dozen steps behind us.

The ground crew saw us coming. They cried out in alarm. Panic spread like lightning.

It wouldn't have happened if we hadn't all been Russians. A gloomy and sensitive people are always ready to believe the worst. And the worst in this case was obvious: total disaster from a late ignition.

They fled like maniacs, but they couldn't escape their expectations. Pale streamers of flame gushed from the engines. More streamers arched from the rocket's peak, the spikes of auroral fire. The gantries shattered like matchsticks, filling the air above us with wheeling black shrapnel. Vlad stumbled to the ground. Somewhere ahead of us I could hear barking.

59

I hauled Vlad to his feet. "Follow the dog!" I bellowed over the roar. "Into the focus of the ellipse, where it's stable!"

Vlad stumbled after me, jabbering with rage. "If only the Americans had gotten the drive! They would have put men on the moon!"

We dashed through a blinding rain of paraffin. The barking grew louder, and now I could see the eager dog of blue light, showing us the way. The rocket was dissolving above us. The blast-seared concrete under our feet pitched and buckled like aspic. Before us the rocket's great nozzles dissolved into flaming webs of spectral whiteness.

Behind us, around us, the paraffin caught in a great flaming sea of deadly heat. I felt my flesh searing in the last instant: the instant when the inferno's shock wave caught us up like straws and flung us into the core of white light.

§

I saw nothing but white for the longest time, seeing nothing, touching nothing. I floated in the timeless void. All the panic, the terror of the event, evaporated from me. All thoughts stopped. It was like death. Maybe it was a kind of death, I still don't know.

And then, somehow, that perfect silence and oneness broke into pieces again. It shattered into millions of grainy atoms, a soundless crawling blizzard. Like phantom, hissing snow.

I stared into the snow, seeing it swirling, resolving into something new, with perfect ease, as if it were following the phase of my own dreams ... A beautiful sheen, a white blur—

§

The white blur of reflections on glass. I was standing in front of a glass window. A department-store window. There were televisions behind the glass, the biggest televisions I had ever seen.

Vlad was standing next to me. A woman was holding my arm, a pretty beatnik girl with a flowered silk blouse and a scandalous short skirt. She was staring raptly at the television. A crowd of well-dressed people filled the pavement around and behind us.

I should have fainted then. But I felt fine. I'd just had a good lunch and my mouth tasted of a fine cigar. I blurted something in confusion, and the girl with Vlad said, "Shhhh!" and suddenly everyone was cheering.

Vlad grabbed me in a bear hug. I noticed then how fat we were. I don't know why, but it just struck me. Our suits were so well-cut that they'd disguised it. "We've done it!" Vlad bellowed. "The moon!"

All around us people were chattering wildly. In French. We were in Paris. And Americans were on the moon.

§

Vlad and I had lost nine years in a moment. Nine years in limbo, as the Artifact flung us through time and space to that moment Vlad had longed so much to see. We were knit back into the world with many convincing details: paunches from years of decadent Western living, apartments in the émigré quarter full of fine suits and well-worn shoes, and even some pop-science articles Vlad had written for the émigré magazines. And of course, our Swiss bank accounts.

It was a disappointment to see the Americans steal our glory. But of course, the Americans would never have made it if we Russians hadn't shown them the way and supplied the vision. The Artifact was very generous to the Americans. If it weren't for the Nedelin Disaster, which killed so many of our best technicians, we would surely have won.

The West still believes that the Nedelin Disaster of October 1960 was caused by the explosion of a conventional rocket. They did not even learn of the disaster until years after the fact. Even now this terrible catastrophe is little known. The Higher Circles forged false statements of death for all concerned: heart attacks, air crashes, and the like. Years passed before the coincidences of so many deaths became obvious.

Sometimes I wonder if even the Higher Circles know the real truth. It's easy to imagine every document about Vlad and myself vanishing into the KGB shredders as soon as the disaster news spread. Where there is no history, there can be no blame. It's an old principle.

Now the Cosmos is stormed every day, but the rockets are nothing more than bread trucks. This is not surprising from Americans, who will always try their best to turn the stars into dollars. But where is our memorial? We had the great dream of Tsiolkovsky right there in our hands. Vlad and I found it ourselves and brought it back from Siberia. We practically threw the Infinite right there at their feet! If only the Higher Circles hadn't been so hasty, things would have been different.

Vlad has always told me not to say anything, now that we're safe and rich and officially dead, but it's just not fair. We deserve our historian, and what's a historian but a fancy kind of snitch? So I wrote this all down while Vlad wasn't looking.

I couldn't help it—I just had to inform somebody. No one has ever known how Vlad Zipkin and I stormed the cosmos, except ourselves and the Higher Circles ... and maybe some American top brass.

And Laika? Yes, the Artifact brought her to Paris, too. She still lives with us—which proves that all of this is true.

Notes on "Storming the Cosmos"

Asimov's Science Fiction, December, 1985.
Written Spring, 1985.

Rudy on "Storming the Cosmos"

The first I heard of Bruce Sterling was in 1982, when he sent me a review of my two novels *Software* and *Spacetime Donuts*. He'd written the review for a free newspaper in Austin. It was about the best review I'd ever gotten. Clearly this guy understood where I was coming from. He also sent me a copy of his novel *Involution Ocean*, a delightful take on *Moby Dick* which features dopers on a sea of sand.

I met Bruce in the flesh at a science-fiction convention in Baltimore in 1983, right after the publication of my fourth SF book, *The Sex Sphere*. He was there with his wife Nancy, plus William Gibson, Lou Shiner, and Lou Shiner's wife. The day after the con, the five of them unexpectedly drove down to visit me in Lynchburg, Virginia, where I was living as an unemployed writer, hoping to support my wife and three children. I came home from my rundown office in shades and a Hawaiian shirt, driving our 1956 Buick, and there they were. I was thrilled that they'd visited me.

Around that time, Bruce started publishing a single-sheet newsletter called *Cheap Truth*, which railed at the plastic artificiality of much SF. This zine—and Gibson's huge commercial success—soon established cyberpunk as a legitimate form of writing. I was grateful to be included.

"Storming the Cosmos" takes off on Bruce's deep interest in all things Soviet. He brought in a huge mass of facts for our story, which was wonderful. And he did more of the work on this one than me.

One way to organize a story collaboration is a transreal approach in which each author owns or in some sense *is* one of the characters. Ultimately Bruce and I organized every single one the *Transreal Cyberpunk* stories in that way. In "Storming the Cosmos," Bruce is Nikita and I'm Vlad.

I was really thrilled that we worked in Laika, the very first space dog. And I still laugh whenever I recall the bit where Nikita is saying, "I did it for Science."

This story got a cover on *Asimov's Science Fiction*.

Bruce on "Storming the Cosmos"

To collaborate with another writer one needs an agenda, because collaboration's not "half the work," it's twice the work, at the least. My agenda in "Storming the Cosmos" was the large problem I had as a Texan science fiction writer coming to terms with "fantastyka," with Soviet science fiction writing.

My interest there was, and is, genuine, but I was rather over-burdened with my autodidactic Soviet erudition. Also, there's something untoward and even tasteless about a Texan fantasist who rashly meddles with Soviet themes, especially when he lacks a humane sympathy for Russians or Marxists, and stares at the vast Soviet historical catastrophe as if it were some lunar ant-pile. As a story, "Storming the Cosmos" is a catalog of Russian catastrophes.

So the work needed a lighter touch, and Rudy supplied that: Russian beatniks.

No state-approved Soviet science fiction writer would ever valorize Russia's bohemian scumbags, erratic dropouts, and wacky refuseniks. But of course Russia did have many genuine counterculture people during the Soviet Space Age: smugglers, stilyagi, jazz listeners, hooligans, parasites, the pampered children of the Red elite. These erratic people would become our Soviet science-fiction heroes.

It's their Kerouackian lightness of heart that gets one through this picaresque tale that is, by any objective measure, terrifying. "Storming the Cosmos" is a perky road-tale, a Hope and Crosby Siberian buddy-movie where either or both of the dual leads can be denounced, arrested, jailed, liquidated, or even annihilated by unspeakable cosmic forces. "Storming the Cosmos" is dreadfully funny. Writing the story with Rudy allowed me to expand that blackly comic sensibility; it came pretty easily to him, but I learned it through imitation, and that was quite a useful, long-lasting lesson for me.

If you have to commit a breach of literary taste, there's no use being coy and camp about that; you've got to be Rabelaisian, Burroughsian, open and big-hearted, it needs to yawp right from the rooftops.

We quickly decided on dual protagonists—that was a whim, but a whim of iron that has persisted through all our joint works. "My" character, Globov the story's narrator, is less interesting than Zipkin, the Rucker character. Globov's best moments, which center on blubbering Slavic self-pity, were written by Rudy. I preferred writing Zipkin, especially those various scenes where Zipkin, a starry-eyed incompetent, tries to harangue and boss his way out of a jam.

We proved something to one another by writing this story together, as we didn't collaborate again for nine years.

Big Jelly

The screaming metal jellyfish dragged long, invisible tentacles across the dry concrete acres of the San Jose airport. Or so it seemed to Tug—Tug Mesoglea, math-drunk programmer and fanatic aquarist. Tug was working on artificial jellyfish, and nearly everything looked like a jellyfish to him, even airplanes. Tug was here in front of the baggage claim to pick up Texas billionaire Revel Pullen.

It had taken a deluge of phone-calls, faxes and email to lure the reclusive Texan venture-capitalist from his decrepit, polluted East Texas oil-fields, but Tug had now coaxed Revel Pullen to a second face-to-face meet in California. At last, it seemed that Tug's unconventional high-tech startup scheme would charge into full-scale production. The prospect of success was sweet.

Tug had first met Revel in Monterey two months earlier, at the Spring symposium of the ACM SIGUSC, that is, the Association for Computing Machinery's Special Interest Group for Underground and Submarine Computation.

At the symposium, Tug had given a badly botched presentation on artificial jellyfish. He'd arrived with 500 copies of a glossy desktop-published brochure: "Artificial Jellyfish: Your Route to Postindustrial Global Competitiveness!" But when it came time for Tug's talk, his 15-terabyte virtual jellyfish-demo had crashed so hideously that he couldn't even reboot his machine—a cheap Indonesian Sun-clone laptop that Tug now used as a bookend. Tug had brought some slides as a backup, but of course the slide-tray had jammed. And, worst of all, the single working prototype of Tug's plastic artificial jellyfish had burst in transit to Monterey. After the talk, Tug, in a red haze of shame, had flushed the sodden rags of decomposing gel down the conference center's john.

Tug had next headed for the cocktail lounge, and there the garrulous young Pullen had sought him out, had a few drinks with him, and had even picked up the tab—Tug's wallet had been stolen the night before by a cute older busboy.

Since Tug's topic was jellyfish, the raucous Pullen had thought it funny to buy rounds of tequila jelly-shots. The slimy jolts of potent boozy Jell-O had combined with Revel's bellowed jokes, brags, and wild promises to ease the pain of Tug's failed speech.

The next day, Tug and Revel had brunched together, and Revel had written Tug a handsome check as earnest money for pre-development expenses. Tug was to develop an artificial jellyfish capable of undersea oil prospecting.

As software applications went, oil-drilling was a little roughnecked and analog for Tug's taste; but the money certainly looked real enough. The only troubling aspect about dealing with Revel was the man's obsession with some new and troublesome organic slime which his family's oldest oil-well had recently tapped. Again and again, the garish Texan had steered the conversation away from jellyfish and onto the subject of ancient subterranean slime.

Perched now on the fire-engine red hood of his expensive Animata sports car, Tug waited for Revel to arrive. Tug had curly dark hair and a pink-cheeked complexion. He wore shorts, a sport shirt, and Birkenstock sandals with argyle socks. He looked like a depraved British schoolboy. He'd bought the Animata with his house-money nest-egg when he'd learned that he would never, ever, be rich enough to buy a house in California. Leaning back against the windshield of his car, Tug stared at the descending airplanes and thought about jellyfish trawling through sky-blue seawater.

Tug had whole tankfuls of jellies at home: one tank with flattish moon jellies each with its four whitish circles of sex organs, another tank with small clear bell jellies from the eel grass of Monterey bay, a large tank with sea nettles that had long frilly oral arms and whiplike purple tentacles covered with stinging cells, a smaller tank of toadstool-like spotted jellies from Jellyfish Lake in Palau, a special tank of spinning comb-jellies with trailing ciliated arms, a Japanese tank with Japanese umbrella jellies—and more.

Next to the arsenal of tanks was the huge color screen of Tug's workstation. Tug was no biologist; he'd blundered under the spell of the jellies while using mathematical algorithms to generate cellular models of vortex sheets. To Tug's mathematician's eye, a jellyfish was a highly perfected relationship between curvature and torsion, just like a vortex sheet, only a jellyfish was working off dynamic tension and osmotic stress. Real jellyfish were gnarlier than Tug's simulations. Tug had become a dedicated amateur of coelenteratology.

Imitating nature to the core, Tug found a way to evolve and improve his vortex sheet models via genetic programming. Tug's artificial jellyfish algorithms competed, mutated, reproduced and died inside the virtual reality of his workstation's sea-green screen. As Tug's algorithms improved, his big computer monitor became a tank of virtual jellyfish, of graphic representations of Tug's equations, pushing at the chip's computational limits, slowly pulsing about in dimly glowing simulation-space.

The living jellies in the tanks of true seawater provided an objective standard towards which Tug's programs could try to evolve. At every hour of the day and night, video cameras peered into the spot-lit water tanks, ceaselessly analyzing the jellyfish motions and feeding data into the workstation.

The recent, crowning step of Tug's investigations was his manufacturing breakthrough. His theoretical equations had become actual piezoplastic constructions—soft, watery, gelatinous robot jellies of real plastic in the real world. These models were produced by using an intersecting pair of laser beams to sinter—that is, to join together by heating without melting—the desired shape within a matrix of piezoplastic microbeads. The sintered microbeads behaved like a mass of cells: each of them could compress or elongate in response to delicate vibratory signals, and each microbead could in turn pass information to its neighbors.

A completed artificial jellyfish model was a floppy little umbrella that beat in steady cellular waves of excitation and relaxation. Tug's best plastic jellyfish could stay active for up to three weeks.

Tug's next requirement for his creations was "a killer application," as the software tycoons called it. And it seemed he might have that killer app in hand, given his recent experiments in making the jellyfish sensitive to chemical scents and signals. Tug had convinced Revel—and half-believed himself—that the artificial jellies could be equipped with radio-signaling chips and set loose beneath the sea floor. They could sniff out oil-seeps in the ocean bottom and work their way deep into the vents. If this were so, then artificial jellyfish would revolutionize undersea oil prospecting.

The only drawback, in Tug's view, was that offshore drilling was a contemptible crime against the wonderful environment that had bred the real jellies in the first place. Yet the plan seemed likely to free up Texas venture capital, enough capital to continue his research for at least another year. And maybe in another year, thought Tug, he would have a more ecologically sound killer app, and he would be able to disentangle himself from the crazy Texan.

Right on cue, Revel Pullen came strolling down the exit ramp, clad in the garb of a white-trash oil-field worker: a flannel shirt and a pair of Can't-Bust-'Em overalls. Revel had a blonde crewcut and smooth dark skin. The shirt was from Nieman-Marcus and the overalls were ironed, but they seemed to be genuinely stained with dirt-fresh Texas crude.

Tug hopped off the hood of his car and stood on tiptoe to wave, deliberately camping it up to jangle the Texan's nerves. He drew up a heel behind him like Marilyn Monroe waving in The Misfits.

Nothing daunted, Revel Pullen headed Tug's way with an exaggerated bowlegged sprawl and a scuff of his python-skin boots. Revel was the scapegrace nephew of Amarillo's billionaire Pullen Brothers. The Pullen clan were malignant market speculators and greenmail raiders who had once tried to corner the world market in molybdenum.

Revel himself, the least predictable of his clan, was in charge of the Pullen Brothers' weakest investments: the failing oil wells that had initially brought the Pullen family to prominence—beginning with the famous Ditheree Gusher, drilled near Spindletop, Texas in 1892.

Revel's quirk was his ambition to become a high-tech tycoon. This was why Revel attended computer-science meetings like SIGUSC, despite his stellar ignorance of everything having to do with the movement of bytes and pixels.

Revel stood ready to sink big money into a technically sexy Silicon Valley start-up. Especially if the start-up could somehow do something for his family's collapsing oil industry and—though this part still puzzled Tug—find a use for some odd clear fluid that Revel's engineers had recently been pumping from the Ditheree hole.

"Shit howdy, Tug," drawled Revel, hoisting his polyester/denim duffel bag from one slim shoulder to another. "Mighty nice of y'all to come meet me."

Beaming, Tug freed his fingers from Revel's insistent grip and gestured toward the Animata. "So, Revel! Ready to start a business? I've decided we should call it Ctenophore, Inc. A ctenophore is a kind of hermaphroditic jellyfish which uses a comb-like feeding organ to filter nutrients from the ocean; they're also called comb-jellies. Don't you think Ctenophore is a perfect name for our company? Raking in the dollars from the economy's mighty sea!"

"Not so loud!" Revel protested, glancing up and down the airport pavement in a parody of wary street-smarts. "As far as any industrial spy knows, I'm here in California on a personal vacation." He heaved his duffel into the back seat of Tug's car. Then he straightened, and reached deep into the baggy trouser-pocket of his Can't-Bust-'Ems.

The Texan dragged out a slender pill-bottle filled with clear viscous jelly and pressed the crotch-warmed vial into Tug's unwilling palm, with a dope-dealer's covert insistence.

"I want you to keep this, Tug. Just in case anything should ... you know ... happen to me."

Revel swiveled his narrow head to scan the passers-by with paranoid alertness, briefly reminding Tug of the last time he'd been here at the San Jose airport: to meet his ailing father, who'd been fingerpaint-the-wall-with-shit senile and had been summarily dumped on the plane by Tug's uncle. Tug had gotten his father into a local nursing home, and last summer Tug's father had died.

Life was sad, and Tug was letting it slip through his fingers—he was an unloved gay man who'd never see thirty again, and now here he was humoring a nutso het from Texas. Humoring people was not something Tug excelled at.

"Do you really have enemies?" said Tug. "Or do you just think so? Am I supposed to think you have enemies? Am I supposed to care?"

"There's money in these plans of ours—real foldin' money," Revel bragged darkly, climbing into the Animata's passenger seat. He waited silently until Tug took the wheel and shut the driver's-side door. "All we really gotta worry about," Revel continued at last, "is controlling the publicity. The environmental impact crap. You didn't tell anybody about what I emailed you, did you?"

"No," snapped Tug. "That cheap public-key encryption you're using has garbled half your messages. What are you so worried about, anyway? Nobody's gonna care about some slime from a played-out oil-well—even if you do call it Urschleim. That's German, right?"

"Shhhhh!" hissed Revel.

Tug started the engine and gunned it with a bluish gust of muscular combustion. They swung out into the endless California traffic.

Revel checked several times to make sure that they weren't being trailed. "Yes, I call it Urschleim," he said at last, portentously. "In fact, I've put in a trademark for that name. Them old-time German professors were onto something. Ur means primeval. All life came from the Urschleim, the original slime! Primeval slime from the inner depths of the planet! You ever bitten into a green almond, Tug? From the tree? There's some green fuzz, a thin little shell and a center of clear, thick slime. That's exactly how our planet is, too. Most of the original Urschleim is still flowing, and oozing, and lyin' there 'way down deep. It's just waitin' for some bright boy to pump it out and exploit its commercial potential. Urschleim is life itself."

"That's pretty grandiose," said Tug evenly.

"Grandiose, hell!" Revel snapped. "It's the only salvation for the Texan oil business, compadre! God damn it, if we Texans don't drill for a living, we'll be reduced to peddling chips and software like a bunch of goddamn Pacific Rim computer weenies! You got me wrong if you think I'll give up the oil business without a fight!"

"Sure, sure, I'm hip," Tug said soothingly. "My jellyfish are going to help you find more oil, remember?" It was easy to tell when Revel had gone nonlinear—his Texan drawl thickened drastically and he began to refer to his beloved oil business as the "Aisle Bidness." But what was the story with this Urschleim?

Tug held up the pill-bottle of clear slime and glanced at it while steering with one hand. The stuff was thixotropic— meaning a gel which becomes liquid when shaken. You'd tilt the vial and all the Urschleim would be stuck in one end, but then, if you shook the bottle a bit, the slime's state would change and it would all run down to the other end like ketchup suddenly gushing from a bottle. Smooth, clear ketchup. Snot.

"The Ditheree hole's oozin' with Urschleim right now!" said Revel, settling a pair of Italian sunglasses onto his freckled nose. He looked no older than twenty-five. "I brought three gallons of it in a tank in my duffel. One of my engineers says it's a new type of deep-lying oil, and another one says it's just water infected with bacteria. But I'm with old Herr Doktor Professor von Stoffman. We've struck the cell fluid of Mother Earth herself: undifferentiated tissue, Tug, primordial ooze. Gaia goo. Urschleim!"

"What did you do to make it start oozing?" asked Tug, suppressing a giggle.

Revel threw back his head and crowed. "Man, if OPEC got wind about our new high-tech extraction techniques ... You don't think I got enemies, son? Them sheiks play for keeps." Revel tapped his knuckles cagily against the car's closed window. "Hell, even Uncle Sam'd be down on us if he knew that we've been twisting genes and seeding those old worn-out oilbeds with designer bacteria! They eat through tar and paraffin, change the oil's viscosity, unblock the pores in the stone and get it all fizzy with methane ... You wouldn't think the ol' Ditheree had it in 'er to blow valves and gush again, but we plumbed her out with a new extra-virulent strain. And what did she gush? Urschleim!"

Revel peered at Tug over the tops of his designer sunglasses, assuming what he seemed to think was a trustworthy expression. "But that ain't the half of it, Tug. Wait till I tell you what we did with the stuff once we had it."

Tug was impatient. Gusher or not, Revel's bizarre maunderings were not going to sell any jellyfish. "What did you think of that artificial jellyfish I sent you?"

Revel frowned. "Well, it looked okay when it showed up. About the size of a deflated football. I dropped in my swimmin' pool. It was floatin' there, kinda rippling and pulsing, for about two days. Didn't you say that sucker would run for weeks? Forty-eight hours and it was gone! Disintegrated I guess. Chlorine melted the plastic or something."

"No way," protested Tug, intensely. "It must have slipped out a crack in the side of your pool. I built that model to last three weeks for sure! It was my best prototype. It was a chemotactic artificial jellyfish designed to slither into undersea vents and find its way to underground oil beds."

"My swimming pool's not in the best condition," allowed Revel. "So I guess it's possible that your jellyfish did squeeze out through a crack. But if this oil-prospecting application of yours is any good, the thing should have come back with some usable geology data. And it never did come back that I noticed. Face it Tug, the thing melted."

Tug wouldn't give in. "My jellyfish didn't send back information because I didn't put a tracer chip in it. If you're going to be so rude about it, I might as well tell you that I don't think oil prospecting is a very honorable application. I'd really rather see the California Water Authority using my jellies to trace leaks in irrigation and sewage lines."

Revel yawned, sinking deeper into the passenger seat. "That's real public-spirited of you, Dr. Mesoglea. But California water ain't worth a dime to me."

Tug pressed onward. "Also, I'd like to see my jellyfish used to examine contaminated wells here in Silicon Valley. If you put an artificial jellyfish down a well, and leave it to pulsate down there for a week or two, it could filter up all kinds of trace pollutants! It'd be a great public-relations gambit to push the jelly's anti-pollution aspects. Considering your family history, it couldn't hurt to get the Pullen family in the good graces of the Environmental Protection people. If we angle it right, we could probably even swing a federal development grant!"

"I dunno, hombre," Revel grumbled. "Somehow it just don't seem sportin' to take money from the Feds ..." He gazed mournfully at the lushly exotic landscape of monkey-puzzle trees, fat pampered yuccas, and orange trees. "Man, everything sure looks green out here."

"Yes," Tug said absently, "thank God there's been a break in the drought. California has plenty of use for a jellyfish that can monitor water-leaks."

"It's not the water that counts," said Revel, "it's the carbon dioxide. Two hundred million years' worth of crude oil, all burned to carbon dioxide and spewed right into the air in just few short decades. Plant life's goin' crazy. Why, all the plant life along this highway has built itself out of car exhausts! You ever think o' that?"

It was clear from the look of glee on Revel's shallow features that this thought pleased him mightily. "I mean, if you traced the history of the carbon in that weirdass lookin' tree over there ... hunnert years ago it was miles down in the primeval bowels of the earth! And since we eat plants to live, it's the same for people! Our flesh, brain and blood is built outa burnt crude-oil! We're creatures of the Urschleim, Tug. All life comes from the primeval goo."

"No way," said Tug heatedly. He took a highway exit to Los Perros, his own local enclave in the massive sprawl that was Silicon Valley. "One carbon atom's just like the next one. And once you're talking artificial life, it doesn't even have to be an 'atom' at all. It can be a byte of information, or a microbead of piezoplastic. It doesn't matter where the material came from—life is just a pattern of behavior."

"That's where you and me part company, boy." They were tooling down the main drag of Los Perros now, and Revel was gaping at some chicly dressed women. "Dig it, Tug, thanks to oil, a lot of the carbon in your yuppie neighbors comes from Texas. Like it or not, most modern life is fundamentally Texan."

"That's pretty appalling news, Revel," smiled Tug. He took the last remaining hilly corners with a squeal of his Michelins, then pulled into his driveway. He parked the Animata under the rotting, fungus-specked redwood deck of the absurdly overpriced suburban home that he rented. The rent was killing him. Ever since his lover had moved out last Christmas, Tug had been meaning to move into a smaller place, but somewhere deep down he nursed a hope that if he kept the house, some nice strong man would come and move in with him.

Next door, Tug's neighbors were flinging water-balloons and roaring with laughter as they sizzled up a huge aromatic rack of barbecued tofu. They were rich Samoans. They had a big green parrot called Toatoa. On fine days, such as today, Toatoa sat squawking on the gable of the house. Toatoa had a large yellow beak and a taste for cuttlebone and pumpkin-seeds.

"This is great," Revel opined, examining the earthquake-split walls and peeling ceiling sheetrock. "I was afraid we'd have some trouble findin' the necessary space for experiments. No problem though, with you rentin' this sorry dump for a workshop."

"I live here," said Tug with dignity. "By California standards this is a very good house."

"No wonder you want to start a company!" Revel climbed the redwood stairs to Tug's outdoor deck, and dragged a yard-long plastic pressure-cylinder from within his duffel bag, flinging aside some balled-up boot socks and a set of watered-silk boxer shorts. "You got a garden hose? And a funnel?" He pulled a roll of silvered duct tape from the bottom of his bag.

Tug supplied a length of hose, prudently choosing one that had been severely scorched during the last hillside brushfire. Revel whipped a French designer pocketknife from within his Can't-Bust-'Ems and slashed off a three-foot length. He then deftly duct-taped the tin funnel to the end of the hose, and blew a few kazoo-like blasts.

Revel then flung the crude horn aside and took up the pressure cylinder. "You don't happen to have a washtub, do you?"

"No problem," Tug said. He went into the house and fetched a large plastic picnic cooler.

Revel opened the petcock of the pressure cylinder and began decanting its contents into the cooler. The black nozzle slowly ejaculated a thick clear gel, rather like silicone putty. Pint after pint of it settled languorously into the white pebbly interior of the hinge-topped cooler. The stuff had a sulfurous, burning-rubber reek that Tug associated with Hawaii—a necessarily brief stay he'd had on the oozing, flaming slopes of Kilauea.

Tug prudently sidled across the deck and stood upwind of the cooler. "How far down did you obtain this sample?"

Revel laughed. "Down? Doc, this stuff broke the safety-valves on old Ditheree and blew drillin' mud over five counties. We had an old-time blue-ball gusher of it. It just kept comin', pourin' out over the ground. Kinda, you know, spasmodic ... Finally ended up with a lake of clear hot pudding higher than the tops of pickups."

"Jesus, what happened then?" Tug asked.

"Some evaporated. Some soaked right into the subsoil. Disappeared. The first sample I scored was out of the back of some good ol' boy's Toyota. Lucky thing he had the tailgate up, or it woulda all run out."

Revel pulled out a handkerchief, wiped sweat from his forehead, and continued talking. "Of course, once we got the rig repaired, we did some serious pump-work. We Pullens happen to own a tank-farm near Nacogdoches, a couple a football field's worth of big steel reservoirs. Haven't seen use since the OPEC embargo of the 70s. They were pretty much abandoned on site. But every one of them babies is brim-full with Revel Pullen's trademark Urschleim right now." He glanced up at the sun, looking a bit wild-eyed, and wiped his forehead again. "You got any beer in this dump?"

"Sure, Revel." Tug went into the kitchen for two bottles of Etna Ale, and brought them out to the deck.

Revel drank thirstily, then gestured with his makeshift horn. "If this don't work, well, you're gonna think I'm crazy." He pushed his Italian shades up onto the top of his narrow crewcut skull, and grinned. He was enjoying himself. "But if it does work, ol' son—you're gonna think *you're* crazy."

Revel dipped the end of the funnel into the quiescent but aromatic mass. He swirled it around, then held it up carefully and puffed.

A fat lozenge-shaped gelatinous bubble appeared at the end of the horn.

"Holy cow, it blows up just like a balloon," Tug said, impressed. "That's some kind of viscosity!"

Revel grinned wider, holding the thing at arm's length. "It gets better."

Tug Mesoglea watched in astonishment as the clear bubble of Urschleim slowly rippled and dimpled. A long double crease sank into the taut outer membrane of the gelatinous sphere, encircling it like the seam on an over-sized baseball.

Now, with a swampy-sounding pop, the bubble came loose from the horn's tin muzzle and began to float in mid-air. A set of cilia emerged along the seam and the airborne jelly began to bob and beat its way upward.

"Urschleim!" whooped Revel.

"Jesus Christ," Tug said, staring in shocked fascination. The air jelly was still changing before his eyes, evolving a set of interior membranes, warping, pulsing, and rippling itself into an ever more precise shape, for all the world like a computer graphics program ray-tracing its image into an elegant counterfeit of reality...

Then a draft of air caught it. It hit the eaves of the house, adhered messily, and broke. Revel prudently stepped aside as a long rope of slime fell to the deck.

"I can hardly believe it," said Tug. "Spontaneous symmetry breaking! A self-actuating reaction/diffusion system. This slime of yours is an excitable medium with emergent behavior, Revel! And that spontaneous fractalization of the structures ... Can you do it again?"

"As many times as you want," said Revel. "With as much Urschleim as you got. Of course, the smell kinda gets to you if you do it indoors."

"But it's so odd," breathed Tug. "That the slime out of your oil-well is forming itself into jellyfish shapes just as I'm starting to build jellyfish out of plastic."

"I figure it for some kind of a morphic resonance thing," nodded Revel. "This primeval slime's been trapped inside the Earth so long it's truly achin' to turn into something live and organic. Kind of like that super-weird worm and bacteria and clam shit that grows out of deep undersea vents."

"You mean around the undersea vents, Revel."

"No Tug, right out of 'em. That's the part most people don't get."

"Whatever. Let me try blowing an Urschleim air jelly."

Tug dabbled the horn's tin rim in the picnic cooler, then huffed away at his own balloon of Urschleim. The sphere began to ripple internally, just as before, with just the same dimples and just the same luscious double crease. Tug had a sudden deja vu. He'd seen this shape on his computer screen.

All of a sudden the treacherous thixotropic stuff broke into a flying burst of clear snot that splashed all over his feet and legs. The magic goo felt tingly on Tug's skin. He wondered nervously if any of the slime might be passing into his bloodstream. He hurriedly toweled it off his body, then used the side of his Birkenstock sandal to push the rest of the slime off the edge of the deck.

"What do you think?" asked Revel.

"I'm overwhelmed," said Tug, shaking his head. "Your Urschleim jellyfish looks so much like the ones I've been building in my lab. Let's go in. I'll show you my jellyfish while we think this through." Tug led Revel into the house.

Revel insisted on bringing the Urschleim-containing cooler and the empty pressure canister into the house. He even got Tug to throw an Indian blanket over them, "in case we get company."

Tug's jellyfish tanks filled up an entire room with great green bubbling glory. The aquarium room had been a domestic video game parlor during the early 1980s, when the home's original builder, a designer of shoot-em-up computer twitch-games, had shored up the floor to accommodate two dozen massive arcade-consoles. This was a good thing too, for Tug's seawater tanks were a serious structural burden, and far outweighed all of Tug's other possessions put together, except maybe the teak waterbed which his ex-lover had left. Tug had bought the tanks themselves at a knockdown auction from the federal-seizure sale of an eccentric Oakland cocaine dealer, who had once used them to store schools of piranha.

Revel mulled silently over the ranks of jellyfish. Backlit by greenish glow from the spotlights of a defunct speed-metal crew, Tug's jellies were at their best. The backlighting brought out their most secret, most hidden interior curvatures, with an unblinking brilliance that was well-nigh pornographic.

Their seawater trace elements and Purina Jellyfish Lab Chow cost more than Tug's own weekly grocery bills, but his jelly menagerie had come to mean more to Tug than his own nourishment, health, money, or even his love-life. He spent long secret hours entranced before the gently spinning, ciliated marvels, watching them reel up their brine shrimp prey in mindless, reflexive elegance, absorbing the food in a silent ecstasy of poisonous goo. Live, digestive goo, that transmuted through secret alchemical biology into pulsating, glassy flesh.

Tug's ex-lover had been pretty sporting about Tug's goo-mania, especially compared to his other complaints about Tug's numerous perceived character flaws, but Tug figured his lover had finally been driven away by some deep rivalry with the barely-organic. Tug had gone to some pains to Windex his noseprints from the aquarium glass before Revel arrived.

"Can you tell which ones are real and which ones I made from scratch?" Tug demanded triumphantly.

"You got me whipped," Revel admitted. "It's a real nice show, Tug. If you can really teach these suckers some tricks, we'll have ourselves a business."

Revel's denim chest emitted a ringing sound. He reached within his overalls, whipped out a cellular phone the size of a cigarette-pack, and answered it. "Pullen here! What? Yeah. Yeah, sure. Okay, see you." He flipped the phone shut and stowed it.

"Got you a visitor coming," he announced. "Business consultant I hired."

Tug frowned.

"My uncle's idea, actually," Revel shrugged. "Just kind of standard Pullen procedure before we sink any real money in a venture. We got ourselves one of the best computer-industry consultants in the business."

"Yeah? Who?"

"Edna Sydney. She's a futurist, she writes a high-finance technology newsletter that's real hot with the boys in suits."

"Some strange woman is going to show up here and decide if my Ctenophore Inc. is worth funding?" Tug's voice was high and shaky with stress. "I don't like it, Revel."

"Just try 'n' act like you know what you're doing, Tug, and then she'll take my Uncle Donny Ray a clean bill of health for us. Just a detail really." Revel laughed falsely. "My uncle's a little over-cautious. Belt-and-suspenders kinda guy. Lot of private investigators on his payroll and stuff. The old boy's just tryin' to keep me outa trouble, basically. Don't worry about it none, Tug."

Revel's phone rang again, this time from the pocket on his left buttock. "Pullen here! What? Yeah, I know his house don't look like much, but this is the place, all right. Yeah, okay, we'll let you in." Revel stowed the phone again, and turned to Tug. "Go get the door, man, and I'll double check that our cooler of Urschleim is out of sight."

Seconds later, Tug's front doorbell rang loudly. Tug opened it to find a woman in blue jeans, jogging shoes and a shapeless gray wool jersey, slipping her own cellular phone into her black nylon satchel.

"Hello," she said. "Are you Dr. Mesoglea?"

"Yes I am. Tug Mesoglea."

"Edna Sydney, Edna Sydney Associates."

Tug shook Edna Sydney's dainty blue-knuckled hand. She had a pointed chin, an impressively large forehead, and a look of extraordinary, almost supernatural intelligence in her dark brown shoebutton eyes. She had a neat cap of gray-streaked brown hair. She looked like a digital pixie leapt full-blown from the brain of Thomas Edison.

While she greeted Revel, Tug dug a business-card from his wallet and forced it on her. Edna Sydney riposted with a card from the satchel that gave office addresses in Washington, Prague, and Chicago.

"Would you care for a latte?" Tug babbled. "Tab? Pineapple-mango soda?"

Edna Sydney settled for a Jolt Cola, then gently maneuvered the two men into the jellyfish lab. She listened attentively as Tug launched into an extensive, arm-waving spiel.

Tug was inspired. Words gushed from him like Revel's Urschleim. He'd never before met anyone who could fully understand him when he talked techie jargon absolutely as fast as he could. Edna Sydney, however, not only comprehended Tug's jabber but actually tapped her foot occasionally and once politely stifled a yawn.

"I've seen artificial life devices before," Edna allowed, as Tug began to run out of verbal ectoplasm. "I knew all those Santa Fe guys before they destroyed the futures exchanges and got sent off to Leavenworth. I wouldn't advise trying to break into the software market with some new genetic algorithm. You don't want to end up like Bill Gates."

Revel snorted. "Gates? Geez, I wouldn't wish that on my worst enemy." He chortled aloud. "To think they used to compare that nerd to Rockefeller! Hell, Rockefeller was an oil business man, a family man! If Gates had been in Rockefeller's class, there'd be kids named Gates running half the states in the Union by now."

"I'm not planning to market the algorithms," Tug told the consultant. "They'll be a trade secret, and I'll market the jelly simulacra themselves. Ctenophore Inc. is basically a manufacturing enterprise."

"What about the threat of reverse engineering?"

"We've got an eighteen-month lead," Revel bragged. "Round these parts, that's like eighteen years anywhere else! Besides, we got a set of ingredients that's gonna be mighty hard to duplicate."

"There hasn't been a lot of, uh, sustained industry development in the artificial jellyfish field before," Tug told her. "We've got a big R&D advantage."

Edna pursed her lips. "Well, that brings us to marketing, then. How are you going to get your products advertised and distributed?"

"Oh, for publicity, we'll do COMDEX, A-Life Developers, BioScience Fair, MONDO 3000, the works," Revel assured her. "And get this—we can ship jellies by the Pullen oil pipelines anywhere in North America for free! Try and match that for ease of distribution and clever use of an installed base! Hell, it'll be almost as easy as downloadin' software from the Internet!"

"That certainly sounds innovative," Edna nodded. "So—let's get to the crux of matters, then. What's the killer app for a robot jellyfish?"

Tug and Revel traded glances. "Our exact application is highly confidential," Tug said tentatively.

"Maybe you could suggest a few apps, Edna," Revel told her, folding his arms cagily over the denim chest of his Can't-Bust-Ems. "Come on and earn your twenty thousand bucks an hour."

"Hmmm," the consultant said. Her brow clouded, and she sat in the armchair at Tug's workstation, her eyes gone distant. "Jellyfish. Industrial jellyfish ..."

Greenish rippling aquarium light played across Edna Sydney's face as she sat in deep thought. The jellyfish kept up their silent, eternal pulsations; kept on bouncing their waves of contraction out and back between the centers and the rims of their bells.

"Housewares application," said Edna presently. "Fill them with lye and flush them through sinks and commodes. They agitate their way through sink traps and hairballs and grease."

"Check," said Tug alertly. He snatched a mechanical pencil from the desktop and began scribbling notes on the back of an unpaid bill.

"Assist fermentation in septic tanks by loading jellies with decomposition bacteria, then setting them to churn the tank sludge. Sell them in packs of thousands for city-sized sewage-installations."

"Outrageous," said Tug.

"Microsurgical applications inside plugged arteries. Pulsates plaque away gently, but disintegrates in the ventrical valves to avoid heart attacks."

"That would need FDA approval," Revel hedged. "Maybe a few years down the road."

"You can get a livestock application done in eighteen months," said Edna. "It's happened in recombinant DNA."

"Gotcha," said Revel. "Lord knows the Pullens got a piece o' the cattle business!"

"If you could manufacture Portuguese man-o-war or other threatening toxic jellies," Edna said, "then you could set a few thousand right offshore in perhaps Hilton Head or Puerto Vallarta. After the tourist trade crashed, you could buy up shoreline property cheap and make a real killing." She paused. "Of course, that would be illegal."

"Right," Tug nodded, pencil scratching away. "Although my plastic jellyfish don't sting. I suppose we could implant pouches of toxins in them ..."

"It would also be unethical. And wrong."

"Yeah, yeah, we get it," Revel assured her. "Anything else?"

"Do the jellyfish reproduce?" asked Edna.

"No they don't," Tug said. "I mean, not by themselves. They don't reproduce and they don't eat. I can manufacture as many as you want to any spec, though."

"So they're not truly alive, then? They don't evolve? They're not Type III a-life?"

"I evolved the algorithms for their behavior in my simulations, but the devices themselves are basically sterile robots with my best algorithms hard-coded in," Tug geeked fluently. "They're jellyfish androids that run my code. Not androids, coelenteroids."

"It's probably just as well if they don't reproduce," said Edna primly. "How big can you make them?"

"Well, not much bigger than a basketball at present. The lasers I'm currently using to sinter them are of limited capacity." Tug neglected to mention that he had the lasers out on unauthorized loan from San Jose State University, thanks to a good friend in lab support at the School of Engineering. "In principle, a jellyfish could be quite large."

"So they're currently too small to live inside," said Edna thoughtfully.

Revel smiled. "'Live inside,' huh? You're really something special, Edna."

"That's what they pay me for," she said crisply. She glanced at the screen of Tug's workstation, with its rich background color drifting from sky-blue to sea-green, and with a vigorous pack of sea-nettles pumping their way forward. "What genetic operators are you using to evolve your algorithms?"

"Standard Holland stuff. Proportional reproduction, crossover, mutation, and inversion."

"The Chicago a-life group came up with a new schemata-sensitive operator last week," said Edna. "Preliminary tests are showing a forty percent speed-up for searching intractable sample spaces."

"Terrific! That would really be useful for me," said Tug. "I need that genetic operator."

Edna scribbled a file location and the electronic address of a downloading site on Tug's business card and gave it back to him. Then she glanced at a dainty wristwatch inside her left wrist. "Revel's uncle paid for a full hour plus travel. You two want to spring for a retainer, or do I go?"

"Uh, thanks a lot, but I don't think we can swing a retainer," Revel said modestly.

Edna nodded slowly, then touched one finger to her pointed chin. "I just thought of an angle for using your jellyfish in hotel swimming-pools. If your jellyfish don't sting, you could play with them like beach balls, they'd filtrate the water, and they could shed off little polyps to look for cracks. I just hate the hotel pools in California. They're surrounded by anorexic bleached blondes drinking margaritas made of chemicals with forty letters in their names. Should we talk some more?"

"If you don't like your pool, maybe you could take a nice dip in one of Tug's tanks," Revel said, with a glance at his own watch.

"Bad idea, Revel," Tug said hastily, "you get a good jolt from those natural sea-nettles and it'll stop your heart."

"Do you have a license for those venomous creatures?" Edna asked coolly.

Tug tugged his forelock in mock contrition. "Well, Ms. Sydney, amateur coelenteratology's kind of a poorly policed field."

Edna stood up briskly, and hefted her nylon bag. "We're out of time, so here's the bottom line," she said. "This is one of the looniest schemes I've ever seen. But I'm going to phone Revel's uncle with the go-ahead as soon as I get back into Illinois airspace. Risk-taking weirdos like you two are what makes this industry great, and the Pullen family can well afford to back you. I'm rooting for you boys. And if you even need any cut-rate Kazakh programmers, send me email."

"Thanks, Edna," Revel said.

"Yes," said Tug, "Thank you for all the good ideas." He saw her to the door.

"She didn't really sound very encouraging," Tug said after she left. "And her ideas were ugly, compared to ours. Fill my jellyfish with lye? Put them in septic tanks and in cow arteries? Fill them with poison to sting families on vacation?" He flung back his head and began camping back and forth across the room imitating Edna in a shrieking falsetto. "They're not Type III a-life? Oh dear! How I hate those anorexic blondes! Oh my!"

"Look, Tug, if Edna was a little underwhelmed it's just 'cause I didn't tell her everything!" said Revel. "A trade secret is a trade secret, boy, and three's always a crowd. That gal's got a brain with the strength o' ten, but even Edna Sydney can't help droppin' certain hints in those pricey little newsletters of hers ..."

Revel whistled briefly, pleased with his own brilliance.

Tug's eyes widened in sudden, cataclysmic comprehension. "I've got it Revel! I think I've got it! When you first saw an Urschleim air-jelly—was it before or after you put my plastic jellyfish in your swimming pool?"

"After, compadre. I only first thought of blowing Urschleim bubbles last week—I was drunk, and I did it to make a woman laugh. But you sent me that sorry-ass melting jellyfish a full six weeks ago."

"That 'sorry-ass melting jellyfish' found its way out a crack in your swimming pool and down through the shale beds into the Ditheree hole!" cried Tug exultantly. "Yes! That's it, Revel! My equations migrated right out into your goo!"

"Your software got into my primeval slime?" said Revel slowly. "How exactly is that s'posed to happen?"

"Mathematics represents optimal form, Revel," said Tug. "That's why it slips in everywhere. But sometimes you need a seed equation. Like if water gets cold, it likes to freeze; it freezes into a mathematical lattice. But if you have really cold water in a smooth tank, the water might not know how to freeze—until maybe a snowflake drifts into it. To make a long story short, the mathematical formations of my sintered jellyfish represent a low-energy phase space configuration that is stably attractive to the dynamics of the Urschleim."

"That story's too long for me," said Revel. "Let's just test if you're right. Why don't we throw one of your artificial jellies into my cooler full of slime?"

"Good idea," Tug said, pleased to see Revel plunging headlong into the scientific method. They returned to the aquaria.

Tug mounted a stepladder festooned with bright-red anti-litigation safety warnings, and used a long-handled aquarium net to fetch up his best artificial jelly, a purple-striped piezoplastic sea nettle that he'd sintered up just that morning, a home-made, stingless *Chrysaora quinquecirrha*.

Revel and Tug strode out to the living room with the plastic sea nettle pulsating gamely against the fine-woven mesh of the net.

"Stand back," Tug warned and flipped the jelly into the four inches of Urschleim still in the plastic picnic cooler.

The slime heaved upward violently at the touch of the little artificial jellyfish. Once again Revel blew some Texan hot air into the goo, only this time it all lifted up at once, all five liters of it, forming a floating sea-nettle the size of a large dog.

"Don't let it hit the ceiling!" Revel shouted. The Urschleim jelly drifted around the room, its white oral arms swaying like the train of a wedding dress.

"Yee haw! Shit howdy! This one's different from all the Urschleim ones I've seen before. People'd buy this one just for fun! Edna's right. It'd be a hell of a pool toy, or, heck, a plain old land toy, as long as it don't fly away."

"A toy?" said Tug. "You think we should go with the recreational application? I like it, Revel! Recreation has positive energy. And there's a lot of money in gaming."

"Just like tag!" Revel hooted, capering. "Blind man's bluff!"

"Watch out, Revel!" One swaying fringe of dog-sized ur-jelly made a sudden whipping snatch at Revel's leg. Revel yelped in alarm and tumbled backward over the living-room hassock.

"Christ! Get it off me!" Revel cried as the enormous jelly reeled at his ankle. Its vast gelatinous bulk hovered menacingly over his upturned face. Tug, with a burst of inspiration, slid open the glass doors to the deck.

Caught in a draft of air, the jelly released Revel and floated out through the doors, and sailed off over Tug's redwood deck. Tug watched the dog-sized jelly ascending serenely over the neighbors' yard. Engrossed in beer and tofu, the neighbors failed to notice it.

Toatoa the parrot swooped off the roof of the Samoans' house and rose to circle the great flying sea nettle. The iridescent green parrot hung in a moment of timeless beauty near the translucent jelly, and then was caught by one of the lashing oral arms. There was a frenzy of green motion inside the Urschleim sea-nettle's bell, and then the parrot had clawed and beaked its way free. The punctured nettle fell into the stiff, gnarly branches of a madrone tree and lay there melting. The moist Toatoa cawed angrily from her roof-top perch, flapping her wings to dry.

"Wow!" said Tug. "I'd like to see that again—on digital video!" He smacked his forehead with the flat of his hand. "But now we've got none left for testing! Except—wait!—that little bit in the vial." He yanked the vial from his pocket and looked at it speculatively. "I could put a tiny Monterey bell jelly in here, and then put in some nanophones to pick up the phonon jitter. Yeah. If I could get even a rough map of the Urschleim's basins of chaotic attraction—"

Revel yawned loudly and stretched his arms. "Sounds fascinatin', Doc. Take me on down to my motel, would you? I'll call Ditheree and get some more Urschleim delivered to your house by, oh, 6 AM tomorrow. And by day after tomorrow I can get you a lot more. A whole lot more."

Tug had rented Revel a room in the Los Perros Inn, a run-down stucco motel where, Tug told Revel as he dropped him off, Joe DiMaggio and Marilyn Monroe had once spent a honeymoon night.

Fearing that Tug harbored a budding romantic notion of a honeymoon night for himself, Revel frowned and muttered, "Now I know why they call this the Granola State: nuts, flakes, and fruits."

"Relax," said Tug. "I know you're not gay. And you're not my type anyway. You're way too young. What I want is a manly older guy who'll cherish me and take care of me. I want to snuggle against his shoulder and feel his strong arms around me in the still of the night." Perhaps the Etna Ale had gone to Tug's head. Or maybe the Urschleim had affected him. In any case, he didn't seem at all embarrassed to be making these revelations.

"See you tomorrow, old son," said Revel, closing his door.

Revel got on the phone and called the home of Hoss Jenks, the old forehand of the Ditheree field.

"Hoss, this is Revel Pullen. Can you messenger me out another pressure tank of that goo?"

"That goo, Revel, that goo! There's been big-ass balloons of it floatin' out of the well. You never should of thrown those gene-splice bacteria down there."

"I told you before, Hoss, it ain't bacteria we're dealing with, it's primeval slime!"

"Ain't many of us here that agree, Revel. What if it's some kind of plague on the oil wells? What if it spreads?"

"Let's stick to the point, Hoss. Has anybody noticed the balloons?"

"Not yet."

"Well, just keep folks off our property, Hoss. And tell the boys not to be shy of firing warning shots—we're on unincorporated land."

"I don't know how long this can stay secret."

"Hoss, we need time to try and find a way to make a buck off this. If I can get the right spin on the Urschleim, folks'll be glad to see it coming out of Ditheree. Just between you and me, I'm out here with the likeliest old boy to figure out what to do. Not that he's much of a regular fella, but that's neither here nor there. Name of Tug Mesoglea. I think we're onto something big. Send that tank of goo out to Mesoglea's address, pronto. Here it is. Yeah, and here's his number, and while we're at it, here's my number at the motel. And, Hoss, let's make that three tanks, the same size as the one you filled up for me yesterday. Yeah. Try and get em out here by six AM tomorrow. And start routing out a Pullen pipeline connection between our Nacogdoches tank farm and Monterey."

"Monterey, California, or Monterrey, Mexico?"

"California. Monterey's handy and it's out of the way. We'll need some place real quiet for the next stage I'm planning. There's way too many professional snoops watching everybody's business here in Silicon Valley, drivin' around scanning cellular phones and stuff—you're receiving this call as encrypted, aren't you, Hoss?"

"Sure thing, boss. Got my Clipper Chip set to maximum scramble."

"Good, good, just making sure. I'm trying to be cautious, Hoss, just like Uncle Donny Ray."

Hoss gave a snort of laughter on the other end of the line, and Revel continued. "Anyhoo, we need someplace kind out of the way, but still convenient. Someplace with some spare capacity, but a little run-down, so's we can rent lots of square footage on the cheap and the city fathers don't ask too many prying questions ... Ask Lucy to sniff around and find me a place like that in Monterey."

"There's already hundreds of towns like that in Texas!"

"Yeah, but I want to do this out here. This deal is a software kind o' thing, so it's gotta be California."

Revel woke around seven AM, stirred by the roar of the morning rush-hour traffic. He got his breakfast at a California coffee-shop that called itself "Southern Kitchen," yet served orange-rind muffins and sliced kiwi-fruits with the eggs. Over breakfast he called Texas, and learned that Lucy had found an abandoned tank farm near a defunct polluted military base just north of Monterey. The tank farm belonged to Felix Quinonez, who had been the base's fuel supplier. The property, on Quinonez's private land, included a large garage. The set-up sounded about perfect.

"Lease it, Lucy," said Revel, slurping his coffee. "And fax Quinonez two copies of the contract so's me and him can sign off down at his property today. I'll get this Tug Mesoglea fella to drive me down there. Let's say two o'clock this afternoon? Lock it in. Now has Hoss found a pipeline connection? He has? Straight to Quinonez's tanks? Bless you, honey. Oh, and one more thing? Draw up incorporation papers for a company called Ctenophore, Inc., register the company, and get the name trademarked. C-T-E-N-O-P-H-O-R-E. What it means? It's a kind of morphodite jellyfish. Swear to God. I learned it from Tug Mesoglea. If you should you put Mesoglea's name on my incorporation papers? Are you teasin' me, Lucy? Are you tryin' to make ol' Revel mad? Now book me and Mesoglea a suite in a Monterey hotel, and fax the incorporation papers to me there. Thanks, darlin'. Talk to ya later."

The rapid-fire wheeling and dealing filled Revel with joy. Expansively swinging his arms, he strolled up the hill to Tug's house, which was only a few blocks off. The air was clear and cool, and the sun was a low bright disk in the immaculate blue sky. Birds fluttered this way and that—sparrows, grackles, robins, humming-birds, and the startlingly large California bluejays. A dog barked in the distance as the exotic leaves and flowers swayed in the gentle morning breeze.

As he drew closer to Tug's house, Revel could hear the steady screeching of the Samoans' parrot. And when he turned the corner of Tug's block, Revel saw something very odd. It was like there was a ripple in the space over Tug's house, an undulating bluish glinting of curved air.

Wheeling about in the midst of the glinting was the furious Toatoa. A school of small airborne bell jellies were circling around and around over Tug's house, now fleeing from and now pursuing the parrot, who was endeavoring to puncture them one by one. Revel yelled at the cloud of jellyfish, but what good would that do? You could as soon yell at a volcano or at a spreadsheet.

To Revel's relief, the parrot retreated to her house with a broken tailfeather, and the jellies did not follow her. But now—were the air bells catching the scent plume of the air off Revel's body? They flocked and spiraled eldritchly. Revel hurried up Tug's steps and into his house, right past the three empty cylinders of Urschleim lying outside Tug's front door.

Inside Tug's house reeked of subterranean sulfur. Air jellies of all kinds pressed this way and that. Sea nettles, comb-jellies, bell jellies, spotted jellies, and even a few giant siphonophores—all the jellies of different sizes, with the smaller ones beating frantically faster than the big ones. It was like a children's birthday party with lighter-than-air balloons. Tug had gone utterly bat-shit with the Urschleim.

"Hey, Tug!" Revel called, slapping a sea nettle away from his face. "What's goin' on, buddy? Is it safe in here?"

Tug appeared from around a corner. He was wearing a long blonde wig. His cheeks were high pink with excitement, and his blue eyes were sparkling. He wore bright lipstick, and a tight red silk dress. "It's a jelly party, Revel!"

A huge siphonophore shaped like a mustachioed rope of mucus came bumping along the ceiling towards Revel, its mane of oral arms soundlessly a-jangle.

"Help!"

"Oh don't worry so," said Tug. "And don't beat up a lot of wind. Air currents are what excites them. Here, if you're scared, come down to my room while I slip into something less confrontational."

Revel sat on a chair in the corner of Tug's bedroom while Tug got back into his shorts and sandals.

"I was so excited when all that slime came this morning that I put on my dress-up clothes," Tug confessed. "I've been dancing with my equations for the last couple of hours. There doesn't seem to be any size limit to the size of the jellyfish I can blow. We can make Urschleim jellyfish as big as anything!"

Revel rubbed his cheek uncertainly. "Did you figure anything more out about them, Tug? I didn't tell you before, but back at Ditheree we're getting spontaneous air jelly releases. I mean—I sure don't understand how the hell they can fly. Did you get that part yet?"

"Well, as I'm sure you know, the scientific word for jellyfish is 'coelenterate'," said Tug, leaning towards the mirror to take off his lipstick. "'Coelenterate' is from 'hollow gut' in Latin. Your average jellyfish has an organ called a coelenteron, which is a saclike cavity within its body. The reason these Urschleim fellows can fly is that somehow the Urschleim vaporizes to fills their coelenterons with, of all things, helium! Nature's noblest gas! Traditionally found seeping out of the shafts of oil wells!" Tug whooped, waggled his ass, and slipped off his wig.

Revel clambered angrily to his feet. "I'm glad you're having fun, Doc, but fun ain't business. We're in retail now, and like they say in retail, you can't do business from an empty truck. We need jellies. All stocks, all sizes. You ready to set up shop seriously?"

"What do you mean?"

"I mean build product, son! I done called my man Hoss Jenkins at Ditheree, and we're gonna be ready to start pumping Urschleim cross-country by pipeline around noon our time tomorrow. That is, if you're man enough to handle the other end of the assembly line here in California."

"Isn't that awfully sudden?" Tug hedged, wiping off his mascara. "I mean, I do have some spreadsheets and business plans for a factory, but ..."

Revel scoffed, and swatted at the jelly-stained leg of his Can't-Bust Ems. "Where have you been, Tug? This is the twenty-first century. Ain't you ever heard of just-in-time manufacturing? Hell, in Singapore or Taiwan they'd have already set up six virtual corporations and had this stuff shipped to global markets yesterday!"

"But I can't run a major manufacturing enterprise out of my house," Tug said, gazing around him. "Even my laser-sintering equipment is on a kind of, uhm, loan, from the University. We'll still need lasers for making the plastic jellies to seed the big ones."

"I'll buy you lasers, Tug. Just give me the part numbers."

"But, but, we'll need workers. People to answer the phone, men to carry things ..." Tug paused. "Though, come to think of it, we could use a simple Turing imitation program to answer the phones. And I know where we can pick up a few industrial robots to do the heavy lifting."

"Now you're talking sense!" Revel nodded. "Let's go on upstairs!"

"But what about the factory building?" Tug called after Revel. "We can't fit the business into my poor house. We'll need a lot of floor space, and a tank to store the Urschleim, with a pipeline depot nearby. We'll need a power hookup, an Internet node and—"

"And it has to be some outta-the-way locale," said Revel, turning to grin down from the head of the stairs. "Which I already leased for us this morning!"

"My stars!" said Tug. "Where is it?"

"Monterey. You're drivin'." Revel glanced around the living-room, taking in the odd menagerie of disparate jellyfish floating about. "Before we go," he cautioned, "You better close the door to your wood-stove. There's a passel of little air jellies who've already slipped out through your chimney. They were hassling your neighbor's parrot."

"Oh!" said Tug, and closed the wood-stove's door. The big siphonophore slimed its arms across Tug. Instead of trying to fight away, Tug dangled his arms limply and began hunching his back rhythmically—like a jellyfish. The siphonophore soon lost interest in him and drifted away. "That's how you do it," said Tug. "Just act like a jellyfish!"

"That's easier for you than it is for me," said Revel, picking up a twitching plastic moon jelly from the floor. "Let's take some of these suckers down to Monterey with us. We can use them for seeds. We can have like a tank of these moon jellies, some comb-jellies, a tank of sea nettles, a tank of those big street-loogie things over there"—he pointed at a siphonophore.

"Sure," said Tug. "We'll bring all my little plastic ones, and figure out which ones make the best Urschleim toys."

They set a sheet of plastic into the Animata's trunk, loaded it up with plastic jellyfish doused in seawater, and set off for Monterey.

All during the trip down the highway, Revel jabbered into his cellular phone, jolting various movers and shakers into action: Pullen family clients, suppliers and gophers, in Dallas, Houston, San Antonio—even a few discreet calls to Djakarta and Macao.

Quinonez's tank farm was just north of Monterey, squeezed up against the boundaries of what had once been Fort Ord. During their occupancy of these rolling dunes, the Army had so thoroughly polluted the soil that the land was now legally unusable. The base, which had been closed since the 1990s, was a nature preserve cum hazardous waste site. Those wishing to stroll the self-guiding nature trails were required to wear respirators and disposable plastic shoe-covers.

Tug guided the Animata along a loop road that led to the back of the Ord Natural Waste Site. Inland from the dunes were huge fields of Brussels sprouts and artichokes. In one of the fields six huge silvery tanks rested like visiting UFOs.

"There it is, Tug," said Revel, putting away his phone. "The home of Ctenophore, Inc!"

As they drew closer, they could see that the great storage tanks were marred with graffiti and pocked with rust. Some of the graffiti were richly psychedelic, but most were Aztec gang-code glyphs about red and blue, South and North, the numbers 13 and 14, and so on. The gangs' points of dispute grew ever more abstract.

Between the tanks and the road there was a vast gravel parking-lot with yellowed thistles pushing up through it. At one side of the lot was a truly enormous steel and concrete garage, practically the size of an airplane hangar. Painted on the wall in fading electric pink, yellow and blue was Quinonez Motorotive—Max Nix We Fix!

"Pull on up there, Tug," said Revel. "Mr. Quinonez is supposed to show up and give us the keys."

"How did you get the lease lined up already?"

"What do you think I've been doing on the phone, Doc? Ordering pizza?"

They got out of the Animata, and stood there in the sudden, startling silence beneath the immense, clear California sky. In the distance a sputtering motor made itself heard, then pushed closer. Revel wandered back towards the nearest oil-tank and peered at it. Now the motor arrived in the form of a battered multicolored pickup truck driven by a rugged older man with iron gray hair and a heavy mustache.

"Hello!" sang Tug, instantly in love.

"Good afternoon," said the man, getting out of his pickup. "I'm Felix Quinonez." He stuck out his hand and Tug eagerly grasped it.

"I'm Tug Mesoglea," said Tug. "I handle the science, and my partner Revel Pullen over there handles the business. I think we're leasing this property from you?"

"I think so too," said Quinonez, baring his strong teeth in a flashing smile. He let go of Tug's hand, giving Tug a thoughtful look. An ambiguous look. Did Tug dare hope?

Now Revel came striding over. "Quinonez? I'm Revel Pullen. Did you bring the contract Lucy faxed you? Muy bueno, my man. Let's sign the papers on the hood of your pickup. Texas style!"

The ceremony completed, Quinonez handed over the keys. "This is the key to garage, this is for the padlock on the pipeline valve, and these here are for the locks on the stairways up onto the tanks. We've been having some trouble keeping kids out of here."

"I can see that from the free paint-jobs you been getting," said Revel, staring over at the graffiti bedecked tanks. "But the rust I'm seeing is what worries me. The corrosion."

"These tanks have been empty and out of use for quite a few years," granted Quinonez. "But you weren't planning on filling them, were you? As I explained to your assistant, the hazardous materials license for this site was revoked the day Fort Ord was closed."

"I certainly am planning on filling these tanks," said Revel, "Or why the hell else would I be renting them? But the materials ain't gonna be hazardous."

"You're dealing in beet-sugar?" inquired Quinonez.

"Never you mind what's going in the tanks, Felix. Just show me around and get me up to speed on your valves and pipelines." He handed the garage key to Tug. "Here,

Doc, scope out the building while Felix here shows me his system."

"Thanks, Revel. But Felix, before you go off with him, just show me how the garage lock works," said Tug. "I don't want to set off an alarm or something."

Revel watched disapprovingly while Tug walked over to the garage with Felix, chattering all the way.

"You must be very successful, Felix," gushed Tug as the leathery-faced Quinonez coaxed the garage's rusty lock open. Grasping for more topics to keep the conversation going, Tug glanced up at the garage's weathered sign. "Motorotive, that's a good word."

"A cholo who worked for me made it up," allowed Quinonez. "Do you know what Max Nix We Fix means?"

"Not really."

"My Dad was in the Army in the sixties. He was stationed in Germany, he had an easy deal. He was in the motor vehicle division, of course, and that was their slogan. Max Nix is German for 'it doesn't matter.'"

"How would you say Max Nix in Spanish?" inquired Tug. "I love Spanish."

"No problema," grinned Felix. Tug felt that there was definitely a good vibration between them. Now the lock on the garage door squeaked open, and Felix held it open so that Tug could pass inside.

"The lights are over here," said Felix, hitting a bank of switches. The cavernous garage was like a vast barn for elephants—there were thirty vehicle-repair bays on either side like stalls; each bay was big enough to have once held a huge green Army truck.

"Hey, Quinonez," came Revel's holler. "I ain't got all day!"

"Thanks so much, Felix," said Tug, reaching out to the handsome older man for another handshake. "I'd love to see more of you."

"Well, maybe you will," said Felix softly. "I am not a married man."

"That's lovely," breathed Tug. The two made full eye contact. No problema.

Later that afternoon, Tug and Revel settled into a top-floor suite of a Monterey seaside hotel. Tug poured a few buckets of hotel ice onto the artificial jellyfish in his trunk. Revel got back into the compulsive wheeler-dealer mode with his portable phone again, his demands becoming more unseemly and grandiose as he and Tug worked their way, inch by amber inch, through a fifth of Gentleman Jack.

At three in the morning, Tug crashed headlong into bed, his last conscious memory the clink and scrape of Revel razoring white powder on the suite's glass-topped coffee-table. He'd hoped to dream that he was in the arms of Felix Quinonez, but instead he dreamed once again about debugging a jellyfish program. He woke with a terrible hangover.

Whatever substance Revel had snorted—it seemed unlikely to be anything so mundane and antiquated as mere cocaine—it didn't seem to be bothering him next morning. Revel lustily ordered a big breakfast from room-service.

As Revel tipped the busboy lavishly and splashed California champagne into their beaker of orange juice, Tug staggered outside the suite to the balcony. The Monterey air was rank with kelp. Large immaculate seagulls slid and twisted along the sea-breeze updrafts at the hotel's walls. In the distance to the north, a line of California seals sprawled on a rocky wharf like brown slugs on broken concrete. Dead tin-roofed canneries lined the shore to the south, some of them retrofitted into tourist gyp-joints and discos, others empty and at near-collapse.

Tug huffed at the sea air until the vice-grip loosened at his temples. The world was bright and chaotic and beautiful. He stumbled into the room, bolted down a champagne mimosa and three forkfuls of scrambled eggs.

"Well, Revel," he said finally, "I've got to hand it to you. Quinonez Motorotive is ideal in every respect."

"Oh, I've had Monterey in mind since the first time we met here at SIGUSC," Revel averred, propping one boot-socked foot on the tabletop. "I took to this place right away. This is my kind of town." With his lean strangler's mitts folded over his shallow chest, the young oilman looked surprisingly at peace, almost philosophical. "You ever read any John Steinbeck, Tug?"

"Steinbeck?"

"Yeah, the Nobel-Prize-winning twentieth-century novelist."

"I never figured you for a reading man, Revel."

"I got into Steinbeck's stuff when I first came to Monterey," Revel said. "Now I'm a big fan of his. Great writer. He wrote a book set right here in Cannery Row ... you ever read it? Well, it's about all these drunks and whores living on the hillsides around here, some pretty interesting folks, and the hero's this guy who's kind of their mentor. He's an ichthyologist who does abortions on the side. Not for the money though, just because it's the 1940s and he likes to have lots of sex, and abortion happens to be this thing he can hack 'cause of his science background ... Y'see, Tug, in Steinbeck's day, Cannery Row actually canned a hell of a lot of fish! Sardines. But all the sardines vanished by 1950. Some kind of eco-disaster thing; the sardines never came back at all, not to this day." He laughed. "So you know what they sell in this town today? Steinbeck."

"Yeah I know," said Tug. "It's kind of a postmodern culture-industry museum-economy tourist thing."

"Yeah. Cannery Row cans Steinbeck now. There's Steinbeck novels, and tapes of the crappy movie adaptations, and Steinbeck beer-mugs, and Steinbeck key-chains, Steinbeck bumper-stickers, Steinbeck iron-on patches, Steinbeck fridge-magnets ... and below the counter, there's Steinbeck blow-up plastic love-dolls so that the air-filled author of *Grapes of Wrath* can be subjected to any number of unspeakable posthumous indignities."

"You're kidding about the love-dolls, right?"

"Heck no, dude! I think what we ought to do is buy one of 'em, blow it up, and throw it into a cooler full of Urschleim. What we'd get is this big Jello Steinbeck, see? Maybe it'd even talk! Like deliver a Nobel Prize oration or something. Except when you go to shake his hand, the hand just snaps off at the wrist like a jelly polyp, a kind of dough-lump of dead author flesh, and floats through the air till it hits some paper and starts writing sequels ..."

"What the hell was that stuff you snorted last night, Revel?"

"Bunch of letters and numbers, old son. Seems like they change 'em every time I score."

Tug groaned as if in physical pain. "In other words you're so fried, you can't remember."

Revel, jolted from his reverie, frowned. "Now, don't go Neanderthal on me, Tug. That stuff is pure competitive edge. You wouldn't act so shocked about it, if you'd spent some time in the boardrooms of the Fortune 500 lately. Smart drugs!" Revel coughed rackingly and laughed again. "The coolest thing about smart drugs is, that if they even barely work, you just gotta take 'em, no matter how square you are! Otherwise, the Japanese CEOs kick your ass!"

"I think it's time to get some fresh air, Revel."

"How right you are, hombre. We gotta settle in at Quinonez's tank farm this morning. We've got a Niagara of Urschleim headed our way." Revel glanced at his watch. "Fact is, the stuff oughta be rollin' in a couple of hours from now. Let's go on down and get ready to watch the tanks fill up."

"What if one of the tanks splits open?"

"Then I expect we won't use that particular tank no more."

When Tug and Revel got to Quinonez Motorotive, they found several crates of newly delivered equipment waiting for them. Tug was as excited as Christmas morning.

"Look, Revel, these two boxes are the industrial robots, that box is the supercomputer, and this one here is the laser-sintering device."

"Yep," said Revel. "And over here's a drum of those piezoplastic beads and here's a pallet of titaniplast sheets for your jellyfish tanks. You start gettin' it all set up, Doc, while I check out the pipeline valves one more time."

Tug unlimbered the robots first. They were built like short squat humanoids, and each came with a telerobotic interface that had the form of a virtual reality helmet. The idea was that you put on the helmet and watched through the robot's eyes, meanwhile talking the robot through some repetitive task that you were going to want it to do. The task in this case was to build jellyfish tanks by lining some of the garage's big truck bays with titaniplast—and to fill up the tanks with water.

The robot controls were of course trickier than Tug had anticipated, but after an hour or so he had one of them slaving away like the Sorcerer's Apprentice. He powered up the second robot and used it to bring in and set up the new computer and the laser-sintering assemblage. Then he crossloaded the first robot's program onto the second robot, and it too got to work turning truck-bays into aquaria.

Tug configured the new computer and did a remote login to his workstation back in Los Perros. In ten minutes he'd siphoned off copies of all the software he needed, and ghostly jellyfish were shimmering across the computer's new screen. Tug went out and looked at the robots; they'd finished five aquaria now, and water was gushing into them from connections the busy robots had made to the Quinonez Motorotive water-main.

Tug opened the trunk of his car and began bringing in artificial jellyfish and throwing them into the new tanks. Meanwhile Revel was moving about on the big storage tanks, crawling all over them like an excited fly on fresh meat. Spotting Tug, Revel whooped and waved from the top of a tank. "The slime's comin' soon," hollered Revel. Tug waved back and returned to his computer.

Checking his email, Tug saw that he'd finally gotten a coelenteratological monograph concerning one of the ctenophores he'd been most eager to model: the Venus's-girdle, or *Cestus veneris*, a comb-jelly native to the Mediterranean that was shaped like a wide, tapering belt covered with cilia. The Venus's-girdle was a true ctenophore, and its water-combing cilia were said to diffract sunlight into gorgeous rainbows. It might be fun to wrap one of them around your waist for dress-up. Ctenophore, Inc., could make fashion accessories as well as toys! Smiling as he worked, Tug began transferring the report's data to his design program.

The roar of the Urschleim coming through the pipeline was like a subway underground. Initially taking it for an earthquake, Tug ran outside and collided with the jubilant Revel.

"Here she comes, pardner!"

The nearest of the giant tanks boomed and shuddered as the slime began coursing into it. "So far, so good!" said Revel.

Tanks two and three filled up uneventfully, but a long vertical seam midway up on tank four began to gape open as the tank was filling. Scampering about like a meth-biker roughneck, Revel yanked at the pipeline valves and diverted the Urschleim flow from tank four into tanks five and six, which tidily absorbed the rest of the shipment.

As the roaring and booming of the pipeline delivery died down, the metal of tank four gave a dying shriek and ripped open from top to bottom. Floundering in vast chaotic motion, the sides of the great tank unrolled to fall outwards like a snipped ribbon, tearing loose from the huge disk top, which glided forward some twenty yards like a giant Frisbee.

An acre or more of slime gushed out of the burst tank to flood the tank farm's dry weedy soil. The thousands of gallons of glistening Urschleim mounded up on the ground like a clear tapioca pudding.

Tug started running toward the spill, fearful for Revel's safety. But, no, there was Revel, standing safe off to one side like a triumphant cockroach. "Come on, Tug!" he called. "Come look at this!" Tug kept running and Revel met him at the edge of the Urschleim spill.

"This is just like the spill at Ditheree!" exclaimed Revel. "But you'll see, spillin' Urschleim on the ground don't mean a thing. You ready start fillin' orders, Tug?" His voice sounded tinny and high, like the voice of an indestructible cartoon character.

"The stuff is warm," said Tug, leaning forward to feel the great knee-high pancake of Urschleim. His voice too had a high, quacking quality. Here and there fat bubbles of gas formed beneath the Urschleim and burst plopping holes in it. The huge Urschleim flapjack was giving off gas like a dough full of yeast. But the gas was helium, which is why their voices were high and—

"I just realized how the Urschleim makes helium," squawked Tug. "Cold fusion! Let's run back in the garage, Revel, and find out whether or not we've got radiation sickness. Come on. I mean it. Run!"

Back in the garage they caught their breath for awhile. "Why would we have radiation sickness?" puffed Revel finally.

"I think your Urschleim is fusing hydrogen atoms together to make helium," said Tug. "Depending on the details of the process, that could mean anything from warming the stuff up, to killing everyone in the county."

"Well, it ain't killed anyone down in Ditheree so far," Revel scoffed. "And come to think of it, one of my techs did check the first batch over with a Geiger counter. It ain't radioactive, Tug. How could it be? We're gonna use it to make toys!"

"Toys? You've already got orders?"

"I got a fella owns a chain of variety stores down in Orange County, wants ten thousand jellies to sell for swimming-pool toys. All shapes and sizes. I told him I'd send 'em out down the pipeline to his warehouse early tomorrow morning. He's takin' out ads in tomorrow's papers."

"Heavens to Betsy!" exclaimed Tug. "How are we going to pull that off?"

"I figure all you need to do is tap off Urschleim a bucketful at a time, and just dip one of your artificial jellyfish into each bucketful. The ur-snot will glom right onto the math and start acting like a jellyfish. You sell the slime jellyfish, and keep the plastic jellyfish to use as a seed again and again."

"We're going to do that ten thousand times by tomorrow morning?"

"Teach the damn robots to do it!"

Just about then, Felix Quinonez showed up in a truck to try and find out what they'd just spilled out of tank four. Revel blustered at him until he went away, but not before Tug managed to set a dinner date with him for that evening.

"Jesus, Tug," snapped Revel. "What in hell you want to have supper with that old man for? I hope to God it ain't because of—"

"Hark," sang Tug. "The love that dare not speak its name! Maybe I can get myself a Venus's-girdle sintered up in time. I think it would be a stunning thing to wear. The Venus's-girdle is a ctenophore native to the Mediterranean. If I can make mine come out anywhere near as gorgeous as the real thing, then we'll sell twenty thousand of them to your man in Orange."

Revel nodded grimly. "Let's git on in the garage and start workin', son."

They tried to get the robots to help with making the ten thousand jellies, but the machines were slow and awkward at this task. Tug and Revel set to work making the jellies themselves—tapping off Urschleim, vivifying it with the magic touch of a plastic jellyfish, and throwing the Urschleim jellyfish into one of the aquaria for storage. They put nets over the storage aquaria to keep the creatures from floating off. Soon the nets bulged upward with a dizzying array of Urschleim coelenteroids.

When dinner time rolled around, Tug, to Revel's displeasure, excused himself for his date with Felix Quinonez.

"I'll just work on through," yelled Revel. "I care about business, Tug!"

"I'll check back with you around midnight."

"Fine!" Revel drew out his packet of white powder and inhaled deeply. "I can go all night, you lazy heifer!"

"Don't overwork yourself, Revel. If we don't finish all the jellyfish tonight we can finish them early tomorrow morning. How many do we have done anyway?"

"I'm counting about three thousand," said Revel. "Damn but those robots are slow."

"Well I'll be back later to drive you back to the hotel. Don't do anything crazy while I'm gone."

"You're the one who's crazy, Tug!"

Tug's dinner with Felix Quinonez went very well, even though Tug hadn't had time to sinter himself that Venus's-girdle. After the meal they went back to Felix's house and got to know each other better. The satiated Tug dropped off to sleep, and by the time he got back to the tank farm to pick up Revel, it was nearly dawn.

A stiff breeze was blowing from the south, and a dying moon hung low in the west over the sea. Patches of fog swept northward across the moon's low disk. The great tanks of Urschleim were creaking and shivering. Tug opened the garage door to find the whole interior space filled with Urschleim jellies. Crouched cackling at one side of the garage was the wasted Revel. Streaming out of five jury-rigged pipes next to Revel were a steady stream of fresh Urschleim jellyfish; blowing out of the pipes like bubbles from a bubble wand. Every now and then an air-bubble would start to swell too large before breaking free, and one of the two robots would step forward and snip it off.

"Reckon we got enough, yet, Tug?" asked Revel. "I done lost count."

Tug did a quick estimation of the volume of the garage divided by the volume of an air-jelly and came up with two hundred thousand.

"Yes, Revel, that's way more than enough. Stop it now. How did you get around having to dip the plastic jellyfish into the slime?"

"The smart nose knows," said Revel, horning up a thumbnail of white powder. "How was your big date?"

"My date was fine," said Tug, pushing past Revel to turn off the valves on the five pipes. "It could even be the beginning of a steady thing. Thank God this garage isn't wood, or these air jellies would lift off the roof. How are you going to feed them all into the pipeline to Orange County, Revel?"

"Got the robots to rig a collector up top there," said Revel, gesturing towards the distant ceiling. "You think it's time to ship 'em out? Can do!" Revel slapped a large toggle switch that one of robots had jury-rigged into the wall. The deep throb of a powerful electric pump began.

"That's good, Revel, let's get the jellies out of here. But you still didn't tell me how you got the jellies to come out of the pipe all ready-made." Tug paused and stared at Revel. "I mean how they could come out ready-made without your having to dip a plastic jellyfish in them. What did you do?"

"Hell, I can tell by your face you already know the answer," snapped Revel defensively. "You want to hear it? Okay, I went and put one of your goddamn precious plastic jellies in each of the big tanks. Same idea as back at Ditheree. Once the whole tank's got your weird math in it, the pieces that bubble out form jellies naturally. We got sea nettles in tank number one, moon jellies in number two, those spotted jellies in tank three, bell jellies in tank five, and ctenophores in tank six. Comb-jellies. Tank four's busted, you recall."

"Busted," said Tug softly. Outside the screeching of metal rose above the sighing of the wind and the chug of the pipeline pump that was sucking the garage's jellies off the ceiling and pipelining them off to Orange County. "Busted."

A huge crash sounded from the tank field.

Tug helped the disoriented Revel out into the driveway in front of the garage. Tank number six was gone, and a spindle-shaped comb-jelly the size of a blimp was bouncing across the sloping field of artichoke plants that lay north of the tank farm. The great moving form was live and shiny in the slanting moonlight. Its transparent flesh glowed faintly from the effects of cold fusion.

"The other tanks are going to break up, too, Revel," Tug murmured. "One by one. It's the helium."

"Them giant air jellies are gonna look plumb beautiful when the sun comes up," said Revel, squinting at his watch. "It'll be great publicity for Ctenophore, Inc. Did I tell you I got the papers for it drawn up?"

"No," said Tug. "Shouldn't I sign them?"

"No need for you to sign, old son," said Revel. "The Urschleim's mine, and so's the company. I'm putting you on salary! You're our chief scientist!"

"God damn it, Revel, don't play me for a sucker. I wanted stock. You knew that."

A dark figure shuffled up behind them and tapped Revel's shoulder with its metal claw. It was one of the industrial robots, carrying Revel's portable phone.

"There's a call on your phone, Mr. Pullen. From Orange County. You set the phone down earlier while you were ingesting narcotics."

"Busy, busy!" exclaimed Revel. "They must be wantin' to transfer payment for our shipment. We're in business, Tug, my man. And just to make sure there's no hard feelings, I'll pay your first year's salary in advance! Tomorrow, that is."

As Revel drew out his portable phone, another of the great metal tanks gave way, releasing a giant, toadstool-like spotted jelly. Outlined against the faint eastern sky, it was an awesome sight. The wind urged the huge quivering thing northwards, and its great stubby tentacles dragged stubbornly across the ground. Tug wished briefly that Revel were screaming in the jelly's grip instead of screaming into his telephone.

"Lost 'em?" Revel was screeching. "What the hell you mean? We shipped 'em to you, and you owe us the money for 'em. Your warehouse roof blew off? That's not my fault, is it? Well, yes, we did ship some extras. Yes, we shipped you twenty to one. We figured you'd have a high demand. So that makes it our fault? Kiss my grits!" He snapped the phone shut and scowled.

"So all the jellies in Orange County got away?" said Tug softly. "It's looking kind of bad for Ctenophore, Inc., isn't it, Revel? It's going to be tough to run that operation alone." With a roar, a third storage tank gave way like a hatching egg, releasing a moon jelly the size of an ice-skating rink. The first rays of the rising sun shimmered on its great surface. In the distance there were sirens.

In rapid succession the two remaining tanks burst open, unleashing a bell jelly and a mammoth sea nettle. A vagary of the dawn breeze swept the sea nettle towards Tug and Revel. Instead of fleeing it, Revel ran crazily towards it, bellowing in mindless anger.

Tug watched Revel for a moment too long, for now the huge sea nettle lashed out two of its dangling oral arms and snagged the both of them. Swelling its hollow gut a bit larger, the vast sea nettle rose a few hundred feet into the air, and began drifting north along Route One towards San Francisco.

By swinging themselves around and climbing frenziedly, Tug and Revel were able to find a perch together in the tangled tissues on the underside of the enormous sea nettle. The effort and the clear morning air seemed finally to have cleared Revel's head.

"We're lucky these things don't sting, eh Doc? I gotta hand it to you. Say, ain't this a hell of a ride?"

The light of the morning sun refracted wonderfully through the giant lens-like tissues of the helium-filled sea nettle.

"I wonder if we can steer it?" said Tug, feeling around in the welter of dangling jelly frills all around them. "It's be pretty cool to set down at Crissy Field right near the Golden Gate Bridge."

"If anyone can steer it, Tug, you're the man."

Using his knowledge of the jelly's basins of chaotic attraction, Tug was indeed able to adjust the giant sea nettle's pulsings so as to bring them to hover over Crissy Field's great grassy sward, right at the mouth of the San Francisco Bay, first making a low pass over the hilly streets of San Francisco. Below were thousands of people, massed to great them.

They descended lower and lower, surrounded by a buzzing pack of TV-station helicopters. Anticipating a deluge of orders for Ctenophore products, Revel phoned up Hoss Jenkins to check his Urschleim supply.

"We've got more goo than oil, Revel," shouted Hoss. "It's showin' up in all our wells and in everybody else's wells all across Texas. Turns out there wasn't nothing primeval about your slime at all. It was just a mess of those gene-splice bacteria like I told you all along. Them germs have floated down from the air jellies and are eatin' up all the oil they can find!"

"Well, keep pumping that goo! We got us a global market here! We got cold fusion happening, Hoss! Not to mention airships, my man, and self-heating housing! And that probably ain't but the half of it."

"I sure hope so, Revel! Because it looks like all the oil business left in Texas is about to turn into the flyin' jelly business. Uncle Donny Ray's asking lots of questions, Revel! I hope you're prepared for this!"

"Hell yes, I'm prepared!" Revel snapped. "I spent all my life waitin' for a chance like this! Me 'n' ol' Tug are the pioneers of a paradigm-shatterin' postindustrial revolution, and anybody who don't like it, can get in the breadlines like those no-neck numbskulls from IBM." Revel snapped the phone shut.

"What's the news, Revel?" asked Tug.

"All the oil in Texas is turning into Urschleim," said Revel. "And we're the only ones who know what to do about it. Let's land this thing and start makin' us some deals."

The giant sea nettle hovered uneasily, rippling a bit in the prop-wash of the anxious helicopters. Tug made no move to bring them lower. "There's no we and no us as long as you're talking that salary bullshit," said Tug angrily. "If you want me to bust ass and take risks in your startup, it has to be fifty-fifty down the line. I want to be fully vested! I want to be on the board! I want to call my share of the shots!"

"I'll think about it," Revel hedged.

"You better think fast, Revel." Tug looked down between his legs at the jostling crowd below. "Look at them all. You don't really know how the hell we got here or what we're doing, Revel. Are you ready to face them alone? It's nice up here in this balloon, but we can't ride a balloon forever. Sooner or later, we're gonna have to walk on our own two feet again, and look people right in the eye." He reached up into the tissues of the giant sea nettle, manipulating it.

Now the sun-baked quake-prone ground began rising up steadily again. Tattooed local hipsters billowed away from beneath them in San Francisco's trademark mélange of ecstasy and dread.

"What are you going to say to them when I land us?" demanded Tug harshly.

"Me?" Revel said, surprised. "You're the scientist! You're the one who's s'posed to explain. Just feed 'em some mathematics. Chaos equations and all that bullshit. It don't matter if they can't understand it. 'There's no such thing as bad publicity,' Tug. P. T. Barnum said that."

"P. T. Barnum wasn't in the artificial life business, Revel."

"Sure he was," said Revel, as the great jellyfish touched down. "And, okay, what the hey, if you'll stick with me and do the talkin', I'll go ahead and cut you in for fifty percent."

Tug and Revel stepped from the jellyfish and shook hands, grinning gamely, in a barrage of exploding flashbulbs.

Notes on "Big Jelly"

Asimov's Science Fiction, November 1994.
Written Fall, 1992.

Rudy on "Big Jelly"

In May, 1992, Bruce and I were panelists in Monterey at a conference about computer user interfaces. At the same time, there was a big show on jellyfish at the Monterey Aquarium, and Bruce and I went and looked at the tanks together. The jellyfish made a big impression on us. So as to ring a change on the classic macho SF two-guys story mode, I made my character be gay this time.

Another element in this story was that, on the way to conference, Bruce visited my house, which was then drawn into the maelstrom of our tale. Bruce did a considerable amount of research on industrial uses for jellyfish while we were working on our story—in fact he discussed this topic with the futurist Esther Dyson.

"Big Jelly" turned out to be one of our favorite stories, and to this day both Bruce and I remain obsessed by the idea of flying jellyfish. It's one of the somewhat rare cases where our obsessions overlap. To this day, Bruce still sends me jellyfish-related links and even toys.

Bruce on "Big Jelly"

As collaborators, our paths rarely cross physically, but when we meet, sparks fly. Monterey, California inspired "Big Jelly," a work which is obviously self-parodistic. Or, rather, it's "transreal" in the strict Rucker sense. In transreal writing, roman a clef elements are jammed into a narrative, not because they're appropriate to the story-line, but because real-life incidents become surreal and provocative within the context of science fiction.

For the addled, fearful protagonists of "Storming the Cosmos," nothing can ever work out. By contrast, the all-American heroes of "Big Jelly" are an effective start-up team, with ambitious goals and complementary talents.

Rudy was again carrying the major burden for both of the characters here—Tug Mesoglea is obviously a Rucker creation, while Revel Pullen is a squalid satire of Texas that no native Texan could have invented. My own big effort here was in framing the work as a social satire of the technology business. "Big Jelly" is about start-up thinking and dot-com boom language, which is easy to science-fictionalize, because it's soaked in the genre's sensibility. The true "big jelly" is not a jellyfish, but the elasticity of high-tech business jargon. Tech rhetoric can be verbally stretched to cover almost any form of excess.

Revel Pullen and Tug Mesoglea do pretty well as inventive entrepreneurs, but whenever either lead is removed from the policing eye of his partner, utter chaos looms. The transreal truth behind this situation is that the authors themselves are tearing their story to shreds. The cage of fiction can barely hold us, and even poor John Steinbeck, a writer who truly knew Monterey, gets sucked into the swirling backwash of gelatin.

The character "Edna Sydney" is, of course, technology consultant and event organizer Esther Dyson. The business applications for our artificial jellyfish were invented by Esther Dyson, when I casually mentioned our story project to her. This fantastic effort took Esther maybe three minutes.

A good egg, Esther Dyson. Her dad and her brother are also swell people. All science fiction writers should study their works with care.

Junk DNA

Life was hard in old Silicon Valley. Little Janna Gutierrez was a native Valley girl, half Vietnamese, half Latino. She had thoughtful eyes and black hair in high ponytails.

Her mother Ahn tried without success to sell California real estate. Her father Ruben plugged away inside cold, giant companies like Ctenophore and Lockheed Biological. The family lived in a charmless bungalow in the endless grid of San Jose.

Janna first learned true bitterness when her parents broke up. Tired of her hard scrabble with a lowly wetware engineer, Anh ran off with Bang Dang, the glamorous owner of an online offshore casino. Dad should have worked hard to win back Mom's lost affection, but, being an engineer, he contented himself with ruining Bang. He found and exploited every unpatched hole in Bang's operating system. Bang never knew what hit him.

Despite Janna's pleas to come home, Mom stubbornly stuck by her online entrepreneur. She bolstered Bang's broken income by retailing network porn. Jaded Americans considered porn to be the commonest and most boring thing on the Internet. However, Hollywood glamour still had a moldy cachet in the innocent Third World. Mom spent her workdays dubbing the ethnic characteristics of tribal Somalis and Baluchis onto porn stars. She found the work far more rewarding than real estate.

Mom's deviant behavior struck a damp and morbid echo in Janna's troubled soul. Janna sidestepped her anxieties by obsessively collecting Goob dolls. Designed by glittery-eyed comix freaks from Hong Kong and Tokyo,

Goobs were wiggly, squeezable, pettable creatures made of trademarked Ctenophore piezoplastic. These avatars of ultra-cuteness sold off wire racks worldwide, to a generation starved for Nature. Thanks to environmental decline, kids of Janna's age had never seen authentic wildlife. So they flipped for the Goob menagerie: marmosets with butterfly wings, starfish that scuttled like earwigs, long, furry frankfurter cat-snakes.

Sometimes Janna broke her Goob toys from their mint-in-the-box condition, and dared to play with them. But she quickly learned to absorb her parents' cultural values, and to live for their business buzz. Janna spent her off-school hours on the Net, pumping-and-dumping collectible Goobs to younger kids in other states.

Eventually, life in the Valley proved too much for Bang Dang. He pulled up stakes and drove away in his solar-powered RV—to pursue a more lucrative career retailing networked toilets. Janna's luckless Mom, her life reduced to ashes, scraped out a bare living marketing mailing lists to mailing list marketers.

Janna ground her way through school and made it into UC Berkeley. She majored in computational genomics. Janna worked hard on software for hardwiring wetware, but her career timing was off. The latest pulse of biotech start-ups had already come and gone. Janna was reduced to a bottle-scrubbing job at Triple Helix, yet another subdivision of the giant Ctenophore conglomerate.

On the social front, Janna still lacked a boyfriend. She'd studied so hard she'd been all but dateless through school and college. In her senior year she'd moved in with this cute Korean boy who was in a band. But then his mother had come to town with, unbelievable, a blushing North Korean bride for him in tow. So much the obvious advice-column weepie!

In her glum and lonely evenings, Janna played you-are-her interactives, romance stories, with a climax where she'd lip-synch a triumphant, tear-jerking video. On other nights Janna would toy wistfully with her decaying Goob collection. The youth market for the dolls had evaporated with the years. Now fanatical adult collectors were trading the Goobs, stiff and dusty artifacts of their lost consumer childhood.

And so life went for Janna Gutierrez, every dreary day on the calendar foreclosing some way out. Until the fateful September when Veruschka Zipkinova arrived from Russia, fresh out of biohazard quarantine.

The zany Zipkinova marched into Triple Helix toting a fancy briefcase with a video display built into its piezo-plastic skin. Veruschka was clear-eyed and firm-jawed, with black hair cut very short. She wore a formal black jogging suit with silk stripes on the legs. Her Baltic pallor was newly reddened by California sunburn. She was very thoroughly made up. Lipstick, eye shadow, nails—the works.

She fiercely demanded a specific slate of bio-hardware and a big wad of start-up money. Janna's boss was appalled at Veruschka's archaic approach—didn't this Russki woman get it that the New Economy was even deader than Leninism? It fell to the luckless Janna to throw Veruschka out of the building.

"You are but a tiny cog," said Veruschka, accurately summing up Janna's cubicle. "But you are intelligent, yes, I see this in your eyes. Your boss gave me the brush-off. I did not realize Triple Helix is run by lazy morons."

"We're all quite happy here," said Janna lightly. The computer was, of course, watching her. "I wonder if we could take this conversation offsite? That's what's required, you see. For me to get you out of the way."

"Let me take you to a fine lunch at Denny's," said Veruschka with sudden enthusiasm. "I love Denny's so much! In Petersburg, our Denny's always has long lines that stretch down the street!"

Janna was touched. She gently countersuggested a happening local coffee shop called the Modelview Matrix. Cute musicians were known to hang out there.

With the roads screwed and power patchy, it took forever to drive anywhere in California, but at least traffic fatalities were rare, given that the average modern vehicle had the mass and speed of a golf cart. As Janna forded

the sunny moonscape of potholes, Veruschka offered her
start-up pitch.

"From Russia, I bring to legendary Silicon Valley a
breakthrough biotechnology! I need a local partner, Janna.
Someone I can trust."

"Yeah?" said Janna.

"It's a collectible pet."

Janna said nothing, but was instantly hooked.

"In Russia, we have mastered genetic hacking," said
Veruschka thoughtfully, "although California is the planet's
legendary source of high-tech marketing."

Janna parked amid a cluster of plastic cars like colored
seedpods. Inside, Janna and Veruschka fetched slices of artichoke quiche.

"So now let me show you," said Veruschka as they took
a seat. She placed a potently quivering object on the tabletop. "I call him Pumpti."

The Pumpti was the size and shape of a Fabergé egg,
pink and red, clearly biological. It was moist, jiggly, and
veined like an internal organ with branching threads of
yellow and purple. Janna started to touch it, then hesitated,
torn between curiosity and disgust.

"It's a toy?" asked Janna. She tugged nervously at a
fanged hairclip. It really wouldn't do to have this blob stain
her lavender silk jeans.

The Pumpti shuddered, as if sensing Janna's hovering
finger. And then it oozed silently across the table, dropped
off the edge, and plopped damply to the diner's checkered
floor.

Veruschka smiled, slitting her cobalt-blue eyes, and
leaned over to fetch her Pumpti. She placed it on a stained
paper napkin.

"All we need is venture capital!"

"Um, what's it made of?" wondered Janna.

"Pumpti's substance is human DNA!"

"Whose DNA?" asked Janna.

"Yours, mine, anyone's. The client's." Tenderly
Veruschka picked up the Pumpti, palpating it with her
lacquered fingertips. "Once I worked at the St. Petersburg

Institute of Molecular Science. My boss—well, he was also my boyfriend…" Veruschka pursed her lips. "Wiktor's true obsession was the junk DNA—you know this technical phrase?"

"Trust me, Vero, I'm a genomics engineer."

"Wiktor found a way for these junk codons to express themselves. The echo from the cradle of life, evolution's roadside picnic! To express junk DNA required a new wetware reader. Wiktor called it the Universal Ribosome." She sighed. "We were so happy until the mafiya wanted the return on their funding."

"No National Science Foundation for you guys," mused Janna.

"Wiktor was supposed to tweak a cabbage plant to make opium for the criminals—but we were both so busy growing our dear Pumpti. Wiktor used my DNA, you see. I was smart and saved the data before the Uzbeks smashed up our lab. Now I'm over here with you, Janna, and we will start a great industry of personal pets! Wiktor's hero fate was not in vain. And—"

What an old-skool, stylin', totally trippy way for Janna to shed her grind-it-out worklife! Janna and Veruschka Zipkinova would create a genomic petware start-up, launch the IPO, and retire by thirty! Then Janna could escape her life-draining servitude and focus on life's real rewards. Take up oil painting, go on a safari, and hook up with some sweet guy who understood her. A guy she could really talk to. Not an engineer, and especially not a musician.

Veruschka pitchforked a glob of quiche past her pointed teeth. For her pilgrimage to the source of the world's largest legal creation of wealth in history, the Russian girl hadn't forgotten to pack her appetite.

"Pumpti still needs little bit of, what you say here, tweaking," said Veruschka. The prototype Pumpti sat shivering on its paper napkin. The thing had gone all goose bumpy, and the bumps were warty: the warts had smaller warts upon them, topped by teensy wartlets with fine, waving hairs. Not exactly a magnet for shoppers.

Stuffed with alfalfa sprouts, Janna put her cutlery aside. Veruschka plucked up Janna's dirty fork, and scratched inside her cheek with the tines.

Janna watched this dubious stunt and decided to stick to business. "How about patents?"

"No one ever inspects Russian gene labs," said Veruschka with a glittery wink. "We Russians are the great world innovators in black market wetware. Our fetal stem cell research, especially rich and good. Plenty of fetus meat in Russia, cheap and easy, all you need! Nothing ever gets patented. To patent is to teach stupid people to copy!"

"Well, do you have a local lab facility?" pressed Janna.

"I have better," said Veruschka, nuzzling her Pumpti. "I have pumptose. The super enzyme of exponential autocatalysis!"

"Pumptose, huh? And that means?" prompted Janna.

"It means the faster it grows, the faster it grows!"

Janna finally reached out and delicately touched the Pumpti. Its surface wasn't wet after all, just shiny like super-slick plastic. But—a pet? It seemed more like something little boys would buy to gross-out their sisters. "It's not exactly cuddly," said Janna.

"Just wait till you have your own Pumpti," said Veruschka with a knowing smile.

"But where's the soft hair and big eyes? That thing's got all the shelf appeal of a scabby knee!"

"It's nice to nibble a scab," said Veruschka softly She cradled her Pumpti, leaned in to sniff it, then showed her strong teeth, and nipped off a bit of it.

"God, Veruschka," said Janna, setting down her coffee.

"Your own Pumpti," said Veruschka, smacking. "You are loving him like pretty new shoes. But so much closer and personal! Because Pumpti is you, and you are Pumpti."

Janna sat up in sudden wonderment. Deep within her soul, a magic casement had opened. "Here's how we'll work it!" she exclaimed. "We give away Pumpti pets almost free. We'll make our money selling rip-off Pumpti-care products and accessories!"

Veruschka nodded, eyes shining. "If we're business partners now, can you find me a place to sleep?"

§

Janna let Veruschka stay in the spare room at her Dad's house. Inertia and lack of capital had kept Janna at home since college.

Ruben Gutierrez was a big, soft man with a failing spine, carpal tunnel, and short, bio-bleached hair he wore moussed into hedgehog spikes. He had a permanent mirthless grin, the side effect of his daily diet of antidepressants.

Dad's tranquil haze broke with the arrival of Veruschka with her go-go arsenal of fishnet tights and scoop-necked Lycra tops. With Veruschka around, the TV blared constantly and there was always an open bottle of liquor. Every night the little trio stayed up late, boozing, making schmaltzy confessions, and engaging in long, earnest sophomore discussions about the meaning of life.

Veruschka's contagious warm heartedness and her easy acceptance of human failing was a tonic for the Gutierrez household. It took Veruschka mere days to worm out the surprising fact that Ruben Gutierrez had a stash of half a million bucks accrued via clever games with his stock options. He'd never breathed a word of this to Anh or to Janna.

Emotionally alive for the first time in years, Dad offered his hoard of retirement cash for Veruschka's longshot crusade. Janna followed suit by getting on the web and selling off her entire Goob collection. When Janna's web money arrived freshly laundered, Dad matched it, and two days later, Janna finally left home, hopefully for good. Company ownership was a three-way split between Veruschka, Janna, and Janna's Dad. Veruschka supplied no cash funding, because she had the intellectual property.

Janna located their Pumpti start-up in San Francisco. They engaged the services of an online lawyer, a virtual realtor, and a genomics supply house, and began to build the buzz that, somehow, was bound to bring them major league venture capital.

Their new HQ was a gray stone structure of columns, arches and spandrels, the stone decorated with explosive graffiti scrawls. The many defunct banks of San Francisco made spectacular dives for the city's genomics start-ups. Veruschka incorporated their business as "Magic Pumpkin, Inc.," and lined up a three-month lease.

San Francisco had weathered so many gold rushes that its real estate values had become permanently bipolar. Provisionary millionaires and drug-addled derelicts shared the same neighborhoods, the same painted-lady Victorians, the same flophouses and anarchist bookstores. Sometimes millionaires and lunatics even roomed together. Sometimes they were the very same person.

Enthusiastic cops spewing pepper gas chased the last downmarket squatters from Janna's derelict bank. To her intense embarrassment, Janna recognized one of the squatter refugees as a former Berkeley classmate named Kelso. Kelso was sitting on the sidewalk amidst his tattered Navajo blankets and a damp-spotted cardboard box of kitchen gear. Hard to believe he'd planned to be a lawyer.

"I'm so sorry, Kelso," Janna told him, wringing her hands. "My Russian friend and I are doing this genomics start-up? I feel like such a gross, rough-shod newbie."

"Oh, you'll be part of the porridge soon enough," said Kelso. He wore a big sexy necklace of shiny junked cell phones. "Just hang with me and get colorful. Want to jam over to the Museum of Digital Art tonight? Free grilled calamari, and nobody cares if you sleep there."

Janna shyly confided a bit about her business plans.

"I bet you're gonna be bigger than Pokemon," said Kelso. "I'd always wanted to hook up with you, but I was busy with my prelaw program and then you got into that cocooning thing with your Korean musician. What happened to him?"

"His mother found him a wife with a dowry from Pyongyang," said Janna. "It was so lovelorn."

"I've had dreams and visions about you, Janna," said Kelso softly. "And now here you are."

"How sweet. I wish we hadn't had you evicted."

"The wheel of fortune, Janna. It never stops."

As if on cue, a delivery truck blocked the street, causing grave annoyance to the local bike messengers. Janna signed for the tight-packed contents of her new office.

"Busy, busy," Janna told Kelso, now more than ready for him to go away. "Be sure and watch our web page. Pumpti dot-bio. You don't want to miss our IPO."

"Who's your venture angel?"

Janna shook her head. "That would be confidential."

"In other words you don't have a backer." Kelso pulled his blanket over his grimy shoulders. "And boy, will you ever need one. You ever heard of Revel Pullen of the Ctenophore Industry Group?"

"Ctenophore?" Janna scoffed. "They're just the biggest piezoplastic outfit on the planet, that's all! My dad used to work for them. And so did I, now that I think about it."

"How about Tug Mesoglea, Ctenophore's chief scientist? I don't mean to name-drop here, but I happen to know Dr. Tug personally."

Janna recognized the names, but there was no way Kelso could really know such heavy players. However, he was cute and he said he'd dreamed about her. "Bring 'em on," she said cheerfully.

"I definitely need to meet your partner," said Kelso, making the most of his self-created opportunity. Hoisting his grimy blanket, Kelso trucked boldly through the bank's great bronze-clad door.

Inside the ex-bank, Veruschka Zipkinova was setting up her own living quarters in a stony niche behind the old teller counter. Veruschka had a secondhand futon, a moldy folding chair, and a stout refugee suitcase. The case was crammed to brimming with the detritus of subsistence tourism: silk scarves, perfumes, stockings, and freeze-dried coffee.

After one glance at Kelso, Veruschka yanked a handgun from her purse. "Out of my house, *rechniki*! No room and board for you here, *maphiya bezprizorniki*!"

"I'm cool, I'm cool," said Kelso, backpedaling. Then he made a run for it. Janna let him go. He'd be back.

Veruschka hid her handgun with a smirk of satisfaction. "So much good progress already!" she told Janna. "At last we command the means of production! Today we will make your own Pumpti," she told Janna.

They unpacked the boxed UPS deliveries. "You make ready that crib vat," said Veruschka. Janna knew the drill; she'd done this kind of work at Triple Helix. She got a wetware crib vat properly filled with base-pairs and warmed it up to standard operating temperature. She opened the valves of the bovine growth serum, and a pink threading began to fill the blood-warm fluid.

Veruschka plugged together the components of an Applied Biosystems oligosynthesis machine. She primed it with a data-stuffed S-cube that she'd rooted out of a twine-tied plastic suitcase.

"In Petersburg, we have unique views of DNA," said Veruschka, pulling on her ladylike data gloves and staring into the synthesizer's screen. Her fingers twitched methodically, nudging virtual molecules. "Alan Turing, you know of him?"

"Sure, the Universal Turing Machine," Janna coredumped. "Foundations of computer science. Breaking the Enigma code. Reaction-diffusion rules. Turing wrote a paper to derive the shapes of patches on brindle cows. He killed himself with a poison apple. Alan Turing was Snow White, Queen, and Prince all at once!"

"I don't want to get too technical for your limited mathematical background," Veruschka hedged.

"You're about to tell me that Alan Turing anticipated the notion of DNA as a program tape that's read by ribosomes. And I'm not gonna be surprised."

"One step further," coaxed Veruschka. "Since the human body uses one kind of ribosome, why not replace that with another? The Universal Ribosome—it reads in its program as well as its data before it begins to act. All from that good junk DNA, yes Janna? And what is junk? Your bottom drawer? My garbage can? Your capitalist attic and my start-up garage!"

"Normal ribosomes skip right over the junk DNA," said Janna. "It's supposed to be meaningless to the modern genome. Junk DNA is just scribbled-over things. Like the crossed-out numbers in an address book. A palimpsest. Junk DNA is the half-erased traces of the original codes—from long before humanity."

"From before, and—maybe *after*, Wiktor was always saying." Veruschka glove-tapped at a long-chain molecule on the screen. "There is pumptose!" The gaudy molecule had seven stubby arms, each of them a tightly wound mass of smaller tendrils. She barked out a command in Russian. The S-cube-enhanced Applied Biosystems unit understood, and an amber bead of oily, fragrant liquid oozed from the output port. Veruschka neatly caught the droplet in a glass pipette.

Then she transferred it to the crib vat that Janna had prepared. The liquid shuddered and roiled, jolly as the gut of Santa Claus.

"That pumptose is rockin' it," said Janna, marveling at the churning rainbow oil slick.

"We going good now, *ptista*," said Veruschka. She opened her purse and tossed her own Pumpti into the vat. "A special bath treat for my pet," she said. Then, with a painful wince, she dug one of her long fingernails into the lining of her mouth.

"Yow," said Janna.

"Oh, it feels so good to pop him loose," said Veruschka indistinctly. "Look at him."

Nestled in the palm of Veruschka's hand was a lentil-shaped little pink thing. A brand-new Pumpti. "That's your own genetics from your dirty fork at the diner," said Veruschka. "All coated with trilobite bile, or some other decoding from your junk DNA. I grew this seedling for you." She dropped the bean into the vat.

"This is starting to seem a little bent, Veruschka."

"Well…you never smelled your own little Pumpti. Or tasted him. How could you not bite him and chew him and grow a new scrap in your mouth? The sweet little Pumpti, you just want to eat him all up!"

Soon a stippling of bumps had formed on the tiny scrap of flesh in the tank. Soft little pimples, twenty or a hundred of them. The lump cratered at the top, getting thicker all around. It formed a dent and invaginated like a sea-squirt. It began pumping itself around in circles, swimming in the murky fluids. Stubby limbs formed momentarily, then faded into an undulating skirt like the mantle of a cuttlefish.

Veruschka's old Pumpti was the size of a grapefruit, and the new one was the size of a golf ball. The two critters rooted around the tank's bottom like rats looking for a drain hole.

Veruschka rolled up her sleeve and plunged her bare arm into the big vat's slimy fluids. She held up the larger Pumpti; it was flipping around like beached fish. Veruschka brought the thing to her face and nuzzled it.

It took Janna a couple of tries to fish her own Pumpti out of the tub, as each time she touched the slimy thing she had to give a little scream and let it go. But finally she had the Pumpti in her grip. It shaped itself to her touch and took on the wet, innocent gleam of a big wad of pink bubble gum.

"Smell it," urged Veruschka.

And, Lord yes, the Pumpti did smell good. Sweet and powdery, like clean towels after a nice hot bath, like a lawn of flowers on a summer morn, like a new dress. Janna smoothed it against her face, so smooth and soft. How could she have thought her Pumpti was gnarly?

"Now you must squeeze him to make him better," said Veruschka, vigorously mashing her Pumpti in her hands. "Knead, knead, knead! The Pumpti pulls skin cells from the surface of your hands, you know. Then pumptose reads more of the junk DNA and makes more good tasty proteins." She pressed her Pumpti to her cheek, and her voice went up an octave. "Getting more of that yummy yummy wetware from me, isn't he? Squeezy-squeezy Pumpti." She gave it a little kiss.

"This doesn't add up," said Janna. "Let's face it, an entire human body only has like ten grams of active DNA.

But this Pumpti, it's solid DNA, like a chunk of rubber, and hey, it's almost half a kilo! I mean, where's *that* at?"

"The more the better," said Veruschka patiently. "It means that very quickly Pumpti can be recombining his code. Like a self-programming Turing machine. Wiktor often spoke of this."

"But it doesn't even look like DNA," said Janna. "I messed with DNA every day at Triple Helix. It looks like lint or dried snot."

"My Pumpti is smooth because he's making nice old proteins from the ancient junk of the DNA. All our human predecessors from the beginning of time, amphibians, lemurs, maybe intelligent jellyfish saucers from Mars—who knows what. But every bit is my very own junk, of my very own DNA. So stop thinking so hard, Janna. Love your Pumpti."

Janna struggled not to kiss her pink glob. The traceries of pink and yellow lines beneath its skin were like the veins of fine marble.

"Your Pumpti is lovely," said Veruschka, reaching for it. "Now, into the freezer with him! We will store him, to show our financial backers."

"What!" said Janna. She felt a sliver of ice in her heart. "Freeze my Pumpti? Freeze your *own* Pumpti, Vero."

"I need mine," snapped Veruschka.

To part from her Pumpti—something within Janna passionately rebelled. In a dizzying moment of raw devotion, she found herself sinking her teeth into the unresisting flesh of her Pumpti. Crisp, tasty, spun cotton candy, deep-fried puffball dough, a sugared beignet. And under that a salty, slightly painful flavor—bringing back the memory of being a kid and sucking the root of a lost tooth.

"Now you understand," said Veruschka with a throaty laugh. "I was only testing you! You can keep your sweet Pumpti, safe and sound. We'll get some dirty street bum to make us a Pumpti for commercial samples. Like that stupid boy you were talking to before." Veruschka stood on tiptoe to peer out of the bank's bronze-mullioned window. "He'll be back. Men always come back when they see a woman making money."

Janna considered this wise assessment. "His name is Kelso," said Janna. "I went to Berkeley with him. He says he's always wanted me. But he never talked to me at school."

"Get some of his body fluid."

"I'm not ready for that," said Janna. "Let's just poke around in the sink for his traces." And, indeed, they quickly found a fresh hair to seed a Kelso Pumpti. It was nasty and testicular, suitable for freezing.

As Veruschka had predicted, Kelso himself returned before long. He made it his business to volunteer his aid and legal counsel. He even claimed that he'd broached the subject of Magic Pumpkin to Tug Mesoglea himself. However, the mysterious mogul failed to show up with his checkbook, so Magic Pumpkin took the path of viral marketing.

Veruschka had tracked down an offshore Chinese ooze farm to supply cheap culture medium. In a week, they had a few dozen Pumpti starter kits for sale. They came as a little plastic tub of pumptose-laced nutrient, all boxed up in a flashy little design that Janna had printed out in color.

Kelso had the kind of slit-eyed street smarts that came only from Berkeley law classes. He chose Fisherman's Wharf to hawk the product. Janna went along to supervise his retail effort.

It was the start of October, a perfect fog-free day. A song of joy seemed to rise from the sparkling waters of San Francisco Bay, echoing from the sapphire dome of the California sky. Even the tourists could sense the sweetness of the occasion. They hustled cheerfully round Kelso's fold-out table, clicking away with little biochip cameras.

Kelso spun a practiced line of patter while Janna publicly adored her Pumpti. She'd decked out Pumpti in a special sailor suit, and she kept tossing him high into the air and laughing.

"Why is this woman so happy?" barked Kelso. "She's got a Pumpti. Better than a baby, better than a pet, your Pumpti is all you! Starter kits on special today for the unbelievably low price of—"

Over the course of a long morning, Kelso kept cutting the offering price of the Pumpti kits. Finally a runny-nosed little girl from Olympia, Washington, took the bait.

"How do I make one?" she wanted to know. "What choo got in that kit?" And, praise the Holy Molecule, her parents didn't drag her away; they just stood there watching their little darling shop.

The First Sale. For Janna, it was a moment to treasure forever. The little girl with her fine brown hair blowing in the warm afternoon wind, the dazedly smiling parents, Kelso's abrupt excited gestures as he explained how to seed and grow the Pumpti by planting a kiss on a scrap of Kleenex and dropping the scrap into the kit's plastic tub. The feel of those worn dollar bills in her hand, and the parting wave of little Customer Number One. Ah, the romance of it!

Now that they'd found their price point, more sales followed. Soon, thanks to word-of-mouth, they began moving units from their website as well.

But now Janna's Dad Ruben, who had a legalistic turn of mind, warned them to hold off on shipments until they had federal approval. Ruben took a sample Pumpti before the San Jose branch office of the Genomics Control Board. He argued that since the Pumptis were neither self-reproducing nor infectious they didn't fall under the Human Heritage provisions of the Homeland Security Act.

The investigation hearings made the Bay Area news shows, especially after the right-wing religious crowd got in on the story. An evangelist from Alameda appeared on San Jose Federal Building's steps, and after an impassioned speech he tore a Pumpti apart with pincers, calling the unresisting little glob the "spawn of Satan." He'd confiscated the poor Pumpti from a young parishioner, who could be seen sobbing at the edge of the screen.

In a few days the Genomics Control Board came through with their blessing. The Pumptis were deemed harmless, placed in the same schedule category as home gene-testing kits. Magic Pumpkin was free to ship throughout the nation! Magic Pumpkin's website gathered a bouquet of orders from eager early adopters.

§

Kelso's art-scene friends were happy to sign up to work for Magic Pumpkin. Buoyed by the chance of worldly success, Kelso began to shave more often and even to use deodorant. But he was so excited about business that he forgot to make passes at Janna.

Every day-jobber in the start-up was issued his or her own free Pumpti. "Magic Pumpkin wants missionaries, not mercenaries," Janna announced from on high, and her growing cluster of troops cheered her on. Owning a personal Pumpti was an item of faith in the little company— the linchpin of their corporate culture. You couldn't place yourself in the proper frame of mind for Magic Pumpkin product development without your very own darling roly-poly.

Cynics had claimed that the male demographic would never go for Pumptis. Why would any guy sacrifice his computer gaming time and his weekend bicycling to nurture something? But once *presented* with their own Pumpti, men found that it filled some deep need in the masculine soul. They swelled up with competitive pride in their Pumptis, and even became quite violent in their defense.

Janna lined up a comprehensive array of related products. First and foremost were costumes. Sailor Pumpti, Baby Pumpti, Pumpti Duckling, Angel Pumpti, Devil Pumpti, and even a Goth Pumpti dress-up kit with press-on tattoos. They shrugged off production to Filipina doll clothes makers in a sweatshop in East LA.

Further up-market came a Pumpti Backpack for transporting your Pumpti in style, protecting it from urban pollution and possibly nasty bacteria. This one seemed like a sure hit, if they could swing the Chinese labor in Shenzhen and Guangdong.

The third idea, Pumpti Energy Crackers, was a no-brainer: crisp collectible cards of munchable amino acid bases to fatten up your Pumpti. If the crackers used the "mechanically recovered meat" common in pet food and cattle feed, then the profit margin would be primo. Kelso had a contact for this in Mexico: they guaranteed their cookies would come crisply printed with the Pumpti name and logo.

Janna's fourth concept was downright metaphysical: a "Psychic Powers Pumpti Training Wand." Except for occasional oozing and plopping, the Pumptis never actually managed conventional pet tricks. But this crystal-topped gizmo could be hawked to the credulous as increasing their Pumpti's "empathy" or "telepathy." A trial mention of this vaporware on the Pumpti-dot-bio website brought in a torrent of excited New Age emails.

The final, sure-thing Pumpti accessory was tie-in books. Two of Kelso's many unemployed writer and paralegal friends set to work on Pumpti user's guides. The firm forecasted an entire library of guides, sucking up shelf space at chain stores and pet stores everywhere. *The Moron's Guide to Computational Genomics. Pumpti Tips, Tricks, and Shortcuts.* The *Three-Week Pumpti Guide*, the *One-Day Pumpti Guide*, and the *Ten Minute Pumpti Guide. Pumpti Security Threats: How to Protect Your Pumpti from Viral DNA Hacks, Trojan Goo, and Strange Genes.* And more, more, more!

Paradoxically, Magic Pumpkin's flowering sales bore the slimy seeds of a smashing fiscal disaster. When an outfit started small, it didn't take much traffic to double demand every week. This constant doubling brought on raging production bottlenecks and serious crimps in their cash flow. In point of fact, in pursuit of market establishment, they were losing money on each Pumpti sold. And the big payback from the Pumpti accessories wasn't happening.

Janna had never quite realized that manufacturing real, physical products was so much harder than just thinking them up. Magic Pumpkin failed to do its own quality control, so the company was constantly screwed by fly-by-nighters. Subcontractors were happy to take their money, but when they failed to deliver, they had Magic Pumpkin over a barrel.

The doll costumes were badly sized. The Pumpti Backpacks were ancient Hello Kitty backpacks with their logos covered by cheap paper Pumpti stickers. The crackers were dog biscuits with the stinging misprint "Pupti." The "telepathic" wand sold some units, but the people buying it tended to write bad checks. As for the user's guides, the manuscripts were rambling and self-indulgent, long on far-fetched jokes yet critically short on objective facts.

Day by day, Janna stomped the problems out. And now that their production lines were stabilized, now that their accessories catalog was properly weeded out, now that their ad campaign was finally in gear, their fifteen minutes of ballroom glamour expired. The pumpkin clock struck midnight. The public revealed its single most predictable trait: fickleness.

Instantly, without a whimper of warning, Magic Pumpkin was deader than pet rocks. They never even shipped to any stores in the Midwest or the East Coast. The folks in those distant markets were sick of hearing about the Pumptis before they ever saw one on a shelf.

Janna and Veruschka couldn't make payroll. Their lease was expiring. They were cringing for cash.

A desperate Janna took the show on the road to potential investors in Hong Kong, the toy capital of the world. She emphasized that Magic Pumpkin had just cracked the biggest single technical problem: the fact that Pumptis looked like slimy blobs. Engineering-wise, it all came down to the pumptose-based Universal Ribosome. By inserting a properly-tweaked look-up string, you could get it to express the junk DNA sequences in customizable forms. Programming this gnarly cruft was, from an abstract computer-science perspective, "unfeasible," meaning that, logically speaking, no human would be able to design such a program within the lifetime of the universe.

But Janna's Dad, fretful about his investment, had done it anyway. In two weeks of inspired round-the-clock hacking, Ruben had implemented a full "OpenAnimator" graphics library, using a palette of previously unused rhodopsin-style proteins. Thanks to OpenAnimator, a whiff of the right long-chain molecule could now give your Pumpti any mesh, texture, color-map, or attitude matrix you chose. Not to mention overloaded frame-animation updates keyed into the pumptose's ribosomal time-steps! It was a techie miracle!

Dad flew along to Hong Kong to back Janna's pitch, but the Hong Kong crowd had little use for software jargon in American English. And the overwrought Ruben killed the one nibble they got by picking a fight over intellectual property—no way to build partnerships in Hong Kong.

Flung back to San Francisco, Janna spent night after night frantically combing the web, looking for any source of second-round venture capital, no matter how far-fetched.

Finally she cast herself sobbing into Kelso's arms. Kelso was her last hope. Kelso just had to come through for them: he had to bring in the seasoned business experts from Ctenophore, Inc., the legendary masters of jellyfish a-life.

"Listen, babe," said Kelso practically, "I think you and the bio-Bolshevik there have already taken this concept just about as far as any sane person oughta push it. Farther, even. I mean, sure, I recruited a lot of my cyberslacker friends into your corporate cult here, and we promised them the moon and everything, so I guess we'll look a little stupid when it Enrons. They'll bitch and whine, and they'll feel all disenchanted, but come on, this is San Francisco. They're used to that here. It's genetic."

"But what about my dad? He'll lose everything! And Veruschka is my best friend. What if she shoots me?"

"I'm thinking Mexico," said Kelso dreamily. "Way down on the Pacific coast—that's where my mother comes from. You and me, we've been working so hard on this start-up that we never got around to the main event. Just dump those ugly Pumptis in the Bay. We'll empty the cash box tonight, and catch a freighter blimp for the South. I got a friend who works for Air Jalisco."

It was Kelso's most attractive offer so far, maybe even sincere, in its way. Janna knew full well that the classic dot-com move was to grab that golden parachute and bail like crazy before the investors and employees caught on. But Magic Pumpkin was Janna's own brain child. She was not yet a serial entrepreneur, and a boyfriend was only a boyfriend. Janna couldn't walk away from the green baize table before that last spin of the wheel.

It had been quite some time since Ctenophore Inc. had been a cutting-edge start-up. The blazing light of media tech-hype no longer beamed from their dense, compact enterprise. The firm's legendary founders, Revel Pullen and Tug Mesoglea, had collapsed in on their own reputations. Not a spark could escape their gravity. They'd become twin black holes of biz weirdness.

Ctenophore's main line of business had always been piezoplastic products. Ctenophore had pumped this protean, blobject material into many crazy scenes in the California boom years. Bathtub toys, bondage clothing, industrial-sized artificial-jellyfish transport blimps—and Goob dolls as well! GoobYoob, creator of the Goob dolls, had been one of Ctenophore's many Asian spin-offs.

As it happened, quite without Janna's awareness, Ctenophore had already taken a professional interest in the workings of Magic Pumpkin. GoobYoob's manufacturing arm, Boogosity, had been the Chinese ooze-farm supplier for Pumpti raw material. Since Boogosity had no advertising or marketing expenses, they'd done much better by the brief Pumpti craze than Magic Pumpkin itself.

Since Magic Pumpkin was going broke, Boogosity faced a production glut. They'd have to move their specialty goo factories back into the usual condoms and truck tires. Some kind of corporate allegiance seemed written in the stars.

Veruschka Zipkinova was transfixed with paranoia about Revel Pullen, Ctenophore's chairman of the board. Veruschka considered major American capitalists to be sinister figures—this conviction was just in her bones, somehow—and she was very worried about what Pullen might do to Russia's oil.

Russia's black gold was the lifeblood of its pathetic, wrecked economy. Years ago Revel Pullen, inventively manic as always, had released gene-spliced bacteria into America's dwindling oil reserves. This fatal attempt to increase oil production had converted millions of barrels of oil into (as chance would have it) raw piezoplastic. Thanks to the powerful Texas lobby in Washington, none of the lawsuits or regulatory actions against Ctenophore had ever succeeded.

Janna sought to calm Veruschka's jitters. If the company hoped to survive, they had to turn Ctenophore into Magic Pumpkin's fairy godmother. The game plan was to flatter Pullen, while focusing their persuasive efforts on the technical expert of the pair. This would be Ctenophore's chief scientist, a far-famed mathematician named Tug Mesoglea.

It turned out that Kelso really did know Tug Mesoglea personally, for Mesoglea lived in a Painted Lady mansion above the Haight. During a protracted absence to the Tweetown district of Manchester (home of the Alan Turing Memorial), Tug had once hired Kelso to babysit his jellyfish aquarium.

Thanks to San Francisco's digital grapevine, Tug knew about the eccentric biomathematics that ran Pumptis. Tug was fascinated, and not by the money involved. Like many mathematicians, Mesoglea considered money to be one boring, merely bookkeeping subset of the vast mental universe of general computation. He'd already blown a fortune endowing chairs in set theory, cellular automata, and higher-dimensional topology. Lately, he'd published widely on the holonomic attractor space of human dreams, producing a remarkable proof that dreams of flight were a mathematical inevitability for a certain fixed percentage of the dreams—this fixed percentage number being none other than Feigenbaum's chaos constant, 4.6692.

§

Veruschka scheduled the meet at a Denny's near the Moffat Field blimp port. Veruschka had an unshakeable conviction that Denny's was a posh place to eat, and the crucial meeting had inspired her to dress to the nines.

"When do they want to have sex with us?" Veruschka fretted, paging through her laminated menu.

"Why would they want to do that?" said Janna.

"Because they are fat capitalist moguls from the West, and we are innocent young women. Evil old men with such

135

fame and money, what else can they want of us? They will scheme to remove our clothing!"

"Well, look, Tug Mesoglea is gay." Janna looked at her friend with concern. Veruschka hadn't been sleeping properly. Stuck on the local grind of junk food and eighty-hour weeks, Veruschka's femme-fatale figure was succumbing to Valley hacker desk-spread. The poor thing barely fit in her designer knockoffs. It would be catty to cast cold water on her seduction fantasies, but really, Veruschka was swiftly becoming a kerchiefed babushka with a string-bag, the outermost shell of some cheap nest of Russian dolls.

Veruschka picked up her Pumpti, just now covered in baroque scrolls like a fin-de-siècle picture frame. "Do like this," she chirped, brushing the plump pet against her fluffy marten-fur hat. The Pumpti changed its surface texture to give an impression of hairiness, and hopped onto the crown.

"Lovely," said Veruschka, smiling into her hand mirror. But her glossy smile was tremulous.

"We simply must believe in our product," said Veruschka, pep-talking to her own mirror. She glanced up wide-eyed at Janna. "Our product is so good a fit for their core business, no? Please tell me more about them, about this Dr. Tug and Mr. Revel. Tell me the very worst. These gray-haired, lecherous fat cats, they are world weary and cynical! Success has corrupted them and narrowed their thinking! They no longer imagine a brighter future, they merely go through the rote. Can they be trusted with our dreams?"

Janna tugged fitfully at the floppy tie she'd donned to match her dress-for-success suit. She always felt overwhelmed by Veruschka's fits of self-serving corn. "It's a biz meeting, Vero. Try to relax."

Just as the waitress brought them some food, the glass door of the Denny's yawned open with a ring and a squeak. A seamy, gray-haired veteran with the battered look of a bronco-buster approached their table with a bowlegged scuff.

"I'm Hoss Jenks, head o' security for Ctenophore." Jenks hauled out a debugging wand and a magnetometer.

He then swept his tools with care over the pair of them. The wand began beeping in frenzy.

"Lemme hold on to your piece for you, ma'am," Jenks suggested placidly.

"It's just a sweet little one," Veruschka demurred, handing over a pistol.

Tug Mesoglea tripped in moments later, sunburned and querulous. The mathematician sported a lavender dress shirt and peach-colored ascot, combined with pleated khaki trail-shorts and worn-out piezoplastic Gripper sandals.

Revel Pullen followed, wearing a black linen business suit, snakeskin boots, and a Stetson. Janna could tell there was a bald pate under that high hat. Jenks faded into a nearby booth, where he could shadow his employers and watch the door.

Mesoglea creaked into the plastic seat beside Veruschka and poured himself a coffee. "I phoned in my order from the limo. Where's my low-fat soy protein?"

"Here you go, then," said Janna, eagerly shoving him the heaped plate of pseudo-meat that the waitress had just set down.

Pullen stared as Mesoglea tucked in. "I don't know how the hell this man eats the food in a sorry-ass chain store." Nevertheless he picked up a fork and speared a piece of it himself.

"I believe in my investments," Mesoglea said, munching. "You see, ladies, this soy protein derives from a patented Ctenophore process." He prodded at Veruschka's plate. "Did you notice that lifelike, organic individuality of your waffle product? That's no accident, darling."

"Did we make any real foldin' money off this crap?" said Revel Pullen, eating one more piece of it.

"Of course we did! You remember all those sintered floating gel rafts in the giant tofu tanks in Chiba?" Mesoglea flicked a blob of molten butter from his ascot.

"Y'all don't pay no never mind to Dr. Mesoglea here," Revel counteradvised, setting down his fork. "Today's economy is all about diversity. Proactive investments. Buying into the next technical wave, before you get cannibalized."

Revel leered. "Now as for me, I get my finger into every techno-pie!" His lipless mouth was like a letter slot, bent slightly upward at the corners to simulate a grin.

"Let me brief you gentlemen on our business model," said Janna warily. "It's much like your famous Goob dolls, but the hook here is that the Pumpti is made of the user's very own DNA. This leads to certain, uh, powerful consumer bonding effects, and…"

"Oh good, let's see your Pumptis, girls," crooned Tug, with a decadent giggle. "Whip out your Pumptis for us."

"You've never seen our product?" asked Janna.

"Tug's got a mess of 'em," said Revel. "But y'all never shipped to Texas. That's another thing I just don't get." Pullen produced a sheaf of printout, and put on his bifocals. "According to these due-diligence filings, Magic Pumpkin's projected online capacity additions were never remotely capable of meeting the residual in-line demand in the total off-line market that you required for breakeven." He tipped back his Stetson, his liver-spotted forehead wrinkling in disbelief. "How in green tarnation could you gals overlook that? How is that even possible?"

"Huh?" said Janna.

Revel chuckled. "Okay, now I get it. Tug, these little gals don't know how to do business. They've never been anywhere near one."

"Sure looks that way," Tug admitted. "No MBAs, no accountants? Nobody doing cost control? No speakers-to-animals in the hacker staff? I'd be pegging your background as entry-level computational genomics," he said, pointing at Janna. Then he waggled his finger at Veruschka, "And you'd be coming from—Slavic mythology and emotional blackmail?"

Veruschka's cobalt blue eyes went hard. "I don't think I want to show you men my Pumpti."

"We kind of have to show our Pumptis, don't we?" said Janna, an edge in her voice. "I mean, we're trying to make a deal here."

"Don't get all balky on the bailout men," added Revel, choking back a yawn of disdain. He tapped a napkin to his wrinkled lips, with a glint of diamond solitaire. He glanced at his Rolex, reached into his coat pocket, and took out a little pill. "That's for high blood pressure, and I got it the hard way, out kickin' ass in the market. I got a flight back to Texas in less than two hours. So let's talk killer app, why don't we? Your toy pitch is dead in the water. But Tug says your science is unique. Okay, but how do we sell the Pumptis?"

"They're getting much prettier," Janna said, swiftly hating herself.

"Do y'all think Pumptis might have an app in home security?"

Janna brightened. "The home market?"

"Yeah, that's right, Strategic Defense for the Home." Pullen outlined his scheme. Ever the bottom-feeder, he'd bought up most of the software patents for the never-completed American missile defense system. Pullen had a long-cherished notion of retrofitting the Star Wars shield into a consumer application for troubled neighborhoods. He was wondering if Pumptis might take the place of the missiles.

Revel figured that a sufficiently tough-minded Pumpti could take a round to the guts, fall to earth, crawl back to its vat in the basement, and come back hungry for more. So if bullets were fired at a private home from some drug-crazed drive-by, then a rubbery unit of the client's Pumpti Star Wars shield would instantly fling itself into the way, guided by that fine old Star Wars software.

Veruschka batted her eyes at Pullen. "I love to hear a strong man talk about security."

"Security always soars along with unemployment," said Pullen, nodding his head at his own wisdom. "We're in a major downturn. I seen this before, so I know the drill. Locks, bolts, Dobermans, they're all market leaders this quarter. That's Capitalism 301, girls."

"And you, Ctenophore, you would finance Magic Pumpkin as a home-defense industry?" probed Veruschka.

"Maybe," said Pullen, his sunken eyes sly. "We'd surely supply you a Washington lobbyist. New public relations. Zoning clearances. Help you write up a genuine budget for once. And of course, if we're on board, then y'all will have to dump all your crappy equipment and become a hunnert-percent Ctenophore shop, technologically. Ctenophore sequencers, PCRs, and bioinformatic software. That's strictly for your own safety, you understand: stringent quality assurance, functional testing and all."

"Uhm, yeah," nodded Tug. "We'd get all your intellectual property copyrighted and patented. The lawyer fees, we'll take care of that. Ctenophore is downright legendary for our quick response times to a market opportunity."

"We gonna help you youngsters catch the fish," said Pullen smugly. "Not just give you a damn fish. What'd be the fun in that? Self-reliance, girls. We wanna see your little outfit get up and walk, under our umbrella. You sign over your founder's stock, put in your orders for our equipment—and we ain't gonna bill for six months—then my men will start to shake the money tree."

"Wait, they still haven't shown us their Pumptis," said Tug, increasingly peevish. "And, Revel, you need to choke it back to a dull roar with the Star Wars attack-Pumptis. Real world ballistic physics is chaotic, dude, which means unsolvable in real time." Tug muffled a body sound with his napkin. "I ate too many waffles."

Janna felt like flipping the table over into their laps. Veruschka shot her a quick, understanding glance and laid a calming hand on her shoulder. Veruschka played a deep game.

Veruschka plucked the Pumpti from her furry hat and set it on the table.

Tug did a double take and leaned forward, transfixed.

Veruschka segued into her cuddly mode. "Pumpti was created in a very special lab in Petersburg. In the top floor of old Moskfilm complex, where my friends make prehistoric amber jewelry. You can see the lovely River Neva while you hunt for dinosaur gnats—"

As she put the squeeze on their would-be sponsors, Veruschka compulsively massaged her Pumpti. She was working it, really getting into it finger and thumb, until suddenly a foul little clot of nonworking protein suddenly gave way inside, like popping bubble wrap.

"Stop it, Vero," said Janna.

Tug daintily averted his gaze as Veruschka licked goo from her fingers.

"Look at mine," offered Janna. She'd programmed her Pumpti to look rubbery and sleek, like a top-end basketball shoe.

"Hey, any normal kid would kill to have one of those," said Revel cheerily. "I'm getting' another product brainstorm! It's risin' in me like a thunderhead across Tornado Alley!"

"The junk DNA is the critical aspect," put in Tug. "Those are traces of early prehuman genomics. If we can really express those primordial codons, we might—"

"Those globbies suck DNA right off people's fingers, right?" demanded Revel.

"Well, yes," said Janna.

"Great! So that's my Plan B. Currency! You smash 'em out flat and color 'em pretty. As they daisy-chain from hand to hand, they record the DNA of every user. Combine those with criminal DNA files, and you got terrorist-proof cash!"

"But the mafiya always wears gloves," said Veruschka.

"No problem, just turn up the amps," said Pullen. "Have 'em suck DNA fragments out of the dang air." He wiggled his lower jaw to simulate deep thought. "Those little East European currencies, they're not real cash money anyways! That user-base won't even know the difference!"

Mesoglea blinked owlishly. "Bear with us, ladies. Revel's always like this right after he takes his meds."

"Now, Tug, we gotta confront the commercial possibilities! You and I, we could hit the lab and make some kind of money that only works for white males over fifty. If anybody else tries to pass it, it just, like—bites their dang hands off!" Pullen chuckled richly, then had another drag off his cig. "Or how about a hunnert-dollar bill that takes your DNA and grows your own face on the front!"

Mesoglea sighed, looked at his watch, and shook it theatrically.

141

"But this is such pure genius!" gushed Veruschka, leaning toward Revel with moistening eyes. "We need your veteran skills. Magic Pumpkin needs grown men in the boardroom. We wasted our money on incompetent artists and profiteers! We had great conceptual breakthroughs, but—"

"Can it with the waterworks and cut to the chase," said Pullen. "It's high time for you amateurs to roll over."

"Make us the offer," said Janna.

"Cards on the table," said Pullen, fixing her with his hard little eyes. "You'll sign all your founder's stock over to us. I'll take your stock, chica, and Tug'll take your pretty Russian friend's. That gives us controlling interest. As for your Dad's third, he might as well keep it since he's too maverick to deal with. Dad's in clover. Okay?"

"You're not offering us any cash?" said Janna. "I don't believe this. The Pumpti was our original idea!"

"You sign on with us, you get a nice salary," said Pullen. Then he broke into such cackles that he had to sip ice water and dab at his eyes with a kerchief.

"You two kids really are better off with a salary," added Tug in a kindly tone. "It won't be anything huge, but better than your last so-called jobs. We already checked into your histories. You'll get some nice vague titles too. That'll be good experience for your next job or, who knows, your next start-up."

"The sexy Russki can be my Pumpti Project Manager," said Pullen. "She can fly down to my ranch tomorrow. I'll be waitin'. And what about the other one, Tug? She's more the techie type."

"Yes, yes, I want Janna," said Tug, beaming. "Executive Assistant to the Chief Scientist."

Janna and Veruschka exchanged unhappy glances.

"How—how big of a salary?" asked Janna, hating herself.

§

After the fabled entrepreneurs departed the Denny's in the company of a watchful Hoss Jenks, Veruschka dropped her glued-on smile and scrambled for the kitchen. She was just in time to save Tug's and Revel's dirty forks before they hit the soapy water.

Shoving a busboy aside, Veruschka wrapped the DNA-soiled trophies in a sheet of newspaper and stuffed them into her purse.

"Veruschka, what do you think you're doing?"

"I'm multiplying our future options. I am seizing the future imperfectly. Visualize, realize, actualize." Veruschka's lower lip trembled. "Leap, and the net will appear."

Stuck in the clattering kitchen of Denny's, feeling sordid and sold-out, Janna felt a moment of true sorrow for herself, for Vero, and even for the Latin and Vietnamese busboys. Poor immigrant Veruschka, stuck in some foreign country, with an alien language—she'd seen her grandest dreams seized, twisted up, and crushed by America, and now, in her valiant struggle to rise from ash heap to princess, she'd signed on to be Pullen's marketeer droid. As for Janna—she'd be little more than a lab assistant.

At least the business was still alive. Even if it wasn't her business anymore.

When they returned to their San Francisco lair, they discovered that Hoss Jenks had arrived with a limo full of men in black suits and mirrorshades. They'd seized the company's computers and fired everyone. To make things worse, Jenks had called the police and put an APB out for Kelso, who had last been seen departing down a back alley with a cardboard box stuffed with the company's petty cash.

"I can't believe that horrible old cowboy called the cops on Kelso," Janna mourned, sitting down in the firm's very last cool, swoopy Blobular Concepts chair. "I'm glad Kelso stole that money, since it's not ours anymore. I hope he'll turn up again. I never even got to make out with him."

"He's gay, you know."

"Look, Kelso is *not gay*," yelled Janna. "He is so totally not gay. There's a definite chemistry between us. We were just too incredibly busy, that's all."

Veruschka sniffed and said nothing. When Janna looked up, her eyes brimming, she realized that Veruschka was actually feeling sorry for her. This was finally it for

Janna; it was too much for flesh and blood to bear. She bent double in her designer chair, racked with sobs.

"Janna, my dear, don't surrender. The business cycle, always, it turns around. And California is the Golden State."

"No it isn't. We've got a market bear stitched right on our flag. We're totally doomed, Veruschka! We've been such fools!"

"I hate those two old men," said Veruschka, after the two of them had exhausted half a box of Kleenex. "They're worse than their reputations. I expected them to be crazy, but not so—greedy and rude."

"Well, we signed all their legal papers. It's a little late to fuss now."

Veruschka let out a low, dark chuckle. "Janna, I want revenge."

Janna looked up. "Tell me."

"It's very high tech and dangerous."

"Yeah?"

"It's completely illegal, or it would be, if any court had the chance to interpret the law in such a matter."

"Spill it, Vero."

"Pumpti Gene Therapy."

Janna felt a twinge, as of seasickness. "That's a no-no, Vero."

"Tell me something," said Veruschka. "If you dose a man with an infectious genomic mutagen, how do you keep him from knowing he's been compromised?"

"You're talking bioterrorism, Vero. They'd chase us to the ends of the earth in a rain of cruise missiles."

"You use a Pumpti virus based on your victim's own DNA," said Veruschka, deftly answering her own rhetorical question. "Because nobody has an immune response to their own DNA. No matter how—how very strange it might be making their body."

"But you're weaponizing the human genome! Can't we just shoot them?"

Veruschka's voice grew soft and low. "Imagine Tug Mesoglea at his desk. He feels uneasy, he begins to complain, his voice is like a rasping locust's. And then his eyeballs—his eyeballs pop out onto his cheeks, driven from his head by the pressure of his bursting brain!"

"You call *that* gene therapy?"

"They *need* it! The shriveled brains of Pullen and Mesoglea are old and stiff! There is plenty of room for new growth in their rattling skulls. You and I, we create the Pumpti Therapy for them. And then they will give us money." Veruschka twirled on one heel and laughed. "We make Pumptis so tiny like a virus! Naked DNA with Universal Ribosome and a nine-plus-two microtubule apparatus to rupture the host's cell walls! One strain for Pullen, and one for Mesoglea. The Therapy is making them smarter, so they are grateful to shower money upon us. Or else," her eyes narrowed, "the Therapy is having some unpleasant effects and they are begging on their knees to purchase an antidote."

"So it's insanity and/or blackmail, in other words."

"These men are rotten bastards," said Veruschka.

"Look, why don't we give a fighting chance to Pullen's home-defense-Pumptis?" asked Janna. "Or his currency-Pumptis? They're nutty ideas, but not all that much crazier than your original scheme about pets. Didn't I hear you call Revel Pullen a marketing genius?"

"Don't you know me yet even a little bit?" said Veruschka, her face frank and open. "Revel's ideas for my Pumptis are like using a beautiful sculpture for a hammer. Or like using a silk scarf to pick up dog doo."

"Too, too true," sighed Janna. "Get the forks out of your purse and let's start on those nanoPumptis."

§

To begin with, they grew some ordinary kilogram-plus Pumptis from Revel and Tug's fork-scrapings, each in its own little vat. Veruschka wanted to be sure they had a whopping big supply of their enemies' DNA.

For fun, Janna added OpenAnimator molecules to shade Revel's Pumpti blue and Tug's red. And then, for weirdness, Vero dumped a new biorhythm accelerator into the vats. The fat lumps began frantically kneading themselves, each of them replicating, garbage-collecting, and decoding their DNA hundreds of times per second. "So

145

perhaps these cavemen can become more highly evolved," remarked Veruschka.

By three in the morning, they'd made their first nanoPumpti. Janna handled the assembly, using the synthesizer's datagloves to control a molecular probe. She took the body of a cold virus and replaced its polyhedral head with a Universal Ribosome and a strand of hyper-evolved DNA from the Pullen Pumpti. And then she made a nanoPumpti for Tug. Veruschka used her hands-on wetware skills to quickly amplify the lone Tug and Revel nanoPumptis into respectable populations.

When the first morning sunlight slanted in the lab window, it lit up two small stoppered glass vials: a blue one for Revel, a red one for Tug.

Veruschka rooted in the cornucopia of her tattered suitcase. She produced a pair of cheap-looking rings, brass things with little chrome balls on them. "These are Lucrezia Borgia rings. I bought them in a tourist stall before I left St. Petersburg." Practicing with water, Veruschka showed Janna how to siphon up a microliter though the ring's cunningly hidden perforations and how—with the crook of a finger—to make the ring squirt the liquid back out as a fine mist.

"Load your ring with Mesoglea's nanoPumptis," said Veruschka, baring her teeth in a hard grin. "I want to see you give Mesoglea his Therapy before my flight to Texas. I'll load my ring for Pullen and when I get down there, I'll take care of him."

"No, no," said Janna, stashing the vials in her purse. "We don't load the rings yet. We have to dose the guys at the exact same time. Otherwise, the one will know when the other one gets it. They've been hanging together for a long time. They're like symbiotes. How soon are you and Pullen coming back from Texas anyway?"

"He says two weeks," said Veruschka, pulling a face. "I hope is less time."

And then Hoss Jenks was there with a limo to take Veruschka to the airport. Janna cleaned up the lab and stashed the vials of nanoPumptis in her office. Before she could lie down to sleep there, Tug Mesoglea arrived for his first day at Magic Pumpkin.

To Janna's surprise, Tug turned out to be a pleasant man to work for. Not only did he have excellent taste in office carpeting and window treatments, but he was a whiz at industrial R&D. Under his leadership, the science of the Pumptis made great strides: improvements in the mechanism of the Universal Ribosome, in the curious sets of proteins encoded by the junk DNA, even in the looping strangeness of Ruben Gutierrez's genomic OpenAnimator graphics library. And then Tug stumbled onto the fact that the Pumptis could send and receive a certain gigahertz radio frequency. Digital I/O.

"The ascended master of R&D does not shoehorn new science into yesterday's apps," the serenely triumphant Tug told Janna. "The product is showing us what it wants to do. Forget the benighted demands of the brutish consumers: we're called to lead them to the sunlit uplands of improved design!"

So Janna pushed ahead, and under Tug's Socratic questioning, she had her breakthrough: Why stop at toys? Once they'd managed to tweak and evolve a new family of forms and functions for the Pumptis, they would no longer be mere amusements, but *personal tools*. Not like Pokemons, not like Goob dolls, but truly *high-end devices*: soft uvvy phones, health monitors, skin-interfaced VR patches, holistic gene maintenance kits, cosmetic body-modifiers! Every gadget would be utterly trustworthy, being made of nothing but you!

As before, they would all but give away the pretty new Pumptis, but this time they'd have serious weight for the aftermarket: "Pumpti Productivity Philtres" containing the molecular codes for the colors, shapes, and functionalities of a half dozen killer apps. Get 'em all! While they last! New Philtres coming soon!

Veruschka's stay in Texas lasted six weeks. She phoned daily to chat with Janna. The laid-back Texan lifestyle on the legendary Pullen spread was having its own kind of seduction. Vero gave up her vodka for blue agave tequila. She surrendered her high heels for snakeskin boots. Her phone conversations became laced with native terms such as "darlin" and "sugar" as she smugly recounted giant barbeques for politicians, distributors, the Ctenophore management, and the Pullen Drilling Company sales force.

By the time Revel and Veruschka came back to San Francisco, Magic Pumpkin had the burn-rate under firm control and was poised for true market success. But, as wage slaves, Janna and Veruschka would share not one whit of the profit. So far as Janna knew, they were still scheduled to poison their bosses.

"Do we really want to give them the Pumpti Therapy?" Janna murmured to Veruschka. They were in Janna's new living quarters, wonderfully carpentered into the space beneath the bank's high dome. It had proved easier to build-in an apartment than to rent one. And Tug had been very good about the expenses.

Veruschka had a new suitcase, a classy Texas item clad in dappled calfskin with the hair still on. As usual, her bag had disgorged itself all over the room. "Mesoglea must certainly be liquidated," she said, cocking her head. Tug's voice was drifting up from the lab below, where he was showing Revel around. "He is fatuous, old, careless. He has lost all his creative fire."

"But I like Tug now," said Janna. "He taught me amazing things in the lab. He's smart."

"I hate him," said Veruschka stubbornly. "Tonight he meets the consequences of his junk DNA."

"Well, your Revel Pullen needs Pumpti Therapy even more," said Janna crossly. "He's a corrupt, lunatic bully—cram-full of huckster double-talk he doesn't even listen to himself."

"Revel and I are in harmony on many issues," allowed Veruschka. "I begin almost to like his style."

"Should—should we let them off the hook?" pleaded Janna.

Veruschka gave her a level stare. "Don't weaken. These men stole our company. We must bend them to our will. It is beyond personalities."

"Oh, all right," sighed Janna, feeling doomed. "You poison Tug and I'll poison Revel. It'll be easier for us that way."

The four of them were scheduled to go out for a celebratory dinner, this time to Popo's, a chi-chi high-end gourmet establishment of Tug's choosing. Pullen's voice could now be heard echoing up from the lab, loudly wondering what was "keeping the heifers." Janna swept downstairs to distract the men while Veruschka loaded her ring. Then Veruschka held the floor while Janna went back up to her room to ready her own ring.

The two little vials of nanoPumpti sat in plain sight amidst the clutter of the women's cosmetics. They could have been perfume bottles, one red, one blue.

As Janna prepared to fill her Borgia ring, she was struck by a wild inspiration. She'd treat Revel Pullen with Tug's Pumptized DNA. Yes! This would civilize the semihuman Pullen, making him be more like Tug—instead of, horrors, even more like himself! There might be certain allergic effects—but the result for the Magic Pumpkin company would be hugely positive. To hell with the risk. No doubt the wretched Pullen would be happy with the change.

It went almost too easily. The old men guzzled enough wine with dinner to become loose and reckless. When the cappuccinos arrived, Janna and Veruschka each found a reason to reach out toward their prey. Janna adjusted Pullen's string-tie. Veruschka dabbed a stain of prawn sauce from Tug's salmon-colored lapel. And each woman gently misted the contents of her ring onto the chocolate-dusted foam of her victim's coffee. The old men, heavy-lidded with booze and digestion, took their medicines without a peep.

Soon after, Pullen retired to his hotel room, Tug caught a cab back to his house in the Haight, and the two women walked the few blocks back to the Magic Pumpkin headquarters, giggling with relief. Janna didn't tell Veruschka about having given Pullen the red Tug Treatment. Better to wait and see how things worked out. Better to sleep on it.

But sleep was slow in coming. Suppose Pullen swelled up horribly and died from toxic Tug effects? The Feds would find the alien DNA in him, and the law would be on Janna right away. And what if the Therapies really did improve the two old men? Risen to some cold, inhuman level of intelligence, they'd think nothing of wiping out Janna and Veruschka like ants.

Janna rubbed her cell phone nervously. Maybe she could give poor old Tug some kind of anonymous warning. But she sensed that Veruschka was also awake, over on the other side of Janna's California King bed.

Suddenly the phone rang. It was Kelso.

"Yo babe," he said airily. "I'm fresh back from sunny Mexico. The heat's off. I bought myself a new identity and an honest-to-God law degree. I'm right outside, Janna. Saw you and Vero go jammin' by on Market Street just now, but I didn't want to come pushing up at you like some desperado tweaker. Let me in. Nice new logo you got on the Magic Pumpkin digs, by the way, good font choice too."

"You're a lawyer now? Well, don't think we've forgotten about that box of petty cash, you sleaze."

Kelso chuckled. "I didn't forget you either, *mi vida*! As for that money—hey, my new papers cost as much as what I took. Paradoxical, no? Here's another mind bender: even though we're hot for each other, you and me have never done the deed."

"I'm not alone," said Janna. "Veruschka's staying with me."

"For God's sake will you two at last get it over," said Veruschka, sleepily burying her head under her pillow. "Wake me up when you're done and maybe the three of us can talk business. We'll need a lawyer tomorrow."

§

The next morning Tug Mesoglea arrived at Magic Pumpkin and started acting—like Revel Pullen.

"Git along little doggies," he crooned, leaning over the incubator where they were keeping their dozen or so new-model Pumptis. And then he reached over and fondled Janna's butt.

Janna raced out of the lab and cornered Veruschka, who was noodling around at her desk trying to look innocent. "You gave Tug the Pullen potion, didn't you? Bitch!"

Before Veruschka could answer, the front door swung open, and in sashayed Pullen. He was dressed, unbelievably, in a caftan and striped Capri pants. "I picked these up in the hotel shop," he said, looking down at one of his spindly shanks. "Do you think it works on me, Janna? I've always admired your fashion sense."

"Double bitch!" cried Veruschka, and yanked at Janna's hair. Janna grabbed back, knocking off the red cowboy hat that Vero was sporting today.

"Don't think we haven't already seen clear through your little game," said the altered Pullen with a toss of his head. "You and your nanoPumptis. Tug and I had a long heart-to-heart talk on the phone this morning. Except we didn't use no phone. We can hear each other in our heads."

"Shit howdy!" called Tug from the lab. "Brother Revel's here. Ready to take it to the next level?"

"Lemme clear out the help," said Revel, sounding Texan again. He leaned into the guard room and sent Hoss Jenks and his mirrorshades assistants out for a long walk. To Jenks's credit, he didn't bat an eye at Revel's new look.

"Let's not even worry about that Kelso boy up in Janna's room," said Tug, reverting to his old accent as well. "He's still asleep." Tug gave Janna an arch look. "Don't look so surprised, we know everything. Thanks to the Pumpti Therapy you gave us. We've got, oh, a couple of million years of evolution on you now. The future of the race, that's us. Telepathy, telekinesis, teleportation, and shape-shifting too."

"You're—you're not mad at us?" said Janna.

"We only gave the Therapy to make you better," babbled Veruschka. "Don't punish us."

"I dunno about that," said Revel. "But I do know I got a powerful hankerin' for some Pumpti meat. Can you smell that stuff?"

"Sure can," sang Tug. "Intoxicating, isn't it? What a seductive perfume!"

Without another word, the two men headed for the lab's vats and incubators. Peeping warily through the open lab doors, Janna and Veruschka saw a blur of activity. The two old men were methodically devouring the stock, gobbling every Pumpti in sight.

There was no way that merely human stomachs could contain all that mass, but that wasn't slowing them down much. Their bodies were puffing up and—just as Veruschka had predicted, the eyeballs were bulging forward out of their heads. Their clothes split and dropped away from their expanding girths. When all the existing Pumptis were gone, the two giants set eagerly to work on the raw materials. And when Tug found the frozen kilograms of their own personal Pumptis, the fireworks really began.

The two great mouths chewed up the red and blue Pumpti meat, spitting, drooling, and passing the globs back and forth. Odd ripples began moving up and down along their bodies like ghost images of ancient flesh.

"What's that a-comin' out of your rib cage, Tuggie?" crowed Revel.

"Cootchy-coo," laughed Tug, twiddling the tendrils protruding from his side. "I'm expressing a jellyfish. My personal best. Feel around in your genome, Revel. It's all there, every species, evolved from our junk DNA right along with our super-duper futuristic new bodies." He paused, watching. "Now you're keyin' it, bro. I say—are those hooves on your shoulder?"

Revel palpated the twitching growth with professional care. "I'd be reckoning that's a quagga. A prehistoric zebra-type thing. And, whoah Nellie, see this over on my other shoulder? It's an eohippus. Ancestor of the horse. The cowboys of the Pullen clan got a long relationship with horseflesh. I reckon there was some genetic bleedover when we was punchin' cattle up the Goodnight-Loving Trail; that's why growin' these ponies comes so natural to me."

"How do you like it now, ladies?" asked Tug, glancing over toward Janna and Veruschka.

"Ask them," hissed Veruschka in Janna's ear.

"No, you," whispered Janna.

Brave Vero spoke up. "My friend is wondering now if you will sign those Magic Pumpkin founders' shares back over to us? And the patents as well if you please?"

"Groink," said Revel, hunching himself over and deforming his mouth into a dinosaur-type jaw.

"Squonk," said Tug, letting his head split into a floppy bouquet of be-suckered tentacles.

"You don't need to own our business anymore," cried Janna. "Please sign it back to us."

The distorted old men whooped and embraced each other, their flesh fusing into one. The meaty mass seethed with possibilities, bubbled with the full repertoire of zoological forms—with feelers, claws, wings, antennae, snouts; with eyes of every shape and color winking on and off; with fleeting mouths that lingered only long enough to bleat, to hiss, to grumble, to whinny, screech, and roar. It wasn't exactly a "no" answer.

"Kelso," shouted Janna up the stairs. "Bring the papers!"

A high, singing sound filled the air. The Pullen-Mesoglea mass sank to the floor as if melting, forming itself into a broad, glistening plate. The middle of the plate swelled like yeasty bread to form a swollen dome. The fused organism was taking on the form of—a living UFO?

"The original genetic Space Friend!" said Veruschka in awe. "It's been waiting in their junk DNA since the dawn of time!"

As Kelso clattered down the stairs, the saucer charged at the three of them, far too fast to escape. Kelso, Janna, and Veruschka were absorbed into the saucer's ethereal bulk.

Everything got white, and in the whiteness, Janna saw a room, a round space expressing wonderful mathematical proto-design: a vast Vernor Panton 1960s hashish den, languidly and repeatedly melting into a Karim Rashid all-plastic lobby.

The room's primary inhabitants were idealized forms of Tug Mesoglea and Revel Pullen. The men's saucer bodies were joyous, sylphlike forms of godlike beauty.

"I say we spin off the company to these girls and their lawyer," intoned the Tug avatar. "Okay by you, Revel? You and I, we're more than ready to transcend the material plane."

"There's better action where we're going," Revel agreed. "We gotta stake a claim in the subdimensions, before the yokels join the gold rush."

A pen appeared in Tug's glowing hand. "We'll shed the surly bonds of incorporation."

It didn't take them long to sign off every interest in Magic Pumpkin. And then the floor of the saucer opened up, dropping Janna, Veruschka, and Kelso onto the street. Over their awestruck heads, the saucer briefly glowed and then sped away, though not in any direction that a merely human being could specify. It was more as if the saucer shrank. Reorganized itself. Corrected. Downsized. And then it was gone from all earthly ken.

And that's how Janna Gutierrez and Veruschka Zipkinova got rich.

Notes on "Junk DNA"

Asimov's Science Fiction, January, 2003.
Written Fall, 2001.

Rudy on "Junk DNA"

This time out, our two chracters are two women; I'm Janna and Bruce is Veruschka. And we also brought back our Tug and Revel characters from "Big Jelly." Bruce found it very easy to write the Revel character—my notion of a comically overbearing Texan.

Due to having two young daughters, Bruce was at this time focused on *Pokemon* characters, which led to the notion of the personal Pumpti pet. It was fine that I found *Pokemon* toys completely repellent and uninteresting, as this gave the story an edge.

The "Junk DNA" collaboration was tumultuous; I began finally to understand why a synergistic pair like, say, Lennon and McCartney might stop working together. Although pleasant and soft spoken in person, both Bruce and I can be bossy collaborators, capable of being very cutting in our emails.

This time out, it was like two guys playing tennis and trying to kill the ball and blast it down the other guy's throat. *Whack!* Some of this abrasive energy shows up in the interactions between the pairs of characters in this story: Janna vs. Veruschka and Tug vs. Revel.

On the upside, I noticed that working with Bruce was having a permanent effect on my writing, and in a good way. I also noticed that bits of his vocabulary were making his way into mine. "Gamely," for instance—that's a word I never used in the past, but now I like to slip it in.

I think my favorite line in this story is, "I got a powerful hankerin' for Pumpti meat."

"Junk DNA" rated a cover illustration when it appeared in *Asimov's*.

Bruce on "Junk DNA"

In our third collaboration, I was determined that we should create a more or less proper science fiction story, a genre work set years distant in the future, with extrapolated technology. "Storming the Cosmos" is historical fiction, it's "atompunk." "Big Jelly" is a technothriller satire more-or-less of its present day. For "Junk DNA" it seemed interesting to combine our earlier stories and drag them both into the future condition, so that "Veruschka Zipkinova" shows up as a grand-daughter of Vlad Zipkin, the hero of "Storming the Cosmos," while Pullen and Mesoglea, the young venture capitalists of "Big Jelly", have aged into seasoned business gurus.

Despite its vivid colors and its obsession with cute kid toys, this is by no means a rollicking, carefree story. "Junk DNA" has a middle-aged bitterness about it, and a pervasive sense that things will never be so good as they once were. Most of the characters are snatching at scraps of happiness that their bleak circumstances have denied them. They're willing to defraud, seduce, embezzle or kill to get a break, and when the two author stand-ins, Pullen and Mesoglea, belatedly show up in the narrative, it's as if they're telling an unhappy, frenzied world to calm down.

I was pleased by the level of invention in this story, but the ending's like a mental breakdown. All Rucker-Sterling collaborations are overheated steam contraptions. They've got their solid, steely components, but also much duct-tape and baling-wire. As you become more familiar with another writer's tricks of composition, you become a sharper critic of his work. That can get painful. Rudy's not a critic by nature, but I most definitely am.

Still, we got it up and running, and it chugs right along.

Hormiga Canyon

Part 1

Stefan Oertel pulled a long strand of salami rind from his teeth. He stared deep into wonderland.

Look at that program go! Flexible vectors swarming in ten-dimensional hyperspace! String theory simulation! Under those colored gouts of special effects, this, at last, was real science!

Stefan munched more of his sandwich and plucked up an old cellphone, one of the ten thousand such units that he'd assembled into a home supercomputer. "Twine dimension seven!" he mumbled around the lunchmeat. "Loop dimension eight!"

The screen continued its eye-warping pastel shapes. Stefan's ultracluster of hacked cellphones was searching Calabi-Yau string theory geometries. The tangling cosmic strings wove gorgeous, abrupt Necker-cube reversals and inversions. His program's output was visually brilliant. And, thus far, useless to anybody. But maybe his latest settings were precisely the right ones and the One True String Theory was about to be unveiled—

"Loop dimension eight," he repeated.

Unfortunately his system seemed to be ignoring his orders. There might be something wrong with the particular phone he was holding—these phones were, after all, junkers that Stefan's pal Jayson Rubio had skimmed from the vast garbage dumps of Los Angeles. Jayson was a junk-hound of the first order.

Ten thousand networked cell phones had given Stefan serious, number-crunching heavy muscle. He needed them to search the staggeringly large state space of all possible string theories. The powerful Unix and RAM chips inside the phones were in constant wireless communication with each other. He kept their ten thousand batteries charged with induction magnets. The whole sprawling shebang was nested in sets of brightly-colored plastic laundry baskets. Stefan dug the eco-fresh beauty of this abracadabra: he'd transformed a waste-disposal mess into a post-Einsteinian theory-incubator.

Stefan had earned his programming skills the hard way: years of labor in the machine-buzzing dungeons of Hollywood. And he'd paid a price: alienated parents in distant Topeka, no wife, no kids, and his best coder pals were just email addresses. Furthermore, typing all that computer graphics code had afflicted him with a burning case of carpal-tunnel syndrome, which was why he preferred yelling his line-commands into phones. Cell phones had kick-ass voice-recognition capabilities.

Stefan dipped into a brimming pink laundry-basket and snagged a fresher phone, an early-90s model with a flapping, half-broken jaw.

"Greetings, wizard!" the phone chirped, showing that it was good to go.

"Twine dimension seven, dammit! Loop dimension eight."

The system was still ignoring him. Now Stefan was worried. Was the TV's wireless chip down? That shouldn't happen. The giant digital flat-screen was new. And, yes, the phones were old junk, but with so many of them in his ultracluster it didn't matter if a few dozen went dead.

He tried another phone and another. Crisis was at hand.

The monster screen flickered and skewed. To his deep horror, the speakers emitted a poisoned death-rattle, prolonged and sizzling and terrible, like the hissing of the Wicked Witch of the West as she dissolved in a puddle of stage-magic.

The flat screen went black. Worse yet, the TV began to smell, a pricey, burnt-meat, molten-plastic odor that any programmer knew as bad juju. Stefan bolted from his armchair and knelt to peer through the ventilation slots.

And there he saw—oh please no—the ants. Ants had always infested Stefan's rental house. Whenever the local droughts got bad, the ants arrived in hordes, trouping out of the thick Mulholland brush, waving their feelers for water. Stefan's decaying cottage had leaky old plumbing. His home was an ant oasis.

He'd never seen the ants in such numbers. Perhaps the frenzied wireless signals from his massive mounds of cell phones had upset them somehow? There were thousands of ants inside his TV, a dark stream of them wending through the overheated circuit cards like the winding Los Angeles River in its manmade canyons of graffiti-bombed cement. The ants were eating the resin off the cards; they were gorging themselves on his TV's guts like six-legged Cub Scouts eating molten s'mores.

Stefan groaned and collapsed back into his overstuffed leather armchair. The gorgeous TV was a write-off, but all was not yet lost. The latest state of his system was still stored in his network of cellphones.

He reached for his sandwich, wincing at a stab of pain in his wrist.

The sandwich was boiling with ants. And then he felt insectile tickling at his neck. He jumped to his feet, banged open the door of his leaky bathroom, and hastily fetched-up an abandoned comb. He managed to tease three jolly ants from his strawy hair, which was dyed in a fading splendor of day-glo orange and traffic-cone red.

Before he'd moved into this old house, Stefan hadn't realized that most everybody in LA had an ant story to tell. Stefan had the ants pretty badly, but nobody sympathized with him. Whenever he reached out to others with his private burden of ant woes, they would snidely one-up him with amazing ant-gripes all their own: ants that ate dog food; ants that ate dogs; ants that carried off children.

Compared to the heroic tales of other Angelenos, Stefan's ant problems seemed mild and low-key. His ants were waxy, rubbery-looking little critters, conspicuously multi-ethnic in fine LA style, of every shape and every shade of black, brown, red and yellow. Stefan had them figured for a multi-caste sugar-ant species. They emerged from the tiniest possible cracks, and they adored sweet, sticky stuff.

Stefan bent over the rusty sink and splashed cold water on his unshaven face. He'd done FX for fantasy movies that had won Oscars and enchanted millions of people on six continents. But now, here he stood: wrists wrecked, vermin-infested, no job, no girlfriend, neck-deep in code for a ten-dimensional string-theory simulation with no commercial potential.

Kind of punk and cool, in a way. It sure beat commuting on the hellish LA freeways. He was free of servitude. And he definitely had a strong feeling that the very last tweak he'd suggested for his Calabi-Yau search program was the big winner.

Just three months ago, he'd been ignoring his growing wrist pains while writing commercial FX code for Square Root Of Not. The outfit was a cutting-edge Venice Beach graphics shop that crafted custom virtual-physics algorithms for movies and the gaming trade.

Of course, Stefan's true interest, dating way back to college, had always been physics, in particular the Holy Grail of finding the correct version of string theory. Pursuing the awesome fantasy of supersymmetric quantum string manifolds felt vastly finer and nobler than crassly tweaking toy worlds. The Hollywood FX work paid a lot, yes, but it made Stefan a beautician for robots, laboring to give animated characters better hair, shinier teeth, and bouncier boobs. String theorists, on the other hand, were the masters of a conceptual universe.

Though the pace of work had nearly killed him, Stefan had had a good run at Square Root Of Not. Their four-person shop had the best fire-and-algebra in Los Angeles, seriously freaky tech chops that lay far beyond the ken of Disney-Pixar and Time-Warner. The Square Rooters' primary client, the anchor-store in the mall of their dreams, had been Eyes Only, a big post-production lab on the Strip.

But Eyes Only had blundered into a legal tar pit. All too typical: the suits always imagined it was cheaper to litigate than to innovate. Disney's Giant Mouse was crushing the copyrighted landscape with the tread of a mastodon.

Stefan hadn't followed the sorry details; the darkside hacking conducted in Hollywood courtrooms wasn't his idea of entertainment. Bottom line: rather than watching their lives tick away in court, the Square Rooters had taken the offered settlement, and had divvied up cash that would otherwise go to lawyers.

Their pay-off had been less than expected, but all four Square Rooters had been worn down by the grueling crunch cycles anyway. Liberated and well-heeled, each Square Root partner had some special spiritual bliss to follow. Lead programmer Marc Geary was puffing souffles at a chef school in Santa Monica. Speaker-to-lawyers Emily Yu was about to sail to Tahiti on an old yacht she'd bought off Craig's List. Handyman Jayson Rubio was roaring around the endless loops of LA's freeways on a vintage red Indian Chief motorcycle. As for Stefan—Stefan was sinking his cash into his living expenses and his home-made ultracluster supercomputer. Finally, freedom and joy. Elite string-theory instead of phony Hollywood rubber physics.

Some days the physics work got Stefan so excited that he could think of nothing else. Just yesterday, when he'd had been feeling especially manic about his code, doll-faced Emily Yu had phoned him with a shy offer to come along on her South Seas adventure. Idiotically, Stefan had blown her off. He'd overlooked a golden chance at romance. Instead of hooking up, he'd geeked out.

Today he was nagged by the sense that he should call Emily back. Emily was smart and decent, just his type. But— the thing was—he couldn't possibly think about Emily without also thinking about work. Those years of servitude were something he wanted to forget. In any case, right this minute he was for sure too busy to call Emily, what with all these friggin' ants.

Stefan glared at his unshaven clown-haired visage in the mirror. He knew in his heart that he was being stupid. How many more women were likely to ask for face-time with him? He'd never get another such offer from kind-hearted

Emily Yu. There were a million pretty women in LA, but never a lot of Emilys. Call her now, Stefan, call her. Do it. You have ten thousand phones in here. Call.

Alright, in a minute, but first he'd call his landlord about the ants.

Back in his living room, long tendrils of ants were spreading out from the TV. Amazingly tiny ants: they looked no bigger than pixels, and their jagged ant-trails were as thin as hairline cracks. They were heading for the laundry baskets.

"Not my cell phones, you little bastards," cried Stefan, hauling his baskets outside to the dilapidated porch.

He found a phone that seemed to hold a charge.

"Call Mr. Noor," Stefan instructed. He'd cloned a single phone account across all ten thousand of his phones.

He heard ringing, and then his landlord's, dry, emotionless voice.

"This is Stefan Oertel, Mr. Noor. From the cottage in the back of your estate? I'm being invaded by ants. I need an exterminator right now."

"Hyperio," said Mr. Noor. "You tell Hyperio, he fixes that." This was Mr. Noor's usual response. Unfortunately Mr. Noor's handyman Hyperio was some kind of illegal, who appeared maybe once a month. Stefan had seen Hyperio just the other day, trimming the bushes and hand-rolling cigarettes. This meant that the ants would rampage unchallenged for weeks.

"Does Hyperio have a telephone?" asked Stefan. "Does he even have a last name?"

"Use poison spray," said Mr. Noor shortly. "I'm very busy now." Mr. Noor was always on the phone to rich friends in the distant Middle East. End of call.

Stefan snorted and squared his shoulders. The ant-war was up to him.

He found his cyber-tool kit and extracted the coil of a flexible flashlight. He poked his instrument through the slots in the back of his TV. The ants had settled right in there, ambitious and adaptable, like childless lawyers lofting-out a downtown high-rise. In the sharp-edged shadows lurked a sugar ant as big a cockroach. The huge ant was tugging at something. A curly bit of wire, maybe. For a crazy, impossible instant the ant looked as big as a hamster.

Stefan rocked back on his heels. These ants were blowing his mind; they were dancing on the surface of his brain. He was losing it. It was very bad for him to be deprived of a computer. He needed some help right away.

"Call Jayson," he told his phone.

Although Jayson Rubio sometimes worked Stefan's nerves, the two of them had a true and lasting bond. During each year they'd spent at Square Root of Not, they'd ventured to Burning Man together, displaying their special-FX wizardry to the festival crowds in the desert.

Both of them had all-devouring hobbies: Stefan's was string theory; Jayson's was memorabilia. Since leaving the FX company, Jayson had started his own little online business, marketing Renaissance-Faire-type costume gear that he made. Stefan maintained Jayson's website.

Jayson was old-school, very analog. At Square Root Of Not, he'd been the go-to guy for everything physical: stringing power cables, putting up drywall, sanding the floors, fixing the plumbing. As a fix-it wizard, Jayson was a human tornado. He always carried a sheathed multitool on his belt: knives, pliers, wrench, saw, scissors, cutters, strippers, punchers, pokers, rippers, pounders, and more. Jayson never lacked for options.

The phone was successfully ringing. Now that Stefan was in a jam, a jam full of sugar-ants, good old Jayson would pitch in.

"Stefan!" shouted Jayson, answering. "Call me back later."

"No no no, listen to me," Stefan babbled. "Ants are eating my hardware!"

Someone else was angrily yelling at Jayson in the background. Jayson had a fetish about holding his cellphone at arm's length, so that the powerful microwave phone-rays wouldn't foment a brain tumor. Whenever you called Jayson Rubio, you weren't calling an individual, you were calling an environment.

Jayson's current environment featured an echoing garage roar of biker engines and snarling heavy-metal music. "What? Not one more dime!" Jayson was barking. "Your ad said 'runs great,' it didn't say 'skips gears!' Are you waving that tire-iron at me, you friggin' grease monkey? What? Sure, go ahead, call the cops, Lester! I love the LA cops!"

Stefan heard more angry demands, and finally the roaring of a motorcycle. The engine noise rose to a crescendo, then it smoothed down. "Stefan, dog," said Jayson at last, wind whipping past his phone. "You still there?"

Stefan explained about the ants.

"Ant-man on the way!" Jayson soothed over the ragged pounding of his motorbike. "Don't even think about poison bug bombs! Bad chemical karma is never the path."

Stefan hung up. His mood had brightened. What the hell, he would fix his system somehow. He'd buy a new TV. The basic program was still in the cell-phone memory chips, also his very last tweak: twine dimension seven, loop dimension eight. For sure that had been the key to the One True String Theory. The One True String Theory was worth every sacrifice he had ever made. Cosmic strings were the key to an endless free source of non-polluting energy. His noble work would be a boon to all mankind.

Stefan wandered outside. It was another ruthlessly sunny June day, the sky blank and blue. The dry hills around Mr. Noor's estate were yellow, with scrubby olive-green oak and laurel trees. Stefan felt glad to be out of the house and away from his crippled hardware. Why did he labor indoors when he lived in California? That was crazy. Comprehending nature was, after all, the end goal of physics. Why not skip the middle-man? Why not go out in nature and comprehend it in the raw?

Maybe the ants were grateful to him for discovering the One True String Theory. In return, the ants had come to teach him a finer way of life. The ants were prodding him to recast his research goals. Maybe, in particular, he could search for a woman to live with? That search was well-known to be solvable in linear time.

He would phone Emily Yu before tonight. Of course he would. How hard could that be? His friend Jayson always seemed to have a partner on his arm, often boozy and tattooed, but undeniably female. All Stefan needed to do was to reach out at a human level. Here he was, unemployed yet still feverishly programming, like the cartoon coyote who skids off a cliff, spinning his legs in mid-air, until finally realizing that, sigh, it's time for that long tumble into the canyon.

Overhead the leaves on a eucalyptus tree shimmered in the hot breeze. Universal computation was everywhere. Behind the facades of everyday life were deep, knotted tangles of meaning. Yes, yes....

Jayson's sturdy red Indian motorcycle putted up the hill and into view, all 1950s curves and streamlining, with a low-skirted rear fender. A beautiful old machine, with Jayson happy on it.

Jayson shed his dusty carapace of helmet and jacket. He wore ragged denim cargo shorts, black engineer's boots, and a black T-shirt bearing a garish cartoon image of a carnivorous Mayan god. Jayson's brawny arms had sleeve-like tribal tattoos under intricate chain mail wristbands. Jayson wove the chain-mail in his idle moments, frenetically knitting away with pliers. Jayson's freaky metal wristbands were the best-selling items on his website. They were beloved by fantasy gamers and Society for Creative Anachronism types.

Stefan offered a cheery wave and hello, but Jayson raised a hand and hauled his phone from his shorts pocket. He listened at arm's length to the tinny bleating of the speaker, lost his temper and began to rage. "Huh? You reported it stolen? So try and find me, Lester! I got no fixed address! You've got a what? Back off, man, or you're never gonna get your money!" Angrily Jayson snapped shut his phone.

"A little trouble with your hog?" said Stefan delicately.

"Aw, that Lester," said Jayson, staring uneasily at his precious red bike. "Nasty old biker, long gray ponytail down his back.... Lester's a crook! He sold me a sick Indian, what it is. A beauty, a rare antique, a New York cop bike with all the original paint... but it shifts rough. On paper I still owe him... but if he won't fix my bike our contract is void. No way he's calling the cops."

Reassured by his own bravado, Jayson grinned and drew a crumpled paper sack from his pants pocket. "Next topic. Your ants are history. I brought ant aromatherapy."

"Didn't you used to have a big tow-trailer for your bike?" said Stefan, studying his friend. "That had all your stuff in it, didn't it?"

A pained scowl furrowed Jayson's bearded face. "Lupe says she's throwing me out. My trailer's locked in her garage in Pasadena until I pay back rent. It's always money, money, money with her. Man, I hate gated communities. Like, why put yourself into a jail?"

"You were pretty serious about Lupe. You told me she was the best woman you ever dated. You said you loved her."

Jayson winced. "Forget Lupe. Forget my stuff. The world's full of stuff. What's the difference who has what?"

"I like where your head's at," said Stefan, feeling empathy for his companion. "Material possessions are mere illusions. Everything we see here, everything we think we own, it all emerges from the knotting and unknotting of a hexadecillion loops of cosmic string."

It was Jayson's turn to offer a pitying look. "Still at that, huh?"

"Jayse, I'm just a few ticks of the clock away from the One True String Theory. In fact I think maybe... I think maybe I already found it. I found the truth exactly when those ants showed up to eat my system. So if I can just publish my science findings in a reputable journal—who knows! It could lead to golf-ball-sized personal suns!"

"Yeah, bro, it's all about the universal Celtic weave," said Jayson. He brandished the chain-mail of his hand-made wristlets, beautifully patterned, with loops in four or five different sizes. Then his indulgent smile faded; he twisted his head uneasily. "Do you, um, hear a helicopter over the valley? Let's hide my bike in your garage. Just in case Lester really did file a report. Those ghetto-birds are hell on stolen vehicles."

"Why don't you just pay the man?" asked Stefan as they wheeled the fine old machine into his tiny, cluttered garage. "This is a beautiful bike. Heavily macho."

Jayson grunted. "Thing is, I spent my Square Root of Not money on primo collectibles. Sci-fi costumes that I picked right off the studio set. They're in my trailer, locked up in Lupe's damn garage. But really, that's okay, because all I need to do is flip those costumes for a profit on my website. Then I can make good on Lupe's rent, and get at the costumes, and also pay off the motorcycle. See, it goes round and round. Loop-like." Another cloud crossed Jayson's face. "My website's still okay, right? Inside your parallel computer?"

"Your site is down. Like I've been telling you—the ants ate a crucial part of my system. Your website still exists." Stefan waved his hands. "It's distributed across the memory chips of ten thousand cell phones. In terms of customer service, though, your website's a lost world."

"I hate computers."

"They love you."

"I hate ants."

"That's what I want to hear," said Stefan. "Let's go get 'em, big guy." He led his friend inside.

They knelt and peered inside the TV, using the flexible light-wand.

"Hey, I've seen lots worse," grunted Jayson in typical LA style. "Your ants are practically too small to see!"

"They come in all sizes, man. I saw one as big as, I dunno, as big a miniature dachshund."

"Get a grip," advised Jayson, and the irony of this insult, coming from him, cheered Stefan no end. Yes, he was having a bad ants-in-your-hair day, but compared to Jayson, he was the picture of bourgeois respectability. He had money in the bank, a roof and a bed. For all his swagger, Jayson was practically living in a dumpster. But—Jayson didn't even care. Jayson wasn't daunted, not a bit. Stefan could learn from him.

Jayson was staring at Stefan's cracked leather armchair. "You gonna finish that sandwich? Is that baloney organic?"

"It's salami," said Stefan. "I'll get you a bottle of beer."

Jayson wolfed down the ant-teeming sandwich in three bites. "Tastes like dill pickles."

"That would be the formic acid."

Jayson chugged the whole bottle of Mexican beer and fetched himself another. He then focused his professional attention on the four little glass phials he'd brought, deftly unlimbering his multitool and twisting off the screw-tops. Jayson loved using his pliers.

"Eucalyptus, peppermint, cinnamon, and verbena," intoned Jayson. He dribbled reeking herbal essences on the floor by the television. "Organic, non-toxic, all-natural, ants hate it. This potion never fails."

The ants tasted of the droplets—and found them good. The trails on the floor thickened as ants seethed out of the TV, so many ants that the trails looked like glittering syrup.

Not wanting to admit defeat, Jayson began stomping the ants. "My essences drew 'em out of hiding. This way we can wipe them out!" One of the old pine floorboards gave a loud crack and split along its length.

"Jayson!"

"Dog, you got so many ants that they gotta be living under your house. You got some serious Los Angeles ants here, man, you got atomic mutant ants like those giant ants in *Them*. We rip up these crappy old floorboards, napalm those little suckers with flaming moth-balls, then float in some plywood and throw down a cheap carpet. Presto, problem solved."

"Save the pyro stunts for Burning Man, Jayson. You're not wrecking my vintage floor."

Jayson knelt and peered through the broken board, getting the ant's-eye view. "That's a great movie, *Them*, it's got those classic rubber-model bug effects. None of your digital crap."

"Digital is not crap," said Stefan with dignity. "Digital is everything. The world is made of ten-dimensional loops of digital cosmic string."

"Sure, sure, but *Bug's Life* and *Antz* were totally lame compared to *Them*."

"That's because they didn't use giant ants," said Stefan. "Certain intellectual lightweights have this wimpy notion that giant ants are physically impossible! Merely because the weight-to-strength ratio scales nonlinearly. But there's so many loopholes. Like negatively curved space, man, or higher dimensions. Lots of elbow room in hyperspace! String theory says there are six extra dimensions of space-time too small for humans to see. The Calabi-Yau vermin dimensions."

"You really know some wack stuff, dog," said Jayson, vindictively mashing ants with his thumb. "If these ants have got their own goddamn dimensions, all the more reason to rip up this floor and pour gallons of burning gasoline into their hive."

"Their nest is not under my house," insisted Stefan. "There's got to be some modern cyber-method to track ants to their true lair. Like if I could laser-scan them, or Google-map them. That would rock."

"Stefan, why did you even call me if you want to talk that kind of crap? It's not like ants have anti-theft labels."

"Hey, that's it!" exclaimed Stefan. "I've got smart dust, man. I've got a whole bag of smart dust in my bedroom."

Jayson grinned loonily and made snorting noises. "Smart dust? Throw down some lines, dog!"

"I do not speak of mere drugs," said Stefan loftily, "I'm talking RFID! Radio frequency ID chips. My smart dust comes out of a lab in Berkeley. You can ping these teensy ID tags with radio, and they give off an ID number. They're computer chips, but they're so much smaller than ants that they're like ant cell phones. Smaller than that, even. Smart dust is like ant pretzel nuggets."

Stefan fetched Jayson a promotional sheet from a heap of tech-conference swag. The glossy ad showed one single ant towering over one single chip of smart dust. The chip was a knitted trackwork of logic circuits, pretty much like any normal computer chip, but the ant standing over it was an armored Godzilla with eyes like hubcaps and feelers big as sewer pipes.

"Whoah," said Jayson. "I'd love to see an ant that big." He drew out his multitool and kinked at a shiny length of his hobby wire.

Stefan rooted through his tangled electronic gear. "Here it is: just what we need. We'll mix this bag of smart-dust with your super-attractive ant repellents, and all the ants will swallow that stuff whole. Luring ants with high-tech bait—that's just like when we did our art installations at Burning Man, back in the day!"

"Yep, those naked hippies were drawn to our tech wizardry like ants to sugar," Jayson concurred. "I'd always get laid right away, but you were obsessed with keeping the demo running."

"I need to change," admitted Stefan.

The ants gathered rapidly around the bait, climbing on top of each other in their eagerness to feed. Stefan squatted to stare. "Wow, we're drawing a matinee crowd!"

"Yeah, we got a big pop hit," observed Jayson. The diverse crowd of ants included little foragers, big-jawed soldiers, curvaceous nurses, boxy undertakers…

Stefan pointed. "That one's big as a rubber beetle! She must be a queen or something!"

"Squash her first," said Jayson, plucking a rumpled pack of cigarettes from his pants pocket.

"I'm gonna capture her! A specimen like this belongs in a science museum." Stefan hopped up and fetched nonconductive plastic tweezers from his electronics toolbox.

But when he leaned in to clutch the biggest ant with the tools of science—*whoa*, the ant shrank to a pencil-dot and disappeared into the floor boards.

"Feeling very strange!" exclaimed Stefan. "Did you see?"

"These ants are shifty mofos; I don't like 'em," said Jayson, lighting his cigarette. He dialed up his lighter's flame to make a small blow-torch. "These website-eaters must have swallowed some chips by now. Tea party's over, girls."

Scorched by Jayson's lighter flame, the ants milled, panicked and dispersed.

Stefan's smart-dust scanner was the size of a pen, with a wireless connection to his laptop. Most of the dust was still half-glued on the floor, so it was hard to find a clear signal. Stefan tapped eagerly at his laptop's keyboard, tweaking the scanner. Enthralled by discovery, he'd forgotten all the pain in his wrists.

The smart-dust signals were vanishing through the walls of his apartment. With some bloodhound-style electronic tracking, Stefan found that the signals converged onto a winding ant highway running through his sun-baked yard.

"See, Jayson, those ants don't live anywhere near my house."

"I'll bring the gasoline," said Jayson, opening the last Mexican beer. "I saw a five gallon can in your garage by the leafblower."

They followed the signals up Mr. Noor's long driveway, the gas sloshing in Jayson's rusty can. The ants were moving with astounding speed, as if they'd mounted tiny broom-sticks.

"I don't like leaving my bike," said Jayson after a bit. "No way these are the same ants that were in your house."

"Smart dust don't lie, compadre."

They arrived at an overgrown pull-off near the gate; Stefan passed it every day. He'd never thought to stop there before, for the spot was bristling with angry yucca and prickly-pear. The trail of cybernetically tagged ants led under a forbidding tangle of dusty cactus, disappearing into a crooked little groove, a mini-arroyo where the fault-tortured dirt of LA had cracked wide open.

A wind-blown newspaper dangled from the spine of an ancient yucca.

Jayson plucked the paper loose. "This might be handy for tinder... Hey, whoa! Look how old this thing is!"

The newspaper dated from 1942; the lead story was about the "zoot suit riots" pitting Latino teens against US sailors on liberty.

"Duck-tail haircuts," murmured Jayson, skimming the article. "I could make a historical zoot suit. This paper is great. I can sell this as memorabilia. There might be a whole trove of old paper under that cactus. Let's hold off on the flaming gasoline attack."

Stefan stared at his laptop. His smart-dusted ant signals were vanishing as fast as movie popcorn. "They're running straight into that crack in the ground. And then their signals just vanish."

"Must be some kinda sink hole," said Jayson. He hunkered down and accurately pitched his empty beer bottle at the crack under the cactus.

The brown Mexican glass bloated like a soap bubble, shrank to the size of a pinhead and disappeared.

"Okay," said Jayson slowly. "That's pretty well torn it."

"It's…that's…wow, it's a localized domain of scale recalibration," said Stefan. "You get that kind of Calabi-Yau effect from a warping of the seventh dimension. You wait here, Jayson. I'm gonna walk right in there. I know how to handle these things."

Clutching his laptop, Stefan ventured forward towards the mysterious furrow. He took a step, two, three. Enormous mammoth-ear blobs of prickly pear cast a weird shade over his computer screen.

Suddenly five enormous fleshy sausages seized his chest with crushing force. He gasped and dropped his laptop. He was yanked backward with blinding speed, then somehow found himself tumbling into Jayson, sending the two of them sprawling on the dry, cracked dirt.

"You shrank, man," Jayson complained, rising and dusting his cargo shorts. "You shrank right to the size of a hobbit. You were the size of Hello friggin' Kitty."

"Where's my computer?"

"You see that little gray matchbook down there? That's your Dell, dude."

"I'm getting it." Stefan darted in, shrinking as he went. He grabbed his laptop and hurried back out.

"Brave man," said Jayson, patting Stefan's shoulder. "How about this for an idea. Instead of walking into that crack, we get my Indian and ride into it."

Stefan considered this, "You really want to risk your precious bike? At this point, it's all you've got left."

Jayson mulled this perhaps unkind remark, and decided to come clean. "Look, I didn't want to tell you this before, because I'd knew you'd get all uptight, but Lester hid one of those satellite locator gizmos inside my Indian's engine block. That's what he told me on the phone. So if he really filed a stolen vehicle report…"

A police helicopter was laboring heavily over the valley. In LA, the cop choppers were always up there. At four AM, above a howl of sirens, you could see them scorching the dark alleys of Hollywood with massive beams of light, like premieres in reverse.

"So I say we ride my bike into this crack in the ground," continued Jayson. "And then we ride off the radio spectrum, just like the ants did. The vehicle disappears. Plus, then we've got some wheels. It's win-win."

"Brilliant," said Stefan, nodding his head. "Let's hurry."

They left the gas can where it was, and ran back to the garage. Jayson kicked his reluctant hog into function. There was room to spare for Stefan behind Jayson on the Indian's enormous seat, which had been built for the generous cop-butts of a simpler era.

They roared up the driveway to the pullout and paused to top up the motorcycle's tank from the can of gas, Jayson recklessly smoking a cigarette all the while.

"I'm, uh, having a moment of hesitation," Stefan confessed when they were back on the seat. "Can two men on a motorcycle possibly fit under a cactus?" He fumbled at his laptop. "I'm thinking maybe some calculations or some Google research would be—"

The rest of his words were lost in the roar of a police helicopter sweeping low over the ridge.

Jayson torqued the throttle and did a wheelie straight towards the bristling chaparral.

Part 2

With the sinister ease of fishline unsnarling, the prickly pear grew to enormous size overhead. The groove in the

173

ground rose up on both sides like a frozen tsunami, then segued into a commodious canyon—a peaceful, timeless place with steep reddish sides and a sweet, grassy floor.

Jayson eased back on the throttle. The canyon cliffs had a certain swoony quality, like a paint-by-numbers canvas done by someone short of oils. The canyon's air was luminous, glowing from within.

Little houses dotted the bucolic valley floor, in rows and clusters. There were fields of corn, chickens in the yards, oranges, and here and there, thriving patches of marijuana.

A dry river snaked along the valley. Livestock grazed the uncertain terrain of the higher slopes, which featured particularly vertiginous, eye-hurting angles. The grazing animals might have been cows and horses—maybe even antelopes and bison.

Up above the slopes the sun was scudding across the sky like a windblown balloon. Jayson braked the bike and cut the engine. "Okay. Okay. What the hell is that up there?"

"That's the sun, Jayson."

"It's falling out of the sky?"

"No, man. Any space warp is a time warp as well. I'd say one minute here in this valley of the ants is about the same as an hour in the workadaddy outer world." Stefan cocked his head, staring at the racing sun, his eyes as bright as an excited bird's. "The deeper we go in, the faster the outer world's time rushes by. We'll be like a couple of Rip van Winkles."

Jayson threw back his head and laughed. "So by now those cops have given up and flown home!" He whooped again, as if recklessly trying to project his voice from the tiny ant crack beneath the cactuses off Mr. Noor's drive. "Kiss my ass, Lester!"

"I have to analyze this situation scientifically," said Stefan, growing fretful. "It's counterintuitive for time to run slower here than in the world outside. That's unexpected. Because usually small things are faster than large ones. Twitchy mice, sluggish elephants. But, oh, I see now, if the component strings of spacetime are *left*-handed seven-dimensional helices, then—"

174

"Then we're free men," said Jayson, kick-starting his bike with a roar. "Let's see if I can find us the local Fatburger. That baloney of yours left a bad taste in my mouth."

But there were no fast-food shacks to be seen in this idyllic landscape. The roads were mere dirt-tracks. No electrical pylons, no power cables. No big LA streetlights. No gutters, no concrete, no plumbing. Even the air smelled different; it had a viscous, sleepy, lotus-land quality, as if it were hard to suck the molecules through one's nose-holes.

In this bucolic stillness, the pop-popping of the old Indian was loud as fireworks. An over-friendly yellow dog came snuffling up behind the slow-moving bike. Stefan turned to confront the stray mutt, and noted its extra, scuttling legs. It wasn't a dog; it was, rather, a yellow ant the size of a dog.

The ant's hooked feet skimmed across the valley floor, leaving neat little ant hoofprints. Intent on Jayson's motorcycle, she moved like a Hong Kong martial artist on wireworks and trampoline.

Jayson hastily pulled his chopper into the gorgeous flowers of a local yard. He killed the engine and the boys leapt from the bike. The ant tapped the bike all over with her baton-sized feelers—trying to initiate a conversation. The motorcycle was, after all, remarkably ant-like in appearance, with its red skin, handlebar feelers, bulging headlight eye, and the gas tank like a thorax. Receiving no response, the yellow ant studied the boys with her compound eyes, then bent her rear end around to smear a drop of sticky ant-goo across the bike's fat rear fender. She bent a bit awkwardly; judging from her lumpy abdomen, she'd recently had a big meal. And now, task done, she scuttled right along.

A weathered man in a white shirt, straw hat and chinos came out of the house and sat down on an old-style dinette chair. The vintage aluminum and vinyl chair was in much better condition than its age would suggest.

"Nice bike," said the old man, beginning to roll a cigarette. "What's it doing in my flowers?"

"Hyperio!" exclaimed Stefan. "I know you—I rent the cottage from Mr. Noor? I'm Stefan Oertel."

"Okay," said Hyperio peaceably. "I used to live in that cottage. Me and my first wife Maria. The gardener's cottage, the owner called it."

"Mr. Noor never told me that."

"Not him. Mr. Hal Roach, fella helped make those fat-man thin-man movies."

"Laurel and Hardy's producer!" said Stefan. "Wow. Serious time dilation. It's a real coincidence to find you here, Hyperio. I was looking for you because I have ant problems."

Hyperio seemed to think this was funny. He laughed so hard that he spilled the tobacco out of his cigarette. It was an odd, desperate kind of laughter, though, and by the end it almost looked like he was in tears.

"I'm sorry, boys," said Hyperio finally. "I'm not myself these days. My wife Lola is sick." He jerked his head towards his door. "My Lola—she's from way up Hormiga Canyon."

"Canyon of the Ants," translated Jayson. "What a great neighborhood. Can I live here? You got an extra room I can rent?"

"You'd pay me?" said Hyperio, looking maybe a little annoyed at Jayson's seeming lack of concern over his sick wife.

"Um, I'm low on funds right now," said Jayson, slapping his pockets. He looked around, sniffing the air for collectibles. "That Deco moderne dinette chair you're sitting on—if I took that over to Silver Lake, I could get you two, three hundred bucks."

"I brought this from the gardener's cottage when I built this place for Lola," said Hyperio. "And I'm keeping it. I like it."

"Hey—do I see a wind-up Victrola through your window? You've got some old 78 records, right? You like that big band accordion sound?"

"You like conjunto, too?" Hyperio said, finally smiling. There was nothing for it but to step inside his house, where he proceeded to treat the boys to a leisurely wind-up rendition of "Muy Sabroso Blues" by Lalo Guerrero And His Five Wolves.

Grown hospitable, Hyperio produced a ceramic jug of room-temperature pulque. He gestured at a rounded lump under a striped Indian blanket on a cot. "My old lady," he said. "My Lola. She's got the real ant problems. Ants living inside her."

"But—" began Stefan.

"They make themselves small," said Hyperio, narrowing his eyes.

"Sure, sure, that figures," nodded Jayson, tapping his booted foot to the music. "How did you end up in Hormiga Canyon, Hyperio?"

"Okay, before Lola, I was living with my first wife Maria in the gardener's cottage," said Hyperio. "One day I found the way in. Yeah, hombre, I had good legs then. I walked the canyon very deep." Hyperio held out his fingers, branching in ten directions, with his cigarette still clamped between two of them. "Hormiga Canyon, it don't go just one way. The rivers run in, the rivers run out. But I didn't stop till I found my Lola. She's a real LA woman. The original." He sat on the creaking cot beside Lola and patted her damp brow.

"So you found Lola and—?" coaxed Stefan, eager to hear more.

"I was crazy in love with her at first sight," said Hyperio. "She was living with this indio, Angon was his name. From the Tongva tribe. Lola was too good for them. The Tongva people, they pray to the ants. They got some big old giant ants back there with legs like redwood trees."

"Wow," said Jayson. "I'd pay plenty to see those ants."

Hyperio got up and changed the record on his Victrola. "This is Lola's favorite song," he said. "'Mambo del Pachuco' by Don Tosti and his band. She could really mambo, my Lola. Back in the day."

The syncopated strains of music poured over the woman on the cot, and she stirred. Hyperio helped her sit up. Lola was stick-thin, and her brown face was slack. She'd been sleeping in a kind of leather shift, hand-beaded with little snail shells. When Lola saw that guests had arrived, however, she rallied a bit. Swaying to the music from the

Victrola, she threw firewood into the stove. She stirred a kettle of soup. She drank water from a big striped pot.

Then she doubled over with a racking cough. She spat up a mass of ants. The ants swarmed all over her hands.

Stefan and Jayson exchanged an alarmed look. But Hyperio wasn't surprised. He herded Lola back into bed, patted her, wrapped her up.

"She's working the Tongvan ant cure," said Hyperio shaking his head. "They eat ants to get well, the Tongvans. Lola eats the ants, lots of them, but she's still no good inside, not yet. That's why she wants me to take her back up canyon."

"Home to her people, eh," said Jayson. "I've heard about that tribe. The Tongvans. They were Californians, but like, before Columbus, basically?"

"The first, yes," said Hyperio. He reached behind a string of dried peppers near the ceiling and produced a leafy sheaf of cured tobacco. With the edge of an abalone shell, he chopped up the brown leaf, then twisted it in scrap of newspaper. "You boys want a good smoke? Have a smoke."

Jayson snatched up Hyperio's hand-rolled cig. "These ants. Is redwood-tree-legs the max size they go?"

"They go bigger," said Hyperio. "The biggest ones live in a monster nest beyond the Tongvans. They say something is wrong with the ground there, like a tar pit. Lola still prays to those tar pit ants. Good cooking, praying to ants, that's my Lola. But pretty soon she likes it better here. She likes the music."

"How did your first wife Maria take it when you showed up with a prehistoric girlfriend?" asked Stefan. It was his fate forever to wonder how romance worked.

"All the way home I worry about that," said Hyperio, nodding sagely. "It only felt like I left Maria a couple of days, maybe a week, but when I get back, Maria is dead! It's twenty years later. I ask around—nobody remembers me. Not a soul. So I moved into Hormiga Canyon and built this little house for Lola and me. She gave me four kids."

"Where are they now?" said Stefan.

"Busy with grandkids," Hyperio shrugged. A metal pot danced and rattled on his iron stove. "Now we eat soup, eh? You want me to warm some tortillas?"

Raw wonder at the way of man and woman had relaxed Stefan's fixation on science for one moment, but now his string-mania came vibrating back at him. "I know why this canyon exists!" he intoned. "There's a fault in the weave of the cosmic strings that make up Los Angeles. And, yeah, that fault is this very canyon. The local Hormiga Canyon ants have co-evolved with the cosmic strings. That's why LA ants are so sneaky! The ants of Los Angeles have a secret nest in that tar pit of cosmic strings."

Jayson looked on him kindly. "Eat something, Stefan."

They had a little of Hyperio's squirrel soup—at least, the soup had some ratlike parts that were probably squirrel—and though the flavors of native Angeleno herbs like yarrow, sage and deer grass were far from subtle, they did seem to brace one internally.

Buoyed by his scientific insight, Stefan was feeling expansive. "You're a fine host, Hyperio! Anything we can do to pay you back?"

Hyperio regarded the boys. "That motorcycle in my flowers—you got some gas in it? Lola wants to go back up canyon to her people. But I don't feel so good about this big trip."

"We can carry Lola in for you," said Jayson grandly.

"Dude," said Stefan to his friend in a low tone. "If we go deep into this canyon, we'll never see our own era again."

"So what?" said Jayson. "When we go up that canyon, we're going to a simpler, cleaner time. No smog. No pesticides. No politicians."

"I can give you boys an old map," said Hyperio, rising from his dinette chair.

Suddenly the room seemed to warp and twist. The walls creaked loudly.

"Earthquake!" yelped Jayson. He bolted from his dinette chair and banged his way through the door.

"Antquake," corrected Hyperio, unperturbed.

RUDY RUCKER & BRUCE STERLING

Stefan rose and peered through the door, clutching his
laptop in both hands. Jayson was hastily rolling his bike away
from Hyperio's house. Certain Angelenos were unnerved by
ground tremors, but the pitching earth beneath his feet had
never much bothered Stefan. In a hyperinflating cosmos
made of humming strings, it was crass to expect stability.

As Stefan stepped outside, it occurred to him to wonder how much time had already passed in Los Angeles, that
city of fast fads, that pen of frantic chickens with their heads
cut off. Although the Hormiga Canyon air was as luminous
as ever, when Stefan peered upwards he saw the night sky
canopy, with a full moon bob-bob-bobbing along, rather
like the bouncy ball in a sing-a-long 40s cartoon.

If Stefan and Jayson went deeper, the spacetime warp
would be even stronger. They'd be visiting a real-world
laboratory of dimensional wonders. Yes, Stefan wanted to
go. There was no choice about that, really.

Up near the dark, blurry lip of the canyon, a black ant
the size of a 1950s prop-job airliner was hard at work. With
an ant's busy clumsiness, her six legs grappled at the fibrous
dirt, setting off little slides. She was groping around in the
fabric of reality with her monster feelers, tugging at the
substance of the canyon wall, pulling stuff loose: it looked
like ropes or pipes. Cosmic strings. This ant was causing
the tremors.

As she worked the fabric of the cosmos, distant houses
shrank and grew as if seen through a shimmer of hot air.
The black ant trundled down the valley wall, carrying a
string in her jaws. The tangled bights of string glowed and
shimmered; the lucid air hummed with a kind of music.
The ant was unsteadily shrinking, first to the size of house,
then to the size of a car, and then to the size of a cow—and
now Stefan realized that those "livestock" upon the hillsides
of Hormiga Canyon were all ants, too.

A herd of them gathered around the big black ant in
a companionable fashion, fiddling with her string, helping
with some dim nest-building agenda. They worked off
instinct and smell.

Lola appeared in the door of Hyperio's shack. She had a hand-woven string-bag over her shoulder. She still looked peaked, but with the promise of a journey home, hope had returned to her haggard face. She and old Hyperio engaged in a tender, rapid-fire farewell in Spanish. She kissed him, and Hyperio picked a red ant from his mustache. With a scowl, he flicked it from his fingertip.

The ant hit the ground scrambling, bounded up and was the size of a panther. It sniffed the fender of Jayson's motorcycle, where the other ant had left its tag of sticky dew. Jayson doubled his fists.

"It's harmless!" Stefan called.

But Stefan was wrong. With an abrupt lunge and a twitch of her big head, the rangy red ant snatched Stefan's laptop from his unsuspecting grasp. She smashed the computer with the clashing machineries of her mouth; the pieces disappeared down her gullet. And then she trotted on her way.

Livid with rage, Stefan took a step or two in pursuit—but then, surprising even himself, he halted. This cosmic-string ant was paying him a compliment by eating his laptop. Somehow she'd sensed the seeds of the One True String Theory within Stefan's flat gray box. Why else had they invaded Stefan's home in the first place? They were there to celebrate the fact that he was King of String!

Weak-kneed with his turbulent flow of emotions, Stefan leaned against the bike.

Jayson began messing with the motorcycle, hiking up the saddlebags to make a platform that could support Lola. "You'll be happier on the open road," he told Stefan. "Without that idiot box leeching your psychic energy."

"Is this bike gonna be big enough?" said Stefan.

"Down in Mexico a family of six would ride," said Hyperio. He laid a board and a folded blanket across the saddlebags, and Lola curled up on it, making herself small. She showed her teeth in pain, then gave the boys a brave smile.

"I bet she used to be beautiful," said Jayson. "I bet she used to look a lot like Lupe."

"You mentioned a map?" Stefan asked Hyperio.

Hyperio handed over a heavy yellow roll of dense, spotted leather. It had a few strands of coarse fur on the edges. It was buffalo hide.

"The Seven Cities of Gold," said Jayson, eagerly unfurling the scroll. "Quivira and Cíbola." Jayson's chain mail wristlets glinted in the light like the armor of a conquistador. "The Spanish never found those 'lost cities.' I bet anything they're in this canyon."

"Los Angeles is the true lost city," said Stefan, peering over Jayson's shoulder. Hyperio's map left a lot to be desired. It had been drawn in blood and berry-juice by some guy who didn't get it about longitude.

The three travelers bid Hyperio a last goodbye.

The road running up the canyon was a much trampled ant-track. The little wooden shacks gave way to simpler dug-out huts and lean-tos. It seemed that the locals had never seen—or heard—a motorcycle before; at the machine's approach, they ran around in circles with their hands over their ears.

Pools of water stood here and there in Hormiga Canyon's dry river, more pools all the time. In certain dank and sticky patches—mud, maybe—huge bison had mired-in hip deep and been butchered by the locals. The boys had to dismount and coax the roaring cycle around these dicey spots, with unsteady Lola grimacing at the jolts.

The beach-ball sun and bouncing moon picked up the pace. The travelers reached a cross-marked spot on Hyperio's map. It was a settlement of low, adobe houses, with a big stone church. The central square smelled of corn tortillas and roast pumpkin seeds. The locals, in dented straw hats and serapes, looked like extras from the set of the Fairbanks silent production of Zorro, except that they were in color, they lacked histrionic gestures, and they were audibly talking.

Eager to mooch some chow, the boys approached the stony well before the church. At the banging sound of their engine, the padre appeared at the church door. Shouting in Latin, he brandished a crucifix and a horse-whip. Jayson cranked up the gas and they rolled on.

They then entered what appeared to be a nature reserve, or, to put it more accurately, a no-kidding primeval wilderness. The human population, what little there was of it, vanished into the trees and scrub. The paths bore bear tracks, cougar tracks, deer tracks, and enormous Jersey-Devil style ant hoofprints. And the river had water in it now.

"One thing bothers me," said Jayson as a ground sloth lumbered by, leaving tufts of reddish hair in the blackberry brambles. "Seems like the ants should get tiny when they come around us humans. Everything else matches our size: the chairs, the tables, the trees. But the ants—the ants are all kinds of sizes."

"The ants can scale themselves to any size they need," said Stefan. "It's because they're in control of the subdimensional cosmic strings."

"Well, how come we can't do that?" said Jayson. "We're special-effects wizards, and ants are just a bunch of insects."

"Twine dimension seven, loop dimension eight," said Stefan thoughtfully. "If we could get hold of some of those strings, we just might find a way."

The glowing air of Hormiga Canyon never quite dimmed, so it was up to the travelers to decide when to bivouac. They gallantly let Lola set their pace, since she was frail and weary. To judge by the way she kept spitting off the side of her little platform, the ants were churning within her.

They made camp atop a little hill above much-trampled edge of river pool. To judge by the fang-marked pigs' knuckles buried in the mud, the pool was an excellent hunting spot.

Stefan gathered dry twigs and Lola expertly stacked a campfire. Jayson had somehow misplaced his cigarette lighter, but thanks to his multitool, he was able to conjure up a bowstring and a drill. Amazingly, a sharp stick spun fast in half-decayed wood really did smolder and ignite.

There were trout in the burbling river, fat and gullible. Stefan was able to harpoon the naive fish with the simplest kind of barbed stick. The boys ate two fire-roasted fish apiece, and when Lola only nibbled at her tasty fish, Jayson ate that one too.

An orgy of ferocious grunts and squeals drifted up from the river pool. Nobody felt quite ready to sleep. Lola lay on her side watching the fire, now and then brushing an ant from her lips. Jayson kept obsessively adjusting the screws on the carburetor.

"I'll stretch out our fuel for as long as possible," he explained. "Us city boys will be in trouble if we run out of gas."

"Did you ever see *Mysterious Island?*" said Stefan, staring dreamily into the flames.

"Of course. If you mean *Jules Verne's Mysterious Island* from 1961, with the giant bird, the giant crab and the giant bees. That's a Ray Harryhausen flick. Harryhausen is the FX god!"

"Precisely. So, you know, the heroes are stranded on a wilderness island with monsters and pirates. They have to, like, totally scrounge for basic food and shelter, and also craft some really hot home-made leather clothes for the female lead..."

"That tight leather dress she had was bitchin'."

"It sure was. So, maybe we run out of gasoline, but I don't see how we have any big problem. I mean, we're FX guys—basically, we are Harryhausen."

"Huh. Maybe *I'm* like Ray Harryhausen," said Jayson. "But you're all digital."

"Don't sell my conceptual skills short, Jayson. We've spent our careers creating lavish fantasies on a limited budget. Working together, we're fully capable of scaring up tools, shelter, food and clothing in a trackless wilderness."

Jayson narrowed his eyes. "What kinda fantasy-adventure costume you need? Nylon, spandex?"

"Antskin would suit our parameters."

"I could do antskin clothes," mused Jayson. "I could craft flexible antskin armor."

"You see?" said Stefan loftily. "I gave you that concept. We're a team. No wonder we feel so much at home here.

This place, Hormiga Canyon, with, like, the monsters and colorful natives—*this* is the soul of Los Angeles. That stuff we left behind, that's nothing but Tinseltown! There today, gone tomorrow."

Jayson looked up thoughtfully at the whizzing sky. Days and weeks were rushing past.

"Why would we want to return to that life of cheap illusion?" added Stefan, sounding braver than he felt.

"Lupe wasn't a cheap illusion," said Jayson. "Other people aren't illusions. Lupe was so real. She was too real for me. I never knew enough real people, Stefan. I was always way too busy feeding the baloney machine." Jayson turned his face away from the fire and scrunched down into the comfortless pillow of his jacket.

Stefan sat in silence, giving his stricken friend some privacy. Soon Jayson's shoulders began twitching. He was crying? No, he was rooting in the dirt with his multitool.

"Look what I just found," said Jayson, studying the scuffed dirt beside the blanket. "This is one of those ant strings. It glows." He gripped the cosmic string with the strong metal jaws of his pliers. Flexing his tattooed arms, he gave it a muscular tug. The string twanged like a badly-tuned harp. A slight shudder went through the fabric of the real.

"Those spoiled academic physicists would trade in their tenure to see this!" crowed Stefan, lying down on his side to observe the phenomena. "You've got hold of a naked cosmic string! And listen to it! It's humming a natural fourth with three overtones. That proves the existence of the Higgs particle!"

Jayson deftly popped the cosmic string loose from the fabric of spacetime. Torn from its context, the string coiled and rippled like a ruined Slinky. Jayson's fingers shrank and grew like ripples in a mirrored pool. "Awesome visual effect, huh?"

The space around them shivered a bit; which seemed to have some effect on the ants in Lola's belly. Abruptly she sat up, yowling in wordless pain. She clutched at her midriff and fled into the woods.

185

"At least she's on her feet," Jayson noted. "Maybe these space-shudders are doing the old girl some good."

"I'm not sure you ought to pluck those strings right out of reality like that. You could set off a major antquake."

"Hey, I'm getting away with it," Jayson shrugged. He clacked the pliers. "I can kink this stuff. I can even cut it. Let's see if it'll make chain-mail."

"Twine dimension seven, loop dimension eight," intoned Stefan.

The air gave tiny, tortured shudders as Jayson obsessed with his craft: "Okay, you coil it into a long spring first, then you cut it into open rings. And, yeah dog, I can kind of see the higher dimensions. Twine 'em, loop 'em, squeeze 'em—and the loose ends stick together like soldering wire. Chain mail."

"I'd never have the patience for all that," said Stefan, shaking his head.

"I'm like a cosmic ant," said Jayson, calmly knitting away.

Stefan left to search for Lola. His tracking skills were none of the best, but when he came across a steady stream of ants, Lola wasn't far. She was leaning against a tree. She'd retched a great bolus of ants from her innards—and her sickness had left with them. She looked much healthier.

They dozed for a few hours, rose and pushed on. Hyperio's map got them past another tricky branching—but then they got hung up at a gnarly crossroads of five arroyos. There was a natural fountain gushing up in the river junction, a subterranean geyser of clear water, with the rivers cheerily running out from it in all five directions. Hormiga Canyon was an Escher ant-maze.

Stefan turned the precious leather map from side to side, like a monkey pretending to read a book. "I wonder if this troglodyte map-maker even knew about North and South."

Jayson was poking in the wet black mud at the river's edge. "Bonanza, dude! This river muck is full of loose strings!"

An orange ant the size of a miniature submarine came churning up out of the river water. Like an implacable homing missile, she ran for Stefan, seized the map and gobbled it down. And then, obeying the dictates of some distant scent signal, she scuttled away.

Stefan's confidence cracked. "Why did you get me into this hopeless mess?" he yelled at Jayson.

"I think this was one of your grand concepts, wasn't it?" said Jayson, not looking up. He was knitting cosmic strings into a wristband.

Lola had never given one glance at the map, so the loss of it did not concern her. She was feeling perkier today, and more than ready to give directions. Perched atop the rear fender, she offered Sacajawea-style pointed hints, and the boys followed her intuitions.

The familiar oak and laurel trees gave way to thirty-foot-tall tree-ferns: palm-like trunks with great punky frizz-bops of fronds. Bright, toxic-looking speckled mushrooms grew from the rich, damp soil. The tops of the cliffs had grown too high to see. And the narrow band of visible sky was flickering from light to dark to light every few seconds.

This crooked branch of Hormiga Canyon was densely cluttered with dun-colored, outsized, primitive herbivores. These prehistoric American megafauna showed little fear of humans. Small ancestral horses were striped like zebras. Long-necked camel-like creatures stank and slobbered. Carnivorous ur-pigs with flesh-rending tusks ran like the wind. The rather small and dainty Californian mastodons were merely twice the size of large elk.

It became clear that Lola was a proud, resourceful woman. Plucking dry reeds from the river's edge, she deftly wove herself a gathering-basket. She imperiously stopped the bike to gather chow, stashing high-fiber Pleistocene bounty in the saddlebags. Cat-tail roots. Freshwater clams. Amaranth grain cut off the tops of pigweeds. When they finally bivouacked, the energized Lola bagged them a fatally innocent antelope by the simple expedient of clubbing it to death with a rock.

Jayson built them a fire, then set to work kinking his cosmic strings.

"You've got to become one with your craft, man," babbled Jayson as a sweating Stefan methodically barbecued an antelope haunch. "My cosmic wristband is talking to me right now. Really. It's saying, like, 'Hi, I'm here.' And, uh, 'Thank you for making me.' I'm fully in tune with its cosmic inner vibrations. I'm on the same cosmic wavelength. Soon I'll be able to focus its cosmic energies." Jayson glared up, daring Stefan to dismiss his claims.

Steadily Stefan spun the dripping, spitted meat. "Jayson, your theory is entirely plausible. These strings are quantum-mechanical. By working with the strings, you, as Man the Toolmaker, entangle yourself in their quantum state. You and your wristband form a coherent system with a unitary wave function."

Jayson nodded, crimping away with his hard steel pliers. "And when this wristband is done and I'm wearing it, I'll be a master of the scale dimension! Like the Hormiga Canyon ants!"

As if on cue, an ant the size of Volkswagen appeared beside the fire, sniffed a bit at the baking amaranth bread, then edged close to Jayson, watching his nimble fingers at work. Seemingly fascinated, the ant went so far as to run one of her feelers over the little swatch of chain mail.

"Shoo," said Jayson mildly, and the ant pattered off.

"Food's ready," said Stefan.

As the three travelers feasted, the luminous canyon air was split with lurid, gurgling screams as monster bears and howling dire wolves culled the herds. Jayson heaped armloads of wood on their bonfire, but they didn't sleep well at all.

When they arose, Stefan took the controls of the motorcycle so that Jayson could focus on finishing his wristlet. Lola, with her basket, sat on the rear fender, bright-eyed and chipper.

They discovered a path that bore heart-cheering human footprints. A river was nearby, running in the same direction they were traveling.

"Dig this," said Jayson over Stefan's shoulder. He shoved his hand forward to show off his completed wristband. It was beautiful; the light that fell upon it shattered into sparks of primary colors.

"Tongva," murmured Lola, sniffing the air.

Part 3

colossal ant burst from a thicket of manzanita, bearing three fierce-looking natives. The riders were clutching the ant's insectile bristles like Mongols holding a horse's mane. They were deeply tanned men with filed teeth, floppy hair and bizarre patterns painted on their faces. Original Californians.

The Tongvans sprang at Jayson and Stefan; seconds later the boys were swathed in woven nets, wrapped up like pupas side by side.

The largest Tongvan leaned over Stefan. He was a wiry, dignified gentleman just over five feet tall. He'd painted an intricate pattern of fern-like scrolls around his eyes and mouth. He had a deeply skeptical, highly judgmental look, very much like an overworked immigration officer at LAX.

Lola sashayed forward and tapped the man on the shoulder. She straightened her time-worn leather shift, preened at her gray hair, and began talking in Tongvan, addressing him as "Angon."

"Her husband!" Stefan hissed to Jayson.

It seemed Lola was telling Angon at length about what had happened to her in the impossibly complicated meantime since they'd last been together.

Angon tried to maintain his hard-guy expression, but as the facts sank in, his face began to quiver. Relative to Angon's experience of time, it had only been a few days since Hyperio had kidnapped his young wife Lola. And now Lola was back—decades older, a sickly crone. Angon cracked and lost his composure. He rubbed his nose against Lola's weathered cheek; the tears flowed.

"Aw," said Jayson.

Angon glared down at the boys. He hollered in Tongvan and raised his flint tomahawk.

"Stick with me," said Jayson, worming himself close to Stefan. "Abracadabra."

Suddenly Jayson and Stefan were the size of rodents. They scampered through the nets and fled into the underbrush. The angry Tongvans crashed about while their ant mowed down ferns with her mandibles—but the boys had deftly taken shelter beneath the red parasol of a toadstool.

The giant ant lumbered off and the Tongvans abandoned their search. From their hiding place the boys watched the Tongvans wheeling Jayson's motorcycle away, with Lola still talking.

"We're not gonna fit in with these people at all," said Stefan, "Hyperio was jiving us. We should head back to town right now. As it is, we're gonna lose thirty years."

"I say we push in further," said Jayson. "I want to see that giant tar pit." He studied his wristband. "What if I make us into giants and we just go grab my bike?" With a sudden popping sound, they grew back up to normal size—but no further. Jayson popped them a couple more times, trying to break through the barrier of normal scale.

"Stop it!" said Stefan, feeling dizzy and whiplashed. He steadied himself by grabbing Jayson's arm. "Look at your wristband, dude, that link-pattern is asymmetric. You're gonna need to weave a mirror image wristband if you want to make us grow."

Jayson dropped them back to small size and cheesed his teeth at Stefan. "Okay, then for now we'll be rats. Let's skulk over and spy on the Tongvans. I want my bike back."

The Tongvans were sitting in a semi-circle before a chiseled stone altar. Perched atop the altar was the red Indian Chief motorcycle. Skinny old Lola was entertaining the tribe by showing them the mambo. Angon looked deeply disheartened.

The boys heard a twitter, a subsonic roar. High above them, huge mandibles stood starkly outlined against the endless, towering cliffs. A monster hooked ant-foot, as thick and red and barky as any sequoia, pounded straight into the ragged fabric of space-time. The great jaws swooped down and snatched up the Indian motorcycle.

The whole canyon shivered as the titanic ant stalked away.

In the stunned excitement, Stefan and Jayson restored themselves to normal size and brazenly stole one of the natives' dugout canoes. They sped down the river with no sign of Tongvan pursuit.

Deprived of his bike and sullen about it, Jayson worked steadily on another wrist band, while Stefan sat in the prow. He used a pointed Tongvan paddle to guide them past the rocks, logs, and silent alligators that adorned the stream.

The time dilation was accelerating. The visible sky was but a bright wriggle, and the days and nights pulsed so fast that the worm of sky was a steady dim glow. The high squiggle reminded Stefan of the tentative smile Emily Yu had worn when she talked of her hopes and dreams—all long gone by now. Decades were flying past, centuries.

Calamitous sounds came from the stream ahead: a roar, a trumpeting, and some sweet, pure music, a primitive universal sound like Peruvian pan pipes or Moroccan flute. And then rapids hove into view. This was the roar. Standing amid the rapids was a herd of twenty-foot-tall mammoths with immense curved tusks. This was the trumpeting.

"The wristband's done! Let me fasten it on you, dog."

"Beautiful."

Upon donning his wristband, Stefan understood all. It took but the slightest effort of his will to grow them both to a height of fifty feet.

Gingerly they sloshed through the minor puddle of the rapids, scattering the little mammoths like poodles. The toy canoe bobbed ahead of them emptily—and suddenly disappeared. The river ended in an immense, scale-free cataract, tumbling into fog. Something vast and gleaming lay beyond.

Stefan shrank them back to a scale that felt more or less normal. They stood on a boulder by the falls, leaning on each other and panting for breath, taking in the staggering view.

It was an immense glistening lake, many miles across, with endless flocks of birds slowly wheeling above it. Ants scampered about on the lake's mirrored surface, elegant as ballet dancers, some as big as ships, others like winged dust motes. Inconceivably vast ant-feelers projected like misty towers from the pit's distant center. In some spots the ants tessellated together to make flowing tiled carpets. Eerie cosmic string music filled the air, the sound almost unbearably haunting and sweet.

"The canyon's core," breathed Jayson.

But here came one last meddling ant, ineluctable as a tax collector, an officious pinkish critter the size of a school-bus. Before the boys could manage to shrink or grow, she'd seized them both in her jaws. She carried them through the mist, squirming and howling—and dropped them like trash by the mouth of a cave near the base of the falls. She hurried off on other errands.

"What the hell?" said Stefan, rubbing his bruised shoulder.

Lying in the cave was Jayson's motorcycle—a bit chewed and bent, but still functional. Next to it were the half-digested pieces of Stefan's laptop, a few scraps of Hyperio's map, and even the debris of that Tongvan canoe they'd just been riding.

"So the goddamned ants know all about us, huh?" said Jayson, rubbing his sore ribcage. "God, I hate them."

"A single ant doesn't know squat," said Stefan. "Ants are like individual neurons. But, yeah, there's some kind of emergent hive mind happening. Like a brain. Like an ultracluster computer. The hive sensed the cosmic harmony emanating from my house. Ants are natural-born collectors; once they got interested in us, they had to gather all the Stefan and Jayson artifacts into one spot."

"They ruined the paint on my motorcycle, man," fumed Jayson, not really listening.

A dog-sized yellow ant trotted up and regurgitated—a few hundred elderly cellphones.

"What is that?" cried Stefan, not wanting to believe what he saw.

"Your homemade supercomputer," said Jayson, shaking his head. "My website."

"My baskets of cell phones?" cried Stefan.. "They're lugging all my phones here?" Stefan picked up a phone and opened it. The phone's components were quite dead; munged by ant jaws and eaten away by stomach acids. Another yellow ant approached and burped up more phones. Perhaps a hundred more yellow ants were following in her wake.

A bit disconsolately, the boys wandered the shore of the giant lake. The edges were treacherous. Thin sheens of water glistened atop a viscous, sticky, string-based equivalent of tar. The string tar had claimed some victims, unfortunate beasts who couldn't take the irregular sudden transitions of scale, their bodies warping like balloon animals, their overloaded tiny hearts bursting from the effort of pumping blood to heads swollen to the size of refrigerators. Tigers and wolves had feasted upon the dying creatures, and had fallen captive to the string-tar themselves. Flies and condors darted and zoomed above the deadly tar pools, their proportions changing in mid-flight. The pools stank of carrion.

It was sickening to even try and imagine how fast the world's time was flowing relative to this forgotten place.

"My Calabi-Yau search program is lost to mankind," mourned Stefan. "How will they ever learn the One True String Theory?"

"Maybe you whiffed on mankind," said Jayson. "But I'd say you went over very big with the ants."

"That's true," said Stefan, brightening just a bit. "And you know what—I bet the ants are in fact using my discovery to weave the world. Our discovery. They learned from touching your chain mail, too, Jayson. Twine dimension seven. Loop dimension eight." Stefan was talking louder, puffing himself up. "The ants built our universe, yes, but we showed them how! It's a closed causal loop. We're the lords of creation."

"If you're God, how come we're so screwed?" said Jayson. "We've gotta get out of here."

Huge, tanker-like ants were skittering across the mirrored lake in a regular rhythm. The big ants were regurgitating food near the pit's wheeling, starry center, then scurrying across the great gleaming lake to mount the inconceivably tall canyon walls, presumably to forage for food in the outer world.

"You thinking what I'm thinking?" said Stefan.

"Yeah," said Jayson. "We hop a tanker ant and we ride it up those cliffs. We end up outside Hormiga Canyon."

"The fast track to far-future L. A.," said Stefan. "Let's do it."

"Help me with the bike." said Jayson, turning back towards the cave.

"The what?"

"Come on, it'll start. They built bikes to last, back then. We'll do a stunt-man number. We'll speed up, ride up that stone ramp over there, and we land on the back of a giant ant. That'll be a bitchin' effect."

Stefan was doubtful, but of course Jayson's plan worked. They landed like ant-lice on the hide of a tanker ant the size of a ship. The behemoth took no notice of them. The boys wedged themselves, and Jayson's machine, among the giant ant's weird organic landscape of chitinous pores and uncanny bristles. Then they held tight.

The tanker ant surged upwards, ever upwards and— emerged onto a sunlit, dusty California hilltop. She hesitated, tasting the air with her feelers. The boys rolled themselves and the bike off the ant's back, sliding onto the familiar yellow grass. For her part, the ant headed into a nearby apricot orchard and began harvesting the fruit-laden trees whole.

Here outside the Canyon, the sun no longer moved in that frenetic fashion. This California sun was setting gently and respectably, in the west, the way a sun ought to set. The sun looked rather too weary, too large and too red. But sunsets were always like that.

Down the hillside was a long, dusty highway, a black, paved, four lane strip with white stripes down the middle. From the distance came a shining, metallic truck. As it passed them by, with a Doppler whoosh, it resolved into a long-haul ant, a rolling monster with a big-eyed head like a truck-cab, a fully-rounded cargo belly, and six stout red leg-axles, adorned with six big whirring black wheels.

Shielding their eyes, the boys followed the departing ant-truck with their gaze. There were sunlit towers scraping the horizon, gleaming and crystalline.

More vehicles passed then, in deft, high-speed cluster-groups of traffic. The whizzing cars and trucks were all segmented, six-wheeled, and scarily fast. Low-slung, gleamy speedsters. Burly station-wagons.

The boys wheeled the motorcycle downhill to the dusty edge of the busy freeway. Their hair was tossed by the backwash of passing ants.

One of the vehicles, a black and white one with large red eyes, slowed to give them a once-over. Luckily it didn't stop.

Jayson sniffed the highway air. It smelled like burning booze poured over a fruitcake. "Well, they've got fuel," he diagnosed.

"I wonder how ants managed to evolve internal combustion engines."

"Heck, dog, I'm wondering how ants managed to evolve wheels."

"In their own diffuse, distributed way, these ants have got some kind of mandible-grip on the laws of nature," said Stefan. Gently he cleared his throat. "That's largely thanks to me, I suppose."

"Gotta be a filling station up this road somewhere," said Jayson, ignoring him. "We're down to our last quart." He kicked his Indian into life. Stefan hopped on.

As they motored into the sprawling heart of Los Angeles, it was clear as the fruit-scented air that they were eons into the future. Stefan had always known his town as a jammed, overloaded, makeshift, somewhat threatening city, with large patches of violent poverty and film-noir urban decline. But the future Los Angeles was as neat as a Le Corbusier sketch: spacey radiant towers, picturesque ragged palms, abundant fruit trees.

Sure enough, they came across a nearly spherical cask-ant dispensing distilled fruit alcohol from her rear

195

end. When prodded by the handlebars of Jayson's bike, she dribbled a handy fill-up into his tank.

Twilight fell, and little ball-shaped lights blinked on. They had no visible source of power.

"String theory on parade," said Stefan, pointing them out to Jayson. "Zero-point energy. I was planning to invent all that some day."

"Sure, dog, sure."

Every ant within this city was a wheeled giant. The ants were clearly the dominant species in town. Most of the city was devoted to their cloverleaves, off ramps and parking-lots.

Then there were the people: gleaming, healthy Californians with amazing skin-tones. There were steady little streams of them, going about their own business, often with bundles on their heads: water-jars and fruit-baskets, mostly.

It seemed that humans as a species had been much harder to kill off than one might have expected. These far-future humans were not making much of a fuss about themselves any more, but given how many were deftly creeping in and out of cracks in the shining towers, they probably had the giant ants outnumbered.

"They're all walking," Stefan noted.

"Nobody walks in L.A! We're the only cats in this town with our own wheels?" Jayson lifted one hand from the throttle. "Hey look! My cosmic string wristband is gone."

"Everything except the ants is the right size here, dude," said Stefan, examining his own bare wrist. "That means our bracelets are smaller than protons now."

Jayson waved his wrist as if this news stung him a little. Then he suddenly veered to the side of the road. "Hey dog, check her out! This rich chick is flagging us down!"

The woman in question was wearing a fetching little antskin cuirass. Her glossy hair was high-piled on her head and she wore a necklace, a belt, and neat platform sandals. She had an unknown flower in her hair and a very nice tan.

"Pleased to meet you," said Jayson gallantly. "Do you speak Eloi?"

The woman thoughtfully caressed the glassy headlight of Jayson's bike. The two boys were dirty, unshaven, and stinking of camp-fires. They also spoke no known language and were riding a mechanical ant, but their new friend seemed willing to overlook all that. She might even think such things were cute and dashing.

She smiled at Jayson in a sunny, mystical fashion, opened her beaded shoulder-bag, and offered him a fresh orange.

Jayson ripped into it, grinning.

"She's not your normal type, Jayson."

"Yeah, she's a cool, classy dame straight outta Beverly Hills! I think my luck is finally changing!"

A small crowd of men, women, even children clustered around the bike. These sidewalk gawkers definitely liked a show. They chatted pleasantly, tapping each other reassuringly on the heads and shoulders.

"We're drawing a big crowd," Stefan said. "Should we split?"

"Are you kidding? This is the public! We'll entertain them!"

Jayson fashioned a bit of his orange peel into a set of jack-o-lantern snaggle teeth and wore them in his mouth. The woman in the antskin cuirass laughed with pleasure.

Stefan picked a smooth pebble off the ground, showed it off to the gawkers, palmed it, and pretended to swallow it. The onlookers were stunned. When he "burped it back up," they applauded him wildly.

Stefan gazed across their pleased, eager faces. "This is a very soft audience, Jayson. I think they're truly starved for techno-wizardry."

A shy girl stood at the back of the crowd. She looked sober and thoughtful. She knew he had done a trick. She wondered why. She was like Emily Yu: smarter than the rest, but too tenderhearted.

Stefan waved at her and offered his best smile. She stood up straighter, startled. She looked from one side of herself to the other, amazed that he was paying attention just to her.

He beckoned at her. He pointed. He waved both his arms. Yes, you. She was so excited by this that he could see her heart beating softly in the side of her throat.

He was instantly in love.

Notes on "Hormiga Canyon"

Asimov's Science Fiction, August, 2007.
Written Fall, 2007.

Rudy on "Hormiga Canyon"

In person, Bruce is very charismatic. I don't actually see him in person very often—usually several years go by between our face-to-face encounters. But whenever I do meet up with him, I always feel like co-authoring a story with him again. Even though I remember how difficult the last collaboration was. So when Bruce turned up at my house for a night or two in the summer of 2007, we eagerly began making new plans. It had been over five years since we'd collaborated on a story.

Bruce's initial idea was that we should write about a city in a large bottle in an apartment in a slum in LA. The city would be a bit like the city of Kandor in the *Superman* comics. For my part, I wanted to write a story about giant ants, a classic SF power chord which has, in my opinion, been insufficiently explored. (*Hormiga* is Spanish for *ant*, you understand.) And never mind any prissy kill-joy claims that giant ants would collapse under their own weight. In SF, you can always invoke whatever rubber physics you need to make your effects work.

So we got the story going. I'm the spaced-out hacker Stefan Oertel, and Bruce is the bluff, can-do, media-savvy Jayson Rubio. The story was a wild run, a roller-coaster ride. Even though it can be hard, it's worthwhile working with Bruce. I think the stories that I've written with him are among my best.

When I collaborate, I get a different texture in the story's prose. This holds whether I'm working with Bruce or with one of my other collaborators—Marc Laidlaw, Paul Di Filippo, John Shirley, Terry Bisson, Eileen Gunn, or my son Rudy Rucker Jr. Co-authoring a story is like being in an intense writer's workshop.

But with Bruce, the transformation is more extreme. Sometimes he'll go in and cut a couple of words out of ©nearly every sentence that I've written. So then—*if it's going to be like that*—I take out his weaker lines. It makes the prose stronger. Of course, after the cuts, there's a lot of broken segues to fix—if you want the story to make logical and emotional sense. It's often me—something of a compulsive perfectionist—who ends up doing the clean-up. And then feeling resentful about it. Like, "I washed all these dishes, and you never said thanks."

So far as I can tell, Bruce himself never feels emotional about our collaborations. He loftily reminds me that it's only ink on paper—or bits in a datastream.

After ten rounds of revisions on "Hormiga Canyon," I was on the point of collapse. And then, like a celestial trumpeter in the sky, Bruce produced a beautiful, visionary, emotionally rich ending. It was what I'd been hoping for all along. A glimpse of heaven.

And once again we scored an *Asimov's* cover illo.

Bruce on "Hormiga Canyon"

Rudy is not likely to show up in my stomping grounds of Austin, Belgrade and Turin, so we generally meet in California. As this story was written, I was spending a year in Los Angeles, so this effort is LA all the way.

The theme of "Hormiga Canyon" is ants. Giant ants are rather often on Rudy's mind. I was willing to indulge him in this conceit, as, from a Los Angeles perspective, there's something cheerfully appropriate and LA pop-sur-realist about giant ants: the classic sci-fi movie *Them* is all about giant ants invading Los Angeles. It was pleasant to invent a couple of Los Angeles special-FX guys who would be entirely willing to accept giant ants on their own terms. The fantasies of Tinseltown are their daily bread, after all.

The story's visual and cinematic, and had to go through a lot of editing, which Rudy hates to do. Still, if you're going to create a B-movie epic with motorcycles and mastodons, the script needs to move right along. Clipped footage littered our cutting room floor, and screening the many rushes was heavy labor for both of us. But it may be our best story as story-telling goes, and it even features a technicolor Hollywood happy ending.

Colliding Branes

"But why call this the end of the universe?" said Rabbiteen Chandra, feeling the dry night air beat against her face. The rollicking hearse stank of cheap fried food, a dense urban reek in the starry emptiness of the Nevada desert. "At dawn our universe's two branes collide in an annihilating sea of light. That's not death, technically speaking—that's a kalpa rebirth."

Angelo Rasmussen tightened his pale, keyboard-punching hands on the hearse's cracked plastic wheel. His hearse was a retrofitted 1978 Volvo, which ran on recycled bio-diesel cooking-oil. "You're switching to your Hindu mystic thing now? After getting me to break that story?"

"I double-checked my physics references," Rabbiteen offered, with an incongruous giggle. "Remember, I have a master's degree from San Jose State."

Rabbiteen knew that this was her final road trip. She'd been a good girl too long. She tapped chewing tobacco into a packet of ground betel-nut. Her tongue and her gums were stained the color of fresh blood.

"The colliding branes will crush the stars and planets to a soup of hard radiation," she assured Angelo. "Then they rebound instantly, forming brand-new particles of matter, and seeding the next cycle of the twelve-dimensional cosmos." She spread her two hands violently, to illustrate. "Our former bodies will expand to the size of galactic superclusters."

Angelo was eyeing her. "I hope our bodies overlap." He wore a shy, eager smile. "Given what you and I know, Rabbiteen, we might as well be the last man and woman on Earth." He laid his hand on her thigh, but not too far up.

"I've thought that issue through," said Rabbiteen, inexpertly jetting betel spit out the window. Blowback stained her hand-stitched paisley blouse. "We'll definitely make love—but not inside this hearse, okay? Let's find some quaint tourist cabins."

As professional bloggers, Rabbiteen and Angelo knew each other well. For three years, they'd zealously followed each other's daily doings via email, text messages, video posts, social networking and comment threads.

Yet they'd never met in the flesh. Until today, their last day on Earth—the last day for the Earth, and, in stark fact, also for Earth's solar system, Earth's galaxy, Earth's Local Group galactic cluster, and Earth's whole twelve-dimensional universe shebang.

The end was near, and Rabbiteen didn't care to watch the cosmos collapse from inside her cramped room in her parents' house in Fremont. Nor did Angelo want to meet the end in his survivalist bunker in the foothills of the Sierras near Fresno—a bunker which, to untrained eyes, resembled an abandoned barn in the middle of a sun-killed almond farm.

So, after a dense flurry of instant-messages, the two bloggers had joined forces and hit the great American road together, blasting one last trump from the hearse's dirge-like horn, a mournful yet powerful blast which echoed from Rabbiteen's parents' pink stucco house and all through the table-flat development of a thousand similar homes.

Chastely sipping biodiesel through the apocalyptic traffic, they'd made it over Tioga Pass onto Nevada's Route 6 by midnight. They were out well ahead of mankind's last lemming-like rush to universal destruction.

"I've been obsessing over Peak Oil for years," Angelo confessed. He was feeling warm and expansive, now that Rabbiteen had promised him some pre-apocalypse sex. "As a search-term, my name is practically synonymous with it. But now I can't believe I was such a sap, such a piss-ant, when it came to comprehending the onrushing scope of this planet's disaster! I was off by...what is it? By a million orders of magnitude?"

Rabbiteen patted his flannelled arm supportively. Angelo was just a political scientist, so he was really cute when he carried on about "orders of magnitude."

He was rueful. "I was so worried about climate change, financial Singularities and terror attacks in the Straits of Hormuz. And all the time the parallel branes were converging!" He smacked the Volvo's cracked dashboard with the flat of his pale hand. "I'm glad we escaped from the dense urban cores before the Apocalypse. Once people fully realize that cosmic string theory is unraveling, they'll butcher each other like vicious animals."

"Don't insult our friends the animals," said Rabbiteen, flirtatiously bending her wrists to hold her hands like little paws.

Rabbiteen's "What Is Karmic Reality?" blog cleverly leveraged her interest in scientific interpretations of the Upanishads into a thriving medium for selling imported Indian clothes, handicrafts and mosaics.

Angelo, unable to complete his political science doctorate due to skyrocketing tuition costs, had left Stanford to run his own busy "Ain't It Awful?" website. His site tracked major indicators for the imminent collapse of American society. The site served to market his print-on-demand tracts about the forthcoming apocalypse, which earned him a meager living.

The end of the Universe had begun with a comment from trusted user "Cody" on Rabbiteen's blog. Cody had linked to a preliminary lab report out of Bangalore's Bahrat University. The arXiv dot-pdf report documented ongoing real-time changes in the fine-structure constant. Subtle dark and light spectral lines hidden in ordinary light were sashaying right up the spectrum.

Rabbiteen had pounced on this surprising news as soon as it hit her monitor, deftly transforming the dry physics paper into an interactive web page with user-friendly graphic design. To spice up her post for user eyeballs, she'd cross-linked it to the well-known Cyclic Universe scenario. This cosmological theory predicted that the fundamental constants of physics would change rapidly whenever two parallel membranes of the cosmic twelve dimensions were about to—as laymen put it—"collide."

Although Rabbiteen didn't feel supremely confident about the cataclysmic Cyclic Universe scenario, that theory was rock-solid compared to the ramshackle Inflationary notion that had grown up to support the corny, old-school Big Bang.

Cosmologists had been tinkering with the tired Big Bang theory for over fifty years. Their rickety overwrought notions had so many patches, upgrades, and downright mythologies that even that the scheme of a cosmos churned from a sea of galactic cow milk by a giant Hindu cobra seemed logical by comparison.

After Rabbiteen's post, Angelo had horned into the act, following a link to Rabbiteen posted by that same user Cody on Angelo's "Ain't It Awful" blog. With the help of vocal contributors from a right-wing activist site, Angelo quickly unearthed a pirated draft of speechwriters' notes for an impending Presidential oration.

Tonight the U. S. President was planning to blandly deny that the cosmos was ending.

The leaked speech made commentary boil like a geyser on Angelo's catastrophe blog—especially since, unable to keep his loyal users in the dark, he'd been forced to announce to them that their entire Universe was kaput. The likelihood of this event was immediately obvious to loyal fans of "Ain't It Awful," and the ripples were spreading fast.

"Listen, Rabbiteen," said Angelo, tentatively slowing the hearse. "Why bother to find a motel? It's not like we want to sleep during our last night on Earth. It'd be crazy to waste those precious few remaining hours."

"Don't you want to dream one more great dream?"

He turned his thin, abstracted face from the bug-splattered windshield, his expression gentler than she'd expected. "I'd rather post one last great blog-post. Exactly how many minutes do we have left in our earthly existence?"

Their Linux laptops nestled together on the gray-carpeted floor of the hearse, the screens glowing hotly, the power cords jacked into a luxurious double-socketed cigarette-lighter extension. USB jacks sucked Internet access from a Fresnel antenna that Angelo had made from metal tape, then jammed on the hearse's roof.

Rabbiteen plopped her warm laptop onto her skirted thighs. She scrolled through a host of frantic posts from her over-excited readers.

"Still almost five hundred minutes," she said thoughtfully. "It's two a.m. here, and the latest doom estimate is for ten-twenty a.m. local time. Hmm. This scientist woman net-friend of mine—Hintika Kuusk from Estonia—she says that, near the end, the force of gravity will become a quantized step function. Six minutes after that, the strong force drops to the point where our quarks and gluons fly apart."

"And then the Big Splat hits us?"

"Full interbrane contact comes seven yoctoseconds after our protons and neutrons decay."

"Seven yoctoseconds?" Angelo's gauzy, policy-oriented knowledge of hard science was such that he couldn't be entirely sure when Rabbiteen was serious.

"That's seven septillionths of a second," clarified Rabbiteen. "A short time, but a definite gap. It's a shame, really. Thanks to our crude nucleon-based human bodies, we'll miss the hottest cosmic action since the start of our universe, fourteen billion years ago. But, Angelo, if we hug each other ever so tightly, our quarks will become as one." And with this, she laughed again.

"You think that's funny?"

"I don't know. Isn't it funny? How could it not be funny? If I let myself cry, that'll be worse."

"There's no time left to weep and mourn, not even for ourselves," mused Angelo. "I realize that you approach the problem of death in your own way. That motto you posted—'the dewdrop slides into the shining sea.'"

Rabbiteen was moved by the proof that he'd been reading her blog. She clapped her glowing laptop shut and gazed out at the stricken moon above a purple ridge of low mountains. "The moon looks so different now, doesn't it? It's redder! The changes in the fundamental constants will affect all electromagnetic phenomena. No more need for fancy big-science instruments, Angelo. We can see the changes in the fundamental constants of physics with our own wet, tender eyeballs."

She wiped her eyes, smudging her lashes. "In a way, it's wonderful that everything will dissolve together. The mountains and the moon, the rich and the poor, all the races and colors."

The road's fevered white line pulsed against Angelo's pale blue eyes. When he spoke again his voice had turned grating and paranoid. "I keep trying for the high road, Rabbiteen, but I can't fully buy that this is the End. I've bot a feeling that certain shadowy figures have been preparing for this. There are so many hints on the Internet... You want to know the real truth about where we're going?"

"Tell me, Angelo." Rabbiteen valued his insights into human society, which was a system she herself had trouble confronting.

"Cody calls it the Black Egg. It's hidden in the Tonopah Test Range, a secret base in Nevada, right near Area 51. He says the fascist slavemasters have built a back-door escape route of our condemned cosmos."

"*That's* where we're headed?" said Rabbiteen, sounding dubious. "On Cody's say-so?"

"Those in the know have an inside track to the Black Egg survival pod against the collapse of the universe. As major intellectual figures on the blogosphere, we should definitely be going there, right? Why should we be left outside the Dr Strangelove mine-shaft bunker when the lords of creation have their own transhuman immortality?"

Rabbiteen was unconvinced. "Oh, Angelo, why do you always blog so much about rulers and power? Everything's emergent. The old white men on top are helpless idiots. They're like foam on a tsunami. Can bacteria stop a bucket of bleach?"

"You're naive," said Angelo loftily. "Do you think it's mere coincidence that we were contacted and guided by a heavy operator like Cody? You're a key blogger on weird physics, and I—I rank with the world's foremost citizen-journalists."

"But Cody is just some blog commenter," said Rabbiteen slowly. The frank lunacy of the Black Egg story made her uneasy. "Cody never seemed like a particularly helpful guy to me. He's more like a snoop, a troll, and a snitch."

"He's just geeky, Rabbiteen. Cody doesn't have a whole lot of human social skills."

"On my blog he comes across like a stalker."

"He told me he's a veteran working physicist employed on black-ops projects by the federal government. A lonely old man whose whole life has been top-secret. I had to work hard at it, but I've won Cody over. He never had any trace of freedom in his life, except for the Internet. He thinks of you and me as his most intimate friends."

"Okay, fine," said Rabbiteen. "Why not the Tonopah Test Range? If that makes you happy."

But rather than smiling at her agreeability, Angelo was antsy. "I wish you hadn't said that. Now you've got me all worried. What if Cody is lying to me? All that amazing physics data could be clever disinformation. Maybe he's just some kind of crazy online pervert who, for whatever twisted reason—"

Rabbiteen aimed a brave smile at her friend's tormented face. "Look, that sign says Tonopah! And there's a nice little motel."

Angelo instantly slewed the heavy hearse into the dark, empty parking lot. Despite the late hour, the motel office door yawned open, with a trapezoid of light on the gravel.

Springy on his sneakered feet, Angelo hopped out of the hearse and into the motel office. Stretching the travel kinks from her back, Rabbiteen noticed a dull glow in the valley beyond this ridge. That must be the whipped old mining town of Tonopah. An all-but-defunct burg like that shouldn't be emitting so much flickering light and hot glare—oh. Tonopah was on fire.

Squinting into the distance, Rabbiteen could make out motorcycles, buzzing Tonopah's back streets like hornets. Some of the night-riders carried torches, leaving spark-spewing trails in the gloom.

"We don't want to stay around here," said Angelo, returning to her. Carefully, disturbingly, he wiped his feet on the gravel, leaving dark stains. Blood.

A vagrant breeze wafted whoops and screams across the dark hills.

"The owner's been killed?" said Rabbiteen. Hollowness filled her chest. "Oh god, oh god, I don't want to be slaughtered by psychos! I want to flash out with the Big Splat!"

"Don't panic," said Angelo, hugging her. "Don't panic yet." He stepped back and showed her a trophy tucked in the back of his belt. A forty-five automatic pistol. "You see, the owner was web-surfing. He had this handgun right next to his mouse—somebody lopped his head clean off while he was staring into his screen." Angelo handed her the pistol, butt-first. "The clip's full; that survival newbie never fired one shot in his own defense!"

Rabbiteen shuddered as she handled the weapon. Beyond the motel's sordid lot, a pair of monster trucks bounced side by side down the two-lane highway, their multiple headlights beaming crazed jittering cones. "Maybe we shouldn't go through Tonopah."

"I'll drive like a maniac, and you'll fire wildly," Angelo advised. "So it'll be fine. Let me give you the précis on this Colt military automatic. As a survivalist, I've logged a lot of hours on this model. It's easy except for the recoil. You hold it in both hands and gently squeeze the trigger. Try that."

Off at the edge of the motel lot, Rabbiteen saw a suspicious shadow. Something looping, boiling, rippling like heat haze. The head lopper? She hastily squeezed off a shot. The pistol kicked upwards with a flash and a deafening bang. The window of a motel unit blew out with a musical crash of glass.

Then, ominous, total silence.

If there had been any guests in this lonely motel, they were all gone. Or murdered. Yet there was still a roiling, phantom shape in the farthest corner of the parking lot. A midnight dust devil, or a smear of tears across her vision.

It was definitely time to go.

"Let's access some mash-up Internet maps," said Angelo, powering up the hearse with a biodiesel splutter. "I know the Test Range is on the far side of Tonopah, but of course the site's fully concealed from the sheep-like American public."

Rabbiteen piled into the paint-blistered hearse with him, suddenly cheered by the utter recklessness of their plan. The last night of mankind's existence—how could it be any other way than this? Car doors locked, and windows up, smelly gun near to hand, she crouched elbow to elbow with her friend, connecting to the global mind, comforted by her talismanic laptop.

"Why do you suppose that Google Maps doesn't even list any super-secret labs?" she complained.

Angelo toyed with the wheel, inching the car across the gravel, waiting patiently as a midnight slew of cars blasted from the darkness down Highway 6. "That's easy. I mean, I'm a dropout from Stanford... and Sergey and Larry are both dropouts from Stanford, too. But unlike me, they're covering for the Man! Because they sold out!"

"Oh, wait," said Rabbiteen, "Google just linked me to a nutcase map site with tons of great info. Hmm. The Tonopah Test Range is just past the Tonopah airport. It butts into Groom Lake where people see, like, aliens from other dimensions. And, get this, the Test Range has their own secret part, and that's *Area 52*."

"Wow," said Angelo. A raging eighteen-wheeler pattered gravel across their windshield. "That's one digit higher than 51."

Rabbiteen's iPhone emitted the stunning CLANK CLANK of a steam-hammer. She'd once missed a vitally important instant-message, so her alert preferences were set to maximum stun.

She bumped her head on the grimy dashboard as she lunged for her sleek device. "It's Cody! Cody is trying to hit me!"

"Hunh," said Angelo. "Don't read it."

"I hot 2 c u 2 n4k3d," read Rabbiteen. She glared at Angelo. "Hot to see you two naked? What does that mean? What on earth did you tell that guy?"

"I had to social-engineer him so we he'd help us break into the Black Egg. Like I said, Cody is a very lonely old man."

"You told him that you'd post photos of us naked?"

"No I didn't say that exactly," said Angelo, his voice almost wistful. "It's worse. I told him I'd stream us having sex on live webcam video." He straightened his shoulders. "I had to tell him something like that, Rabbiteen. I lied to him. And, really, at this point, so what? What possible difference does it make? The whole universe is about to melt."

Rabbiteen frowned down at her pistol, turning it over in her hands. She was momentarily tempted to shoot Angelo, but stifled the impulse. It was amazing how many user-friendly little clicks and snicks the pistol had.

"Anyway, my gambit worked on him," said Angelo. He patted the iPhone, which lay on the seat, its message still showing. "See the digits on the bottom of the screen? Cody also sent you the GPS coordinates to the site."

He punched tiny buttons on a squat plastic gizmo suction-cupped to the dash of his hearse.

"Continue Highway 6 through Tonopah," said the genteel female voice of Angelo's GPS navigation unit. "Turn right at unmarked dirt road number 37A."

Jaw set, Angelo peeled out of the lot and barreled through the crumbling heart of the stricken desert settlement. Knots of drunken, flare-wielding marauders were barricading the streets with smoldering debris. Angelo accelerated through a flaming police sawhorse, and Rabbiteen braced her heavy pistol in both hands, firing wildly and shrieking flamewar abuse through the open window.

Overawed by the style of the loons in the hearse, the rioters let them pass.

Then they motored sedately through the eastern outskirts of blacked-out Tonopah, past burning tract homes and empty desert shacks, past the silent airport and the abandoned mines.

As they turned off onto the dirt side road, Rabbiteen mimicked the feminine voice of the GPS navigator. "Suggestion. What if I posted naked pictures of myself with this gun?" She shoveled in a fresh chew of betel. "What kind of user response would I get?"

"You mean if your users weren't torn apart into their constituent quarks?" Angelo smiled and took her hand.

He was feeling buoyant. The world was definitely ending, in fire and blood just as he'd always guessed, yet he'd finally found a woman meant for him. With that sweet, frank way she had of cutting to the core of an issue without ever delivering anything useful, Rabbiteen Chandra was the very soul of bloggerdom.

His last night on Earth felt as vast and endless as a crumpled galaxy, while the full moon had gone the shape and color of a dry-squeezed blood orange. The clumps of sage were pale purple. The world Angelo inhabited had finally come to look and feel just like the inside of his own head. Incredible to think that he and Rabbiteen might be the last human beings ever to witness this landscape. It was as if they owned it.

"Isn't that a guard house ahead?" said Rabbiteen. "If you want to crash through that, I can lay down some covering fire. At least till I run out of bullets."

The GPS crooned sedately from the dash. "Proceed though Security Gate 233-X, traveling twenty-two miles further into the Tonopah Test Range to destination Area 52."

"I'd hoped Cody would be waiting for us at this security gate," said Angelo, slowing the hearse. "But I guess he never leaves his supercomputer console." His nerves were fraying again. "The guards around here are brainwashed killing machines. Mindlessly devoted to the fugitive neoconservatives of the Area 52 escape pod. If I stop, they'll extradite us to Guantanamo. If I pull a U-turn, they'll chase us down with Predator aircraft. If I barrel through the gate, we'll smash head-on into their truck-bomb tank traps."

"Oh, stop talking like that," said Rabbiteen. "It's 3 a.m. on their last night on Earth! How devoted to duty can those guys be? Don't they have any girlfriends? Or kids?"

The glum little concrete guardhouse that defended the Test Range was in fact deserted. The razor-wire chain-link moaned in the wind and the striped traffic arm pointed uselessly at the starry sky.

The hearse rolled into the empty desert compound, the narrow military road gently curving around peaks that sat on the sand like giant Zen boulders. Here and there old war-gamed jeeps had been shot to pieces from helicopters. Except for this ritualized military debris, there was only the moon and the mountains, the silence broken by periodic updates from the GPS unit.

To cover his growing embarrassment, Angelo propped his laptop on the dash. Automatically he clicked for his blog. "Oh my God!"

Terror gripped Rabbiteen's heart. "What? What now?"

"Look at my traffic spike! My Webalizer stats are right off the charts! *Drudge Report, Boing Boing, Huffington Post*, they're all sucking my dust! I rule the net tonight! Everybody's linking to me!"

"How about *my* blog?" she asked. "I blogged the Big Splat before you did—"

"This is fantastic!" continued Angelo. "I'm finally fully validated as an independent citizen journalist!"

Rabbiteen jealously moused around his screen. "Dammit, my own site has totally crashed! Why doesn't your traffic max out when you get Slashdotted so hard?"

"My 'Ain't It Awful' site is scalable, babe. I pay full service on the Amazon web-cloud and they just keep adding servers. This is the last night on Earth. No one will ever beat my post for traffic. I'm the greatest blogger in the history of the planet."

Rabbiteen considered this boast. Though galling, it had to be true. Her boyfriend was the greatest blogger in the world. Except nobody would really call Angelo her boyfriend, because they'd never even kissed.

Feeling let-down, she stroked the glossy screen of her iPhone, scroll-flicking her way through a rolling list of friends and landing on, why not, Prof. Dr. Hintika Kuusk, the Estonian string theorist. Dr. Kuusk was a kindly, grandmotherly scholar; a woman of the world who'd always been very kind to the gawky physics enthusiast named "Rabbiteen Chandra."

Rabbiteen pecked out a text message on the phone's eerie virtual keyboard. "About to have sex with Angelo Rasmussen inside Area 52."

She thumb-smeared SEND and launched her confession into cellphonespace. She was glad she'd told a confidante. Blogger that she was, it always felt better to tell somebody than to do something.

Moments passed, and then the phone emitted its signature clank. A sober incoming reply from Hintika Kuusk: "Fare thee well, Rabbiteen."

"Farewell 4ever Dr. Kuusk," typed Rabbiteen, her heart filling. She slid a glance over at Angelo, who was steering with one hand while trying to type with the other. She considered cozying up to him and working her wiles, but just then, with another clank, here came a mass-mailing to Hintika Kuusk's extensive buddy list: "OMG OMG OMG! Rabbiteen-Karmic-Reality is hooking up with Angelo-Aint-It-Awful!"

Within seconds, a follow-up fusillade tumbled onto Rabbiteen's phone display and laptop screen—from handhelds, from Twitterstreams, from MySpace pages—gossipy whoops and snarks, cheerful shout-outs and me-toos, messages from half the women Rabbiteen knew.

Angelo glanced over, his eyebrows kinked. "What's the excitement?"

"Oh, it's just my silly, romantic women friends. Don't let me distract you from fondling your famous blog."

Angelo was gentlemanly enough to close his laptop. "We're being fools. What do you say we pull over now?"

He tapped a button on the GPS unit for a distance update. "Area 52 is now twelve miiiii—" The robotic voice twisted into a sudden anguished squawk. The device sputtered, chirped, and went dark.

Reflexively concerned about any loss in connectivity, Rabbiteen lifted her cell phone. Its display had gone black. "Those wonky Apple batteries..."

"Try your laptop?" said Angelo.

Rabbiteen read from its screen. "You are not connected to the Internet." And then, like a cranky, spoiled child finally falling asleep, her laptop, too, went dark.

And then—oh dear—the car died.

Wrestling the stiff power steering, Angelo guided them to rest in a curved billow of roadside sand.

It was quiet here, so very quiet. The wind whispered, the red moon glowed.

Rabbiteen spoke aloud, just to hear her own voice. "I was sort of expecting this. Electrical circuits can't work anymore. Too much drift in the fundamental constants of electromagnetism."

"Like a power failure affecting the whole Earth?" said Angelo.

"It's much more than a power failure. And it's not just our sweet little Earth. It's the entire universe."

Angelo sighed. "For years people called me paranoid. Now I finally know I was a realist. I was truly perceptive and insightful. I was never a fringe crank intellectual, I was a major public thinker! I should have had a wife, kids... I should have had tenure and a MacArthur Grant."

Should Rabbiteen declare her love for him? It was on the tip of her tongue. He was oh so close in the rosily moon-dappled car. She reached out and touched his face.

"There's one important part I still don't get," said Angelo doggedly. "Aren't our nerves electrical? We should be fainting or passing out. But I'm still thinking—and my heart's still beating.... It's beating for you."

"Human nerves are mostly chemical," said Rabbiteen, her voice rising to a squeak. She made a lunge for him. At last they kissed.

"We could lose our ability to think and feel at any moment," Angelo said presently. "So it's the back of my hearse, or it's the sand. Unless you want to get out and hunt for Cody's Black Easter Egg."

Rabbiteen turned and gazed behind herself. The hearse did have white silk ruffles. In the weirdly altered moonlight, those were kind of—romantic.

As they bucked against each other, bellies slapping, vivid and relentless, it occurred to Rabbiteen that she and Angelo were just like the two cosmic branes.

It could be claimed that the once-distant branes were violently colliding, but that was a very male way to frame what was happening. If you laid out your twelve-dimensional coordinate system differently, the branes passed through one another and emerged reenergized and fecund on the other side of that event.

It was like the urge to have sex, which was loud and pestering and got all the press, as opposed to the urge to have children, which was even more powerful, obliteratingly powerful, only nobody could sell that to men.

Afterward came the urge to abandon all awareness and slide into deep black sleep, which no one could resist. Cuddled in the sweaty crook of Angelo's arm, Rabbiteen tumbled straight over the edge of nightmare.

She saw a lipless, billowing, yellow-eyed face peering into the side window of the hearse. Its enormous mouth gaped in woozy appetite, yawning and slamming like some drug-drenched door of perception. The otherworldly visitation of a Hindu demon. Had she dreamed that?

"Angelo!" She poked his ribs.

But he was off-line, a blissful, snoring mass. She retrieved the gun from the front seat, and stared with grainy-eyed, murderous intent into the moonlit desert. Despite her fear and wariness, she couldn't keep her lids open.

Red distorted sunlight woke them through the windows of the hearse.

"Oh no, here it comes!" yipped Angelo, sitting up with a start. He'd mistaken the rising sun for the final cosmic conflagration, and not without reason, for the solar disk was ten times its usual diameter, and the light it shed was as dim as the clouded gaze of a stroke victim.

The world outside their hearse was rendered in faded Technicolor. The skewed interaction between light, matter, and their human retinas was tinting the sage red, the sand a pale green, the sky canary yellow.

With icy, tingling fingers, Rabbiteen grabbed Angelo's wrist, trying to read his watch. "It can't already be time for the end, can it?"

"My watch has a wrecked battery now," said Angelo. "But if the sun's coming up, then it must about six a.m., right? We've still got, what, four hours to hunt for the Black Egg."

Rabbiteen's bare belly rumbled. "Do you have any breakfast?"

"Of course! Angelo Rasmussen is the Compleat Survivalist. I don't always have great sex with gorgeous Californian tech chicks, but I always have food and water."

As she preened a little, he dug into the wheel-well. "Here we go. Fruit-leather and freeze-dried granola."

They munched companionably, sitting with their legs dangling out the hearse's open back door. Rabbiteen felt happier than ever before in her life, out of her mind with head-over-heels, neck-yourself-silly romantic bonding. It was beyond ironic that this would happen to her just now.

"Do you really think a lame stalker like Cody could dodge the Big Splat?" she essayed. "I'd love to hope that's the truth. I mean, now that we're together, it would be such a great ending if somehow—"

"Not looking good," said Angelo, staring into the particolored desert gloom. "If Cody's story was for real, we should see scads of black helicopters flying in here, with all kinds of fat cats saving themselves from destruction."

"Even your *black* helicopters can't work today," said Rabbiteen a little impatiently. "It's not just the batteries, Angelo. It's spark-plugs, ignition, control chips—everything. No electrical machine will ever function again." Seeing his stricken look, she tried to soothe him. "Maybe all the refugees are here already. Maybe they're all crowded into the brane collision survival pod. Imagine the fun when they see us."

"The Black Egg of Area 52," said Angelo, drawing fresh strength from the idea. "Let's walk there."

"I'm ready. We'll walk to the end of the earth."

Angelo loaded a stained khaki knapsack with food and water, daintily lotioned his skin, and even produced a couple of wide-brimmed hats, blister packs and a telescoping metal walking-stick.

"Rabbiteen Rasmussen," he murmured as they gamely trudged the sandy road. "What a fantastic name. That would be a king-hell blogger handle."

Rabbiteen's heart glowed with joy.

They came to a fork in the troubled road—with both alternatives equally bleak. "My compass is useless now," Angelo griped. "Also, I think the sun is exploding."

Indeed the swollen, ruddy sun was spiky with fractalized flares. Its face was mottled with dark writhing sunspots, vast cavities into the star's inner layers. Old Man Sol was visibly breathing his last. It was like seeing a beloved parent succumb to a disfiguring disease.

They picked the road to the left and slogged forward.

Rabbiteen's love-smitten psyche was bubbling over with happy thoughts, yet the fear goblins ran fast behind, eating them. Compulsively, her mind returned to that demonic toad face she'd glimpsed in the midnight of her soul—but she didn't share this inner terror with Angelo. He'd only make fun of her or, worse, drive himself frantic with speculation.

Their few remaining moments of togetherness were passing all too fast. There was no sign of any secret base, or of any human beings at all. They were trudging endless, badly-colored terrain in utter forlornness, like the last two holdout players in some outdated Internet game.

Angelo was stumbling, leaning heavily on his fancy high-tech walking-stick.

"My feet are asleep," he complained.

"Me too." Rabbiteen rubbed one tingling hand against another. "I guess—I guess the changes in the electrical constants are finally getting to our nerves and our bodies."

Against her will, a sudden wail forced itself from her. "Oh, Angelo, do you love me?"

"Did I forget to say that? I get so distracted sometimes. Yes, I love you. I do love you. I'd post it in letters of fire bigger than the sun."

This declaration revived her a little; they wobbled on, teetering on their rubbery ankles.

Angelo was thinking hard. How strange it was that a woman's welcoming body could nail a man to the fabric of space and time. This was a mystical proof to him that sexual intercourse was an inherent part of the fabric of the universe. His brain was working very fast—as if some kind of electrochemical friction had vanished inside his skull—but the fringes of his nervous system were fading. It was terrible to know he would soon die, and worse to know that Rabbiteen's kindly, ardent body would smear across the cosmos like a spin-painting.

"Look!" she cried. Another unguarded, open gate. They tottered through, their knees wobbling. In the fractured, crystalline distance they could see sun-blasted buildings and a sandy airstrip. "It's too far," added Rabbiteen, bursting into tears. "And we're too slow! We won't make it."

They sat in the shadow of a boulder, arms around each other, awaiting the end—or the strength to rise and slog on. But now a deep rumble filled their ears. Sand rose into the air as if blown by an impalpable gale; rocks flew off the mountains with the ease of tumbling dice.

The two lovers fell upwards.

There was frantic, incomprehensible activity all around them, as if they were mice in the grinding engine of a merry-go-round. Like the maculated sun overhead, the planet's surface had come unmoored. Geological strata had gently unpacked like the baked layers of a baklava, sending the surface debris crashing about in search of new equilibria.

Eerie pink sunlight glittered from the hearse's window as, plucked from beyond the horizon, it tumbled past them, its hood and doors slamming rhythmically, bouncing up the slopes of the nearest peak.

In ordinary times, the earthquake noise alone might have crushed their clinging bodies, but the booming of this planetary destruction was oddly muted and gentle. The fundamental constants had plateaued for a moment. A new order of gravity settled in, with everything that could come loose from the Earth being messily sorted according to its mass.

Belatedly, a reluctant mountain tore itself loose and rose ponderously into the lemon sky.

Rabbiteen and Angelo were floating a few score yards above the remains of the ancient desert—a patch of fine dust beneath a layer of sand with pebbles admixed, topped by bones, sticks, stones and target-range military rubble.

A venomous little Gila monster tumbled past them, dislodged from some flying mountain redoubt, its stubby tail twisting, its skin glittering like a beaded arm-band.

Angelo's blown mind irritably snatched for facts. "Are those nerve-gas canisters up there? They're like weather balloons." He beat his helpless legs against the empty air and began to twist in place. "Can you explain this to me, Ms. Karmic Science?"

Rabbiteen's mind had frozen with awe. The mountains of the firmament were floating across the spotted face of the bloated sun. She had no way to think clearly—with thunderhead shelves of granite and feldspar poised to crush her.

"Hold me, Angelo! You're drifting away! I want to be with you till the very end!"

"We're doomed," said Angelo. He squinted into the hazy, polymorphous distances. The stark concrete hangers and wooden shacks of Area 52 were piled in midair like badly-assembled Ikea shelving.

The humbled remnants of the secret federal base showed no signs of life. No super scientists, no fat cats there, no Black Egg. All those cogent hints about close encounters in the American Southwest with psychic saucer-craft, and nobody was even here. People were so cynical about the miraculous that they couldn't even bother to show up.

"I can almost feel that other brane arriving now," said Rabbiteen. "Once the force of gravity has changed, we only have six minutes."

"Cody!" hollered Angelo, his voice echoing off the floating islands of stone. He cupped his hands around his mouth. "Help us, Cody!"

"Come on, Cody!" shrieked Rabbiteen. Giggling shrilly, she grappled at Angelo. Her fingers were numb, and the flesh of his neck and shoulders felt spongy and strange. "The desert's so beautiful, Cody! Especially upside down! We had great sex, and next time you can watch us, I promise!"

"Cody, Cody, Cody!!!"

A lens-like shape formed in mid-air, magnifying the tumbleweeds and boulders. Slowly, it opened a dark throat.

"Hello?" said Angelo.

The blackness folded in on itself and took form. The hole became crooked, then everted, like a giant origami tentacle. It swayed around in mid-air like a hungry feeler.

It took note of the two of them.

The warped tentacle wriggled and dimpled; the tip flexed to assume the shape of a staring, glistening face. Complex forces within the bulging shape were manipulating it like a sock puppet. The eyes bulged like a rubber mask, the mouth stretched and gaped like a toad's.

"Cody?" said Angelo, yet again, one arm wrapped around Rabbiteen. "Are you here to save us?"

The demonic toad twisted his head this way and that. He had large, golden eyes. "Do I look properly embodied within your planet's three spatial dimensions?"

"No!" Rabbiteen squeaked, stiff with unearthly terror. "You look like hell!"

"Interaction was so much easier on the Internet," said the toad, smacking his thin lips. "It's a lot of trouble to manifest this low-dimensional form to you." The creature's voice was modulated white noise, like sand sculpted into letters.

"I saw him last night, Angelo," cried Rabbiteen. "I saw him peeking into the hearse! And he was in the motel parking lot. Cody was stalking us."

"I was monitoring you," said Cody, his head billowing like a black pillowcase. "You two alone have reached Area 52, naturally selected from the many billions on your planet. You are like sperm cells beating their way up a long canal—"

"—to reach the Black Egg," completed Angelo hurriedly. His molecules felt overstretched. "Okay, yes! Here we are! Let us inside!"

Cody leered at them provokingly. "The Cosmic Mother," he said, "is the immortal entity that fills the band of hyperspace between the twin branes of the cosmos. I am the tip of one of Mother's many tentacles. If you can imagine that."

"Of course we can imagine that!" jabbered Rabbiteen. "Don't let us die!"

"Let us in," repeated Angelo. His fingers felt and looked like orange circus peanuts.

"This Black Egg is prepared for you, my blogger friends," said Cody simply. "The universe is collapsing, so the Cosmic Mother has placed a Black Egg on every space and place that supports intelligence. Billions of eggs, spewed in the cosmos like dewdrops in the shining sea."

"Oh Cody," said Rabbiteen. "You read my blog too."

"Of course I do. Physics is collapsing, but the network will persist. All the Black Eggs are linked via quantum entanglement. Telepathy, if you will."

Momentarily, Angelo forgot his fears. "Wow, I always wanted some telepathy."

"There's also infinite connectivity and infinite storage in the network of eggs," Cody evangelized. "The network has an infinite number of users. They're all upset and angry, just like you, because they're all indignant to see their universe collapse. They all believed they were the most important aspect of the universe. Imagine the confusion. We have an infinite number of anthropic principles—one for each race!"

"Then you'll need moderators," said Rabbiteen practically. "You need some users that know how to link and comment."

"Absolutely we do," said Cody. "This cosmic cycle was planned-out and architected rather poorly. It's closing down much earlier than the Cosmic Mother expected. Instead of crashing like this, the universes are supposed to get more stable with each new release."

"We're just the kickass bloggers you need!" crowed Angelo. "We can keep up our moaning and complaining for millions of years! Assuming that we're rewarded for our efforts. I mean—is there any kind of revenue stream inside there?"

"You'll lack for nothing inside your race's Black Egg," leered Cody. "Except your human need to eat or breathe. There will be sex, of course. There's always sex on the Net. The Cosmic Mother adores sex."

"Wow," said Rabbiteen.

"Now come closer to me," said the toad-headed tentacle. "Technical detail: your Black Egg is a hyperdisk where the branes are riveted together via a wormhole link in the twelfth dimension. In this one special region—it's down my gullet—the branes can't collide. I know your primitive minds can't understand that. Think of me as a pinecone that protects a tree's seeds from the heat of a fierce wildfire."

Angelo shook his bloating hands. "Never mind the license agreements, just sign us up and log us in!"

Rabbiteen had to annotate. "Really, Cody, I think it's more accurate to say the cosmic branes pass through each other serenely."

"Ah, you refer to the Twisterman coordinatization," said Cody, his bloated demon head expanding with a ragged jolt. "Yes, under that viewpoint, we'll all be transformed into our mirror-images. If you calculate in terms of the diffeomorphic quiver bundles, then it's—"

"Hurry up!" screamed Angelo—losing his composure as his left thumb snapped off.

"Fine," said Cody. "Over the next ten million years we can discuss these issues fully." His wide mouth gaped open. The inside looked dank and slimy.

Rabbiteen felt another flicker of unease. Could it be that Cody was an underworld demon after all? Under his promise of cosmic transformation, was he luring them to a fate infinitely worse than mere death? How would the toad behave any differently, if he were doing that?

Cody waited with his silent mouth agape.

Up in the sky, the sun went out. The stars and moon were gone as well. Utter darkness reigned. A shrill buzz filled the nonexistent air and slid menacingly down the scale.

Pressing together, Angelo and Rabbiteen crawled into the toad's mouth. Pushing and pulling, moving as one, the lovers wriggled their way down to the womb of the Black Egg. And of our world they saw no more.

Within the Egg's twelve-dimensional kalpas, time and space regressed. There was neither room nor duration in which to hunger, to tire, or draw a human breath. Yet in another sense, this was a weightless and limitless utopian paradise in which happy Neetibbar and wry Olegna could gambol and embrace.

The mortal races of the next universe would occasionally comment on two glorious superclusters, titanic arcs of creative energy stenciling the void like a net—sharp and sleek, stable and sweet, weaving the warp and weft of the reborn cosmos.

Notes on "Colliding Branes"

Asimov's Science Fiction, February, 2009
Written May - July, 2008.

Rudy on "Colliding Branes"

In April, 2008, I fell under the spell of a popular science book, *The Endless Universe*, by Paul Steinhardt and Neil Turok. I got Bruce to help me work the ideas into this science fiction story, "Colliding Branes." Bruce had the excellent idea of making the main characters be bloggers, and later he came up with the killer twist of having the space between branes be in some sense a living thing—like a Lovecraftian Great Old One.

I decided it was finally time to have our transreal stand-ins for our tale be a man and a woman. My character is the woman, that is, Rabbiteen. Bruce is the politically involved guy Angelo. Once again we went through ten drafts, with the usual wrangling, interspersed with rewarding moments of visionary joy.

I especially love a phrase that Bruce wrote into our ending for this tale: "...a weightless and limitless utopian paradise in which happy Neetibbar and wry Olegna could gambol and embrace."

After the last week of the collaboration I went to the hospital with a cerebral hemorrhage—what used to be called a fit of apoplexy. I nearly died, but then I rebounded and went back to being my old self, essentially unscathed.

Later I told Bruce that the attack was his fault. It told him he'd pushed me over the edge. I didn't literally think this was true, but it seemed like a good thing to tell him. I was, like, testing to see if I could evoke any hint of human empathy from the man.

Bruce imperturbably replied that I wouldn't have any further problems if I would just accept that he's always right.

Bruce on "Colliding Branes"

Since every Rucker-Sterling story has dual characters— sometimes men, sometimes women—it seemed inevitable that the dual leads would eventually have a romantic interest. "Colliding Branes" is a love story, although it's entirely about death. Mere everyday death couldn't possibly be enough for a Rucker-Sterling composition, so it's visionary, grandiose, universal death, death that outdoes the Lovecraftian scale of cosmic horror.

Writers are mortal. But bloggers, who are pitifully dependent on their Rube Goldberg tangle of obsolescent software and hardware, are even more mortal than other writers. So if "love against death" is a grand, time-honored literary theme, then "blogging against cosmic annihilation" must surely be even more touching and pitiful.

There are scenes in "Colliding Branes" that are a down-market sci-fi version of the Dantean vision of Paolo and Francesca, as those doomed, posthumous lovers waft through the fierce winds of Hell. These two star-crossed lovers get much more humane sympathy than most protagonists of Rucker-Sterling stories; they're comic figures, but they're more emotionally open, better-rounded people, and they fully share the story's dualized point-of-view, which switches from boyfriend to girlfriend at the drop of a proton.

Death tends to be a major advance in a writer's career. I've learned a lot of useful things from long-dead writers. I don't care much for the work of Dante, but Boccaccio's *Decameron* opens with the horrific, totalizing slaughter of the Black Death, and then proceeds to shuck, jive and wisecrack through dozens of weird anecdotes and comic set-ups. Boccaccio left us a great legacy; he swept up a bunch of raunchy Renaissance bar-stories, and then even Shakespeare ripped him off.

They say that Geoffrey Chaucer may have met Petrarch. I quite like the idea of these two old-school maestros getting together, swapping a few opinions over the mead, then writing an inventive travel-tale together. Maybe they did that, and maybe they decided that, although collaboration is a pretty intense experience, it would be more discreet not to publish it.

Good Night, Moon

"They say the Moon's gone missing," said Carlo Morse. He set another fabule on the checkered tablecloth at Schwarz's Deli.

Jimmy Ganzer examined the growing collection of dream nuggets. The fabules were tightly patterned little pastel spheres, pockmarked and seamed, scattered across the tabletop like wads of gum. "Nobody goes for space travel dreams anymore," said Ganzer. "I don't want to work on that."

"I don't mean the Moon's supposed to be in our new fabule for *Skaken Recurrent Nightmare*," said Morse. "I'm telling you that the Moon has really gone missing. Reports from Shanghai say the Moon faded from the sky a few hours ago. Like a burnt-out firework. Everyone's waiting to see what happens when night hits Europe and the US."

Ganzer grunted.

Morse adjusted his augmented-reality necktie, whose dots were in a steady state of undulation. "That's gotta mean something, don't ya think?"

"It's not even sunset yet in LA," said Ganzer carelessly. "So what if there's no Moon?"

Schwarz's Deli had fed generations of Hollywood creative talent. The gold-framed celebrity photos on the walls were clustered thick as goldfish scales. The joint's historic clientele included vaudeville hams, silent film divas, radio crooners, movie studio titans, TV soap-stars, computer-game moguls, and social networkers. The augmented-reality mavens were memorialized by holographic busts on the ceiling. Business was in the air, but it was bypassing Morse and Ganzer. Especially Ganzer.

"We've got our own problems," admitted Morse.

With a practiced gesture, Ganzer formed a vortex in the deli's all-pervasive bosonic fluxon entertainment field. Then he plucked a lint-covered fabule from the pocket of his baggy sports pants. "Check out my brand-new giant paramecium here."

Ganzer's creation oozed from the everting seahorse-valleys that gnarled the fabule's surface.

Morse rotated the floating dream with his manicured fingertips, admiring it. "I can see every wiggly cilia! This dream is, like, realer than you, man."

Ganzer nodded, in a superior, craftsmanlike fashion. "Yeah, the blank for this fabule uses high-end Chinese nano-goo. It's got more sensory affect than the human brain can parse."

Morse smiled at his collaborator. "Jimmy, you've brought in the awesome, once again. I knew that you could pull it off. I can't wait till Presburg shows up to sample this."

Ganzer's plain face wrinkled with a sheepish grin of triumph. With a sweep of both his arms, he corralled the dozen other fabules on the tabletop. "Lemme admit something to you," he said, stuffing the wrinkly spheres into a logo-bearing plastic storage tube. "I haven't viewed all these episodes of *Skaken Recurrent Nightmare*. I did pick up on the basic gimmick, though. Bugs."

"Yeah, *Skaken Recurrent Nightmare* conveys a different stark raving insect terror every night. The haunting dream you can't escape."

"A little corny, though, huh?" said Ganzer.

"I scraped my skull down the rind for those insects," said Morse, looking haggard and worn. "They're festering in my unconscious right now. I can see bugs in the daylight sometimes. They're in my food. They're in my shower."

"Your praying-mantis riff in the first episode was pretty classy," said Ganzer, using his finger to scrape the last glob of cream-cheese off his plate. "Having the woman you love devouring your face, bite by bite, while you're mating? A primal riff like that one hits home. Kind of a turn-on, too."

"Can I level with you?" said Morse. "We haven't had another megahit since that first episode of *Skaken*. Every night, half the human race falls asleep and boots up a total mental inferno. If this new episode doesn't strike big and—"

"You were right to call on me," Ganzer assured him.

"Jimmy, are you sure you're up for this job? I mean— *Skaken* isn't like our old indie scene. I'm working with sponsors. We're government licensed. We've got global distribution."

"Speaking of global—should I try that Chinese oneirine?" said Ganzer. "You gotta respect the rate at which those Chinese fabbers churn out the dream product."

"I use that stuff when I'm working," said Morse with a shrug. "On oneirine, I can start work the instant I close my eyes. I lucid-dream while I sleepwalk around my home office. But you do that anyway, Jimmy. You don't need oneirine. You can hardly tell dreaming from waking."

"People make too much of that distinction," shrugged Ganzer. "Reality is socially constructed."

"The Moon isn't socially constructed," said Morse.

"Then why's it gone?"

"The Moon's still up there, Jimmy. The Moon has gotta exist in one form or another. The Moon is a huge physical object. The Moon is like half the size of a planet, even. The Moon has gravity and tides."

Ganzer smiled indulgently and leaned back in his seat. "I bet you think the dark side of the Moon really existed before we took pictures of the dark side of the Moon."

"Don't start on me with the dreamer head games, Jimmy. Presburg is gonna be here any minute. Bitch about the biz, talk about the pastrami, act normal, listen to his rap. Bobby Presburg is easy if you let him talk."

Under this scolding, Ganzer shifted restlessly in his seat. "The pro dream biz is all about relentless mental focus," he declared. He wiped his greasy hands on his stained football jersey. "You know what our real problem is? Presburg doesn't respect our craft! Presburg thinks that us fabbers just idly slumber around, waiting for inspiration! He doesn't get it about us creatives! We plunge to the red-hot core of the psyche and we seize the deeper reality! That's how I deliver unique material like my giant, flying paramecium."

"You're a good guy," said Morse, with a short laugh.

"These days, any punk eight-year-old kid can dream up zombies and vampires! No wonder a pimp like Presburg likes to peddle insect paranoia."

"Look, Presburg is smarter than you know. The insect theme has been good for *Skaken Recurrent Nightmare*. We're getting ads from insecticide manufacturers and exterminator services."

Ganzer pounded at the checkered café table with his pudgy fist. "Carlo, the truth is that guys like Presburg have polluted dreamland—made it dull! You know why I'm dreaming about single-celled monsters now? Because Presburg hasn't been there. Germs are special. They're real, but you can't see them."

"You've always been the go-to guy for lurking invisible menaces," Morse admitted.

"Deconstructing reality's physical subtext is the core of my art! Seeing the unseen, naming the unnamable, and dreaming the undreamable—that's what Mr. Jimmy Ganzer is all about!"

"Yeah, yeah," said Morse, fondling Ganzer's new fabule. The dream-recording had a knobby surface, with clefts between the knobs, and the knobs themselves were tight clusters of smaller knobs. "I've been around the dance floor with you a few times. You're the ultimate old-school indy dreamer, Jimmy. You're the session man. You're the fixer."

"Yeah, okay, sure," Ganzer admitted, mopping his plate with a last scrap of whole wheat bagel. "I'm a cynical outsider artist, curiously endowed with an ability to slip reality's surly bonds."

Morse looked up as the deli's door jangled aloud. The sun was low in the sky outside, gilding the dusty streets. A strikingly handsome pair of youngsters had slipped into the cafe, bribing their way past the gateman—a mocking, weatherbeaten, Ukrainian named Yokl.

"Look at those wannabes," said Morse. "The kid with the pink tentacles growing out of his neck? And his girl's got a third eye in the middle of her forehead. They're here to flash their demos and beg for a deal."

Ganzer tugged at the elastic waist of his velour track pants. Ganzer always wore sports gear, despite the fact that he never exercised, and spent his creative working life soundly asleep. "She's hot. Costume-play sure has changed, hasn't it? We've gone from dorky hats to riding the bosonic flux."

The aspiring fabbers slipped into a nearby empty booth. The boy shoved the dirty plates and cups aside with a busy flurry of his pink tentacles.

"Whoa," Morse remarked.

"That's a pretty good augment," said Ganzer. "For a punk wannabe. Moving real objects with his dreams."

"A ribbonware plug-in for the bosonic flux medium," said Morse. "From China."

Ganzer glanced over his shoulder. "Nice projected glow from the girlfriend's third eye. It's sweet to see two noobs yearning to get discovered around Schwartz's."

"Presburg would eat those kids like pink-elephant cotton candy," said Morse.

"That reminds me," said Ganzer. "If your bossman's picking up our supper tab, we should order something pricey."

"We just had supper, man. You went through that lox and bagel like a horde of locusts."

"On come on, that bagel wasn't supper! That was just a nutritional restorative to sharpen my oneiric brain chemistry."

Morse lifted his elegant hand and signaled for Maya, their favorite Schwarz's waitress. The deli was slowly filling up with the early evening crowd.

"They put dreams on cereal boxes now," Morse muttered, straightening his tailored sleeves. "Dreams are on bubble-gum cards. Remember when our users had to load dreams off a server the size of a beer keg? And the low fidelity—hell, I look back at my old works now, way back in the 2040s, and they're like crazy-bum finger paintings made with coffee and ketchup."

"I don't like to hear you dismiss your best work," said Ganzer. "Those low-fi dreams that you used to bash out—they had a bright, childlike gusto! I mean, sure, they bombed in the marketplace. But in those days, there was nothing like a dream marketplace."

"It's all the work of Hollywood hustlers," Morse griped. "The lamestream media for the mundane sheeple... Sure, we always knew we were selling our souls, but how come we couldn't get better residuals?"

"Because we were artists once," Ganzer pointed out. "But we've matured into hard-ass bosonic pros. We're like full-tackle rugby players by now, Carlo. We gotta scrum. Scrum, scrum, scrum. That's such a great mantra, *scrum*, my unconscious creative mind finds that word really evocative. Oh, hi, Maya. What've you got for us in the way of appetizers? I'm starving."

Maya the waitress struck a pose at the table and twitched her fingers. Gleaming images of diner chow sprang into life, bright as neon in midair. "We gotcha some nice kosher spring rolls, Mr. Ganzer. Filled with tilapia liver."

"Could you sprinkle on a little brewer's yeast? And bring me a big ginseng root-beer."

"Not a problem," said Maya, steadily chewing her dreamgum. "And how about some unicorn bacon for you, Mr. Morse?"

"Is it *real* unicorn bacon?"

"Real as unicorn bacon can get!"

Morse nodded. Maya dismissed the menu images with a flip of her wrist, and sashayed off.

Morse leaned forward, cracking his knuckles. "How exactly do I frame your episode for Presburg? Just in case he actually asks."

"The dreamer turns into a paramecium," said Ganzer. "It's the classic dream-transformation riff. We should keep it sharp and simple."

Morse narrowed his eyes, with a critical stare. "Does our average dream consumer really want to be a paramecium? Is this, like, the fulfillment of an unconscious urge? An urge to become single-celled?"

"It's one of those classic dream situations where the central figure is beset by demonic mishaps," Ganzer explained. "Let's call our lead Franz Kafka. *Skaken Recurrent Nightmare* can use the class."

"But how exactly is Franz turning into a paramecium? I mean, I can totally get it about transforming into your spirit-animal—like a vampire bat, or a werewolf, or a cockroach. But a paramecium? Is that even scary?"

"It's cellular," Ganzer explained.

"What's cellular?"

"All of it," said Ganzer. "Everything is cellular. Reality is cellular. I really love that word, cellular. Cellular phone, cellular foam, sleeper cell, cellulite, cellular automata... A cell can be anything! For a solid week, I wore augment goggles with a live feed from the microscopic world. I saw cells floating around in mixed-reality, twenty-four seven."

Morse thought this over. "You've got a lot of time on your hands, since the divorce."

"Last night when I created this fabule, I chanted *cellular* to myself before I fell asleep. Just a simple creative trick, but I know how to get into a working groove."

Morse nodded. "I used wool blankets for bedsheets when I was fabbing about the lice with the black plague. Sure, I had to sleep alone, but great dreams can only come from creative suffering. Great dreams come from *spiritual* suffering. The fabule artist is like Saint Anthony, all alone in the desert, tempted by demons. Weird chimerical beasts, naked demonic chicks, eggs with legs..."

"Yeah man, we're both like saintly hermits, if only people knew," said Ganzer, wobbling his head in sympathy. "Those snot-fop critics say that dream-fabbing is a cheap fad! Well, dreams get fabbed in the Bible, man! Dreams get fabbed in Shakespeare's *Macbeth*! Dream-fabbing has very deep cultural and philosophical roots, the deepest of any art form ever! Those critics just don't get us because we're *too profound*."

Morse nodded and glanced at his watch. "Yeah. You bet."

Carried away by his own eloquence, Ganzer was bouncing eagerly on the red leather of his café seat. "Let's really ramp this fabule, okay? Like the old days when we were giving dreams away. Forget Presburg's mainstream soda-pop audience! I want our fabule users to feel their every cell coming into visionary synch! This new fabule can bust our users totally loose from consensus reality!"

"How do you plan to pull that stunt off?"

"It's cellular. It's quantum dots. It's quantum and cellular and bosonic. It's bosonic cellular quantum dottiness. With ribbons on."

Morse gazed down at Ganzer's gnarly fabule, which sat innocently on the table like a wadded piece of bread. "Yeah, those quantum dots. I loved those in your hot demo here. The quantum dots were that floating pepper I saw all around the paramecium, right? That cool, crackly, visual effect, like Marvel comics from a hundred years ago."

Ganzer was pleased. "I like having chaos and dirt in my dreams. I'm like a bluesman with a distorted amp."

A pink tentacle touched the tabletop. "Hi guys," said the tentacle's owner. The newbie was a handsome, bright-looking kid with olive skin and spiky hair. "Aren't you Carlo Morse and Jimmy Ganzer?"

"That's James Ganzer, to you," Ganzer said.

"I'm Rollo," said the kid. "And this is Tigra," who was his girlfriend with the third eye. Ganzer couldn't stop staring at that eye.

"I'm a ribbonware hacker," said Tigra, blinking flirtatiously. "Rollo and I are viral."

"We couldn't help but overhear you discussing your work with quantum dots," said Rollo. "Back in Kentucky, I did a lot of work with quantum dots. In film school."

"You went to *film school*?" said Morse, wrinkling his nose.

"Of course I didn't study *film*," said the kid, wide-eyed. "More like ribbon theory and subdimensional bosonics."

"Look, Kentucky, you're talking to guys who cut their teeth on piezotrodes," challenged Morse. "I got a closet full of fabules older than you."

"Tigra and I have been around in Hollywood for a while," said Rollo. "We're underground artists." He used his writhing hot-pink tentacles to set a doll-like figurine on the table. His tentacle brushed against Morse's hand. Morse jerked his hand away.

"You made a naked statue of your girlfriend?" said Ganzer, nudging the figurine. "Yeah, that's, uh, real avant-garde."

"It's made of pumice," snickered Rollo. "Green cheese."

"He means it's refabulated ribbons from Moon rocks," put in Tigra. "The new plug-in is coded into me. I mean, into my little statue there. You guys plug that in, drop out, take off, and you'll join us."

"What's up with the Moon, anyway?" asked Morse.

"Psychogeographic revolution," said Tigra. "No more second-hand reality. We're taking control with our dreams."

Ganzer stared hopefully at the attractive three-eyed woman. "My dreams can get pretty wild."

"I'd be glad to help you guys realize some wild dreams," said Tigra, batting her three eyes in rotation. "I mean, the famous dream-drama-comedy team of Morse and Ganzer? I'd do you two just for the experience!"

"We don't do any tutoring sessions," Morse said. "Do you mind? Our producer will be here any minute."

"Can we talk to him?" said Rollo.

"No way."

Wounded, Rollo looked defiant. "Well, producers aren't gonna matter anymore. Not when reality hacking is finally here."

Maya the waitress reappeared, both her arms laden with plates. She was used to defending celebrity guests, and she chased the noobs back to their booth.

Maya deftly served them fresh cutlery on kosher burdock leaves.

"Look, how could the Moon transform overnight?" said Morse. "I'm a veteran of this business, but I don't see how that's remotely possible. I mean, I know that the fabule biz is completely unregulated. But—

"The Moon waxes and wanes all the time," said Ganzer, busy dipping his spring rolls in fish sauce. "Sometimes it's up there, sometimes it isn't, and the vast majority of the user base has no idea where it is. And I don't know why anyone should bother. I mean, the Moon can take care of itself. The Moon is the very archetype of mankind's nocturnal dream life."

"I always hated archetypes," nodded Morse, munching his unicorn bacon. "Strip-mining other people's work, that's what I call that. Archetypes are pure theft of our collective-unconscious pre-intellectual property."

"Yadda yadda," said Ganzer. "Play your tiny, sobbing violin."

They ate silently for a few minutes.

Eventually Morse shoved his plate of unicorn bacon aside. "My wife used to worship my dreams. I can't even get her to look at a fabule, nowadays. My wife's gotten way into musicals. All-singing, all-dancing, lot of bright color—there's no plausibility, and no plots either. But much better set design. So she says. I think she's having an affair with one of her clients. Over at the stroke center. I think our marriage is—"

Ganzer held up a greasy finger for attention. "Franz Kafka awoke from uneasy dreams to find himself transformed into a giant paramecium."

"Okay. Go for it. Then what?"

"Then a big burst of violent action. Resolution of the inner conflict. Franz Kafka's maid walks in on him while he's single-celled. She screams. She attacks him."

"Who has a 'maid,' these days?"

"Kafka's in a hotel. She's the hotel maid. She knocks, and she doesn't hear any answer because all that Franz the giant paramecium can do is rock back and forth in midair above the bed, wallowing and slobbering."

"I've been there," said Morse. "Coming off oneirine."

"The maid sees the giant flying paramecium and she freaks," continued Ganzer. "An explosive return of repression. She thwacks him with a mop, *whack-whack-whack*. She's an attractive woman, somewhat coarse, a motherly, sympathetic person with a sense of humor—but this paramecium beast, she blindly wants to kill it, it's befouling the room that she cleans every day. *Whack-whack-whack.* Franz is trying to excuse himself with his floppy paramecium slipper-mouth. He's like, '*Bluh glub groo.*' The maid finds his voice menacing and incomprehensible. He's a slimy man-sized attack-zeppelin. '*Grumma fleep smee.*'"

"That's the grand finale of million monster movies," said Morse. "The monster must be killed. Before it, like, multiplies, finds a job, and gets motor-voter registration."

"Do you want to hear my pitch, or don't you?"

"Want a piece of my unicorn bacon?" asked Morse.

Ganzer took a sample. "It's good," he observed, then chewed in silence for a moment. "I think the hotel maid should have sex with Franz Kafka the flying paramecium."

"Oh, sure, why not?" said Morse expansively. "Let the giant paramecium grow suitable protuberances, and manage, against all odds, to win his lady's favor. After all, we're talking about a fabule from Jimmy Ganzer, so people's expectations are way down in the gutter. Jimmy Ganzer's dreams are the sewer that the gutter drains into."

"I'll dream it in, and you can handle the parental-guidance rating," said Ganzer, raiding Morse's plate for more bacon. "I'm lonely, so it'll be hot. Are we done yet?"

"Give me more plot," said Morse.

"Sex scenes never have plots," protested Ganzer. "Dreams, musicals, and porn—three utopias of irrational gratification. But you—you want a little logic, right? Do it yourself."

"Fine," said Morse. "I'll fab some pillow-talk afterwards between the maid and the paramecium. They're lying on the bathroom floor. He's cozily blubbering to her, maybe praising the limpid beauty of her female mitochondria. I'm thinking she sees him as a friendly talking toy. But then—"

"But then!" interrupted Ganzer, getting excited again. "In a spasm of remorse and disgust, the maid slashes Franz open with—with a scythe. And his jelly-flesh pours into the bathtub. No, the toilet—better. More *noir.*"

"The gelatinous contents of his sack-like body pours into the whirling stony vortex," mused Morse. "I like it. But it shouldn't be a scythe. They're five feet long."

"I love the sound of the word *scythe*," said Ganzer loftily. "That primal, agricultural quality. That grim reaping."

"Make it a sickle," said Morse. "A little curved sickle, corroded, but with a pink plastic handle. Something vengeful, but girly."

"Now we've got it nailed," said Ganzer, breaking into a grin. "The maid flushes the toilet and she washes Franz into the sewer. He pollutes the city's water supply, and everyone catches a bad case of being him."

"Perfect ending," said Morse, leaning back in triumph. "That's a vintage move. Dreams infiltrating real life. Every fabber's dream. We do the fadeout. We play the *Skaken Recurrent Nightmare* theme song and we leave the user with a burning urge to browse into our store and buy some anti-bacterial lotion. The business model is happy, Presburg's happy, I'm happy, you're happy. We're gonna pull this off."

"Fine," said Ganzer. "We're still on top of the game, bro. At least until this ribbonware stuff brings it to a whole new level." He fondled the figurine of Tigra and glanced around. "Looks like our underground pair got evicted. That's great. That means that the ribbonware plug-in from this—"

"Here comes the man," said Morse, straightening.

Presburg had entered the deli. Yokl the floor manager greeted him personally, and effusively led the big wheel the ten steps across the red-and-black linoleum tiling, to the booth where Morse and Ganzer sat.

Morse stood up and shook hands. Ganzer contented himself with a casual "How's it going, Bobby?"

"Scoot over," Presburg told Ganzer, seating himself beside him. Presburg was young and whippet-thin. He wore a sprayed-on layer of cotton, which showed off his gym-toned torso.

"So," he said. "Are we gonna to save this freakin' wreck of a series? What's your game plan?"

"I can get you guys through the next episode," said Ganzer, knocking the little statue against the table. "If you don't mind some, uh, stylistic innovations."

"Innovations aren't gonna cut it," said Presburg, shaking his head. "I need something more ontological. More hermeneutic."

Morse groaned. "Why do you always say that, Bobby? What does those words even mean?"

"It means get off the mattress! Guy buys a dream about a car—he sees it in his driveway when he wakes! Girl buys a dream about a diamond necklace—she's wearing it in the morning!"

"For all intents and purposes," said Morse. "In her mind."

Presburg shook his head. "Not when the studio gets that Chinese ribbonware. You get a billion dreamers all focused on one thing, the sky's the limit. Like the Moon, baby."

Maya the waitress simpered up and set down a cup of tea. "The usual, Mr. Presburg?"

"Surprise me," said Presburg with irritation. "I mean, if you can surprise me. Try real hard."

Maya crossed her eyes and dramatically stuck out her tongue. Presburg ignored her. Maya flounced off.

Presburg reached for the sexy little Tigra figurine. "Whatcha got there?" Ganzer kept it in his hand.

"It's a tie-in toy," Morse lied. "Can we talk about my contract, Bobby? And, like I was telling you, I want to bring in Jimmy here as a consultant."

"No more contracts for *Skaken*," said Presburg flatly. "We're in a paradigm shift. Best I can offer you is boys is a consulting fee. No residuals. And it's up to you how you split it."

"I'll walk," said Morse.

Presburg rolled his eyes.

"I'll float out the goddamn keyhole! " ranted Morse. "Working on *Skaken* makes me feel like a grubworm paralyzed by parasitic wasps. That frikkin' bug metropolis has been filling my brain like maggots in a rotten piece of meat!"

Presburg stopped with his cup of tea halfway to his lips. "Look, I'm about to eat a meal here. You screwballs want a better deal? Bring some serious action to the table! You know a lot of low-lifes, Ganzer. Get me a hot ribbonware plug-in."

"You're sure that stuff works?" said Ganzer, giving Morse a look.

Maya the waitress slapped down a plate of twitching live shrimp. Their bodies were shelled, but their heads were still in place. "You can drip Tabasco on them if they slow down kicking, Mr. Presburg."

"My compliments to the chef," said Presburg, examining the writhing mass of tortured arthropods. "I was wrong to ever doubt the crew at Schwartz's. You guys are pros."

Maya dimpled. "Thanks a lot, Mr. Presburg. You're a charmer."

"Maya, you work the noon-to-nine shift, right? Did you happen to notice the Moon last night?"

"I don't care about the Moon," said Maya. "Here in LA, the sky's a solid dreamy dome of urban glare. The Moon's way out of style."

"Thank you," said Presburg. "You may go. Next witness? Carlo Morse?"

"I see what you're getting at," said Morse. "The Moon's goddamn gone."

Presburg sampled a live, vigorously kicking shrimp. "Not exactly gone," he said, his mouth full. "Real different. The Chinese ribbonhackers have been dreamfabbing on it. You tell me what that means for our business."

"No more tides?" said Morse.

"Oh we'd get decent tides from the Sun's gravity anyway," said Presburg dismissively. "Think harder." He bit the body off another shrimp. "Meanwhile, you should try some of these. With that hot sauce, they're fantastic."

"Pretty soon food will be totally free," said Ganzer, intently studying his figurine of Tigra. "We'll be dreaming garbage into food."

"The new market," said Presburg with a quick nod. "Reality is the ultimate medium to productize."

"If dreams become real—" put in Ganzer, still fiddling with the figurine. "Well, I'd like to be an amorphous blob. I wanna fly, too. Remember flying dreams, Carlo? Nobody buys those these days."

"I always really wanted to fly," mused Morse. "In my flying dreams, I'll be hovering over people, and talking down to them, and they just answer back in a normal, everyday fashion. There's no panic, no corny sense of wonder about it—"

"Hey!" exclaimed Ganzer. He'd managed to twist the little Tigra-figure's head loose. He pulled it off the little body. Attached to the head was a gleaming ribbon, like a tiny sword.

"That's a ribbonware plug-in!" exclaimed Presburg.

With a smooth, nimble motion, Ganzer stabbed the ribbon into the side of his own head.

His gut bulged out, his neck shrank, his head merged into his body. His stained sportswear burst and dropped to floor in scraps. Ganzer slumped across the table—jiggly, shiny, ciliated, magnificent. A huge paramecium with his slipper-mouth agape.

Presburg jumped to his feet and screamed—a rich scream, filled with vibrato and with a ragged crackle in the upper registers.

"I can fly," blubbered Ganzer. He floated off the tabletop and drifted towards the room's low ceiling.

As if guided by fate, Maya came racing across the deli, carrying a big carving knife from the countermen. With a quick gesture, she slit Ganzer open like a hog.

Flying ribbonware shards tumbled out like viruses from an infected cell. Nimble as dragonflies, some of the ribbons plunged themselves into the heads of the people in the deli. And the rest of them surged out the deli door and into the early evening streets.

Yokl the doorman politely ushered them outside, where the populace was gently floating over their abandoned cars.

"Can we fly up there and get a decent dessert on the Moon?" said Presburg, his voice sounding odd. He was turning into Jimmy Ganzer. "I mean, this all stands to reason, right? We'll find Tigra up there, too."

Morse patted his old friend on the back and gazed into the lambent sky. Something was rising over the dark horizon. A cosmic jewel, with its facets etched in light, slowly turning and unfolding.

"Dream on," said Morse. "Dream on."

Notes on "Good Night, Moon"

Tor.com, October, 2010.
Written May - June, 2010.

Rudy on "Good Night, Moon"

Two years went by and I started to miss collaborating with Bruce. And then he passed through San Jose, California, near where I live. He was in town for a conference on augmented reality—the idea being to overlay computer-generated images upon real-world views. I went to hear Bruce's keynote speech at the conference, and I brought him home to spend a day at our house in Los Gatos. As always I was dazzled by his charisma—and we agreed to do another story.

As I've mentioned, I'm always very pleased with the way our collaborations come out. Our intense give and take generates something quite unlike the stories that either of us writes alone. The stories feel like gifts from the muse.

In "Good Night, Moon" we went back to the default of having two guys for the main characters. Bruce is the market-savvy Carlo Morse, and I'm his flaky wildman pal Jimmy Ganzer. We mixed in some augmented reality, but the real core of the story is to discuss what it's like to be a pair of aging science-fiction writers. Transrealism in action. It was Bruce who came up with the great title, "Good Night, Moon."

We'd sent all of our previous collaborations to good old *Asimov's SF Magazine*, but this time out, we went to the *Tor.com* online science-fiction site—at this point *Tor.com* seemed to have more visibility, and they were paying more.

Bruce on "Good Night, Moon"

Of course we had to get around to metafiction about two writers collaborating. The story makes as little rational sense as dreams do, but the tone is completely on-pitch. That Ruckerian transreal mix of the visionary and the mundane—I can never accomplish that alone. We're not television writers, but that's some snappy sit-com dialogue sitting on the page there. Also, the story's the right length for what's basically a one-off joke.

The science fiction critic Damon Knight used to call science fiction "The Old Baloney Factory." Science fiction writers are pop-cultural figures, they're something like Nashville acts or maybe graffiti street artists. However, I never met a science fiction writer who didn't have some astral and profound disturbance of the psyche—and I've met plenty.

Loco

"Waverly's dead?" said Becka, verging towards a shriek. "How can Waverly be dead? Without him to cover our ass, we're finished! They'll rub us out and say we never existed!"

"You hear that rumbling outside?" said Gordo. "A steamroller. That's how they got him." Gordo's breath misted the frigid air, for Dr. Waverly had ignored paying the power bills to heat their safehouse.

"What kind of bodyguard are you anyway? Hopeless ape! We're doomed." With one burgundy fingernail, Becka slit a spy-hole through the aluminum foil duct-taped to the window. "What is that monster doing out there?"

Gordo rubbed his chapped hands. "I was watching Dr Waverly like a hawk. Who knew a steamroller could pounce?" Laughing darkly, Gordo dropped into a leather executive armchair. From this throne, Dr. Fred Waverly had once ruled a federal research empire. The chair's glossy arms were cracked and its casters were flat as broken feet.

"This means we're on a hit-list," said Becka.

"Lighten up," said Gordo, his voice echoing in the unheated room. "This means we're on our own. We'll close down Project Loco. Sell off the secrets. And get the hell out while we can."

"Was it Yellco who got Waverly?"

"Not likely," said Gordo, blinking at her. "But I'm glad we've got a barricade. In case that roller makes a charge." He gestured at the walls, stacked with debris.

The contents of Project Loco's offices had been manhandled by forklift robots and crammed into their hideout: a derelict McMansion in dismal Middleburg, Virginia.

During the seven weeks of their increasingly uneasy confinement, Gordo and Becka had passed the time by piling the federal debris against the walls. Graceless steel desks, empty water-coolers, dead coffeemakers, and oddly angled surge-protectors—plus their specialized locative-science equipment: GPS units, atomic sextants, flux oscillators, nanolasers, and neutrino sieves.

The house was a jumble of crazed debris—except for one shining treasure, the culmination of years of off-the-books black-budget research, a bubbling, green-lit aquarium-tank, with glassy little cells subdividing it like an uneasy high-rise—a tenement for leeches.

Eight or nine species of leeches. Careful Loco research had proved that leeches in particular excelled as plug-and-play biotech implants. Leeches were simple and rugged, they ran off human blood, and their boneless flesh could hold a fine payload of wetware programming. Plus, once you got used to the concept of interfacing with leeches, it didn't hurt all that much to stick them on.

Happier than clams and flexing in slimy topological ease, the bioprogrammed invertebrates were the ultimate product of the Loco Project. They carried the experimental Loco translocation apps. The parasites' aquarium boasted its own battery-operated power supply to keep the creatures at a comfortable blood-warm heat.

Gordo pressed his chilly hands against the warm green glass. Outside the safehouse walls, the steamroller clattered on like a coffee grinder, casually, remorselessly. Every once in a while a ragged stranger would wobble by on a bike, but nobody seemed much bothered by the goings-on at a derelict house.

Meanwhile the steamroller was methodically flattening everything near the safe house's garage. With digital efficiency, it crushed the abandoned doghouse. Then the thorn-tangled rose bushes. Then some cheap concrete garden statuary.

So much for the anonymous safety of the Loco Project's final redoubt. The front yard was a maze of roller-marks in snow.

Uneasily, Becka rubbed the back of her neck. "What actually happened? Did Waverly morph into a giant leech? Like Patel did at the lab? Waverly was claiming he'd fixed that in his latest wetware build?"

"He slumped to the ground," said Gordo thoughtfully. "That's all I know for sure."

"Was he writhing at all? Did he display spastic invertebrate activity?"

"The way it came down—" Excited now, Gordo crouched in the middle of the room, his heavy body nimble as he moved his hands, mapping things out. "He went soft. The steamroller attacked. And Waverly was like a gingerbread man under a rolling pin. A thirty-foot smear of smashed mathematical physicist. No blood, no bones. I used my hands to pry him off the lawn. I rolled him up like a tortilla and carried him into the garage."

"Not much like Patel," mused Becka.

"I can't say," replied Gordo. "Remember, I only joined your team after the Patel incident."

"I wish you'd stop bitching about 'the Patel incident.'"

"Look," said Gordo, "you can't just morph a federal scientist into a giant invertebrate that catches fire. That's not an acceptable protocol."

"Security guys like you can never keep your traps shut," said Becka, angrily pacing back and forth through the debris. "Forget about Patel, he's stuffed in a nuclear waste barrel. Let's talk about Waverly. Even if a steamroller crushed him, it's not scientifically established that he's dead."

"Where do you get that idea? Of course he's dead. I saw his brains come out of his eye sockets."

"I need facts," insisted Becka. "Not your interpretations."

"Oooh," said Gordo. "The dragon lady. Okay, as soon as we stepped outside the safehouse, Waverly started babbling. He said, 'I'm going everywhere.' He was slobbering. Then he lost his muscle tone. His hands pulled up into his sleeves, and he went all boneless. And then—wham! That steamroller comes out of nowhere and runs him over."

"Just like that?" said Becka skeptically.

"That's how I saw it. That's the machine that killed him, still tooling around out there. It's like a remote-controlled drone." Gordo peeped out the window. "Look, it keeps backing in and out of our garage. That's where I dragged Waverly. It's still running over him. Again and again."

Bathed in the warm green light of the leech aquarium, Becka stared at Gordo. She looked cute and serious with her short dark hair. Pitiable shadows of rage and despair played across her face. As long as Dr Waverly had been in charge, Becka, ever the faithful post-doc, had been full of hope. But now, with Waverly flattened, her illusions were crushed like so many asphalt pebbles.

"Where do steamrollers come from?" she mused. "Oh. The city construction yard."

"I guess," said Gordo, still peering out the window. "But I can tell you it didn't drive here. Someone got hold of our loco and teleported it in. Take a close look, it's cruising right by our house again."

Becka hastened to the window.

"It's motor isn't on at all," Gordo pointed out. "It's drone control isn't active. You can tell from the lights on top. They're all off. The things running on pure loco. Someone's teleporting it all around!"

"Translocating, not teleporting," snapped Becka. "Can't you get that one thing straight? Loco applies affine transformations to the subdimensional pregeometry that underlies the spacetime foam. Loco edits our reality from the outside. Loco is nothing like 'teleportation'."

"Sure it is," said Gordo, baiting her. "It's like on Star Trek."

"Christ, you're a moron."

"Maybe so, baby. But this moron has what you want." Gordo attempted a leer.

"As if," said Becka, looking away.

"Anyway," said Gordo, beginning to enjoy himself. "The steamroller spread out fat Waverly like pizza dough."

Becka scowled, "I told you that Waverly should never leave our safehouse."

Gordo picked absently at the masking tape on an office cartoon, taped to the side of an upended desk. An archaic folk-xerox of some guy unscrewing his belly-button and having his ass drop off.

Becka rooted in the debris that braced the safehouse walls. She found a federally-approved orange and silver pilot survival blanket. It was sixty years old and rattled like burnt parchment, but she wrapped it around her sloping shoulders.

"Don't get that look on your face again," said Gordo, adjusting the buttons of his overcoat. "None of this is my fault. Waverly insisted on taking a walk today. You know he was stir-crazy. He said an outing might reduce his bloat. We snuck out while you were sleeping."

Becka wrung her blue-knuckled hands. "God damn it! We've been stuck here for weeks in this crappy, nameless, unheated, dead-end, foreclosed house, playing Dad and Junior and Sis. We shattered every limit of space and time and stuck our software into leeches, and after all our fine work, what do we get?"

"We get a steamroller popped out of thin air," said Gordo practically.

"With the Pentagon waiting for us to turn our beautiful invention into a killing machine."

Gordo grunted.

"Or for some sleazy web-biz morons to productize us commercially. I'm talking about Yellco. They hired a bunch of our disgruntled staffers. Yellco and their stupid cloud."

"The cloud's ubiquitous," said Gordo cozily. "The cloud is everywhere, all the time. That's what's good about the Yellco cloud."

"The cloud spies on everybody," said Becka. "How come the cloud is bigger than the government? This is all so unfair!"

Silently, Gordo blew on his hands, then rubbed his right shoulder. He opened a desk, revealing half a crate of army-surplus beef stew.

"How can you possibly eat at a time like this?"

"When's a man supposed to eat?" retorted Gordo, searching through a tangle of cable-dripping debris. He produced one stained, misshapen plastic container and pulled a tab at its base. The stew began to hum and rattle.

"That can is seriously past its expiration date," remarked Becka.

"Desperate times," nodded Gordo.

"Did you set Waverly up?" asked Becka, slitting her eyes.

Taken aback by the wild accusation, Gordo was silent for a long moment. "Why are you always like this?" he said, his voice nearly a whine. "Everything's always so complicated with you."

"I'll make it simple." Becka stood up and poked him in the chest with her finger. "Our boss is a pancake. Who's next?"

"You!" said Gordo, abruptly clamping her in an embrace.

Becka wriggled one hand free. She slapped Gordo so hard that the sound echoed from the clutter on the walls.

"Go ahead, hit me," muttered Gordo, releasing her and gingerly feeling his inflamed cheek. "Because I'm a mole, all right? You might as well know—I'm a mole from Yellco. I've been wanting to tell you that for a long time."

Becka gaped in amazement, still catching up. "You work for Yellco? All this time?"

"Yeah. When I spread the word about that Patel incident, your staffers scattered in all directions. You ended up exiled and alone, and I came along to pick up the intellectual property. That's the pay-off, and that's why I'm still here, all cozy with you."

"Oh, it's all so dark-side," said Becka despairingly. "So sleazy. So sold-out."

"You academics never have any street-smarts," said Gordo, still rubbing his cheek. He looked at his reflection in the glass of the gleaming aquarium. "Me, I'm a street-hardened security op. That's what Waverly asked for—after you guys vitrified Patel's ashes into a glassy barrel of nuclear waste. Waverly figured a guy like me would know how to hush things up. That shows how much you losers knew about real-life federal security."

"What were you doing before?" asked Becka, intrigued. "Where do people like you come from?"

"Oh, I was the top security man at Dulles airport. Humiliating passengers. It was great work, but I screwed up, and strip-searched a congressman's son. You guys were my disgrace posting. Project Loco is my personal Siberia."

"But you should have loved your new job!" Becka protested. "We got such superb results in unconventional physics! Sure, Patel turned into a leech and underwent spontaneous combustion—but that only happened one time! All the rest of those wiggling things locked in the penthouse, those were just animal subjects. Dogs, mostly. Leeches love dogs."

Silently, Gordo thought this over. "What was Patel like?" he said at last. "I mean, before he got all flexible and tubular."

"Patel was cute. He had a crush on me, actually. That's why he volunteered to pioneer the science of translocation. The test went fine at first, but after the leech hit an artery, Patel started heating up inside. Like a runaway reactor. We locked him into the shower-room, hoping he'd damp down. But he crawled out through the keyhole and slithered upstairs to my office."

"I never heard this part," said Gordo.

"It was such a mess," said Becka. She tightened her voice and pressed on. "That pathetic Patel was telling me that he'd done the test to show he loved me. With those leechy, toothy mouth-parts, I could barely understand him. Like bluh bluh bluh. And he was hot as a furnace. I was yelling and backing away from him. And then, oh God, he caught fire in my office. Men came in haz-mat suits, I never used that office again. That was the room we turned into your office, actually. After we hired you to keep things mum with your sleazy dark-side connections."

"So you could turn more volunteers into giant leeches."

"Not actual leeches!" exploded Becka. "Subdimensional pregeometric assemblages!"

"What's the diff? They're both boneless, wormy and wobbly."

Becka put her hands on her hips. "That's a typical ignorant layperson's confusion."

Right then Gordo's can of self-heating beef-stew popped open. The putrid smell of spoiled meat wafted out.

"You can't eat that rubbish," said Becka impatiently. "Let me show you some real food."

"Now you're being nice," said Gordo, wrapping a rag around the spoiled stew and sequestering it within a file cabinet. He walked back, gently smiling, his voice soft. "Show me what you've got for me, baby. People always eat a lot at wakes. And after that—they have sex. It's life against death. Very human."

"You wish," said Becka, her cheeks pinkening.

"I didn't mean you in particular were human," said Gordo.

"You can't have red-hot funeral sex with just anybody," said Becka, deciding to flirt. She lowered her head, placing a delicate finger on a small bump on the base of her neck, up by the hairline. "As for the food, I made Waverly fit me with a loco leech. Call me crazy."

"I'll volunteer too," said Gordo reflexively.

"You might morph into a pregeometric assemblage that resembles a slimy bloodsucker," Becka warned him, a flicker of a smile on her face.

Gordo shook his head. "I'm thinking that when Waverly morphed this morning, he willed it to happen. The guy was so cornered and stir-crazy, he wanted to morph. Right before the big change, Waverly said, 'I'm going everywhere.' Well, I'm going where's right for me. Fish one of those little bastards out of the tank for me. I'll take my own chances."

"I just wish I could pry my own leech loose and give it to you," said Becka uneasily. "But check out my awesome food demo first. It'll blow your mind."

Becka pulled two chairs over the flimsy card-table that Waverly used as a desk. Improbably yet deftly, she extracted a loaf of bread from a meager pencil-holder. The bread puffed up as she pulled it upwards, like toothpaste oozing from a tube.

"Now watch," crowed Becka. "No keyboards, no commands, not even a gestural interface." She cocked her head, staring at the crisp loaf of flaky bread on the table. The baguette spontaneously opened up with a laser-sliced precision. It rapidly bedecked itself with thin, slot-like wafers of colorful ham and brie.

Becka blinked her sharply focused eyes, and the spatial substance of the sandwich rotated upon itself, like the slats of a Venetian blind. A tidy row of colorful ham and cheese canapés sat on the wobbling table in the chilly room.

"I always wondered how you fed the boss behind my back," exclaimed Gordo.

Becka proudly nibbled a shred of the gourmet ham.

"That came out of nowhere, like the steamroller?" nodded Gordo. Outside their walls, the machine was still busily clanking around. "Here, but not really here?"

"Where is anything?" said Becka. "An object is just a mesh of pregeometric locative architectures—instantiated via a spatial transform. This food started as a baguette sandwich in Fort Meade, over where we used to work. I edited the baguette loco myself."

Gordo scarfed up the little treats as fast as his cold-stiffened fingers could pluck them from the table.

"You're eating eight sextillion affine transformations for every canapé," Becka told him, delicately choosing a few for herself. "Loco tech is super processing-intensive. Each of these tasty morsels is a zettaflop of cloud crunch."

"A zettaflop?"

"That's one higher than exaflop. So don't get all greedy. The cloud-load for this snack creates info lag all up and down the Eastern Seaboard."

"A secret chow-line through the cloud's back door," mused Gordo. "That's some kinda management perk."

"That's how life has to be nowadays," Becka shrugged. "Looks great, tastes yummy. It's provisionally real. Of course if the loco crashes before you've metabolized your lunch—tough! You've got a bellyful of subdimensional quantum foam."

Gordo looked up hopefully, licking translocated mayonnaise from his fingers. "So we can glom free lunches from random delis forever, whenever we want?"

"Burn Before Thinking, is what Dr. Waverly said about that idea. We were supposed to feed Special Forces paratroops with this. And then there was our death-ray app. We were supposed to translocate raw energy from the core of the sun. And blast it out in a beam."

"Awesome," said Gordo. "How did that work out?"

"It's technically feasible. But we kept having problems getting the coordinates right. Hassles with the gravitational warp—it's very chaotic at the center of a star, what with general relativity coming into play. Very unstable. We tested the process on dogs, taking them outside to bark at the sun. And of course that body-morphing issue was a big problem with the dogs. Quite a few caught fire."

"Burning dog-shaped giant leeches with death-ray eyes," said Gordo.

Becka plucked at her full lower lip. "I really wouldn't put it that way."

"You and Waverly were a pair of loose cannons."

"We wanted to hit some goddamn development milestones, okay?" said Becka. "We were finally turning the corner. Waverly found a superior West Virginia leech that was free of the morph effect! He'd been wearing his leech with no trouble for two full months. I've had my own leech for just a few days less than him, and I feel perfectly fine."

"So far, so good," said Gordo. "Just look how far you've come, you and Dr. Waverly."

Becka flopped into Waverly's stuffed chair beside the sparkling aquarium-tank of the loco leeches. She closed her eyes and rested her hands on her temples. Presently she lifted her head and bleakly stared at him.

"Whether you want to admit it or not, Waverly's still alive. He's undulating. Even though that steamroller keeps rolling on him, making him thinner and thinner."

"How would you know that?" asked Gordo cautiously.

"I can see him through my loco leech. Not see him, exactly. It's more like proprioception—I know ultraprecisely where he is. Like the way you know where your elbow is, or your bedroom furniture when you get up in the night."

"Well, I saw him with my own human eyes, and I didn't see any undulating. He looked deader than hell."

"What a blind, coarse, unfeeling man you are. What a nightmare this is for me," Becka intoned. "The girl with the highest SAT in the history of Minneapolis. I should have paid more attention to reading Mary Shelley. Frankenstein? I always loved Mary Shelley. I mean, she was super-brainy, but really romantic and hot."

Becka's face quivered with despair. She reached under her flimsy card-table desk. She heaved out the overstuffed, derelict-style backpack she used as her raw-panic bug-out-bag. It held some choice packs of blueberry people-chow in there, a half-pint of ouzo, even a plush stuffed turtle. Finding a mass of crumpled tissue, she wiped the tears from her smooth, olive-skinned cheeks.

"That pitiful trembling tortilla was the greatest physics genius of our time," she whispered.

"Yeah," Gordo said gruffly, "I know, it's a shame."

"At the end of his life, you and I were the only friends he had left. We're like his next-of-kin. We should do the decent thing by him. Go fetch a piece of Waverly from the garage."

"Your mentor's mortal remains are kinda crumbly," said Gordo.

"Crumbly?"

"Majorly."

"Like—just like dead-organic, squashed crumbly? Or like subatomic degenerate-matter blue-Cerenkov-radiation glow-in-the-dark Los Alamos crumbly?"

Gordo looked glum. "What you said." He pulled back the frayed cuffs of his overcoat, studying the peeling skin of his hands. "Look at this. And the rays cooked my shoulder, too."

"I'd better not go into the garage at all," said Becka quickly. "Not with him decaying into pregeometric subdimensional Feynman diagrams. So, okay, well, you can go in there again. Because you've already been exposed. Run to the garage pronto and fetch in a piece of the boss."

"No way."

"Don't be stupid! You already touched him. Just hold your breath and flake off a small piece. I don't need much for a forensic study."

"That's such a lame word, forensic," said Gordo, rebelling. "Why not truck him over to Dulles and feed him through the airport scanners?"

"I know he's still alive," insisted Becka. "I just need a way to prove my hypothesis. And—" Becka jumped to her feet, her face alight. "Eureka!"

"What?"

"I just realized! Dr. Waverly translocated that steamroller here himself! He's the one who brought it in. He's using the steamroller to flatten himself, so he won't go critical. He's reducing his bloat so he won't catch fire."

"What then?" said Gordo, really doubting her.

"He's aiming for a higher type of phase transition! Our simulations predicted that was theoretically possible, but— if he's actually achieved it, he's entered a whole new level of existence! Be a man and go into that garage, Gordo. Or at least call out to Dr. Waverly from the garage door."

"I've had it," Gordo snapped. "You know what? I'm out of here. I just made up my mind. Waverly is stone dead. I'd be crazy to stay in this meat-locker one minute longer. I can outrun that steamroller. I'm a tough guy, I'll take my own chances out in the real world." Gordo flipped up his collar, pulled down his hat, and ambled toward the door.

Becka rose to her sneakered feet and scampered hastily after him. "Wait, Gordo. You're abandoning years of research by brilliant scholars."

Gordo looked Becka up and down, from her ironic Goob Dolls hairpins to her skatepunk Converse sneakers. "Research by mixed nuts, more like. What good did you get out of any of this research? Ever? Maybe you're gonna find out the personal phone number of the Higgs boson, but meanwhile you're a blacklisted junior professor who was shitcanned for science fraud."

Cut to the quick, Becka retorted. "Well, you're a big ugly goon who gropes helpless females in airports."

They studied one another, awaiting some next, consequential move.

After a dreadful interval, Gordo realized he would have to be the one to speak up. "Look. Don't get mad. Maybe we could work something out. You and me. We could blow this bad scene and make a run for it. There's a lot of good security jobs in Qatar and Kazakhstan."

"What am I supposed to do in those countries, swathe my face in a Hermes scarf? I'm a brilliant American federal scientist with years of loyal service! I'm staying right here in my own country. My only problem is that Project Loco is so freaking astral it makes LSD look like Medicare."

"The feds aren't going to fund you anymore. Not when your boss is a self-flattening radioactive pancake."

"It's not exactly radioactivity," said Becka. "But, yeah, I know."

"So, how about we hook up with private enterprise," suggested Gordo. "My pals at Yellco. They're in big business, they can deal with the feds. You go and do the kabuki for them. A live demo. Lay sample loco leeches on those awestruck investor geeks. Then I can close the venture deal."

"Selling government-funded research results is unethical," said Becka in a lofty tone. "Since you're not a scientist like me, you know nothing of the proper research and development protocols."

Gordo nodded quietly, grimly. "Oh, I agree with you. I appreciate that, the way you just put me down. I'd love to see you cut a deal for yourself." He stroked his stubbled chin, pooching out his lips to assume a wise expression. "You're guilty of warping the fabric of spacetime with a leech stuck to your neck. You'll get the gas chamber. The networks will run it live."

"Oh god, oh god, oh god!"

"You're fine if I'm here to protect you," said Gordo, stout and manly. "Waverly's flatter than toast, but nothing's happened to you yet. You know what we need? A drink. A drink, two trench coats and a handgun."

"How can you even talk about booze when we're in so much trouble?"

"Bust out that ouzo you've got hidden in your knapsack. Translocate us an apple pie."

"No pie for you," said Becka primly. "It's not even ten in the morning." She turned to the coffee maker that sat atop an unstable heap of lab equipment. "I'll make you a nice strong coffee."

"Whatever," said Gordo. "Rough day. I hate seeing dead people. Especially when I have to clean them up."

Becka sniffed. "The noise of that steamroller is giving me such a headache."

Gordo reached absently into his shirt pocket. "Hey, you want some aspirin? I copped it last week in that shell of a mall. It's German! Really pure."

"You can be a handy guy sometimes, El Gordo," said Becka, gratefully eating a painkiller.

"Real soon now, we burst into action," said Gordo, "Caffeine and sugar, aspirin and ouzo! We're gonna take the war to the world outside!"

Just then they heard a clumsy scratching at the front door, followed by a series of light, precise knocks.

Gordo peered through the fisheye spyhole in the center of the mansion's bolted door. "This is the living end," he said. "Now someone sent us a robot."

"You're kidding me."

"No way, look for yourself. It's one of those Japanese quadruped things, those herky-jerky origami dogs. I've never seen one outside a YouTube video."

"I can see it through my loco leech," said Becka with an inward look. "Maybe we'd better find out what it wants."

Gordo opened the door to reveal a disposable droid, a creature that had been created as a 3D-printed construction of grid-wired plastic. It was cheap and flimsy, tidily folded to balance on four pointed feet. Graphic displays flowed across its surfaces.

The closest surface resolved into the plump face of their landlord. His name was Yonnie Noe, and he was famed for having bought up three thousand houses in the blasted Northern Virginia suburbs. Keen on personal service, Mr. Noe printed out fresh rent-collector droids every day.

"I need to speak with Dr Fred Waverly," said Yonnie's face, his tone peremptory. The sound emanated via vibrations from the collector droid's surfaces. The creature cocked its head, aiming its photosensitive patches into the house, sampling the air with a roughened surface near the tip of its triangular nose.

"Dr Waverly's in the garage," said Gordo. "He's getting a massage."

"That's nice, but I smell burnt wiring," announced Yonnie. The bot slid a papery leg through the open door. "Did you use a two-prong plug in a three-prong hole, sir? I'll have to inspect for that."

This was a ruse. Once a collector droid had somehow folded and slithered its way into a deadbeat's sanctum, valves would open and it would emit a spray.

"You can't evict us," bellowed Gordo, giving the droid a savage kick.

"You didn't pay your landlord," chirped the paper robot, skittering right back. "Allow me to display your deadbeat financial status." A series of charts, blueprints, progress bars and spycam views scrolled rapidly across its back and its legs.

Yonnie's face reappeared, threatening and serious. "The ambient biometric feeds shows the renter of record to be lying on floor of the garage."

"I just told you that," said Gordo. "But you weren't listening."

"Dr. Fred Waverly's brainwaves arc subnominal," intoned Yonnie. "I deem him incapacitated. Your evident failure to file a police report is a crime! Prepare for immediate eviction, followed by arrest!"

"Dr. Waverly's only resting," babbled Becka over Gordo's shoulder. "He's in a deep trance. He's an ascended master. I know you want your back rent, Mr. Noe, but we don't have the password to activate Professor Waverly's credit account."

"This is unacceptable," snapped Yonnie.

"You can't arrest us," said Gordo. "You're made of paper and coat-hangers." He gripped the robot by its papery mid-riff and threw it into the snow. He slammed the door and shot the steel bolts.

The robot pattered and scratched at the door, emitting a buzzing series of escalating threats. And they could hear a second droid fumbling at the window.

With trembling hands, Becka stuffed a few things into her backpack and shrugged it onto her shoulders. "I'm not strong enough for this," she said. "I can't beat up robots. I'm a scholar."

"I can handle this crisis," said Gordo, watching her. "Pick me out a loco leech."

"Okay, try the top left box in the tank," Becka counseled. "Put a leech straight up your nostril and it'll hook to your brain immediately. It takes a whole hour to interface it if you stick it on your neck."

Leaning over the aquarium, Gordo pincered out a writhing brown West Virginia leech. Holding it tight between finger and thumb, he snorted it up.

"Oof," said Gordo, staggering. He held up his hands, staring at them like he'd never seen fingers before. "Sextillion," he muttered. "I'm counting the molecules, yeah. Septillion."

The collector droids were scritch-scratching at the door and the window, earnestly trying to slide in through the cracks. But this algorithm failed them. They were quiet for a minute, and then they emitted two tightly collimated chirps. One of the window panes shattered into shards. Instantly two folded-up shapes glided through the empty pane like paper airplanes. The droids unfolded themselves to stand on all fours, wavering like drunken hat stands.

One of the collector bots lifted his tail and began to spew a thin stream of repulsive gas.

With a savage effort of his will, Gordo dove into the locative mental spaces of his leech. Immediately he found the city construction yard. Translocating physical objects was as easy as lifting a fork from a table.

"Roar," Gordo declared.

A bulldozer crashed gloriously through the wall into the littered dining room, its blade raised like a tear-stained guillotine. The dozer's tracks and blade made a lethal, pig-slaughtering racket. Fresh, cold air streamed in.

"This all goes on your bill," screeched Yonnie No's voice, and then his origami droid was crushed.

Gordo bobbled his head, manipulating the bulldozer as effortlessly as a wire-frame graphic. Its dirt-stained teeth knocked the aquarium from its stand in a geyser of shattered glass and wallowing parasites. The dozer whirled, its dirt-stained treads gouging the floor.

"I'm voiding your deposit," chirped Yonnie Noe's remaining collector droid, scuttling out of reach. It hid in the crannies of the junk piled against the walls, preparing to vent its own supply of gas.

The bulldozer rotated in place, lining up for an attack. Gordo zoomed the dozer's dimensions down to a nimbler size. With a blur of motion, the miniaturized bulldozer darted like a rabid terrier to crush the last droid to bits.

And then, with a smooth affine transformation, Gordo restored the dozer to its full stature. It trundled outside, making another yawning hole in the wall, opening a Pompeii-like vista.

Silence fell. The dozer was motionless beneath the pearly winter sky. In the garage, the steamroller was silent too. A few dark dots of snow began to fall. The frigid air smelled somehow like steel.

"You overdid it," said Becka critically.

"Women always say that," shrugged Gordo. "You wanted me to solve your problem... Hey, problem solved now, it's all rubble."

"Look," said Becka, pointing.

A wide, flat sheet was creeping across the snowy winter lawn, reflecting glints of rainbow color from the low, gray clouds.

"He's like a flounder," said Becka. " Or no, he's like a soap film."

Waverly the soap-film man undulated and rose into the air. As if seen through a haze of static on a clouded video screen, he twinkled, stuttered, jaggified, and broke up—into frantic dots. A swarm of Waverly gnats. Bright and glittering, the gnats swirled in a slow tornado.

"He's going everywhere," said Becka. "He predicted this. He's encysted himself into a quintillion particles."

With a dip and salute, the swarm of Waverlys scattered itself to the vagrant breezes of winter.

"I don't think that's an attractive career choice," said Gordo.

"Do you want to try and pry your leech loose, before it really digs in?" asked Becka. "I think it's too late for me."

"I'm riding this all the way," said Gordo. "Wherever it leads. Having this superpower—it feels like the first time I've ever really been alive. It's just you and just me against the world. So first, before anyone else shows up—" He nodded his head towards the house.

"Hot funeral sex?" said Becka, her expression unreadable.

"Please," said Gordo.

Notes on "Loco"

Tor.com, June, 2012.
Written December, 2011.

Rudy on "Loco"

Bruce emailed me an idea for a story that would some-how be related to locative art, that is, to virtual-reality art providing an experience that relates to a viewer's specific location. I wasn't exactly sure where to go with this notion, but I knew it would be fun to work with him again. As is customary for our collaborations, "Loco," is a two-person story, with the characters loosely based on Bruce and me.

This time, instead of directly arguing with each other about the story via email, Bruce and I transrealized our bickering into actual dialog within the story. I'm the punky woman, and Bruce is the tough, hard-bitten man. There's also a bit of me in the professor who's been run over by a steam-roller.

Having a guy be flattened like a pancake without actu-ally dying was one of those odd story-twists that simply occurs to a writer like me—and then, just for the hell of it, I throw it in and see if I can make it work within a tale's internal logic. The tank of leeches, the attack of the road-grader, and the paper robots are what-the-hell ideas too—it was Bruce who came up with those three.

In the end, the story has a fine, mad logic. I relish Bruce's rich vocabulary, his contrarian attitude, and his obsessions—refreshingly different from mine. Cory Doctorow wrote a nice bit about our story on the *Boing Boing* blog:

"'Loco,' a new story by Rudy Rucker and Bruce Sterling is the weirdest fucking thing I've ever read that managed to still make sense. I've read pretty much every word both of them ever published and together, they are infinitely weirder and more interesting than they are on their own. I'm willing to bet that writing this was half euphoric loony-laughter, half weird-out contest, and 100 percent awesome."

Bruce on "Loco"

This story might have been a rather standard cyberpunk technothriller about federal research scientists who blunder into their own Manhattan Project. I had an idea along that line—because I'm beset with ideas, I have thousands of them—but I've done work of that sort before, and I didn't know where such a story might go.

Rudy immediately attacked the story with brazen cartoon elements—a living man smashed flat by a bulldozer, an attack of paper robots from an angry landlord. The trick in "Loco" is to subsume these aggressive provocations without breaking character. The two leads are government workers, and they stay feds no matter what. The result is some spectacularly weird cyberpunk-transreal dialogue, almost certainly the best such exchanges we've written.

"Loco" is not a great science fiction story, but it features some unearthly scenes that convey the world-smashing feeling of a Surrealist exquisite corpse. Two conceptual worlds have been collaged together, and the jagged edges are smoothed out nicely. So the sentences work, they're grammatical and even rational, but they state weird things that are simply unheard-of, unthinkable thoughts that no single human brain could produce.

I don't like to play the suffering tortured artist as Rudy does, because I don't write from the heart; I'm critical and analytical, and for me it's all about text construction. Nevertheless, I dare to declare that "Loco," for all its extreme daffiness, is deadly-serious sci-fi high-artwork. This is pulverizing psychedelia jam-band action where the guitars get bulldozed live on stage.

Totem Poles

Dirt Complaining and Dirt Harkening were a long-buried married couple.

"I haven't minded being dead one bit," said Dirt Complaining. "But now we've got space aliens nosing around. And they're curious about totem poles? Why did you men even make those things?"

"We were great artists," said Dirt Harkening.

"Fools conjuring up cosmic forces."

"I miss potlatch," said Dirt Harkening. "That's what I've missed most, down here in the Earth's dirt."

"Potlatch again," said Dirt Complaining. "Ha! All you big chiefs, pretending to be above all wealth, so spiritual, so potent! Whose robes and amulets were you burning and throwing into the sea? Women's crafts, women's treasures!"

"Easy come, easy go," said Dirt Harkening. "With flying saucers in the sky, our whole Earth is in play. But come what may, dear wife—our squabbles don't matter anymore."

"The heirs of our dead flesh still walk the Earth, husband."

"The living take no account of us. People have forgotten that sacred truth was captured in the mighty symbolism of our totem poles. Even though the saucers understand."

"Your totem poles were vulgar," said Dirt Complaining. "Big phallic brags !"

"We artists like that sort of thing. A totem pole that stands up good and stiff—very fine."

"Let's see how this ends," said Dirt Complaining.

§

Ida lowered her combat binoculars. She had pale skin, a heart-shaped face and a bob of lustrous dark hair. "It's a shame that nobody sees the point of our struggle. What if we're wrong?"

Kalinin adjusted his brimless fur Cossack hat. He was a bony, waxy-skinned warrior with high cheekbones and a great beak of a nose. "You and I will be heroes," he said, looking tenderly upon Ida. "Once we learn how to kill this race of flying saucers."

"But the saucers are saving the very Earth that mankind destroyed!"

"If you wash an apple before eating it, do you do that for the apple's good?"

Heaped with garbage, a chain of filthy diesel trucks lumbered toward the vast scar of the coal mine, here in the Donbass region of the Ukraine. One after another, with distant groans and screeches, the great trucks dumped their trash. It was high noon, with a glaring sun.

The alien creatures had three primary forms—one for the air, one for the sea, and one fearsome form that infested the Earth itself.

The air invaders resembled classic flying saucers. They haunted Earth's skylines, absorbing pollutants. In their sea-going form, the saucers took on shapes like whales. They devoured poison gyres of floating plastic with their ivory teeth, and filtered toxins with their dark baleen. And the subterranean saucers were colossal, rubbery, saucer worms. They infested mankind's mines and landfills, erasing every scrap of poison they found.

Thanks to the aliens, the withered fields and rain forests, stricken by every form of human rapacity, were blooming again. Happy dolphins and gallant tuna swam the open seas. Wild pigs roamed the taiga like the wind. The planet's molten poles were freezing again as the rising seas receded.

The very largest of the chthonic saucer worms was here in a Donbass coal mine. Kalinin's sworn goal in life was to kill this worm. For weeks, militarized Russian diesel trucks had been dumping nuclear waste into the mine, filling it with choice bait for the saucers. Lured by this bonanza of filth, an armada of the flying saucers had burrowed into the shaft and had merged their bodies to form a vast and lumpy worm.

Sheltered by a rampart of wet sandbags, Kalanin and Ida watched one of the great, silvery saucers fly by overhead. Kalinin's ragtag paramilitary warriors set up a rousing antiaircraft fire from their muddy ambush holes. But they weren't firing bullets.

The living saucers, it seemed, had a weakness. They carried within them some prime directive about intelligent life, some ethic that manifested itself as a tenderness towards human beings. The saucers were unwilling or even unable to harm people. They had an especial loathing for dead people. Therefore Kalinin's paramilitary troops fired human body-parts at any saucer within range—making the innocent blue sky above the radioactive coal-mine into an aerial graveyard of human carrion.

The saucer flexed, ducked, and dodged its way through the sprays of gore. The fierce militia-men concentrated their bloody fire the more. The saucer's capacities, although great, were not infinite. Under the harassment of flying carnage, the saucer's smooth seamless edges grew rough. The alien invader slowed, faltered, and broke into a hailstorm of twitching mirror-scraps. These were saucer grubs, actually quite good to eat.

The paramilitary troops howled with glee, and fired off celebratory blasts from their small arms. Their hot bullets would fall to earth somewhere, often killing civilians. No matter. Graveyards were a useful source for the body-parts. Flying saucers might spurn killing people, but no cosmic rule decreed that the Russians couldn't kill themselves.

"Our best warriors are our dead," remarked Ida, shaking her head.

"Only the dead stay true," said Kalinin. His corps of armed volunteers was dwindling day by day. They shared Ida's sense that the saucers were good. They feared the battle was unwinnable. And the local Ukrainian peasants were filling the warriors with wild tales. Supposedly a salamander-shaped saucer-being had resurrected a farm wife from her grave. The villagers were calling the old woman a saint.

"I do wonder why the saucers are so kind to us," said Ida. "We've done nothing to deserve redemption."

"They're saving us up," said Kalanin. "For a last supper."

Silently Ida studied Kalanin, her expression a mixture of cunning and tenderness. A former painter turned Kremlin intriguer, Ida was Kalinin's state-support liaison in his desperate, unauthorized war. She brought Kalinin black money, grim volunteers, experimental weapons, and deniable orders from the Kremlin.

Kalinin was a veteran of the Russian nuclear-missile corps. During his military career, he'd been at ease with the idea of human beings destroying the Earth. And he felt an instinctive hatred for the flying saucers and their campaign to heal the world. It was a horror to see beings who were immune to human malice.

When the saucers first invaded, Kalinin had been commanding a nuclear launch center. His hydrogen bombs had failed to impress the space invaders. The saucers merely shimmered and swayed through the thermonuclear shockwaves—insolent as striptease dancers. Russian military lasers did nothing to faze them. Particle beams, the same. Meanwhile the other nations were making peace with the aliens.

The Kremlin's Higher Circles had encouraged Kalanin to resign from the Russian army, and to strike out on his own. And now Ida was the only ally he trusted.

A talented portraitist, Ida had at one time enjoyed the intimate patronage of the Russian Minister of the Environment. But then the flying saucers had cruelly dissolved her oligarch's pipelines and nuclear plants. The Minister had shot himself. Casting about for a new role, Ida had found her place as Kalinin's liaison. But now she was ready to move on, and Kalanin knew it. She had a stash of jewelry to help her along. But what about Kalanin?

The nuclear-waste trucks retreated to fetch more garbage. The harsh sun beat upon the rutted earth.

"Let's eat," said Kalanin, and produced a loaf of tainted Chernobyl bread. He cut off a slice with his ever-ready bayonet.

Ida unsheathed a chunk of dried sausage. The meat within its casing was the flesh of a Przewalski horse. Methodically, the couple chewed their meager rations.

"That giant saucer worm likes you," Ida told Kalanin. "You've fed it so much trash that it thinks you're its best friend on Earth."

"I've spoiled the worm, yes," said Kalinin with a thin smile. "It's like a decadent intellectual. A lazy gourmand that never spent a day on duty."

"Don't hate intellectuals, Kalinin. I'm one too. An artist, don't you remember?"

Kalinin's face reddened with a sudden access of rage. "Why do you ally yourself with decadent parasites? They only want to lord it over those who fight!"

"Are they so wrong?" said Ida gently. "Is war so wonderful?"

"We should liquidate any wretch who collaborates with the saucers," cried Kalanin, maddened at the thought of Ida's impending defection. Below his furry hat-brim, his narrow eyes filled with tears. Wildly he ranted. "Spineless bastards! Double-domes! Where's their sense of destiny? Life to them is nothing but hashish and vulvas!"

"Let's suppose the saucers are here to raise everyone's level, dear Kalanin. Come with me now. Let's see how our pet saucer worm has grown on its diet of poison rubbish."

Kalinin and Ida made their way down from their overlook, following the debris-strewn tracks of the diesel trucks. The ragged lip of the former coal-mine was a variegated crust of crushed and flattened junkyard debris, smoldering like an overbaked pie. Moving with care, Ida and Kalinin tottered close to the unstable edge.

"What if a great hero chose this hole as his grave?" mused Ida. "A great man whom the worm loved. Such a hero might single-handedly transform the worm. Just as the mortar-blasted corpse debris transforms the flying saucers." She gave Kalinin a calculating look. "How much do you love me?"

"What are you after?" said Kalanin, stepping back from the hole. The sun was beating on his head. The world seemed to spin around him. The rubble, the fruitless battles, Ida's betrayal.

"It's your best way out of here," said Ida, nudging him forward once more. "Death in battle is a path to immortality. To resurrection, even. I'll bring you back to life, and I'll finally share your bed."

They were at the very brink of the mineshaft, with the rubble shifting and rattling beneath their feet. Below them the gigantic worm stirred, liquid, exultant, entirely happy in its garbage.

Drunk with love, helplessly wanting to impress Ida, Kalinin leapt out into the air and slashed his own throat with his razor-sharp bayonet. He dropped down the shaft amid a spinning gush of blood.

Kalanin hit the bottom so fast that his substance merged into that of the startled saucer worm. And then—so great was the creature's revulsion for human death—it explosively shattered into grubs. The sky-darkening plume of eruption was visible for hundreds of miles.

Ida was unharmed. Quickly and decisively, she took command of the paramilitary rabble—declaring a cease-fire and dismissing them all.

That night she set off for Mumbai, India. Following Kalinin's plume.

§

"Mumbai is the greatest city mankind has ever seen," Puneet remarked to his business associate, Leela. "We nearly wrecked the planet with filth, but that was just our subcontinental exuberance. And now, thanks to the saucers, all is well. Our business is an integral part of Mumbai's greatness."

Leela had brought in a bright stainless-steel tiffin-box full of free-range saucer grubs, fresh from the Ukraine. The edible grubs had blown in on the monsoon winds. They were unusually tasty. Leela offered one to Puneet, who gobbled it with his usual avidity.

Leela and Puneet were from the district of Maharashtra—elite school friends and now in business together. Their initial funding had come from Puneet's prosperous family. Leela and Puneet had rocketed to commercial success by marketing saucer worms as a general house-cleaning product called Kleen Kobras.

The source of the worms? Lucky Puneet had managed to stable a saucer-creature inside a Mumbai warehouse, an anomalous silver being the size and shape of a crocodile. There was no knowing why the creature had approached him, but there it was. He fed it a steady diet of human garbage, and the obliging lizard budded off as many Kleen Kobras as Puneet and Leela could use.

It was Leela who'd thought of selling the worms. An image of the saucer salamander was an integral part of her marketing campaign—it appeared in all the ads. These days in India, there was a fad for all things relating to the beneficent saucers.

"Our trade is indeed bringing us fine success," said Leela. "And now we should seek entree to high society. Philanthropy, Puneet. Highly upscale. We do something momentous for dear old Mumbai, and then we are in the social register."

"A stupendous civic gift," mused Puneet. "With the proviso that we spend no cash. Commercial moguls such as us are too slick for that."

"Agreed," said Leela. "What if you petition our saucer lizard on behalf of Mumbai? Perhaps a public feast upon our worms? Surely the lizard will honor the astral grandiosity of your soul."

"You are a most agreeable woman," said Puneet. He raised his finger. "I have indeed been envisioning a saucer gambit. A grand stroke for urban development. Presenting it as a philanthropy would be genial indeed."

Leela crossed her stockinged legs and opened a paper notebook. "Tell me your raga to riches, Puneet."

Puneet toyed with a cufflink, suddenly shy. But then, warmed by the sun of Leela's smile, he found his voice. "I am proposing that we colonize Mumbai's outlying districts with eleven duplicate copies of the city center."

"*What?*"

"A Dodeca-Mumbai. Twelve supercities united in one magical, intricate graffito of urbanism. We're far too crowded within our one small Mumbai. Once I issue my commands, we'll enjoy a megasprawl of twelve. This is a good thing. The saucer lizard can accomplish it."

"Truly so?" said Leela. "All I've seen the lizard do is hatch Kleen Kobra worms. Exceedingly many of them, yes, but—"

"Our saucer lizard is deeply sensitive to my kundalini," replied Puneet. "The only limits are those within my mind!" Warming to the sound of his own voice, Puneet waved his spotless cotton sleeve at the view from their penthouse office's window. "We'll make the Dodeca-Mumbai of your dreams, Leela."

"But I've dreamed no such thing."

"The lizard and I will cut-and-paste our entire downtown, warping and squeezing where need be."

"And you said—twelve in all?"

"I have conceptualized a keen workflow," said Puneet, glowing with pride. "We copy Mumbai once, and that makes two Mumbais. Then we copy the two Mumbais, so there are four. And then—" Puneet rose from behind his teakwood desk and rapped his Kleen Kobra distribution map with a swagger-stick. "Then we make two fresh copies of the four, arriving at twelve altogether!"

"I understand," said Leela, her expression studiously blank. She would never want the wealthy Puneet to know she thought he was an idiot.

"Imagine our tourism," crowed Puneet. "Our exotic Indian fastness—twelve times as magical as before. Dodecaduplicated by saucer aliens! What a place for a honeymoon."

Leela tapped her front teeth with her mechanical pencil. "But—twelve Mumbais means twelve times the slums. Dodgy to promote."

"We won't be copying the *people* of Mumbai," said Puneet. "Human reproduction is for the likes of you and I. The saucer lizard will only be replicating the infrastructure. Dodeca-Mumbai will have twelve classic Royal Taj Hotels.

Twelve Bombay Stock Exchanges. Twelve Marine Drives. Each and every Mumbai dweller will have twelve times as much room!"

Leela made jotting gestures in her notebook. She gazed up at Puneet, widening her eyes. "Brilliance! The lowest slumdog sleeping on the pavement will prosper as a landlord. Imagine the looks on their faces in Dubai! The Arabs have a mile-high skyscraper, yes, but our metropolis will be twelve times so flat as ever before!"

"It's good to have you as my business soulmate, Leela. Our brainpower is more than doubled. Dodeca-Leela-Puneet!" Puneet paused, studying Leela's fair form. "May I venture another idea? What if we launch the first wave of Dodeca-Mumbai tourism with a fertility festival?"

Leela frowned. "Sex tourism?"

"Nothing so hole-and-corner as that," said Puneet, adjusting his coiffure with his manicured fingertips. "In Dodeca-Mumbai we are looking for the stars." His voice grew soft. "Listen to me, Leela. You and I might inaugurate the fertility festival, should you permit. We two have been selling saucer worms for months. Isn't it time we discovered our mutual humanity? Carnal yet noble—like the conjugal sculptures of Khajuraho. Stirring the milk of life with the cosmic cobra."

"This is a marriage proposal?"

"Who but Leela can be a worthy mate for the architect of Dodeca-Mumbai!"

"Very jolly," said Leela.

Their nuptial ceremony was glamorous and elaborate. But in the midst of greeting the mass of wedding guests, and tying his robe together with Leela's, and circling the sacred nuptial fire—all this while talking to the saucer salamander on his phone—well, Puneet made some slip-ups.

The twelve copies of Mumbai failed to appear. Instead, there was only one copy of Mumbai, botched and glitchy, and shoehorned higgledy-piggledy into the streets and intersections of an existing sector of the town. The intended replica of the core metropolis consisted of 7,777 Royal Taj hotels.

These sumptuous and vacant lodgings were immediately set upon by the angry Indians whose access streets had been built over. They now had to climb over the tops of buildings to get in and out of their homes. The citizens didn't know whom to blame for their urban mishap, but they knew they'd been disadvantaged by some typical big-city swindle. Some of them settled into the massed new hotels' million-plus rooms. Others began diligently stripping out carpets, doorknobs, towels, soap, and brass bathroom fixtures.

Adroitly dodging the burst of public anger, Puneet and Leela crept incognito into one of the 7,777 bridal suites. They were drained by their intricate marriage ceremony—and dejected over Puneet's bungling. Their initial attempt at sexual congress was desultory.

"Let's lie low," said Puneet, sprawling on the wadded satin sheets. "Until the Mumbai corruption squads become bored with searching for scapegoats. Our fresh new married life should be about propriety, stability and impeccable Hindu values. No more saucer grubs. Just rice, coriander and chamomile tea."

Leela clumsily adjusted her incendiary wedding-night nylon-and-satin lingerie, which was a rumpled splash of sexy vermilion in the hotel's saffron sheets. "I can write a press release blaming the Dodeca-Mumbai mix-up on that plume of grubs from the Ukraine. I've been in touch with a Russian woman who just arrived from there. She noticed our saucer lizard logo and she wants to meet the lizard herself. She has some odd notion about rebirth. Anyway, she's offering me diamond earrings."

"Birth?" said Puneet, always a half-step behind. "This reminds me of the fertility festival I'd mentioned. All singing, all-dancing, very fine. I'll take the stage and announce that my new bride is on the way to bearing me a son and heir! Thereby bringing us sympathy. The sooner the better, Leela."

"I knew you would request this, Puneet, but the time is not right. I'm a successful businesswoman, embroiled with international intrigue."

Puneet raised a chiding finger. "Human fertility is the one blessing that flying saucers can never bring! You must bear us two sons, seven, twelve!"

Leela immediately locked herself in the suite's large bathroom.

"What are you doing in there?" called Puneet plaintively.

"All will be well, dear husband," said Leela. Her voice was indistinct through the heavy, gilt door. "I'm consulting expert counsel."

Time passed. Puneet watched television, which consisted entirely of 20th century satellite reruns from China and Brazil. And now someone was pounding on the hallway door. Puneet opened up to find an attractive white woman standing there. She had smooth, pale skin, a lustrous bob of dark hair, and a writhing, bandage-wrapped package cradled in both her arms. It resembled a mummified crocodile.

"Did you lose this?" said Ida, in Russian-accented English.

"That's mine!" cried Puneet. "That's my magic saucer lizard, it's the source of all my business!"

The Russian woman tenderly set the writhing mummy onto the marital bed.

Leela unlocked the bathroom door and pranced into the hotel suite. She was still in her wedding lingerie, and had tidied her hair and make-up.

"This is the Russian woman you were talking about?" Puneet asked Leela.

"I phoned her for help," said Leela.

"Help with what?" said Puneet. "We were doing fine here! We just got married!"

"Does that make you the master of life and death?" put in Ida, rolling her glorious eyes in disdain. "While you frolic in satin sheets, a Russian hero gave his life for mankind!" She turned to Leela. "Open the windows. A miracle is at hand. A redemption. A resurrection."

Leela obeyed at once. The low, city-lit clouds were roiling with dark energy, swirling with an almighty monsoon of flying scraps and silver shreds. Ukrainian saucer grubs hailed in through the open windows, mounding upon the twitching silver crocodile in the bed. The grubs merged into a mass that split open, and—

"A son for me?" cried Puneet.

No. It was Kalinin. His eyes glowed like the staring orbs of a painted Byzantine icon.

"Oh darling," said Ida, hurrying forward and kissing his pale lips.

"We're going to America," said Kalanin, pulling free.

§

Ida and Kalinin walked hand-in hand down a water-front street in the grotty south end of San Francisco. It was a fine summer night, nearly dawn, with a full moon on the horizon. They'd been to an art party. There had been wine. And a smorgasbord of barbecued saucer grubs.

"I love the sight of saucers now," said Kalinin, gazing into the haunted, moonlit sky. He still had his beaky nose and his high cheekbones. His teeth were straighter than before, and he spoke English. His passage through the phantom world of the saucer-beings had changed him other, less definable ways. He said odd things, and he had a heavy aura.

Kalinin had told Ida that he was one of twelve res-urrected saucer saints—twelve saints scattered across the surface of the Earth—and that he could hear the voices of the other saints within his head at all times. But Ida and Kalinin kept these secrets from those around them. They walked among humankind like an ordinary woman and man.

Silvered by the low moon, a nearby saucer's energetic surface was a ceaseless flurry of subtle, mercurial patterns, like wave-chop, or like the scales of a swimming fish.

"You always understood them better than anyone else, Kalinin," said Ida. "Do they plan to annihilate us? Is that why they sent you back?"

"They're refining us," said Kalinin. "Like ore within a crucible. Like vapor in an alembic. Life and death are phil-osophical mistakes."

"Sometimes I miss the old Kalinin," said Ida. "It was noble to be so stubborn. Fighting the inevitable, no matter what."

"Discarded dross," said Kalinin. "Economics, government, military power—nonsensical, distorted, irrelevant." Imposing as he seemed to others, when he gazed at Ida, his eyes were as warm as ever before. "Love remains. Art is the path to the final unification."

"Everyone at the party was saying things like that," said Ida, shrugging her bared shoulders in her shining gown. "People are so full of themselves in America! They talk as if they were demigods, but what do they do? They crank themselves up on grubs and watch someone's thousand-hour video in ten minutes."

"A mirage that flies by, half-seen, half-sensed," said Kalanin. "The saucers want a richer kind of art. They want us to change the world."

"But Kalinin, what if the saucers are like children who poke sticks into anthills to watch the ants seethe? The ants build and build, they strive and strive—but are any of them famous artists?"

"We'll craft a great work of ant," said Kalanin.

"Everyone at the party was talking about totem poles," said Ida. "In the old days, the Native Americans of the northwest carved faces on sticks with stone knives. That was their art. But then, one day—one strange day—the sailing ships came to them, and strangers brought them steel axes. How did they respond? They made huge totem pole logs, from Oregon to Alaska!"

"Totem poles," said Kalinin slowly. "Yes. Of course. Totem poles are good."

"But the story is tragic! The old world that the natives knew by heart became someone else's New World. A world of syphilis and smallpox, with the totem poles stored in museums."

"The grubs are our steel axes," said Kalanin.

"Why don't the saucers speak to us, Kalinin? Will they let us join their world? Can we join the Higher Circles of galactic citizenship?"

Kalinin gave a dry laugh. "Higher than the Kremlin."

They walked along in silence for a few minutes, bringing their minds into synch. They even got a levitation thing going, loping along in long strides, laughing at each other.

"You see it too?" said Kalanin, coming to a stop, panting for breath. "You'll make a painting. Monumental. And then—"

"The end of the world," said Ida. "Brought to you by a crazy woman who made her crazy boyfriend slit his own throat with a bayonet."

"And who brought him back to life. This is holy, Ida. No need to joke."

Ida held out her hands. "I laugh because I'm scared."

The two of them embraced, lit by the moon and the silver saucers and the first rays of the rising sun. A gentle puff of breeze came off the bay.

"I'll paint now," said Ida.

"Paint everything," said Kalanin. "Can it fit?"

"I'll use—poetic compression," replied Ida. "Room to spare."

She raised her arms and the skies opened. Tens of thousands of saucer grubs rained down upon her. Some of the grubs became brushes, others formed pools of paint.

Ida and her living brushes set to work, painting on the street, on the sidewalks, on the nearby warehouse walls, Ida swinging her arm from the shoulder, carving sweeps of color and form. Her loose strokes limned buildings and people and trees. She depicted the insides of the buildings as well as the outsides, and the meanings of the things to be found in there, and the lives of those who'd made the things.

"Be sure to include an image of your painting," urged Kalinin.

Ida nodded, uninterruptedly busy, sharpening the identities of her scribbles and blots. A tight spiral of darkly energetic grubs began converging onto a certain section of her mural. Ida was crafting a secondary world-mural within the main one.

Just like the main mural, the secondary mural held a image of the entire world. And within it you could see a third mural, with a yet tinier fourth mural inside that, and so on and on.

"Keep going," said Kalinin.

"We've only begun," said Ida. Flecks of paint bedizened her bobbed dark hair like stars in a night sky.

Kalinin closed his eyes and his lips moved. Rays of light flickered into life, one of them stellating out from Ida's regress—the others from points across the globe.

Twelve poles of supernal light, needles of prismatic brilliance, radiating into the cosmos, dissolving the substance of our world. Bathing in its native glow, the Earth became a silver, dodecahedral orb, a mysterious cosmic traveler.

§

"I like this potlatch," said Dirt Complaining.

"The best ever," Dirt Harkening agreed.

Notes on "Totem Poles"

Tor.com.
Written June - December, 2014.

Rudy on "Totem Poles"

"Totem Poles" began with me emailing Bruce about how the advent of European traders with steel axes had set the Northwest First Nations people to making large totem poles in the early 1900s, and about how the Europeans then crushed the tribal cultures. I wanted to create an analogous SF scenario in which cryptic aliens arrive and give us radically powerful creative tools with catastrophic consequences.

To get things rolling, I sent Bruce a scene featuring a woman painter in San Francisco. Bruce responded with a scene about a male Russian soldier and a female Russian administrator. Also a scene with two dead First Nations people talking. We couldn't immediately see a good way to connect the scenes. For the next few revisions we kept tweaking each other's scenes and repairing our own scenes.

We also toyed with the idea of adding on more scenes, wondering if we might make the story itself a kind of totem pole—and Bruce came up with a scene in India involving a man and a woman. At this point we'd done six versions of the story.

I did an extreme push, thinking about the story day and night until I'd found a plausible through-line for our tale. At this point, I was the woman painter and the woman Russian—who by now were the same person. Bruce was the Russian soldier. I thought the story was finished. Bruce approved of what I'd done, but even so he made changes—and so the process went on. We did four more revisions. It didn't feel like we were converging. Bruce said it was like we were baking bread while floating in thin air. Or like we were cartoonists creating a jam strip for *Zap Comix*.

After version eleven, Bruce said he didn't want to work on the story anymore, but that he didn't think it was properly finished. I viewed this as my opportunity for an unsupervised final cut. I went into a blood-lust revision frenzy, and sent the resulting version twelve to the editor Patrick Nielsen Hayden at *Tor.com*. Patrick's quick response: "This may be the weirdest thing we'll have published yet, but I like it and I want it." *Whew*. I was glad for this validation.

So, okay, *Tor.com* paid us for the story, but then a year went by, and they kept not actually publishing it, who knows why, and then it was time for *Transreal Cyberpunk* to appear in our antho, and I'm finalizing this note, and I'm not sure if *Tor.com* is going to post the story or not. I've been having a hard time getting info out of them. Oh well! I'll update this info in a later edition...

Anyway, I think "Totem Poles" is trippy and cool, with a couple of great shock-cut scenes, and a lot of different levels working in it. Bruce wan't happy with the story, but you can decide for yourself.

By the way, "Totem Poles" was our fourth story in a row that ends with the world as we know it coming to an end. Kind of tells you something about where we're at. In the evening of our lives.

Bruce on "Totem Poles"

Rudy and I have been at it quite a while, so for "Totem Poles" we had little in the way of conceptual framework, and decided just to jam around a loose theme, and see what happened. The result was a violently disordered series of drafts which were rather more interesting than the resultant final text. You sort of had to be there, and nobody else was there, so, well, no one else will ever know how brilliant this scheme was; all we've got left is this burnt soufflé from a kitchen on fire.

"Totem Poles" is formally interesting, but it strongly reminds me of one of those Brian Eno "curiosities" recordings where Eno sets up loops and tracks on his hacked equipment and then deserts the studio to go ponder Long Now clocks. I happen to be quite the Brian Eno fan, and I will cheerfully forgive Professor Eno most anything, but even Jove nods. "Totem Poles" is our worst story. It's the most disjointed and threadbare of our works, but it does have the virtue of revealing our compositional methods. If you can work your way through the haze of free-jazz distortion, you might see us flinging our favorite fantasy-riffs, Jackson-Pollack style, splattering onto the page. We were making soup from a single iron nail, and the two quarreling chefs smashed every spice-rack in sight.

Although it's morbid, "Totem Poles" doesn't feel like a proper conclusion to anything; on the contrary, it feels like a teenage garage band rehearsal for something that might become really good, after a thousand hours of practice. I hope we write at least one more story. We may not have the time, but we've got the power. *Ars longa, vita brevis*, folks.

Kraken and Sage

Early in his career, Jorge Jones turned himself into a supercomputer. By deftly biohacking the Golgi apparatus and mitochondria power molecules of his cells, Jorge brought every part of his body into his mental network. With a little hacker yoga, he pushed his mathematical thinking out of his busy brain-matter, down his spine and nervous system, and into the flexing meat of his muscles and tendons. He used his fat cells for data storage.

Soon after this feat, Jorge's activated ponderings allowed him to create an organic programming tool he called the Hydra. A user could design a Hydra program, download the code into a customizable virus known as the "Jones Flu," and then infect some hapless plant or animal to carry out whatever strange demands possessed the programmer.

Thanks to the Hydra, life on Earth could be forced to serve Mammon's passing whim.

Whales carried passengers. Sheep grew colored wool. Jones flu cows were milk-emitting silos, big enough to live in. Feverish chickens could fire up within their insulating feathers and roast themselves on the spot. Exquisite glass bottles grew upon winery vines, slowly filling themselves with champagne. Clean water and snug shelter were as trivial as disposable phones.

The Jorge Jones Hydra was the dominant, global-scale tool of biotech—patented, licensed, and the only platform of its kind. The Hydra supported armies of engineers, divisions of lawyers, battalions of designers, and conspiracies of investors. A stack, a network, a global octopus.

Then the bubble burst.

§

It was a misty morning in the mountains, blessedly quiet. Jorge Jones was surrounded by living timber, graciously bent to his will. His possessions were few, but perfect: a polished wooden bowl, a voluptuously curved chair, a carved table, a horn spoon, and garments of down and spider-silk. Jorge Jones, the guru of organic computation, had no more need for copper, silicon, or plastic.

Other than his organically programmed crows and squirrels—and the occasional freebooter nuthatch, woodpecker, or beetle—the visitors to Jorge's sequoia tree were few and far between, and he liked life that way. Jorge Jones liked life to go entirely his own way. And he still had his Hydra working for him.

He'd infected his crows with the Jones flu virus, and they ferried raisin bran to him. And he'd coaxed this sequoia tree into hollowing out a spacious two-story apartment within its massive trunk. A hidden cave, with a few choice pieces of elegant temperfoam Milanese furniture, and a generous balcony with swirling art-deco railings. Design was important to Jorge. His last marriage had broken up over his wife's horrid appliance choices.

So here he was, after the revolution, living alone in his sequoia—in an ascended state of computation and meditation. He'd become a sage of pure science and lofty conceptual metaphysics, with no annoying legal, ethical, social, economic, or military complications. He was finally free of nagging hassles from his best friend, or more likely his worst enemy, Frank Sharp.

But even in the trackless, bird-chirping depths of the redwood forest, Jorge could never get Sharp's wiseguy voice entirely out of his head. "Why not turn your dog into a methane tank?" Sharp had said once. "And burn its farts for a space heater."

But Jorge's dear old dog was long dead now. Jorge had become a forest sage, and he had no time for Sharp's worldly antics any more, nor for any mundane thing that wasn't serious.

§

A foggy spot of light bumbled around in the damp, green branches of his primeval tree.

This glowing apparition moved with a considered urgency, like the Zen butterfly that never hastens, even when pursued. It drifted on the air like ancient plankton—a floating thing of many soccer-ball facets, a gleaming polyhedron. Its planes were wobbly and bubbly, a stripped-down, minimal, ultra-primitive life-form, its grip on life so tentative that a bubble-pop would annihilate it.

Slowly yet steadily, the luminous herald drew closer, tracing a path through the three-dimensional maze of Jorge's great tree. The uncanny cyst was feeling its way toward him with wiry, delicate cilia that writhed from its tinted geometric corners.

The plankton-bubble bumped the sharp tip of a broken branch. Jorge held his breath, but the blob didn't burst. Those shining membranes were tougher than they looked.

Jorge grew uneasy, watching the creature draw closer. No use trying to enjoy his morning tea and cereal. The floating entity was homing in on him. But who knew that he lived thirty meters up a tree in the middle of nowhere? Even the government spooks who'd spirited him to this mountain redoubt had agreed to forget about him. Frank Sharp had arranged that deal.

§

Frank Sharp, dealmaker. Not exactly a government agent, not exactly a criminal, not exactly a lawyer. Frank presented himself to the world as a high-paid consultant, offering services worldwide to high-tech industries who'd lost their way in the tangled jungles of humanity.

Jorge called out to the shining, airborne bubble. "Frank Sharp? No more schemes. You have nothing I want."

In response, the lantern-like creature dipped and drew closer, its facets swirling with color. And just then something touched Jorge on the back of his neck.

"Fuck!" screamed Jorge, whirling around, all traces of sagely aplomb gone.

It was a second levitating polyhedron, all in shades of black and gray. This dark floater had crept up from behind him in utter dewy silence, arriving at Jorge's bare neck with the stealth of a vampire bat. And this one was indeed the avatar of Frank Sharp, hired to escort the first blob, the colorful one. Step by computational step, that first bubble shaped itself into a model of the head of Jorge's former student, Betty Yee.

§

Delicate, intelligent, and more plain than beautiful, Betty Yee was a techie of the Pacific Rim. Although her floating head was merely a mockup made of taut organic membranes, Betty had her usual expression: an ingratiating yet self-serving look. Betty had always been ambitious to change the world in her own direction.

"I'm honored to meet you again, Dr. Jones," said the floating head of Betty Yee. "A wild storm, then a day of sun! Seeing you lifts my heart."

"You know my policy about leaving the world behind," Jorge scolded. "I told you my plans back at the Stanford Biological Accelerator."

"Yo, yo, yo!" yelled the dark Frank Sharp floater, maneuvering to wedge in bubble-like between Jorge and the head of Betty Yee. "Don't forget what she did to you, professor! She robbed your lab and stole your ideas."

"You said you would let me explain the crisis to him," admonished Betty Yee.

"I said I would let you plead, yes," said the Frank Sharp floater. "If Gold Lucky pays by the minute. And the clock started when our bubbles drifted up this tree."

"I can be brief," said Betty Yee. "Dear, good, wise Doctor Jones: you changed the world. In China, we adopted your changes to our methods. We embraced them, we extended them. Mistakes were made."

"Back up," said Jorge. "Did Frank just say he was renting me out by the minute?"

"We must have your help in Shenzhen. We've aroused a dangerous computational form of life. We set that process running—now we can't shut it off without your skill."

"I named this new outbreak the Kraken," Frank confided. "After Tennyson's poem. The primordial sleeping monster of the deep. Roused by the folly of man. Arising for the end of human days."

Jorge's gaze flicked between the pretty glowing lantern and the vampire bubble that had poked him. "Betty, why are you bobbling around with this guy? Don't you know any better?"

"Gold Lucky Company hired Mr. Sharp as our connection man," Betty confessed. "It was the only way that I could find you in time to save the world."

"Her problem is giant monsters made of intelligent mud," said Frank.

Betty Yee nodded her floating head. "Awkward."

Jorge considered the situation. "What's in this for me?"

"Let me explain that face to face," Frank offered. "Betty's not around here, because she's fighting for her life in the Shenzhen disaster zone. As for me, though, I'm running this floating bubble while I'm actually standing right down at the base of your tree."

Frank Sharp had arrived in the flesh. There had never been one episode when that situation hadn't turned out to be crap.

§

Jorge's windlass wheel was powered by three hundred organically computing squirrels. Once Betty's Chinese bubble had burst in a glowing patch of slime, the rodents set to work with brisk muscular efficiency. They were a jostling tide of fur inside the squeaking wheel. The sequoia's little-used wooden lift cage hauled Frank Sharp straight up the trunk.

His character armor well in place, Frank Sharp stepped into the treehouse and raised his elegant brows. "It's a privilege to visit your sequoia retreat, Jorge. I know you deserve your serenity, after all we've been through together. I told the big boys back at the Agency, I told 'em: yo, we can't squeeze blood out of a redwood stump. Let Professor Jones be. He's old, he's lost it, he's pretty near death. Forget him. We'll find some younger math genius who can avert this Lovecraft-scale catastrophe."

Jorge looked at his stained fingertips, seeing them very clearly just now. They were dirty, with a glossy sheen over the dirt. A bum's hands. He hadn't bathed or shaved in days, or maybe weeks. Was his chosen life so great? Frank Sharp, by contrast, looked like he'd just stepped out of a five-star hotel lobby.

"*What* other genius?" Jorge said.

"Oh, well, we both know about you math guys. You always do your best work before thirty."

"Maybe so, but we live to be a hundred," countered Jorge. "Can you tell me again who you're working for this time?"

"I work for the high-enders on any given day," smiled Frank. "Whenever an industry peaks, they start to die—so they call in a futurist. I serve them their final cheese course."

"Me, I'm not an industry anymore," said Jorge sourly. "I'm a lonely, resentful old man with some broken patents."

"That's all thanks to Betty Yee and geopolitics. Be fair, Jorge, it was never easy to keep a guy like you out of prison or the nuthouse."

Jorge glared at Frank. "Before you showed up here in my sequoia tree, I had a chance to end my days in dignity."

"What the hell do you with yourself, way up here? Besides feeding your squirrels."

"I perform gedankenexperiments," said Jorge. "I confront great conundrums that can only be resolved by sheer Einstein-style chin-stroking."

Sharp stared blankly into the gently waving redwood foliage, baffled by this assertion. Finally he shrugged. "Fine! Feel sorry for yourself. Sulk. Me, I'm a man of the world, okay? Because if I don't take power, I'm a dirt-common schnook. I'm the nameless ox that dies in harness. Cut to the chase, Jorge. Save the world for me. I need the world."

Jorge had a crushing rejoinder ready, but when he saw the obscure pain haunting Sharp's darting, dishonest eyes, a moment of sagely compassion touched him. Despite all that had happened between the two of them, he found it within himself to know pity.

"All right, Frank. We should love the world. Keep your world off my back, and I'll debug your problems on principle."

§

The disaster-stricken city of Shenzhen was entirely closed to air traffic and internet access. An industrial region beset with giant mud monsters had to clamp down on unharmonious thinking. However, Frank Sharp, hired Chinese agent, was able to lay out the full, uncensored story for the ears of Jorge Jones, global disaster consultant.

While working R&D for the potent Gold Lucky Corp, Betty Yee had abused Jorge's patented technology of organic computation in a self-referential and radically improper manner.

Gold Lucky had planned to recreate the so-called "Cambrian Explosion" of Earthly evolution—an ancient geologic epoch, reborn in the form of creatures generated by Jorge's organic computations. Let a thousand mutants bloom. Gold Lucky's software engineers, feverish at the prospect of productivity bonuses, had imagined that they might extract a master program from China's enormous Big Data fossil record of primeval worm tracks, ammonite shells and algae stains. This was a straightforward matter of collating the entire Cambrian fossil record and stochastically interpreting the fossils as ideograms.

Unfortunately, this brilliant scheme, like most software startups, had been an abject bust.

When Betty Yee took over the research program, she went much smaller, more nano-scale. She focused on a special class of fossils known as "stromatolites." Stromatolites were pancaked stacks of calcified primitive algae.

Betty's efforts revealed that these fossilized microbial mats were a computational archive. The fossil stromatolites were the historical record of millions of years of super-advanced single-celled life—a full core-dump, source-code, and stack-trace for the primeval cellular-automata soup that had covered planet Earth for nameless geologic eons, long before nature had evolved any spines, mouths or bones.

The dense primeval brew, the oldest form of life on earth, had been a hot and sour soup of computation.

Of course no one had believed Betty's science findings, so she'd boldly ported this fossilized database straight into the Gold Lucky medicated-mud factory. Then everybody believed, because behold: the Kraken awoke.

§

Frank and Jorge were quickly ushered past customs in Shenzhen, because no mere functionaries were allowed to inspect Jorge's latest version of his Hydra tool—newly revamped for battlefield action. Betty Yee met them with an armored Chinese limousine.

"Why did you publish that paper in the *Hong Kong Journal of Genomics* about stochastic flows across membrane diffusors?" Jorge promptly demanded. "Was it to break my patents?" He'd been brooding over the issue during the long trans-Pacific flight.

"Then you remember my work!" said Betty Yee. She sounded pleased, but in person she looked careworn. Betty was dressed in standard global nerd style: pink jeans, white athletic shoes, a sweatshirt with a corny graphic, a purple windbreaker. Her hair was newly streaked with gray and she had dry crowsfeet at her temples.

"My patents were not about commercial advantage," lectured Jorge. "I put the patents there to protect this world from things men were not meant to know."

"Your patents weren't stopping anyone," said Betty. "Especially not your National Security Agency and our Chinese cyberwar units. While you've been living in your tall woods like an exiled Taoist poet, everyone here in China has been building Hydra units for years."

Jorge locked eyes with his former student. He was angry, but she steadily returned his gaze. As man and woman, they were of different generations and had once had an entirely decent, productive teacher-student relationship. However, many years had passed. Betty had become a woman of discretion, while Jorge, although ancient, was not entirely dead to male lust.

"Yo, what's up with the stromatolite codes?" Frank interrupted, seeking some normalized conversation.

Betty blinked and cleared her throat. "Imagine the unthinkable patience of plankton, passing endless yugas under the sun," she offered. "The legacy of the living Earth before plants and animals. Much like the placid, stable, civilized Middle Kingdom, before the West showed up and wrecked the Confucian utopia."

"A nanotech-style gray-goo singularity is a legacy?" said Frank Sharp. "Like, thanks a lot."

"The singularity was never ahead of us," said Betty. "It was always behind us. On hold, deep in the limestone strata."

§

In the distance, towards the battered metropolis, the Chinese earth shook with disaster. Hoarse and loud. Military observation planes were flying in slow circles. Dozens of helicopters swarmed overhead—some of them napalm bombers, some of them carrying tanks of water and fire retardant, some of them medics carrying off the wounded.

The armored robot limo rolled with cybernetic slickness toward the Gold Lucky plant, swerving to avoid the bomb craters in the road, skirting the slumped rubble of charred, collapsed buildings, sometimes taking a detour to avoid the urban structures that were still in flames. The earlier airstrikes were releasing their bent, stinking billows into the glowering sky, spark-filled pillars of dust and toxic urban smoke.

The first Kraken mud-monster caught Jorge and Frank by surprise, stepping out from behind a glass office building, like a threatening ghoul in a funhouse ghost ride. And then another, another and another, ten meters, twenty meters, thirty meters tall. Although they were faceless and eyeless, the Kraken monsters were very alive. They stank powerfully of digestion and sewage.

They walked the terrified Earth, huge, slimy, shaggy, bipedal golems of computational mud, flaking off writhing chunks in the crude shapes of horseshoe crabs, scorpions, sea worms, sea cucumbers. The cellular computers were recruiting modern germs from the local peasants' synergistic duck, fish, and pig manure ponds. And the monsters promptly assimilated any bewildered animals or hapless human locals that fell into their slimy grip.

"They're made of smart cells, embedded in flowing mud," said Betty Yee. "They compute in parallel. Each cell processes food scents and physical contacts. Gradients of wetness and light. I released them from the fossil stones with Professor Jones's language for organic computation. I freed the Kraken with a Chinese Hydra, and now, I know: mistakes were made."

The slick clay golems rose up much faster than the angry choppers could burn them down to Chinese porcelain. A herd of the salty, reeking, stop-action claymation monsters rumbled past and over the limousine, powerful on their vast dented legs. The Kraken monsters were huge, and with every astounding step on the Chinese soil, they grew visibly bigger.

Frank straightened his tie and gave a thin smile. "Betty, your military attacks don't even hurt their feelings." His exquisitely tailored, black suit made the leather of the limo look cheap. "They're generating body forms like they're leafing through Charles Darwin and highlighting the hot parts."

"Let us join the welcome banquet at the Gold Lucky plant," Betty recited. "We must formulate a war plan."

§

The Gold Lucky welcome banquet was a spartan emergency lunch where terrified employees wolfed down cold noodles from stamped aluminum bowls.

"Jorge here can degrade, attrit, and suppress your Krakens, I have no doubt," Frank Sharp told Betty Yee. "The American press calls him the John von Neumann of organic computation."

"Do you still read the American press?" said Betty doubtfully.

"That's not what matters," said Frank, deftly chopsticking his chilly ramen. "Because Jonny von Neumann was a shadowy, zoned out guy who was in there, at the start, with the players. Von Neumann created the first digital computer. Also, the first atomic bomb. That's the American way: throw the big brainiac at the big problem. Save the moral indignation for when you can pay for it. One man against the universe. Just keep moving his bar, extending his finish line, until he comes up with some ecstatic, dreadful breakthrough that can cap it all. If he fails, and his brain turns to slush in his hospital bed, that's all part of his legend."

Betty decanted a plastic squeeze bottle of hot-sauce into her lukewarm noodle bowl. "Why do you say such painful things, Frank?" she said, meeting his eyes. "Dr. Jorge Jones is a great man. You torment him. You mock him. Why?"

"Free speech won't kill a great man," said Frank. "Your mud monsters might kill him."

"You know what killed von Neumann?" said Jorge. "The hydrogen bomb tests. He had to go and gawk at all of them, he didn't have the sense to stay home."

For two minutes they ate in silence.

There were certain matters that Jorge Jones and Frank Sharp never talked about. Like the treason charge that had hung for years over Jorge's head, for his ruining spook encryption with his massive stash of secret and heretofore unknown prime numbers. Through a Byzantine legal maneuver, Sharp had finally gotten the hacker charges dismissed.

As a quid pro quo, the secrets of the Hydra, Jorge's programming tool, had been handed over to the Washington security establishment. Jorge himself, legally scot-free, and carefully stripped of any possible role in government, business or academe, had been given control of a nice, tall sequoia tree in a quiet, misty, federal park.

An ingenious secret arrangement, but of course it could not last. The vampire that was power might be buried, but then every living thing around it would rot. The Hydra's design specs and its proprietary control software, had been released by a malcontent at the NSA. Or else hacked by Chinese military disguised as computer-science students. Or maybe just sold off by Frank Sharp, who rarely asked for more than ten percent on a deal.

All that pain and trouble to keep things tight and shipshape, and the genie still blew out of the bottle. The genie whistled howling through the bottleneck and flew worldwide on the cloudy winds. They were like that, genies.

"John von Neumann transformed this world, and so did I," said Jorge over the candied bean cakes. "If some obscure Hungarian exile can turn America into an atomic, computational superpower, then it'll be easy for me to obliterate Chinese Kraken monsters with my Hydra." Jorge wiped his mouth and set down his chopsticks. "So what? The reward for being a low-empathy know-it-all."

Sensing Jorge's moment of self-doubt, Frank leaned forward over the flimsy folding table. "To live alone, a man must be very like a god—or very like a wild beast."

"This Chinese banquet wasn't supposed to have a cheese course," said Jorge.

"Our conversation would be easier if you'd ever studied literature," said Frank. "Politicians adore the classic quotes from ancient Greek. But for you, old geek: what is it? Differential equations?"

Jorge stared him down. "Being rescued by you is worse than prison."

Betty Yee looked from one to the other. "Gentlemen, we have a problem in the field."

§

Shenzhen had been a prosperous city where an industrious people pursued their own happiness and minded their own business. Now it looked like Godzilla's birthday cake.

Betty Yee herded Frank and Jorge into a robot helicopter, which promptly rose aloft. "I feel so ashamed," she announced. "The world would be a happier place if this had only happened in Washington instead. Where you vainly seek to control the rest of us. And where men like Frank Sharp make dirty money."

"I am the king-hell futurist!" barked Frank Sharp over the noise of the rotors. "You wanted to bring in Jorge Jones, the sage of organic computation, you had to suit up a cowboy first! Take us to the front lines!"

During the brief flight, Jorge hastily prepared the Hydra that he'd brought along. Jorge's Hydra had four bright blue eyes set into its waist, and a working mouth inside its ring of eight tentacles. Each tentacle had an opening at its tip for puffing out viral spores. This Hydra's interface consisted of EEG patches that could monitor Jorge's brain impulses and thus, to some extent, read his thoughts. Jorge wore the Hydra atop his head.

"Fun," said the Hydra, settling into place. Its inhuman voice was high and cheerful.

"Good boy," said Jorge, brushing tentacles from his eyes.

A battlefield was a young man's arena, but in a cyberwar an old man was ferocious. Firing from the chopper with the advantages of air supremacy, Jorge destroyed twenty-five of the Krakens in rapid succession, poofing them with aerial squirts of Hydra mist. The Krakens crumbled below him like sandcastles in the tide. The remaining monsters absorbed this battlefield fact on the ground. Stumbling and lumbering, they retreated, redesigned themselves, and returned to combat.

The second wave of mud golems were armored lumps. They resembled dog-sized trilobites and cow-sized ankylosaurus dinos—each with a spiky ball on its tail. There was even one ghastly thing like a rolling, gawping human head that, Frank Sharp boldly insisted, was clearly modeled on himself.

Solving the relevant reaction-diffusion equations in his head, Jorge reprogrammed his Hydra's viral mist—and began picking off Krakens again. He'd fly low, get close to one of them, and *poof*.

Frank Sharp began yelling unwanted advice, a target observer calling the shots on the slaughter. "Zap that one who's a crooked pig, melt that ugly sucker looks like a snail, and then get the slobbering kangaroo. God, they're ugly!"

Then, with covert suddenness, there were no more Krakens in sight.

"I seriously doubt this is—mission accomplished," said Jorge. "With me killing them and Frank insulting them, these Cambrian mud monsters are going to want to build a Kraken a kilometer high."

But for now all was calm.

§

Back at Gold Lucky's damaged, smoke-stinking headquarters, the uniformed employees were gleefully celebrating Jorge's swift victory with rounds of sorghum liquor. Betty shyly proffered an attache case loaded with high denomination bills.

"That'll do for earnest money," said Frank, stuffing the sheaves of money into his pigskin bag.

"The Chinese invented paper money," said Betty. "The old ways are simple and strong."

"It's world-changing stuff, money," nodded Frank. "A shame what Jorge did to crypto-money and electronic funds transfer. I warned him to knock it off with that prime-number research, but he was a wild man. Jorge had no brakes, in his younger days. He didn't even know what brakes were."

The victory party was as brief as a stock-market rally. A short distance from the corporate HQ, the Krakens' roaring and burbling had resumed.

"Oh wow," said Jorge, realizing something."I've been dissolving them, but their spores become seeds. They rise back up like a battalion of Chinese clay soldiers!"

"I'm losing the thread here, Jorge," Frank complained. "Plankton, stromatolites, horseshoe crabs, trilobites, dinosaurs—everything but jellyfish and ants. And now it's clay soldiers?"

Betty was regaining her confidence. "Our brave pilots are improving with the napalm. Although the Kraken is made of germs that compute, germs are just germs. We can't lose with Professor Jones and his Hydra."

"Thing is," put in Frank Sharp. "It's the Hydra itself that's the real Kraken. The Hydra, metaphorically, is the American Kraken."

Jorge wanted to protest, but Frank forestalled him with an upraised hand.

"Consider the prophetic words of *The Kraken*, by Alfred, Lord Tennyson," said Frank, in full lecture mode. "I shall quote this visionary Victorian work *in extenso*."

Below the thunders of the upper deep,
Far, far beneath in the abysmal sea,
His ancient, dreamless, uninvaded sleep
The Kraken sleepeth: faintest sunlights flee
About his shadowy sides; above him swell
Huge sponges of millennial growth and height;
And far away into the sickly light,
From many a wondrous grot and secret cell
Unnumbered and enormous polypi
Winnow with giant arms the slumbering green.
There hath he lain for ages, and will lie
Battening upon huge sea worms in his sleep,
Until the latter fire shall heat the deep;
Then once by man and angels to be seen,
In roaring he shall rise and on the surface die."

A ringing silence followed.

"Only a fatuous English major would call a Kraken a metaphor," said Jorge, fighting his way clear of Tennyson's spell. "Organic computation is real."

"Scientist," spat Frank Sharp. "Robot."

Betty Yee was upset. "You foolish men will never save China. Why do you quarrel as if our catastrophe is all about you?"

"Frank should *become* the Kraken, if he thinks it's poetry," said Jorge. "Would make me laugh. You, a Kraken, like a trademarked balloon of hot air in a Thanksgiving parade."

"Is this the sage of computation talking?" said Frank Sharp. "You're no sage, you're California granola, Jorge, you're a nut, a fruit, and a flake. All the time kvetching like some granny who spilled tea on her embroidery."

"We'll see," said Jorge, sending cool, War-of-the-Worlds-alien type thoughts into his personal Hydra unit, still hibernating atop his head. "We'll see who spills what."

He puffed a newly programmed cloud of viruses into the room.

Frank Sharp tried to hold his breath, failed, grew apoplectic. "What are you doing? That stinks."

"We'll feel feverish for a few minutes," said Jorge. "And then we're good. Jones flu. The new subprogram will give us somatic compatibility with the Krakens. That way, even if it devours us, we'll retain autonomy."

"Can we get back to the fighting now?" asked Betty Yee. "Our tanks are waiting."

"Take us to where the Krakens roar."

§

Their armored tank clanked across a kilometer of wasteland to their next battlefield encounter.

This time Betty had brought along her own Chinese-built knock-off of the Hydra. She was getting maybe a little dubious about the military merits of Frank and Jorge. Her rig was a full two meters long, a stumpy torpedo, with twelve snaky viral-spore-puffing tentacles at one end.

"I like the look of production-level biotech military gear," said Frank Sharp, studying the Chinese Hydra. "Milspec design—it's so functional and conservative. And you load it up with—what? Did I hear you talking about glass ampules of powdered computation?"

"I have ammunition on hand, yes," said Betty Yee, opening a small wooden case. "My lab synthesized a batch of the viruses that Professor Jones used in the battlefield before our break. One single ampule of them is enough. The Hydra will remember. I'll activate it now." She tossed the little glass tube into the Hydra's mouth. It chomped up the glass round as if it were a peanut.

"But we, hey, we need to stay loose," said Jorge. "Change tactics on the fly, with our boots on the ground. This Hydra of yours, you can program it?"

"Certainly," said Betty Yee. "Its interface is voice-activated. However, since this is classified military hardware, it only speaks Chinese."

Frank Sharp looked smug. "Hell, I know enough Mandarin to order up a two-day party with sword-swallowers and dancing girls."

Frank, and Jorge found their places inside the squat Chinese tank, with an anxious Betty offering final advice on its interfaces and affordances. Just then another slimy giant Kraken lurched up from the muddy soil, implacable as a Frankenstein monster assembling itself in a grave. It rose a hundred meters high, roughly humanoid, and flaking off fractal chunks as before. The newly spawned stromatolites were continually and obsessively recruiting fresh germs from the dirt. Slurping shit up, knocking shit down.

Frank barked broken Mandarin at the tank's complex dashboard, and the tank roared forward. Their heavyweight Chinese Hydra puffed out a vast cloud of viral stink-gas. The collapse of the shambling hundred-meter-high Kraken was total and abrupt. From the bottom up, its flesh deliquesced into diarrhea. A sudden, awful, computational crash into a vast sewer-puddle of shit-germs.

"Next?" crowed Frank Sharp.

A passing military helicopter framed another Kraken in a target beam. This monster resembled a giant starfish humping across the tormented soil. Jorge lowered the tank's muzzle and picked it off, letting the over-engineered military-grade Hydra puff its cloud of viruses out through tank's barrel. On they rolled, crunching a swath through a killing-zone of bursting stromatolites.

"Let me kill that giant scorpion on my own!" said Frank Sharp, hankering for a big-game-hunter-type personal kill.

Exhausted by the horrific stench of the infected mire, Jorge let Frank tend to the massive Hydra. Frenzied with battle lust, Frank somehow felt it necessary to give the weapon a rousing pep talk in his pidgin Chinese.

The Hydra misinterpreted Frank's jabber as a series of commands regarding its program codes. It reformulated the virus that it was squirting. The result? Far from being destroyed by the randomly tweaked Hydra spores, the scorpion golem was galvanically energized. Moving with unholy, frenetic speed, it dug into the topsoil, scratching out a massive hole—shooting up clouds of dust and then fractured rock.

Deep its newly dug stone den, the scorpion proceeded to infect the landscape. The dirt and stone underfoot were morphing into a supernal Kraken, a litho-being that heaved the ground like an earthquake. The tremors tossed the mighty tank around like a Hong Kong plastic toy. Frank and Jorge were battered against its harsh interior like two wasps trapped in a bottle. Clawing their way through the hatch, they abandoned the Hydra and sprinted for higher ground.

§

"Nice work," Jorge jibed at Frank Sharp. "Very professionally done."

Panting and rubbing their bruises, they were wobbling weak-kneed on a hilly parking lot, surveying the growing havoc. The ground was erupting with long, stony arms of bursting rubble. These violent tendrils of fracked rock could easily swat down a helicopter.

"It wasn't acting like that before," said Frank uneasily. "What'd I do?"

"Those are Frank-Sharp-modified scorpion cells."

Silently, Frank unwrapped a pack of Panda brand Chinese cigarettes, lit one, and offered it to Jorge, who was still talking.

"The Kraken cells wriggled down between the grains of sand and soil, down through the cracks in the rocks, all the way down to the water table. A natural paradise for the right kind of microbe. Your new cells multiplied in darkness. Hyperexponentially. And they roared back. Nice fast turnaround on that cycle, Frank. Hats off."

"I'm sure this is all for the good," said Frank, coughing on rock dust as he struggled to light his own cig. "Take a big-picture perspective, man. What we formerly thought of as organic life on Earth arose as a local glitch. The Cambrian explosion was a matter of moving a stalled system to a higher level of efficiency. Initially, our kinds of multi-cellular bodies were monsters. Our ancestors were glitches in the cell-colony status quo. And then the system rolled down a hill, through a valley of chaos, and up to the top of a higher peak. Producing us."

"*Sure* we say we're higher forms of life," said Jorge. "Both sides of a morphogenetic bifurcation always say that."

"You can't compare human beings to primeval mud monsters."

"Yes I can. Because I just now did the math."

"Did the math? That's—"

"I did the math with my ass muscles while we're standing here smoking bad Chinese cigarettes."

Unsteadily Frank Sharp lit a new cigarette from the stained butt of the last. "I guess you're saying—that we're different, but not any better. We're all creatures of Earth. Figures in the dance."

"Exactly. And now that your tweaked scorpion has fracked itself into the water table, we'll never kill the Kraken. We need to cut a deal here."

"Okay. How?"

"Surely we humans have something that immortal Kraken mud monsters would want."

"But how would we even talk with them?" asked Frank. "They're made of germs and dirt. They don't have eyes and ears."

"I'm thinking they hear us anyhow," said Jorge. "We could talk about prime numbers and the Riemann Hypothesis," he added, blowing smoke. "Or maybe the poetry of Tennyson. Because Tennyson is fucking buried. Like them."

Frank tried to take offense, then laughed sourly.

"We could tell the stromatolites about quantum entanglement-based networks," continued Jorge. "Being virus-based, they must be closer to that issue than us."

"Maybe we could interest this intelligent mud in establishing a broader global presence," said Frank. "More followers. A ubiquitous brand. The mud could come out of the underground and go mainstream."

"Yeah!" said Jorge, livening up. "You're on it, Frank! Promo. Buzz. Offer them a deal. You yourself would have to turn Kraken for the big meeting, you understand."

"I'm game," said Frank. With insouciant bravado, he dabbed his finger against one of the fallen mud monsters—and took a taste.

§

Frank's voice grew louder and more insistent as the cellular computation invaded his body tissues. Riddled with viral activism, he was lecturing on and on. About media and sociology in the modern Chinese novel. About the long-dead expat Japan-based author, Lafcadio Hearn. About viral push-pull cool-hunting web-bots. About the archetypal nature of industrial design, even for cellular entities.

The palpitating mound that had once been Frank Sharp grew upwards at supersonic speed, drawing dirt into itself. As a comradely gesture, the Frank Sharp mountain had a sharp valley set into one side—and this left a field where Jorge Jones could survive the tectonic devastation.

Tiny Chinese fighter jets buzzed around Frank like biplanes swarming King Kong. No no, much smaller than that. Like butterflies above the slopes of Mount Fujiyama.

And then—the eruption. A deep, subsonic rumble, and a sharp, explosive crack. Starting from the top, the Frank Sharp mountain dissolved into the sky. The peak was shattering into dust. The eruption continued for half an hour, volcanic, unstoppable, spawning a vast plume that mingled with the jet streams, sowing the Kraken substance across every square centimeter of the old planet Earth. The Chinese urban landscape on the far side of the mountain was as lava-engulfed as ancient Pompeii or Herculaneum. And Jorge Jones still stood in the valley along the near edge.

"A very tasty world," rumbled Frank, slowly subsiding back to his old self. "I'm the One. I've got the answers."

§

The shock and awe subsides. Everyone is a Kraken, all the time, everywhere. Sermons in the stones, and good in everything.

Jorge, Frank, and Betty spend some quality time discussing matters in the hot springs near Jorge's sequoia. Playing with the freaky minnows. Looking at rocks and fossils. Revisiting that idea that the sedimentary stones are archives. Jorge and Betty getting closer than before.

Turns out there's an entire Golden Age literary and cultural archive down there in the geological strata. It's like cave paintings or cuneiform or hieroglyphs—or even like the cool old paper SF magazines, the ones that primeval sci-fi fans used to root through in the 1950s, before computers were invented. The protocols of the Old Ones.

Betty finds she can use the profound Confucian-style New Age teachings of the prehistoric worm-tracks to educate the global biotech Kraken. And thereby to rectify all names and to set forces in harmony. And even to live with Jorge, in his tree, for awhile. But then she goes home to rebuild her city.

Frank throws in his lot with the trilobites. He retrofits his mitochondria, and becomes a half-billion-year old cultural relic. Occasionally he appears in a five-gallon goldfish tank at an ultra-elite gathering of the planet's new trillionaires, emitting long speeches via a piezoplastic hookup on his primitive, chitinous shell. Mostly, though, Frank dwells at the bottom of the hot springs by Jorge's sequoia, where the heavy action is chemosynthetic and the cultural movers and shakers are so far underground that they don't even need eyes.

Jorge gets Frank registered as an endangered species, to assure his friend of long-term peace. Then Jorge takes to painting Taoist ink-wash scrolls. The great misty Kraken mountains, and the little old man in the robe. The mountains are vast and eldritch and timeless, and the sage is just a passing figure, crabbed and energetic in his wise little niche.

Now and then Frank surfaces in the springs and jets out some sepia for Jorge's inkhorn.

The Kraken and Sage, they don't compete, or quarrel, or annul one another's being. They just make the scene: they're just plain there.

Notes on "Kraken and Sage"

Original for *Transreal Cyberpunk*.
Written March - August, 2015.

Rudy on "Kraken and Sage"

I wanted to publish our joint stories in an anthology, *Transreal Cyberpunk*. But Bruce didn't feel like "Totem Poles" was a worthy story to end with. We wanted to go bigger. So once again we started corresponding about possible ideas. Bruce was interested in something relating to the so-called Cambrian explosion of new species in the fossil record. And I had an image of an old scientist living in a sequoia tree. Bruce and I had an illusion that this time we'd finally write a really tight plot outline before starting our tale.

It's always best if I can see Bruce in person when we write a story together, and we were in fact slated to be on a panel about the legacy of cyberpunk, held at UCLA in March, 2015. So I wrote up the first page of a story and did a painting of an old man encountering a floating jellyfish in a tree. And then Bruce and I talked some more about our story while in LA.

In the end, of course, we didn't hew very closely to any of our plans. But we did use the plans in a different kind of way. Around the fourth revision, when things were bogging down, I went ahead and did a Burroughs-inspired cut-up. I combined in a single document two successive drafts of our story plus a lot of passages taken from our email threads about possible scenes. And then I removed randomly selected blocks of text from the document and shuffled the remaining blocks around. And sent that to Bruce.

Nothing daunted, Bruce removed even more material, arranged the remaining chunks in something like a chronological order, and numbered the chunks. It looked a little like his wonderful Ballardian 1984 story, ""Life in the Shaper/Mechanist Era: Twenty Evocations."

For our joint story, the numbering scheme didn't really seem to work. We did however keep the hip-hop / jump-cut style of a narrative broken into chunks. This framework lightened the load, and made us more nimble. We worked through four more revisions—improving the voices, the eyeball kicks, the flow—and then we were done.

One funny thing. Just before we started our work in late March, 2015, Bruce sent me an email with this line: "I'm wondering if maybe we could write just one story that doesn't involve huge kraken-style catastrophes or both the authors transreally dropping dead." I started laughing to myself about the word *kraken*, and I decided that not only should our story include a kraken, but our "Bruce" character should *become* a kraken.

Along the way, Bruce unearthed Alfred Tennyson's amazing poem, "The Kraken," and we collaged that into our text for texture. A Victorian hip-hop sample. Battening upon huge sea worms in our sleep.

The ending is drawn from another of Bruce's' emails—it was a dreamy, early idea for a scene, and a nice place to wind up. It's like we're walking offstage hand in hand after our fierce Punch & Judy show. A sweet, mellow, real-time moment; a break from the punk guitar sludge and the insane screaming.

And there you have it. *Transreal Cyberpunk.*

What's the overarching subject of our nine tales? Well, as I keep repeating, the stories are transreal. They're about Bruce and me, about our friendship, and about what it was like to be working as SF writers over the last thirty years.

It's been an awesome run.

Bruce on "Kraken and Sage"

Most Rucker-Sterling stories are about ridiculous catastrophes. That's because, transreally, our composition process is itself a ridiculous catastrophe. However, we'd never written a story where the catastrophe is finished, complete, over and done with: end of the book, turn the page, finally close the covers.

Once upon a time, it was a big gaudy deal, but now it's in the past. The weird and dire events have been subsumed, become one with the passing parade of life. Because the participants are elderly people, or better yet, they're dead. They properly belong to the ages, like William Burroughs or J. G. Ballard, two idols of our cyberpunk youth.

"Kraken and Sage" is about a guy who has survived ridiculous catastrophe and reached a state of mature serenity. Or, at least, it would be about that grand theme, if Rudy or I possessed any maturity or serenity. However, we just don't. Maybe some day. There's hope for us, I think.

We created a pretty good framework plot for this tale: our hero is this Californian sage who has retreated from the unseemly hurly-burly of wealth and power, and become a kind of Taoist. Then his own creations rise from their slumbers in some new catastrophe—(let's say a disaster in China, why not, they've got plenty)—and he arrives on-scene to restore the world's calm. He's not an agent of freak-out, an aid and abettor to the sci-fi krakens who harshly disrupt our reality. On the contrary: the wise sage is a classic, conservative figure.

What an exciting departure from our norm, because no Rucker-Sterling protagonist is ever on the side of order, ethical responsibility, legality and proper social roles. People like that do exist—(fewer of them all the time, but some do)—yet they always had a marked absence from the extensive Rucker-Sterling oeuvre.

Could we even imagine such a person? A placid sage who calms Krakens? Maybe the Kraken is his sidekick, an entity he can pat on the head!

Keen to tackle this creative challenge, I envisioned a protagonist rather like the late-in-life Vaclav Havel. Not the dramatic, street-rally, revolutionary hippie Vaclav Havel of 1989, but the wise but waning, been-there-done-that narrator of the little-known Havel book "To the Castle and Back." This is certainly the best memoir ever written by a guy who was once a nation's President. There's no politicized frenzy, special-pleading or moral chest-beating in Havel's final book. It's all about furniture, state dinners, press coverage, how to dress, scheduling problems, over-booking the state helicopter, the stuff of lived presidential experience. It's a severely unromantic and super-convincing text. I was pretty sure I could steal a lot of it and no one would know.

So we created a draft that was basically about a guy like the elderly Havel—he's very hip, but he can no longer be much bothered, he just sees right through the technicolor sci-fi bluster. Giant jellyfish, huge ants, Soviet UFOs, he knows these wacky advents just come and go in the long run. However, well, that story was boring. Rudy couldn't put up with it, the narrative was too dull. And he was right, because it was passionless, very gray ink-wash. It read like a respectful obituary.

Something had to be done to get this monochrome text off its sickbed, so we hauled in the defibrillators and the electroshock cables. First Rudy vividly tore it up with some Burroughs cut-and-paste sampling. Then I cut all the fat and gristle out of it and violently squeezed it into a Ballard condensed novel.

The story survived these devastating attacks, but it became mighty hectic and bedraggled. Oddly, this made the story feel very 2015 AD: it became an authentically contemporary work. "Kraken and Sage" features grinding low-level aerial warfare. Industrial and ecological catastrophes. Obvious charlatans with all the wealth and power. Scientists as a victim class. And some mud monsters, because, well, mud monsters.

"When you cut up the present, the future leaks out." "Earth is the only truly alien planet." When you're a science fiction writer, you need to pretty well throw the bread way out on the water. Once the seas rise, you never know what oozy relic will be left to a wondering mankind: floating on the slow blue waves out there, or half-buried in the dark and muddy shore.

www.ingramcontent.com/pod-product-compliance
Lightning Source LLC
Chambersburg PA
CBHW070846280626
47161CB00017B/2683